PENGUIN BOOKS

THE GATES OF THORBARDIN

DRAGONLANCE™ SAGA HEROES II,
VOLUME TWO

Dan Parkinson is best known as a top-selling Western writer, though in recent years his subjects have expanded to include, among others, high seas adventures and historical novels. A personal favourite among his twenty books is the science-fiction love story, *Starsong*, also published by Penguin.

D0994074

DragonLance® Saga

H•E•R•O•E•S II

VOLUME TWO

The Gates of Thorbardin

Dan Parkinson

Cover Art
JEFF EASLEY

Interior Illustrations
VALERIE VALUSEK

PENGUIN BOOKS
in association with TSR, Inc.

PENGUIN BOOKS

Published by the Penguin Group
Penguin Books Ltd, 27 Wrights Lane, London W8 5TZ, England
Penguin Books USA Inc., 375 Hudson Street, New York, New York 10014, USA
Penguin Books Australia Ltd, Ringwood, Victoria, Australia
Penguin Books Canada Ltd, 2801 John Street, Markham, Ontario, Canada L3R 1B4
Penguin Books (NZ) Ltd, 182–190 Wairau Road, Auckland 10, New Zealand

Penguin Books Ltd, Registered Offices: Harmondsworth, Middlesex, England

First published in the USA by TSR, Inc. 1990
Distributed to the book trade in the United States by Random House, Inc.
and in Canada by Random House of Canada Ltd.
Distributed to the toy and hobby trade by regional distributors.
First published in Great Britain by Penguin Books 1991
3 5 7 9 10 8 6 4 2

Dedication

Stories grow from stories told,
So no tale's ever ended
While there's yet new among the old.
It's thus that lore's extended.

The Gates of Thorbardin is dedicated to whomever finds
the gnomish island-vessel, or solves the mystery of
Garon Wendesthalas, or tells the whole tale of Caliban
and Kolanda, or can chronicle the entire Battle of Waykeep.

PLAINS OF DERGOTH

SKULLCAP

BREAKS

Sky's
End
Peak

The
Bridge

Lost Gate

The Bog

Northgate

THORBARDIN

OUTE

Southgate

Part I

THE DREAM CHASER

Chapter 1

Even here, in this cold crevasse split deep and narrow into living mountain stone . . . even here, where he could go no farther, where his aching body squeezed so tightly between serrated walls of cutting stone that his back was raw and bleeding . . . even here, where no roads came and the only trails were paths of small things passing. . . .

Even here, he knew they would find him.

At least one of them would come, drawn by the scent of his blood—would come up through the riven rock and find him cornered. There were too many of them on the slopes below, too well spread as they hunted upward, for all of them to miss him where he hid. One would come. One would come to kill him.

He had watched them coursing the field like a hunter's pack. From a ledge where the tumbled stone lay grotesque in the shadows of the sheers above, he had seen them lose his scent. They had spread wide, casting about almost as wolves might, seeking movement, great blunt noses dipping to sweep the ground and rising to test the air, thick, sleek tails swishing graceful arcs as they wound and curved through the diminishing brush of the mountain slope. Long and lithe, immensely powerful and as graceful as dark zephyrs on the wind, they moved upward in silent unison, missing nothing as they came. Sunlight on the black fur rippling over mighty muscles was a tapestry of iridescence.

How many were there? He hadn't been able to tell. They were never all in sight at once. He'd judged that there were thirty down there, seeking him. But it didn't matter. Of the hunting cats he had seen, one would be enough.

Hunger had knotted his stomach as he turned upward again, seeking a place to go to ground. Or a weapon. His hands craved the touch of a weapon—any kind of weapon. He had then found a palm-sized rock with a cutting edge and balanced it in his hand. It was no proper weapon, only a sharp stone. But to hands long-comforted by the tools they held, it was better than nothing at all.

Clambering into tumblestone mazes, he'd used his rock to cut a strip from the leather kilt he wore, and concentrated on binding the strip about the rock to make a grip that would fit his hand. He stumbled, fell against a spur of stone, and felt it gash his shoulder. Warm blood ran down his arm, bright droplets spattering the rock beneath his feet. He paused for only a moment, looking at the blood, and raised one eyebrow in ironic salute. Then he had moved on.

Above the tumblestone rose the sheer faces of rock cliffs, and among the cliffs he had found the crevasse, and now he waited there. He had seen them coursing up through the mazes, had seen the one that paused and sniffed where it found the droplets of his blood. One, at least, would find him here. That one had the scent and would not lose it again.

The crevasse was a great slit, deep into the standing cliff. Far above was open sky, but the walls were sheer, with no place to climb. For a time the cut had run on, inward and upward, even widening at one point, where a tiny cold spring dripped from a sandstone cleft to pool in the sand below then disappear into the rising ground. He had stopped there for a moment, trying to quench a thirst that tortured him. Then he had gone on, and could almost feel the hot breath of the hunting cat closing in behind him. From the spring, the crevasse wound back into sheer stone, narrowing as it went. Finally he could go no farther. He had pushed himself into the final rift as tightly as he could, holding his breath, and he felt the cold rock scraping at his flesh.

He tilted his head to peer upward. Far above was sky, and its path was wider than the cleft that swallowed him front and back. Using the rock walls as pressing surfaces, he raised himself a few inches, bracing with his elbows at the rock before him, with his feet at the rock behind. His breath was a cloud of steam, hanging in the cold, still air around him, condensing on chill stone as he worked.

By inches he crept upward, levering himself between two surfaces. A foot, then three, then seven he climbed, using his forearms thrust ahead of him—then his hands as the chimney widened above. When he could no longer climb, when his outthrust arms would not reach farther and give purchase, he looked down. He was fifteen feet above the bottom of the crevasse and could go no higher.

He was still within reach of a hunting cat, he knew. Any one of the great beasts, as tall at the shoulder as he was at the ears, could leap this high. His chest heaving, his breath a cloud in the shadows of dark stone, he clung and waited. He could go no farther.

"Come on, then, pouncer," he muttered. "You have my scent and you know where I am, so you are the chosen one. Come along, now, and let's get it done. I'm tired."

Tiny clickings echoed up the split, needle tips of great claws tapping at stone as the beast padded nearer. Now he could hear its breath, the deep-chested, rumbling purr of a huge cat closing on its prey.

Shadows shifted in the cleft, and he looked upward. High above, where the walls opened upon sky, something moved. A face was there, tiny and distant, looking down at him. It was there, then it withdrew. Someone was atop the escarpment, above the rended cliffs, someone curious enough to look down and see what was happening below. But whoever it was, it meant nothing to him, here. All that mattered in this moment was that he was here, the cat was coming . . . and in a place far away Jilian waited for him. He had promised her he would return.

In the cold mist of his breath, he now saw her face. Of them all, she was the only one who had truly believed him. The only one with faith in him. He had told her about the dreams. He had told several others, as well, but of them all, Jilian believed.

Rogar Goldbuckle might have believed about the dreams, but not about their portent. Goldbuckle had listened, stood for a time in thought, then shook his head. "Who's to know what a dream means?" he had sighed. "I've had dreams, too, Chane. But that's all they were. Just dreams."

It had been worse when he told Slag Firestoke what he wanted to do. Old Firestoke was not fond of him anyway and was not happy about an empty-pursed orphan spending time with his daughter. It had been Jilian's idea to tell her father about Chane's premonitions, in the hope that Firestoke might outfit him for his quest. He didn't need much. Just warm clothing, arms and provisions, and a few of Firestoke's hirelings to accompany him.

"Thorbardin is in jeopardy," Chane had told him. "I know it, and in dreams I've been told that I must find the key to save it."

"Dreams!" Firestoke had rumbled, glaring at him. "You're daft as a warren-bat."

"I know I'm right," Chane had insisted. "I don't know exactly what I'm to find, but I'll know when I find it."

Firestoke had laughed at that, a cruel, victorious

laugh. "So you come to me for money? Well, you can wait until your whiskers rust. You won't see a brass coin from me, Chane Feldstone. Now get out of my house . . . and stay away from my daughter! She'll have better than the likes of you."

Then, it seemed that old Firestoke had changed his mind. At the time, Chane believed that Jilian had persuaded him . . . and Jilian had believed it, too.

The cat sounds were closer now, momentarily hesitant while the big beast tasted the air. Chane clung to his braced position and felt chill beads of sweat among his whiskers.

She probably still believes it, he thought. How would she know that her father's villains accompanied me to the edge of the wilderness, then waylaid me?

They had beaten and pummeled him, enjoying the sport. They had taken his weapons, his coins, his boots, his warm clothing. Everything that Firestoke had provided, they took—and everything else he had, as well.

"Don't come back to Thorbardin," they'd told him. "Our sponsor doesn't want to ever see you again."

And they had harried his trail, to make sure he didn't turn back. Day after miserable, hungry day they had followed him, until he had crossed beyond Thorbardin's realm into the wild lands.

Hunger weakened him, and he felt his braced arms trembling. The purring rumble of the great cat was very near, just beyond the final bend in the chasm. He took a deep breath. "Come on, you blasted cat," Chane said aloud. "Come kitty-kitty-kitty, you tarnish-pitted carnivore. Come on and get it over with!"

Then it was there, thirty feet away, a sleek, stalking predator of midnight black. Gold eyes spotted him, and it paused, ears flattening back atop an ebony head as wide as his body.

Its mouth opened wide to clear front fangs the size of daggers. Its purr became a low roar, and it bunched its massive body, long tail twitching. Then it charged . . . two long bounds and a leap, front paws reaching for its prey.

In the last instant, he released his hold and dropped. A heavy paw the span of his own hand brushed his head. Needle-sharp claws cut shallow furrows from his hair to his brow. Then he was below it, and he heard the heavy thump as the cat wedged itself into the slanting cut where he had been.

He fell, rolled away, scrambled upright, and caught its writhing tail in both hands, pulling himself upward. Feet braced against stone, he climbed and swung himself to its rump, dodging its thrashing hind claws. Hands full of black fur, he pulled himself forward. The cat's roar became a howl of rage. Its head came up and turned, great teeth glinting as he grabbed the cat's head and threw himself over its shoulder, clinging for life. The cat shrieked. He heard the snapping of bone.

For an instant he dangled between clawed paws that had ceased to move, and felt the hot breath of the beast on his face as its lungs emptied themselves. It did not breathe again. Its neck was broken.

Feeling weak with hunger and exertion, he pulled himself atop the beast once more, sat there long enough to let his muscles stop trembling, then raised himself above it, feet braced against rock faces on either side. He began prying the cat loose from the grip of the stone. When finally the huge body was free, he dragged it back to where there was a little space, rolled it onto its back, got out the wrapped shard of rock and set about dressing and skinning the body.

He had almost completed the task when a voice behind him said, "Take the tenderloin. Best part of a cat."

He turned, crouching. The person who stood there, a few yards away, was nearly his own height, but slighter of build. He was beardless, though the great mane of his hair had been caught up in leather wraps at one side and was looped around his neck like a fur collar. He leaned casually on a staff with a fork at its end, and gazed sardonically at the skinned beast on the ground. "I don't believe I ever saw a body go to so much trouble for his supper," he said. "You are a mess. Blood all over you, and I expect some of it's yours."

The newcomer was looking him over unabashedly, and Chane glared back. "A kender," he growled. "You're a blasted kender."

"So I am," the newcomer said, feigning surprise. "But then you're a dwarf. I guess everybody is something. Chestal Thicketsway's the name. You can call me 'Chess' if you want to. Why *did* you lead that cat in here, anyway?"

"Because I couldn't think of any better way to kill it, and I'm hungry."

"So am I," the kender grinned. "Did you notice the little canyon back there, with the spring in it? I'll get a fire started there, if you'll bring the meat. And don't forget the tenderloins . . . and the backstrap. Those are the best meat, you know."

* * * * *

By evening firelight, the little spring canyon in the cleft seemed almost a homey place. His belly full of roast hunting cat, sage tea, and a bit of hard cheese that the kender had produced from his pouch—he said he had found it somewhere—the dwarf pegged down the catskin and began to work the flesh from it, using his edged stone as a scraper, while the kender watched curiously. All through supper the kender had chatted sociably, not seeming to care that his companion rarely answered except for an occasional grunt or growl. Chestal Thicketsway was not bothered by that, it seemed. He enjoyed the sound of his own voice, and rarely ran out of new ideas and opinions with which to amuse and amaze himself.

But as the dwarf worked steadily over the staked-down hide, scraping, rubbing, and dressing it, Chess gradually went silent . . . or nearly so. He sat by the fire and watched in lively curiosity, now and then muttering to himself. "Not that," he said. "Wrong color." Then, "No, I don't think so. It is far too big." And, "Well, possibly for formal occasions, but hardly for every day."

Finally the dwarf turned to glare at him. "What are you muttering about?"

"I'm trying to decide what you plan to do with that pelt," the smaller person explained. "So far I have pretty well eliminated any ideas of a tent or a rug, and I can't see a dwarf flying a black fur flag . . . unless, of course, he plans to take up taxidermy, which is an unusual occupation for dwarves as far as I have seen. If you were a gnome, now—"

"I need a coat," the dwarf said gruffly, returning to his scraping.

"—You might have some notion of lacing poles into it to make a flying machine, or punching holes in it to sift gravel for a—"

"Shut up," the dwarf said.

"—sliding stairway. What?"

"I wish you would be quiet. I'm trying to work here."

"I can see that. Why don't you make yourself a coat? You could certainly use one, I'd say. Maybe some boots, too. Most dwarves I've met prefer bullhide boots with iron soles, but just some simple fur boots would be better than those rags you have bound around your feet. I don't think I've ever seen a worse-dressed dwarf than you. I've seen goblins with better attire. Did you lose your clothes somewhere?"

"They were stolen. . . ."

"And aren't you supposed to carry a hammer or an axe or something? Most dwarves are pretty tight-fisted about tools and weapons. I'd say you have a story to tell. How about your name?"

"What about my name?"

"Do you remember it?"

"Well, of course I remember it!"

"What is it?"

"Chane Feldstone."

Chane turned back to his pelt, growling. When it was cleaned to his satisfaction, he put more wood on the fire and went to retrieve the two longest teeth from the carcass of the cat. They were the center incisors of the upper jaw, and like incisors they were sharp along the edges. Unlike incisors, though, they tapered to keen points at the ends . . . and unlike the teeth of most creatures—

even creatures as large as the hunting cat—they were nearly ten inches long.

He worked at them for a time, wrenching them this way and that with strong hands, until finally they were loose enough for him to pull them out of the jaw. Chane carried them back to the fire and laid their root ends in the flame to clean them while he cut hardwood for grips and lengths of thong for binding.

"Most dwarves prefer metal daggers," the kender pointed out. "Most dwarves don't care for ivory."

"This is the best that's available right now," Chane snapped. "It will do until I can find something better."

"Things aren't hard to find," Chess agreed. "People are always leaving things just lying around—"

"Don't you have somewhere to go?" Chane asked.

The kender leaned back against a rock, cupping his hands behind his head. "I thought I'd have a look around that valley down there . . . the one the cats chased you out of. It's called Waykeep, or some such thing."

"The valley?"

"Or some part of it. No one seems to know very much about it. Hardly anyone goes there."

Chane looked at the great pelt, pegged out for curing, and at the daggerlike fang he was fitting with a handle. "I can see why," he said.

"Actually, I was on my way to Pax Tharkas, but I got sidetracked," the kender admitted. "There's a lot to see in these mountains. And a lot not to see. Did you notice that valley the cats came from, how it just sort of fades out of sight when you try to see it? Pretty mysterious if you ask me."

Even if you *don't* ask, Chane was thinking.

"I had a nice talk with a hill dwarf a few months ago. He'd lost an amulet and I helped him find it, and when I showed him my map he said the blank space between the west ranges and the Vale of Respite must be the Valley of Waykeep. He doesn't know anything about it, except it doesn't show on maps and nobody goes there. Especially wizards. So that's why I'm sidetracked and not on my way to Pax Tharkas. You don't look like a hill dwarf. You look a little different. Are you a mountain dwarf?"

"I'm from Thorbardin," Chane said, paying scant attention to the chattering kender. The more the creature talked, the more glassy-eyed he felt. It was like trying to listen to twenty or thirty anvils, all at once.

"Is that why your beard grows back that way?" Chess stared at him in bright-eyed curiosity. "Do all Thorbardin dwarves have swept-back whiskers?"

"No, but I do. It's just the way they grow." He looked up from his work, thoughtfully. "What kind of maps do you have?"

"Oh, all kinds," the kender spread his hands. "Big ones and little ones, some drawn on linen, some on parchment—I even have one drawn on a . . . no, I used to have that, but I don't now. I ate it." He glanced at the remains of their meal.

"Maps of what?" Chane growled.

The kender blinked at him. "Places. That's what maps are. They're pictures of places. I make a lot of maps. Of places. When I go home to Hylo someday . . . that's where I'm from, did I tell you that?"

"I don't know." The dwarf's scowl was becoming fierce. "What places?"

"—I'll be able to show everybody where I've been." The kender blinked again. "What places would you like?"

"I don't know, exactly," Chane sighed. "I've never seen it . . . except in dreams. But it's outside of Thorbardin . . . someplace beyond Northgate."

The kender shifted his voluminous belt-pouch around so that it rested on his lap, and began rummaging inside it. The pouch seemed to have endless capacity, and the dwarf stared at the horde of treasure the kender's busy hands brought to light. Bright baubles of countless kinds, small stones, bits of twine, an old turtle shell, various metal objects, a wooden cube, an old and battered bird's nest—this the kender stared at for a moment, then tossed aside—a broken spoon, a scrap of cloth. . . . The treasures went on and on.

Then Chess drew forth a fat sheath of drawings and his

eyes brightened. "Ah," he said. "Maps." He thumbed through them. "If the place you want to see is north of Northgate, that means it's east of here," he explained, then looked up, glanced at Chane and pointed. "East is that way."

"What do the maps show to the east?" Chane squinted, trying to see what the drawings said.

Chess looked up, surprised. "Nothing," he said. "I thought I told you about that. The first thing east of here is the Valley of Waykeep, and it isn't on maps. Maybe I can draw one on the way."

"I don't want to go to the Valley of Waykeep," the dwarf snorted.

"If you want to go east, you do," Chess said amicably, then reached into his pouch and drew out another shiny bauble. "How about that?" He held it up and gazed at it in surprise.

"How about what? What is that?"

"It's that hill dwarf's amulet. The one I helped him find. He must have lost it again. That's where I found it the first time, too. Right in here, under the troll's sandal. What do you know!"

Chapter 2

"What kind of dream was it? I mean the one where you saw a place outside of Thorbardin, and now you want to find it?" Chestal Thicketsway scrambled to the crest of a stone ledge and squinted, peering at misty distances. Fogs and low clouds seemed to span the Valley of Waykeep, a trough of sun-dappled gray mist miles across and tens of miles in length. He noted again how the valley seemed to just . . . lose itself from sight, even when one stood directly above it and looked down.

Chane Feldstone hoisted himself to the ledge-top, a black-clad dwarf burdened by black packs slung from each shoulder. The dead cat had provided more than a meal. It had provided a good, black fur coat, two packs, and a supply of smoked meat. "It was just a dream," he said. "At least that's what almost everybody tells me. Maybe they're right, too. But it's my dream, and I don't think that's all it is."

"Well, what do you think it was?" The kender shaded his bright eyes, gazing at the distant, craggy mountains that rose above the mists several miles eastward, across the valley.

"I think it was a message," Chane sighed. "It's like a dream that I've had a hundred times over the years, only this time it seemed to almost make sense, and there was this face—I felt like I should know who he was, but I can't quite grasp it. He told me that I had a destiny and the fate of Thorbardin depends on me, and he showed me a place where I must go."

"Why?"

"I don't know. He didn't say, but it must have something to do with the helmet, because that's what I always dream about."

The kender glanced around at the dwarf, raising an eyebrow quizzically. "What helmet?"

"The same one I always dream about. Ever since I was half-grown."

"A helmet," Chess breathed. "Gee, I usually just dream about butterflies and leeches and things. I don't think I ever dreamed about a helmet." He raised his forked staff, twirled it in his fingers for a moment, then tossed it into the air and caught it, still twirling, as it fell. "Dreams are important, though. My cousin dreamed he was a doormat one time, and a week later an ogre stepped on him."

Chane stared at the twirling staff. "What is that thing, anyway?"

"What?" Chess blinked and stopped twirling the stick. "Oh, this? It's a hoopak. Tell me some more about your helmet dream."

"Well, it's just a dream. I've had it now and then, most of my life. I dream I'm in a place I've never seen before, and there's something there. Sometimes it's a locked chest, sometimes a bag, sometimes a pile of stones or a wooden box. But I open it, and there is an old helmet inside. A war helm, with horns and a spire, cheekplates, noseguard . . .

it always looks the same, and every time I start to put it on my head there is a voice that says, " 'No, not now. Not yet. When the time comes, you will know.' "

"Is that all?" the kender frowned in disappointment. "That isn't very exciting."

"That's all of it," Chane admitted. "Or it was until a few weeks ago, when I started having that dream almost every night. But now it's different. There's a great, high bridge, and nothing at all beneath it. I cross the bridge, and then I find the helmet. I start to put it on, and there is someone there with me. A warrior, like the old Hylar warriors back in the time of the great war. He looks at me and says, 'The time approaches. Thorbardin is at risk. Chane Feldstone, you must become who you are and who you are meant to be. It is your destiny.' " Chane growled and scuffed a fur-clad foot against the stone. "Old Firestoke laughed when I told him about it."

"Is he the one who chased you out of Thorbardin?"

"Nobody chased me out of Thorbardin!" Chane rumbled. "I went because I wanted to go. But his villains beat me up and robbed me and told me never to come back."

"Why do you suppose they did that?"

"Because Slag Firestoke is a miserable old rust-pit, and he wants Jilian to marry somebody wealthy or famous."

"I don't suppose you are either of those?"

"No, I'm not. But I'll go back when I'm ready, and I'll go on my own terms, and Slag Firestoke can go to corrosion for all I care."

"But you're going to find the helmet first."

"I intend to try. Maybe it was just a dream, but I want to find out."

"Maybe the helmet will make you rich and famous," the kender suggested.

Still seething at the recent memory of betrayal and humiliation, Chane squinted and peered at the misted valley. The kender was right about one thing, he decided. The valley seemed to try to hide itself, as though it didn't want company. But to reach the mountains east of there he would have to cross it.

They had seen no further sign of the big cats. If the

beasts lived in the valley, they had obviously gone home during the night. In the distance, beyond the mists, morning sun haloed the caps of tall peaks that jutted upward like lizards' teeth. At one point, somewhat to the north, there was a gap that might be a pass.

"Does your map say what's beyond those next mountains?" he asked.

"Another valley," the kender said. "It's called the Vale of Respite. And beyond it are more mountains. Some really big ones. According to one of the maps, the northern gate of Thorbardin is over there someplace. I've never seen that. Have you?"

"Not from outside," Chane admitted. He growled again, thinking about Firestoke's "armsmen"—actually just a gang of toughs, the sort who were all too common in some of the warrens and even parts of some of the clan cities in the undermountain domain. Firestoke! The old rustbucket had made Chane believe that he was helping him, outfitting him for a journey, providing armed companions . . . and had betrayed him. What must Jilian think? Thinking of Jilian he became so melancholy that he went back to thinking about her father instead.

"Yes, by the Great Anvil!" he growled. "Yes, I will go back, and maybe I'll shove Slag Firestoke's pretensions right down his throat."

"Being rich and famous might help," Chess allowed. He shifted his pouch to a more comfortable position at his belt, gripped his hoopak, and scuffed an impatient foot. "Look at it, will you? I never saw a valley so reluctant to be seen."

Chane picked up his packs. "Maybe it's a spell."

"I don't think so," the kender said. "I heard magicians don't like to come here because it makes them itch or something. The hill dwarf told me that." He glanced at the fur-clad dwarf, then tipped his head to study Chane critically. Clad entirely in black cat-fur, the only parts of the dwarf that were visible were the top half of his face—swept-back whiskers nearly as dark as the cat fur covered everything below his nose—his hands, and his knees between kilt and boot-tops. Chess decided he looked like a dwarf in a black bunny suit.

Chane stepped to the edge of the ridge and looked down. Rough, fissured rock fell away in a vertical drop, and through the mists he thought he saw water below.

Wings beat the air, and a dark shadow flitted across the ledge. They looked up. A large bird, as black as midnight but with iridescent flashes where sunlight caught its sleek feathers, had swooped down from somewhere above and now rested on a gnarled snag just overhead. It preened itself, shifted its footing on the snag, and cocked its head to stare at them with one golden eye. "Go away," it said.

Chane blinked. "What?"

"It said, 'go away,' " the kender repeated. "I never heard a bird say 'go away' before, have you? For that matter, I've never heard a bird say a word of any kind—except once, when a messenger bird in the service of some wizard got lost in a crosswind or something and landed on the flagstaff at Hylo Village. It talked for five or ten minutes. Nobody knew what it was talking about, but half the folks in the village were invisible for several days afterward." He paused, remembering. "Lot of things got misplaced about then. Old Ferman Wanderweed never did find his front door—"

"Will you be quiet?" Chane snapped. "This bird just talked to us."

"I know that. It said, 'go away.' I told you."

"But birds can't talk!"

"Generally not." Curiously, the kender raised his forked staff and poked at the bird. It glared at him, first with one eye and then with the other, and shifted its position on the snag. "Go away," it said again.

"Do you suppose that's all it knows how to say?" Chess wondered aloud. "Just, 'go away'? If I were teaching a bird to talk, I think I'd come up with something better than—"

"Go away or keep the Way," the bird said.

"That's much better," Chess nodded.

"What does it mean by that?" Chane glared at the bird, which glared back with a malicious yellow eye.

"Go away or keep the Way," the bird squawked. "Go away or keep the Way! Go away or keep the Way!" Having had its say then, the bird glared at them one more time, relieved itself on the snag, spread wide wings, and launched itself out over the valley.

They watched it shrink to a dot in the distance, then Chane settled his packs on sturdy shoulders and stepped to the edge of the cliff again.

"You're still going?" the kender asked.

"Of course I am. Why not?"

"You heard what that bird said."

"I don't take orders from birds. Are you coming?"

"Sure, but I bet there's an easier way down than where you're heading." Turning away from the sheer ledge, the small creature started off, down the far slope, angling away from the ledge.

Chane frowned and called after him, "That isn't the way the bird went."

Chess glanced back. "So what?"

"The bird said, 'keep the Way.' Maybe we're supposed to follow it."

"I thought you didn't take orders from birds."

"I don't, but I'm open to suggestions when they lead in the direction I want to go."

"Well, I'll meet you in the valley, then," Chess said. "This looks like a nice, easy path around this way. A person could get hurt climbing down that cliff."

"Suit yourself." The dwarf shrugged, eased himself over the sheer ledge, and found handholds and acceptable, if precarious, holds for his feet. As a mountain dwarf, climbing was second nature to him, and he had little patience for detours.

The sheer face was almost vertical, but it was rough and broken, and Chane could find purchase. As he lowered himself below the edge, he saw the kender strolling happily away, down the easy slope to the north.

It was eighty feet to the bottom of the rock, as nearly as Chane could judge. Slow going, but he kept at it, working his way down with the stubborn dexterity of his kind. Born in Thorbardin, largest kingdom of the moun-

tain dwarves of Krynn—and maybe the only one, for all
Chane knew—swarming over rock faces was as natural
to him as delving caverns and tunnels. Dug from the bedrock of a mountain range, Thorbardin was more than a
city. It was an entire complex of cities, all deep within the
mountains. And it had many levels. In one way or another, Chane had been climbing rock all his life.

The dwarf was nearing the bottom when he heard
shouts and scuffling above. A rain of pebbles pelted
Chane. He looked up to see the kender flinging himself
over the ledge, seeming to fly out into thin air for a moment before he twisted around, thrust his forked staff at
the face of the cliff, wedged it into a crack, and swung
from it. Above Chess a great black head with feral yellow eyes looked down. A big, padded paw with ranked
claws extended and swatted downward, trying to reach
him. The kender pulled himself hand over hand to the
rock face, clung there, released his staff, and thrust it
into another crack farther down. "The bird was right," he
called. "I think I'll try it your way."

Chane let himself down another set of holds, and suddenly it was raining gravel again. From above came the
sound of splintering rock, and another yell. The next instant, Chane was knocked from his holds as the kender
landed on him. A tangle of arms and legs, pack, pouch,
and forked staff, the kender and the dwarf thumped onto
the slope at the foot of the cliff and rolled downward,
gathering momentum—a black-and-motley ball heading
for the maze of tumblestone below, leaving a cloud of
dust in its wake. Through the fallen rock they went,
threading this way and that among boulders as the rise
and fall of the slope guided them. They bounded off a
boulder, careened from another, shot through a hole in
the base of two coupled stones, and zoomed off a lower
ledge. Water glinted below, rising to meet them, then
closed over them with a splash.

The kender surfaced, bobbing like a cork. He sputtered, blinked, and headed for the nearest solid surface—
a jutting creek bank a few feet away. Reaching it, he
pulled himself up, water sheeting from him. "Wow," he

said. "Your way down is certainly faster than mine."

When there was no answer, he looked around. There was no sign of the dwarf. The surface of the stream—a deep, cold little river no more than twenty feet wide—shivered with converging ripples and resumed its flow. He looked downstream, then upstream. No one was in sight. He waded out as far as he could and began thrusting about beneath the surface, poking here and there with his hoopak.

Nothing.

"Now where did that dwarf get off to?" Chess muttered. He waded in another step, fighting the current, and prodded deep into the stream, finding nothing but water.

Several yards downstream, near the bank, waters parted and a pair of black cat-ears emerged, followed by a black head-pelt and then the face of Chane Feldstone, dripping wet. The dwarf got his whiskers above water and blew out a long-held breath, then plodded up the shallows and out of the creek.

"What are you doing over there?" Chess snapped at him. "I was getting worried. I didn't know whether you could swim."

The dwarf turned, glaring at him with hot-eyed fury. "I *can't* swim! I had to walk." He sat down to empty water out of his boots and his pack, then put them on again and stood, plodding toward the kender with the look of mayhem in his eyes. "Why did you jump on me up there? If you can't scale cliffs, why don't you just stay off of them?"

"I didn't jump on you," Chess said. "I fell on you. It's a different thing entirely. It. . . ." He looked past the drenched dwarf and pointed. "Do you know that you have a following?"

Where thickets began, fifty yards downstream, four of the great black hunting cats had emerged. Ears laid back, eyes blazing with feline anticipation, they padded toward the pair, their rumbling purrs like distant thunder.

"Don't talk about it," Chane said. "Run!"

They ran up the creek bank, across a gravel bed, and

onto meadowgrass where thickets converged ahead of them. The kender, in the lead, dove into the thickets, as quick and as limber as a rabbit taking cover. The dwarf, slower of foot, felt hot breath on his back as he bumbled into a viny wilderness that clawed and pulled at him from all sides. With one arm up to protect his feet, he pushed on, short, brawny legs making up in power what they lacked in speed. Directly behind him he heard cats circling, testing, slinking into the thickets by hidden ways, spreading to flank him on both sides, converging to head him off. Chane tripped and sprawled, suspended for a moment in a nest of thorny brush. He pushed on and stumbled again, and abruptly a fork of seasoned hardwood was in his hand. He gripped it and followed as it pulled him forward another step, then two.

"Come on!" the kender shouted. "We don't have all day!"

With Chess pulling and his own legs pushing, Chane burst from the entwining thickets and rolled onto clear ground. He could see nothing except a mass of vines and thorns in front of his face. He tried to stand, tripped over vines tangled around his face, and fell again. Behind him, to the right and left, were the rumbling purrs of big cats. He braced himself for their attack, and waited.

And nothing happened.

Near at hand, the kender said, "Well, how about that! I think we've found the 'Way.' "

Pulling and cutting at Chane's cloak of vegetation, the kender cleared a viewport for him. He looked around. They were near the center of a wide, open path that led into forest. The path's surface was black gravel, its stones glinting in the spangled light like bits of coal. And alongside the path were several of the huge hunting cats, glaring and whining, padding this way and that along the verge of the gravel.

"They don't want to come onto the path," the kender said. "I guess this is what the bird was talking about." He turned his attention again to clearing thorny vines from Chane, pulling and slicing at them, discarding them by lengths and armloads. "You really are a mess," he noted cheerfully. "Given a little time, I'll bet you could grow berries."

Chane's arms were free then, and he set about untangling himself, shrugging off the kender's attempts to help.

"This works pretty well for that," Chess said, holding up the implement he had been using. Chane stared at it—a dagger made from a cat's tooth.

"What are you doing with that?" he demanded. "That's mine."

"Is it?" the kender looked at it closely. "I found it somewhere, while we were rolling down the hill. Do you suppose you lost it?"

"Give it back!"

"All right." Chess handed over the knife. "If that's how you feel about it, here. It's all right. I still have another, just like it."

Above the blackstone path an iridescent raven wheeled, circled, then flew off to the north as though showing them the direction to take.

Other eyes also watched the bird, but not directly. High on a wind-scoured crag, among the peaks east of the Valley of Waykeep, a man knelt beside an ice pool, gazing intently at its surface. A dark bison-pelt robe pulled tight around his shoulders shielded him from the cold, only here and there exposing the color of the long robe he wore beneath it—a robe that had once been vermilion, but whose hood, cape, and hems now were faded to the red of twilight. The color blended, in the shadow of his hood, with unkempt whiskers the gray of winter wind.

In the ice pool was an image: two beings on a black path where black cats prowled the edges and a black bird beckoned above. The image wavered and misted as an errant wind scattered hard, dry snow across the ice. Without looking up, the man raised a long staff with a crystal device at its peak. Sunlight glinted in the crystal and concentrated through it to glow on the surface of the ice. The misted surface smoothed itself, melted, and refroze bright and clear. The two in the valley were on the move, following the bird. Like a deadly honor guard, great black cats plodded along both sides of the pathway, flanking them.

The image shifted then. In the ice was a great, vaulted chamber hewn from living stone. Dim and deserted, the chamber contained various structures and articles, largest of which was a great dais upon which rested a crypt. Here and there on the shadowed walls hung paintings, all done in the finest dwarven style. The view held on one painting and seemed to approach it as the vision magnified: a fighting dwarf in emblazoned armor, leading a charge of dwarven warriors across a blasted mountainscape. Again the vision grew, focusing on the face of the dwarf in the lead.

Peering closely into the ice, the man studied the features of that face—wide, strong dwarven features of a face that had known power and had known pain; wide-set, intelligent eyes that had seen much of life and had cherished most of it; a face chiseled for patience, twisted now in fury as he led his armies in final assault.

The man studied the features as he had in many viewings, then twitched his staff. The view changed again, back to the black pathway in the Valley of Waykeep. This time the vision moved close, sighting on the irritated, frowning face of a dwarf in black furs with cat ears atop his head.

Just as he had studied the face in the painting, the man at the ice pool now examined the features of the dwarf in the valley below.

Chapter 3

The blackstone path wound and curved as it wandered deeper into the Valley of Waykeep. It twisted and turned oddly, often for no apparent reason. Sometimes it nearly doubled back on itself, so that the travelers found themselves walking southward within easy reach—sometimes even within sight—of where they had just passed going northward. Then again, it would straighten for a time, only to abruptly veer off to the east or west, as though circling around some obstacle that neither the dwarf nor the kender could see.

At times the path narrowed, becoming only six or eight feet wide. In these places the big cats gathered along its edges—sometimes a dozen or more, rumbling and purring in feral anticipation—and the two were forced to go in single file, running a gauntlet of swatting, searching claws as the animals balanced just at the borders of the path and strained forward, trying to reach them.

"These creatures are most decidedly unfriendly," Chess mentioned as he dodged a huge, needle-clawed paw. As it whipped past him, he rapped it sharply with his hoopak. "Bad kitty!" he snapped. The cat's responding growl was thunderous.

Just behind him, Chane ducked as a cat swatted at him. "Stop stirring them up," he ordered the kender. "You're just making matters worse."

"I don't know why they have to be so surly." The kender shrugged. "Maybe they don't get fed regularly. I wonder why this path twists and turns so much. Doesn't it seem odd to you that a path should go to so much trouble to go around things, if there aren't any things to go around? I'll bet we've walked ten miles so far, and haven't gained more than a mile or two. You see, there it goes again." He pointed with his hoopak. Ahead, the black road turned abruptly to the left and disappeared into forest. "Do you see any reason why we shouldn't just go straight ahead?"

"I see about a dozen very good reasons," Chane snapped, counting cats.

"I mean besides them. What do you suppose is ahead there, that this path doesn't want us to see?"

Chane felt an extended claw graze his boot-top and skipped away from it, then ducked as a cat on the other side tried to knock off his head. He spun, lost his balance, and sprawled, pellets of black gravel sheeting ahead of him. The cats there dodged aside, retreating. Chane got to his knees and scraped at the gravel with his hand. The gravel was spread evenly over a smooth surface, as though it had been swept. It was only inches deep, with bare dirt below. He gathered a handful of gravel and tossed it toward a cat. The cat veered aside, as though panicked.

"They don't like this stuff," Chane muttered. "I think they're afraid of it."

Chess had come back to watch. "Well, then, that's

easy," he said. "All we need to do is move the road."

"Move it how?" Chane's brows lowered in disgust.

"I don't know," Chess shrugged. "You're a dwarf. You're supposed to know about things like moving gravel. How would *you* do it?"

"If I wanted to, I'd use a skid. Something flat and heavy to drag it from one place to another. But we don't have a skid."

"Then maybe you could build one," Chess suggested. "There are all sorts of things around here to use."

Chane sighed, looking off into the forest beyond the path. Yes, there were plenty of materials, readily available. There also were plenty of giant black cats just itching for one of them to step off the path and within reach. "Sure," he said. "That deadfall log over there could be a dragsled, with vines attached. But it's over there, not here."

"Then go get it," the kender said. "Just a minute, though. I'll see if I can give you a little space." Without hesitating, he stepped to the edge of the path, lifted his staff and brought it down between the ears of a cat. While that one still was recoiling, Chess thumped two more of them, prodded a fourth one in the ribs, then moved away along the path, his feet flying, swerving on and off of the carpet of black gravel. All of the cats on that side bounded after him, snarling and spitting. "Hurry!" he shouted.

For a moment, Chane stood stunned, staring after the departing chase. "Rust and tarnish!" he muttered. "That kender is crazy." Then he hurried off the path to gather materials for a dragsled skid. "I don't know why I'm doing this," he grumped as he dragged things back to safety. "It wasn't my idea to change the road. It was his."

Still, when the kender reappeared at the curve in the path, strolling along with a pack of angry cats pacing him, Chane was already binding vines to a log and weighting it with stones. Chess came to watch him work, peering over his shoulder. "Do you think it will work?" he asked.

"Of course not," Chane snapped. "I'm just doing this

for practice."

"What's wrong with it?"

"To start with, in order for a skid to move gravel, somebody has to get out in front of it and pull it. And whoever does that is going to be eight feet past the edge of the path before the gravel load gets there."

"That could be a little chancy," Chess admitted, looking around at the patrolling cats. "But if you don't pull too fast, I can come along behind you and . . ."

"*Me* pull?"

"It's your skid," the kender pointed out. "Besides, you're bigger than me. Anyway, I can follow along and throw gravel out ahead of you, enough to keep the cats back while you reroute the road."

"I don't see anything wrong with just leaving the blasted road where it is!"

"We've already been over that," the kender said.

Considering the circumstances of its construction, the skid worked fairly well. The black gravel on the path was only a few inches deep, with ordinary clay below, and when Chane put his shoulders to the tow-vines and dragged the sled, it plowed up a growing mound of black pebbles in front, and left bare clay behind.

"That's perfect," Chess grinned. "Just head for the curve, and keep going straight ahead when you get there. I'm right behind you."

"That's comforting to know," the dwarf growled.

When he came to the curve, Chane was barely moving. The load of gravel ahead of the skid had grown so that it took all his strength to move it. He hesitated at the edge of the path, confronted by cats. Then showers of black gravel began to fly over his shoulders, some of it pelting him from behind as the kender flung enthusiastic handfuls as fast as he could. The cats snarled and snapped, but backed away. "Take the weights off the skid," the dwarf called.

"Why?" Another handful of gravel flew, one fair-sized pebble catching Chane on the cheek as he turned.

"So it will spread the gravel instead of scooping it! Don't argue, just do it!"

Chess removed the weights, then resumed showering gravel as Chane took up his harness again.

By the time the skid was exhausted, the pathway south of the curve had a bare clay stripe angling from its center to the turning edge, and a new black path the width of the strip extended fifty feet into the forest. Chess scampered back and forth along the new path, peering off into the forest. "Nothing interesting yet," he said, finally. "We'd better go back for another load."

The second stripe taken from the main path extended the new road another fifty feet, and the third stripe put them well into the forest, almost out of sight of the road where they had been. Poised at the very end of the gravel, the kender peered and squinted, looking ahead. "There *is* something over there," he pointed. "But I can't see what it is. It's something big, though. Another load, and we should be there."

"Another load and we'll have wiped out the original path back there," Chane pointed out.

"Oh, come on. Where's your spirit of adventure? Just one more haul."

They started back, and Chane was almost at the clearing when he stopped. "Now see what we've done," he grunted. Ahead, black cats were crossing the main road freely. Whatever the black gravel did to stop them, there wasn't enough left on the skidded section to work.

The kender studied the problem solemnly, pursing his lips as his pointed ears twitched slightly in thought. Then he shrugged. "It's all right. We weren't going that way, anyway."

"We can't go back, either," the dwarf pointed out. "We might want to, you know. We. . . ." He paused, then caught the kender by the shoulder. "That business you did before, leading the cats off . . . can you do that again?"

"I suppose so. Won't be as much fun the second time, though. Things like that get to be routine after a while."

"I don't care," the dwarf said. "Just do it."

The kender shrugged. "I guess one more time won't hurt. Come along, kitties. Time for another run." Poking and prodding at snarling predators, Chess circled the stump of the road, gathering more than a dozen cats on the far side. With a final swat of his staff, he took off around the curve, great cats bounding after him. Left alone, Chane wrapped his harness over his shoulders and set about replacing gravel on the main road. Some time passed before the kender returned, a long line of irritated cats slinking along abreast of him. When he saw what the dwarf was doing, Chess shouted and ran toward him. "What are you doing?" he demanded. "We need that gravel. Why are you putting it back?"

Panting, Chane slipped out of his vine harness and inspected his work. The road here was not as neatly graded as it had been, but it was black again and hemmed in the cats. "Because we *don't* need it any longer," the dwarf said. Picking up his pack, he strode to the east verge of the road and walked off into the forest. Behind him, across the road, the cat pack snarled and rumbled, unable to cross.

"Well, come on," Chane glanced back. "Let's see what it was that you wanted to look at."

It might once have been a machine, in some incredibly ancient time. Or it might have been a building. Perhaps even both. Now it was a great heap of rubble and broken metal things, slowly surrendering to the landscape. Trees hundreds of years old grew from its crest, vines and brush obscured its slopes, and a carpeting of forest leaves and grassy loam was well along toward burying it.

Chane and Chess wandered over and around it, peering, poking, and prying.

"This looks like part of a wheel," the kender chattered. "But why would anybody make a wheel fifteen feet across? Wow! Look at those things sticking out of the mess. What are they, drills? They're as big around as— and here's some old, rusty chain. Must have weighed a ton per link when it was still good iron. I wonder what this was, over here. A furnace of some kind? Did you notice that all these stones scattered over here are square? They might have been paving blocks. What do you suppose this thing was when it was something?"

"I haven't the vaguest idea." Chane was digging through a reddish heap of vaguely-shaped rust tumbles, raising a cloud of thin red dust that settled on his black furs like rust-colored snow. After several minutes he straightened, holding up a long, slim object to have a better look at it. It was a rod, nearly six feet long, gnarly and misshapen from centuries of rust. He knew by its heft, though, that there was good metal within it. He set it aside and began digging again.

For some time the kender explored the ancient heap, his bright eyes shining in wonder at each new mystery. He moved things here and there, on the thought that whatever all this was the outside of might also have an inside, and somewhere there might be an entrance. Finding none, he scampered here and there over the surface of the thing, tugging and pushing at everything that protruded, seeing what would move. Where a broken shaft of heavily corroded metal angled upward, he cleared away broken stone, then braced his feet and pulled at the stub. Deep beneath him, something groaned and large parts of the mound shifted slightly. Beyond the crest, the dwarf shouted, then appeared at the top.

"Sorry about that." Chess waved at him. "I guess whatever this was, it doesn't work any more."

With a warning scowl, the dwarf went back to what he was doing. Chess continued his exploration. Near one edge of the mound, tugging away a rock, he found a thick, ragged sheet of green-black stuff that might once have been bronze. Wiping it with his tunic, he saw letters on its surface and sat down to read them aloud. Most were corroded beyond recognition, but here and there a few words could be partially deciphered:

". . . velous Wallbreacher, equipped with secondary ar . . . iple-geared self-propel . . . ba . . . not included . . ."

And elsewhere, ". . . Model one of—"

"Gnomes," Chess said, nodding at the revelation. He climbed to the top of the mound. Beyond, Chane was moving stones around, arranging them in a circle. Chess cupped his hands and shouted, "Gnomes!"

The dwarf raised his head. "What?"

"Gnomes!" the kender repeated. "This was a gnomish machine of some kind. I found its label."

"What was it supposed to do?"

"I don't know. But gnomes built it, so it probably didn't do anything right."

Chane turned away and resumed the moving of stones.

For a bit longer, Chess explored the ancient wreckage, then he brushed down his tunic, shouldered his pouch, picked up his staff, and went to find the dwarf. "This was interesting," he said. "Now let's go on, and see what else there is to find."

"I'm busy," Chess grunted, setting a block of stone atop another.

"What are you doing?"

"I found some usable metal. I'm setting up a forge to work it."

"Oh." The kender walked all the way around the circle of stone, wide-eyed. "What do you want to make?"

"A hammer, of course. The only thing I know of that can be made without a hammer is a hammer, though it won't be a very good one, without a hammer to work with."

"A hammer," Chess nodded, taken with the logic of it. "Then what?"

"What?"

"What are you going to make once you've made your hammer?"

"Another hammer. Once I have a rough hammer to use, I can make a perfectly good hammer with it. Then, if that rod there will stew out and take a temper, I'll make a sword."

"Is this part of your plan for becoming rich and famous?"

"I don't have any such plan," the dwarf growled. "I don't have a hammer or sword, either, so first things first."

"I have a feeling this is going to take a while."

"It will take as long as it takes."

For the rest of the day, Chestal Thicketsway prowled about, exploring the silent forest, becoming more and more impatient. At nightfall he returned to the wreckage heap, took fire from Chane's now-operating forge and made a meal of cured cat meat and bark tea, then went to sleep to the sound of dwarven craft echoing in the night.

At first light of morning, the kender awakened, stretched, and strolled over to watch the dwarf again. Chane now had a serviceable—if crude—hammer, and was using it to make a better hammer from a chunk of iron he had found.

Finally the kender had seen enough. "I'm going on ahead," he said. "I want to see what else is interesting around here."

"Have a nice trip," Chane said without looking up.

"Yourself, as well," Chess replied. He started off, northward, then turned back and made several trips back and forth between the mound and the black road where great cats prowled the far border.

Chane was thoroughly engrossed in what he was doing. The good hammer was taking shape nicely, and he had scraped away enough age from the long rod to see the metal beneath, and to taste it. It was good steel. It would make a blade . . . maybe more than one.

The kender paused once more beside the forge. "Luck with your quest," he said.

"You, too," Chane glanced up. "See you."

"Sure," Chess waved and headed north. Long after he had gone, the dwarf looked up from his work and his eyes went thoughtful. Entirely ringing him and his forge was a circle of black gravel scattered on the ground. The kender had left a shield for him, in case any of the hunting cats found a way to cross the road or to go around it.

Chapter 4

Through that day and most of the next, Chane worked at his forge in the forest. In a buried firepit he coaled bits of hardwood for the bed of his flame, and a foot-bellows of sapling lengths and catskin fed it to a pulsing glow. His first hammer was no more than a lump of iron remelted, skimmed clean and shaped in a clay mold. But with its help he crafted a second one—a hammer that even a Hylar prince or Daewar merchant in the finest halls of Thorbardin might have envied. For though Chane Feldstone—orphaned and without a known lineage—had been relegated to the lowly ranks of common delver and sometimes outsman in the teeming realm within the Kharolis Mountains, still the high crafts came to him easily when he turned his hand to them.

Often through the years of childhood he had watched others of his age go off to apprentice at the trades of metalsmithy, stonecutting, and other such high callings. Sometimes he had been envious that those so chosen had someone of note to sponsor them. His hands had longed for the feel of good tools, and his heart had yearned for the chance to do such works as those more fortunate would one day do. Still, he had not been alone in his circumstances. Among the seven cities of the undermountain kingdom there always were thousands of children without access to great name or the comfort of wealth. Children of the warrens and the ways, the offspring of warriors who didn't come home or traders lost to the outlands, orphans and waifs of all sorts. It was the way of the dwarves of Thorbardin that these children be cared for and receive at least some basic education so they would never lack for work or the basic needs.

Chane had grown up like the rest, and had learned a host of lesser skills that served him well. Only, there had been times—times all through the years when some secret part within him raged and strove for recognition. Times there had been. . . .

When he was yet a youngster, inches short of his full growth of four feet six, Chane had been employed to clean the smithing stalls of the ironworker, Barak Chiselcut. A piece of nickeliron had been cast aside, and Chane retrieved it, put a high polish on it and returned it to the master.

"A nice bauble," old Chiselcut had said, approving. "So you enjoy metals, youngster?"

"Yes, sir. I like the feel of good metals, and the sound and taste."

"Then keep this," the old dwarf told him. "Play with it at the forge and anvil, if you like. But mind you get your work done first."

For weeks, Chane had shaped the bit of nickeliron, late in the sleeping hours when no one else was about, and the small dagger he crafted from it had so pleased Barak Chiselcut that the shopmaster gave the youth some brass and ebony with which to make a handle for it.

"You have skill at making weapons, Chane," Chiselcut told him. "Maybe some ancestor of yours was a craftsman. It's too bad you don't have a known lineage. But then, most orphans don't. Keep the dagger, and keep learning. Having craft is more important than knowing who you are."

For fifteen years Chane had carried and cherished the knife, and sometimes at odd moments it seemed to whisper to him, "Look at me, Chane Feldstone. I am no ordinary dagger, and you are no ordinary dwarf. See your reflection in my steel. Perhaps someday your reflection will tell you who you really are."

He had looked at his reflection and wondered. Even then, in the years before his shoulders broadened and his whiskers grew, he had been aware that he looked subtly different from most of those around him . . . not quite typical of the ordinary day-to-day Daewar he met in the trade centers. In some respects, he even resembled the Hylar dwarves—not that it made any difference, since there was no more likelihood of his tracing lineage among the Hylar than among the Daewar. A foundling is a foundling, anywhere in Thorbardin.

It was in those years, too, that the dreams began. The same insistent dream, over and over, sometimes no more than a week apart. The mysterious place, the mysterious container, and the old, horned battle helmet that he held in his hands but somehow never managed to place upon his head.

The years had passed, and he had come of age and found work with Rogar Goldbuckle, the trader. He had served as a packer and sometimes as an outsman, going beyond Southgate to help with the gear and goods of trading parties bound for Barter or some other gathering place of merchants. Chane had made the journey to Barter himself once. He had met elves and humans, gnomes and kender. He had seen the rising and setting of the sun, had seen the moons in the night sky, had felt the vastness of *outside*, a world not contained beneath mountains.

Back in Thorbardin, full of worldliness and wonder,

Chane had walked as tall as any dwarf for the first time in his life. And it had been then that he'd met Jilian. Jilian Firestoke. His eyes grew moist now, remembering how she had made his heart melt . . . and how he had worked to win her affections. He had known from the first that her father despised him, but that hadn't seemed important. Jilian knew her own mind, and what Slag Firestoke thought about anything didn't seem to matter. . . .

Until the dream had come again, this time with urgency. This time the dream had spoken to him of destiny, and he couldn't help but believe it.

And old Firestoke had used the opportunity to teach Chane who he truly was—a lowly foundling who had reached beyond his grasp.

The nickeliron dagger was gone now. It was one of the things Slag Firestoke's thugs had robbed from him when they drove him into the wilderness. Maybe Jilian was gone as well. Chane was certain that Slag Firestoke wouldn't tell his daughter what he had done, so all Jilian could know was that Chane had gone away and not come back. Maybe she even thought he was dead. He was still tempted to head right back for Southgate, to give those toughs a taste of honest iron, and to shake Slag Firestoke until his teeth rattled. The devious old rust-bucket.

But the dream called. There was something he was supposed to do, and he knew deep inside that he could not return to Thorbardin until he had done it . . . or at least tried his best.

"Become rich and famous," the kender had said. Chane rumbled his irritation at the thought. What could a kender know about anything?

The new hammer shaped itself on his makeshift anvil. Four pounds would be its weight. His hands told him that, and he knew there was no mistake. A head that was a shaping maul at one end with a tapered balancing spike at the other. A hammer that could bend the strongest drawbar or shape the daintiest filigree . . . and could serve as a formidable weapon should the need arise. He put the final touches to it, tempered its face and its spike, and set it on a shaft of sturdy darkwood, with rawhide lashing for the hand to grip. Then he fashioned a thong to carry it, took a deep breath, and looked around for the metal that would make a sword.

A man stood a few feet away, leaning casually on a staff, watching the dwarf. Chane had no idea how long the man had been there. He had not heard him approach. But the faded red robe beneath the bison-pelt cape told him *what* the man was, and the dwarf felt a twinge of distaste . . . distaste and more than a bit of caution. A wizard.

"I see nothing wrong with becoming rich and famous, Chane Feldstone," the wizard said in a voice as thin and as cold as winter wind. "It is a proper approach to some worthwhile goals."

The dwarf frowned at him, backing off a step. "Have you been listening to my thoughts? If you have, you know it wasn't me who said that, it was some kender."

"There'd be no need to read the thoughts of one who speaks them to himself while he is working, Chane Feldstone."

"How do you know who I am? I didn't tell myself my name."

"Oh, I know of you, Chane Feldstone," the wizard said. "I might even know more of who you are than you do."

"Who are you, that you know about me?"

The man sighed, bowing his head, and whiskers of sleet gray bobbed as he nodded. "I have been called many things, young dwarf. Some call me Glenshadow the Wanderer. If you want a name for me, that will do." He stepped closer to the still-glowing forge and spread his hands as though to warm himself. He glanced at the new hammer. "Have you set a crest or a device upon that? Have you named it or made it yours?"

Again the dwarf edged away, but he took the hammer from his belt and turned it in the light. "I've only initialed it. See for yourself. What device would I use?"

The wizard squinted at the hammer. "Ah, yes. I see. C. F. Chane Feldstone. It is truly your hammer, then."

"What do you want of me?"

"Why, I am going with you. I thought you would know that."

"Why would I have known any such thing?"

"You're right, of course," the man admitted. "Well, first we must go see the Irda."

"The who?"

"The Irda."

"Why?"

"We will know more about that when we get there. Come along, now."

"Come along nothing!" Chane's whiskers twitched with exasperation. "I have a sword to make."

The wizard looked at the ancient, rusted metal bar. "That isn't the stuff of your sword, Chane Feldstone. There's better along the way. Come on, now. This valley is not a happy place for me, and I don't want to spend more time here than I have to."

Chane shook his head violently, clenching his teeth in frustration. "I don't know what you're talking about, and I don't want to go!"

"I think you had better," the wizard said quietly.

"Why?"

"Because of them." The wizard tilted his head to one side, gesturing."

Chane looked where the man indicated, then sucked in a whistling breath, grabbed his pack, and ran, barely aware that the robed man was pacing him alongside. Behind them came a leaping, bounding, slinking flood of huge black cats.

The wizard was half again as tall as Chane, and when he lifted his hems and sprinted, he left the dwarf in his wake. "This way!" he called. "The road curves back, just ahead!"

Chane ran for all he was worth, but with each step the cats were closer behind him, their deep, rumbling purrs mounting like the roll of charging drums. When he felt their breath warming his back he clasped his hammer in one hand, his cat-tooth dagger in the other, skidded to a stop, and spun around. The dwarf crouched and roared a battle cry. As he faced them, the cats hesitated. Other cats coming up behind collided with the leaders. In an instant the glade was atumble with clawing, spitting cats, swatting at one another, sidling and rearing, grappling and rolling. Chane raised his hammer and started forward, set to wade in among them, but a hand caught him by the nape, turned him, and shoved.

"Run!" the wizard snapped. "This is no time for games!"

The logic of that statement was inescapable. Chane ran. Beyond the glade was forest, and beyond the forest the blackstone path. They arrived there with cats pounding at their heels, and the dwarf strode back and forth along the edge of safety, growling as ferociously as the frustrated predators that strained toward him. Finally Chane got his temper under control, slung his hammer at his belt, and turned to the wizard. "How do you suppose those cats got across the road? They were supposed to all be on the other side."

The man shrugged disinterestedly. "An ancient question, that. Why *does* a cat cross the road?"

"Rust and corruption!" Chane glared at him. "That's chickens, not cats! And don't change the subject. What I asked was *how* they got across."

"Oh, that. You left your log skid back there. Someone simply moved the gravel again."

"But who would—" the dwarf's face went dark with fury. "You! You did that! Why?"

"Would you have come along with me otherwise?"

Chane tried to say something, could think of nothing appropriate, and merely sputtered.

"No need to apologize," the wizard said. "Any dwarf worth his salt would rather cook iron than travel. It's your nature. You might have dawdled there for weeks, when you should be seeking the Irda. You *do* want answers to your questions, don't you?"

"I don't have any questions!"

"Of course you do." The wizard drew himself up to his full height, and the gray eyes above his gray beard seemed to focus on something far away. "Everyone has questions." At first, Chane had thought the man looked old. Now he realized it was not old he looked, but . . . ageless. "You can learn to be what you've always been," the wizard said, "if you've the gift of knowing. But you can't learn from whence you came 'til you learn where you're going."

Chane felt a chill creep up his spine. "Are you working a spell, wizard?"

"Oh, mercy, no," the man said, turning away. "Didn't your little friend tell you? Spells are dangerous and unreliable here. This is the Valley of Waykeep."

* * * * *

For days Jilian Firestoke had watched the ways of the Daewar city, going often to the market centers at the tenth and thirteenth roads and finding excuses even to visit the bustling ware-room district near the eleventh road gate, where goods from other clan cities in Thorbardin were gathered and traded. She had ridden a cable-train to the east warrens, where Chane Feldstone worked the fields sometimes when neither Barak Chiselcut nor Rogar Goldbuckle had employment for him.

Wherever she went, she had asked about Chane, but no one had seen him lately. Maybe, some suggested, he had gone to carry dispatches for Rogar Goldbuckle to his commodity camp west of Thorbardin in the Kharolis Mountains. But, no, one of Goldbuckle's guardsmen had said that he was sure there had been no dispatches lately, and since Goldbuckle was preparing for a pack-trip to Barter, he would carry any such messages himself.

She had become more worried by the day. It was not like Chane to just disappear without telling her where he was going. Yet, since the day she had taken him to see her father—she had been sure her father would help him, but he had flatly refused—Chane had been absent. Someone said they thought Chane might have gone back again, alone, to talk with Slag Firestoke. But her father said he hadn't seen the whelp again and, furthermore, didn't want to.

Jilian had only recently—as they said in the polite

sectors—"come of age," and had no shortage of admirers among the young male dwarves of Thorbardin. A petite and sturdy four feet three, with the wide, subtly chiseled face of a dwarven angel and a curvaceous shape that even the most modest of clothing could not hide, it was natural that she should have suitors. And she did. They came by the dozens, and Slag Firestoke busied himself investigating the family lineage and financial means of each one. But he was wasting his time. Jilian had already decided. Even when young males of the noble-blooded Hylar clans stared after her in the market, with open mouths and enchanted eyes, she was no more than amused. In Chane Feldstone she saw something that no one else seemed to see, but that didn't matter. She saw it, and had no intention of letting him get away.

And she had told her father so, in no uncertain terms. In that straightforward way of hers that always seemed to infuriate him, Jilian had made it clear that she would, by Reorx, decide for herself what male she wanted. And she had, by Reorx, decided it was Chane Feldstone.

It wasn't that Chane was the most handsome young dwarf she had seen—although his broad shoulders, his somber, wide-set dark eyes, and the way his near-black whiskers swept back in feral lines along each sloping cheek reminded her of old pictures she had seen, paintings of the fierce Hylar warriors of ancient times. It wasn't that he was the most entertaining; at times, when the mood was on him, Chane was nearly impossible to talk to, and seemed to lose himself in dark, hidden thoughts that he wouldn't—or couldn't—express.

He was, in fact, a waif.

Orphaned in some manner that left no clear record of his lineage, Chane was a bit of an enigma to those whose duty it was, or whose inclination it was, to keep track of people in the dwarven realm. Clearly a citizen of Thorbardin, he yet had no definable status except that of orphan and common worker.

But now Jilian was worried. He had simply disappeared, and no one had seen him. And when she had asked her father to make inquiries, old Firestoke just sneered and said, "Good riddance. He's nothing but an upstart who's never learned his place."

She would have argued with her father, except for the arrival of that bunch of rough-looking armsmen who were waiting to see him on some sort of business and wouldn't go away until they had. By the time they were gone, Jilian's anger at her father had jelled. She didn't want to argue with him. She didn't want to talk to him at all. In fact, she had hardly seen him since the incident, having gone about her own business and staying out of his sight when he was at home.

Until today.

With communication at a minimum in the Firestoke quarters, certain necessities such as paying the tap fees and keeping the larder stocked—things Jilian normally did—had piled up so that she had to do something about it or face such problems as late penalties on water and oil bills. So she had gone to her father's chamber for the money she needed, and found that he was away on business.

For the first time in months Jilian had opened the old dwarf's private locker.

Now she stood over the locker, holding a dagger in her hands—a small, nickeliron dagger with an ebony-and-brass hilt. It was a dagger she had seen many times, but not in her father's things. It belonged to Chane Feldstone.

Chapter 5

Chestal Thicketsway had been a little miffed that the dwarf had abandoned what promised to be an interesting exploration in favor of playing with fire and iron and such things. But, in the way of all kender, he hadn't stayed miffed very long. The world held far too many new and fascinating things to see for any kender to dwell for long on any one subject . . . even such a novelty as a fugitive dwarf who could kill a giant cat with his bare hands and make himself a bunny suit.

Before he had gone a mile, Chess found a new fascination. The forest of this valley, what he had seen of it so far, was an ancient forest. The gnarled and twisted hardwood trees, some still wearing their fall colors though many now were bare, spoke of ages of time, while the deep loam beneath them, under a thick carpet of fallen leaves, whispered of countless generations of such trees that had grown and fallen before them. Thousands upon thousands of years have passed here, the forest seemed to say, and nothing of note has occurred. Nothing here has changed.

And yet, where the rolling lands came down to a little rock-bound stream, the forest did change. Across the stream was a different sort of forest, younger and less brooding. The kender crossed, climbed the far bank, and prowled around, looking at everything. The trees were large here too, but younger and more varied. The forest here spoke of hundreds of years . . . but not of thousands.

"It burned," something said . . . or seemed to say. Chess was not sure whether he had heard words or imagined them. He looked around and there was no one there. He was alone.

"It might very well have," he told himself. "This might once have been a forest fire, and all the old trees burned and the ones here now grew later."

"Much later," something seemed to say.

"I beg your pardon?" The kender turned full circle, holding his forked staff at the ready. There was no one there, nor any sign that anyone had been there—at least in a very long time. The only sound was the fitful breeze rustling the treetops. He squatted, peering under the nearby bush, then walked in a wide circle, looking behind trees and under stones. There was no one anywhere about.

Perplexed and curious, he went on, turning often to look behind him. He wasn't sure at all that he had heard anything, but he didn't remember thinking the words that he had seemed to hear until after he seemed to hear them. Talking to himself was nothing unusual for Chess. As a traveler, he was often alone, and even in company he often preferred to talk to himself. But he didn't recall ever not being in complete charge of one of his own conversations.

The younger forest—he thought of it now as Afterburn Woods—rose away before the kender, and he kept traveling more or less northward, recalling from time to time that his original purpose—at least the most recent one—had been to go east across the valley with Chane Feldstone, to see if the dwarf could find his dream-helmet.

The forest thickened, then broke away, and the black road was before him, curving in from the east to wind northward again. The path almost immediately lost itself in the forest as it curved once more, again to the east.

"I wonder what it's trying to stay away from now," the kender muttered.

"Death and birth," something nearby seemed to say.

Chess spun around. As before, there was no one there. "Death and birth?" he repeated.

"Birth and death," something almost certainly said.

This time Chess strolled about, squinting as he peered upward. Maybe the talking bird has come back, he thought. But there was no sign of it anywhere. Besides, it had *talked*—clearly and without mistake. Whatever was talking here just kind of *seemed* to talk. It wasn't the same.

With a grunt of exasperation, he put his hands on his hips and asked, "Whose birth and death?"

"Mine and theirs," something seemed to respond.

"Theirs and yours?" As the kender asked the question, his bright eyes were darting from one side to the other, looking for a clue as to who was talking to him.

For a moment there was silence, then the silence whispered, "Death and birth. Go and see." And a few yards away, just where the trees began, there was a brief shifting of light—as though the air there had moved.

"Probably something truly dreadful over there somewhere," Chess decided. "Maybe even a deathtrap for kender. I guess I had better go and see."

He turned his back on the black road and entered the verge of forest where the odd shifting of air had been. A few feet into the woods he saw it again—a little way ahead and beckoning.

"Ogres, maybe," the kender told himself cheerfully. "A

beckoning vesper to lead the unwary into a nest of ogres. Or hobgoblins, perhaps? No, probably not. They aren't smart enough to think of something like that." He paused for a moment, searched in his pouch, and withdrew a sling—a small, soft-leather pocket with elastic loops attached to either end. He secured the loops to the ends of the fork on his hoopak, kicked around in the fallen leaves until he found a few good pebbles, then hurried on, following where the vesper had been. He went on, not seeing the strange air-shift again, but keeping to its original direction.

After a time the forest broke away, and Chess found himself on a low, broken ridge with a clearing extending from its base. A great shallow bowl of ground, broken here and there by groves of trees and grassy knolls, the clearing extended into distances where herds of animals grazed. Beyond them, forests rose toward the tumbles and steeps of the valley's east wall.

Nearer, though, in the bottom of the bowl, was a wide field of what looked like ice—flat around the edges, but distorted within by many random shapes and lumps that seemed to grow from it.

The kender scrambled down the ledge and approached the field of ice. All around it, the air was cold and silent.

"Old," the silence seemed to say.

"Right," the kender agreed. He knelt at the edge of the field and rapped at it with his staff. The stuff looked and sounded like ice, and when a sliver of it broke away he tasted it. It was ice. "It's ice," he said.

"Fire and ice," the silence seemed to say. "Old."

Encouraged, Chess wandered out onto the ice. A few steps brought him to the nearest of the weird shapes—a tangled mound of crystals and spires higher than his head and twenty feet long. He knelt, looking into it, seeing twisted dark shadows inside. He rapped at it with the heel of his staff. Little cracks formed, then a hole, larger than his head, appeared in it as bits of ice fell away. Inside was a blackened tangle of burned branches, and a mist like ancient woodsmoke rose from the hole. He stuck his head through for a better look. Inside the ice was a burned tree.

"Fire and ice," he said to himself. It looked as though the tree had burned and toppled, then been caked with ice while it still burned.

All around were other interesting ice mounds. The kender wandered among them, peering here and there, his eyes wide with the pure delight of a kender amidst a mystery. Sometimes he could not see what the ice held, but sometimes he could. One small lump contained a dead dwarf—a short, thick-set body armored with mail and visored helm. A bolt from a crossbow had pierced him. He lay across an emblazoned shield, preserved by the ice so that the blood of his wound was still bright red. Hill dwarf, the kender thought. He looks as though he might have died just minutes ago.

"Old," something seemed to say.

Chess stood and turned away, but stopped as something in the flat ice underfoot caught his attention. He knelt again, brushing at the surface. Just beneath it, things glittered and shone. He went to work with his staff.

Breaking away the shallow ice, he found a broadsword, its edge notched by combat but still as shiny as when it was new. He lifted it, then set it aside. A good dwarven weapon, it was too heavy and awkward to suit a kender. But there were other interesting things there, as well. One by one, he lifted out a pewter mug, a string of marble beads, and a little glass ball. He looked them over, then moved on. Under other ice mounds were other dead dwarves, some standing, some kneeling and some fallen. Dwarves with hammers and swords, frozen in mortal combat. Hill dwarves and mountain dwarves, locked now in solid ice in a battle that would never end.

"What ever could they have been fighting about?" the kender wondered.

"The gates," something seemed to say.

Chess peered all around, shading his eyes. He saw nothing anywhere that looked like gates. "Gates? What gates?"

"The gates of Thorbardin," the silence seemed to say.

"That dwarf should have come with me," the kender muttered. "I'll bet he never saw anything like this."

At the thought of Chane Feldstone, Chess looked back the way he had come. The dwarf had said something about wanting a sword. Chess snooped for a while longer, then decided there was nothing to see here that was more unusual than what he had already seen. He went back to where he had left the dwarven sword, hoisted it on his shoulder, and started back, more or less retracing his steps. Chess had in mind to leave the sword somewhere that the dwarf would be likely to pass—if he came north at all—so he decided he would retrace his steps to the black road.

"So long," something seemed to say.

Chess turned, looking all around, yet no longer expecting to see someone. "Oh, yes," he said. "So long to you, too."

The silence seemed puzzled and suddenly very sad. "So very long," it seemed to say.

Chess didn't know what to say to that, so he said nothing and went on his way. The sun sank below the valley's west wall, and the forest became a shadowy place. Here and there, little mists formed above the leaf mold to drift vague tendrils among the trees. Chess wandered, pausing to look at a bright stone, a bird's nest, a scattering of bones where some predator had fed. Whatever caught his eye, he inspected. Whatever came to hand, he picked up. Whatever appealed to him—if there was space for it—went into his pouch. It was the way of all the kender, and Chestal Thicketsway was no exception.

In evening shadows, somewhere near where he expected to find the black road, he came across another gnomish artifact—an ancient, fallen construct that might once have been a catapult, except that no one could conceivably have operated a catapult so huge and complex. He walked around and through the overgrown wreckage, trying to imagine how the thing might once have looked—a huge, impossibly complex machine standing at least a hundred feet tall on four gigantic wheels with spiked iron rims . . . endlessly intricate systems of pulleys and gears, levers and winding mechanisms, steam boilers and windvanes . . . and probably half a hundred whistles, bells, and ratchet-rattles.

Little was left of it now. What had been wood was entirely gone. What had been stone was rubble. What had been iron was designs of rust imbedded in the ground. But he traced it out, and could surmise what had happened. Here an army of gnomes had built a siege engine and had set it off. Possibly it had thrown a missile, but definitely it had thrown itself. The entire machine had climbed up onto its throwing arm, flipped over and landed on its back. And there it lay to this day, what was left of it.

Such a long, long time ago. So inconceivably old.

"Ages," something seemed to say.

Chess jumped, then turned full circle again, squinting into the twilight. "I thought I had left you back there," he snapped.

"All the ages since the first," the breeze whispered. "Old. Very old."

"Well, I can see that," the kender agreed. "Are you following me?"

"With you," something whispered.

"Why?"

"By your doing," the voice that was no voice said.

"By my—" Chess strode to where he had set the dwarven sword and picked it up. "Aha!" he said. Then he raised a puzzled brow and rubbed at his cheek. "Funny, though. I'd heard that magic doesn't work right in this valley."

"I don't," something very wistful seemed to say.

It was growing dark, and there was nothing more to see here, so Chess set the sword on his shoulder and headed west. The black road should be near now, he decided.

The forest became deeper and more shadowy, and the kender stopped abruptly, his pointed ears twitching. Somewhere to his left, things were moving, coming his way. Among the shadows were darker shadows, big shadows flowing and bounding toward him on great padded paws . . . shadows that purred as they came, like the rumbling of distant thunder.

"Oops!" Chess said, and ran.

*　　*　　*　　*　　*

In evening's dusk, Chane Feldstone and Glenshadow the Wanderer rounded a curve of the black road and saw ahead of them a conclave of cats. Feral eyes and dagger teeth glinted where the brutes prowled and crouched at each side of the path, while a small figure danced and darted from side to side, shouting threats and taunts. As the two approached, the taunter saw them and waved. "Hello!" he called. "I wondered where you were! Who's that with you?"

"There's that kender," the dwarf told the wizard, then turned. Glenshadow had stopped. The man stood now, holding his staff before him as though to protect himself. Chane cocked his head, the tilting ears on his cat-cape cap giving a quizzical look to his scowl. "What's the matter? It's only a kender."

"There's more," the wizard said. "But I can't see . . ."

"More? I don't see anybody except a kender. And of course a bunch of cats, but that's no surprise."

"Not a person," the wizard said slowly, looking one way and then another, peering into the gloom. "No, not a person, but an . . . an event."

The dwarf growled, deep in his chest. Kender and wizards . . . birds and hunting cats . . . Chane was beginning to miss the sensible, logical life of Thorbardin. Out here, it seemed, no one ever really made sense. "What event? I don't see any event."

"It hasn't happened yet," Glenshadow said softly. "But it wants to."

"Needs to," something seemed to say in a voice that was not a voice.

Chane felt a chill crawl up his spine as he whirled around, looking for the source of the sound. He felt as though he had heard a voice, but his ears had not. The mage behind him had raised his staff higher, but he didn't seem to see anything, either.

The kender trotted up to them, grinning. "I see you've met whatsit," he said. "I think he comes with the sword." He lifted a dwarven broadsword from his shoulder and extended it, hilt first. "Here. I found this for you. Now you can stop complaining about not having a sword."

Surprised, Chane took the sword and held it in both hands, turning it over, squinting in the poor light.

"Of course, there's a ghost or something attached to it," Chess said brightly. "But I can't see how that would matter. Who's that with you? He looks like a wizard."

"He is, I guess," the dwarf said. "Haven't seen him do any magic, but I'd just as soon he didn't, anyway." He lifted the sword to his mouth and tasted its blade. "Old," he muttered. "Good steel, though. And it doesn't *look* old."

"It's been on ice," the kender explained. "What's wrong with your wizard? He looks like he's seen a ghost."

"I don't know what's wrong with him." Chane busied himself, slicing a strip of cathide from his cape to make a belt for the sword. "He said he saw an event."

"Well, I've seen a few of those." The kender nodded. "But I try not to let them bother me. Pretty good sword, huh?"

"A fine sword," the dwarf agreed. "Thank you. Where did you get it?"

"I found an old battlefield, over east of here. There's a lot of good stuff just lying around. And frozen dwarves all over the place, too. Probably nobody you know, though. They've been there a long time. Maybe the ghost is a dwarven ghost. I've never met any sort of ghost before, so I don't know. But if he bothers you, just ignore him."

As one coming out of a trance, the wizard Glenshadow shook himself and lowered his staff. He stepped close to them, leaned down, and squinted at Chane's sword, then turned to the kender. "Not a ghost," he said, in a voice that was like winter. "And not fixed to the sword, either. It follows you, Chestal Thicketsway."

The kender blinked. "What does?"

"You picked up more than a sword on that battlefield,

kender. You picked up an unexploded spell."

Before Chess could respond, Chane pointed down the path. "The cats are gone," he said.

Then on an errant breeze, coming from somewhere ahead, all three of them heard a sound that seemed to float among the treetops and drift down like crystal snow. The mage seemed to stiffen, the kender's eyes went huge, and even the stolid, pragmatic dwarf felt the sound take hold of his heart and tug at it.

Somewhere off there, to the north, someone was singing. The voice was more lovely than anything Chane Feldstone had ever heard.

Chapter 6

Though it had no king—no regent had acceded to the throne since the death of King Duncan two centuries before—the fortified realm of Thorbardin, deep beneath the surface of the central Kharolis Mountains, considered itself a kingdom. And without a king, it fell upon the Council of Thanes to sit as a Board of Regents, deciding such matters as were not governed within the separate cities and warrens that made up the undermountain realm.

Seven cities lay within the bedrock of the mountains, each a major community in its own right, as well as three farming warrens, two Halls of Justice, and a massive fortification at each of the realm's two main gates.

In the more than three centuries since the great Cataclysm that had forever changed the continent of Ansalon, the dwarves of Thorbardin had mostly abandoned the manning of Northgate. The Cataclysm had left the northern approaches virtually inaccessible, providing better security to the north than even the massive gate that plugged the mountainside there ever had.

For a century, rumors had persisted about a secret way to Thorbardin from the north, and the dwarves had kept the fortifications there operational. Chaos and pestilence had followed the Cataclysm, and for most of that century the threats to Thorbardin from outside were frighteningly real. Plague and famine had spread across the known world, migrations were under way across the continent, and no unfortified place could long survive.

But then the gates of Thorbardin had faced their hardest test . . . and held firm. The bloody Dwarfgate War raged through the Kharolis Mountains, hill dwarf armies pitted against those of the mountain dwarves—cousin against cousin, like against like. Those outside were determined to break through to the inside of Thorbardin, incited, some said, by the evil archmage Fistandantilus, whom many held to be the most powerful magician the world of Krynn had ever known.

Against these forces, Thorbardin had fought a defensive action. Then, under King Duncan and his sons—with Prince Grallen leading the Hylar dwarves—the armies of Thorbardin went out to carry the fight to their enemies, right to the mountain called Skullcap, lair of the great wizard himself.

What came to pass then—the tragic end of both armies in one last, terrible act of magic by Fistandantilus—was now old history. Of those who might be old enough to remember, few cared to.

But through it all, the shattered north portal had held, as had all of Thorbardin's defenses. More than two centuries later, the undermountain kingdom still stood. Concerns about threats from outside were no longer acute. In very recent times there had been unsettling rumors, of course—rumors the traders brought, about migrations of goblins and ogres to the north, about whole villages disappearing in distant places beyond the northern wilderness. Some suspected that, far off somewhere, armies were being amassed, and there were whispered comments about "Highlords" and infamous plots. Someone had even claimed to have seen a dragon, but no one believed that. There were no dragons, not anywhere on the entire world of Krynn. It was common knowledge.

There were rumors, and a few were concerned, but life went on in Thorbardin as it had for two hundred years. Some trade had been restored—not as in the fabled past, before the War of the Gates, when open trade roads had linked Thorbardin with Pax Tharkas and other realms— but some trade with other places and other races outside. Time had passed, and the old legends of a secret gate somewhere passed also into oblivion. The old tales of untold evils that might yet lurk about the blasted and glazed grotesqueries of Skullcap Mountain to the north—the legends of the glory of King Duncan and the noble Prince Grallen—grew dim.

It was not in the nature of mountain dwarves to dwell upon the past. And certainly, in the teeming cities of Thorbardin, few cared to reflect upon such antiquities.

Under the Kharolis Mountains, Thorbardin was what it had always been—hundreds of square miles of busy, bustling, squabbling, and delving dwarfdom, where the past was past and the problems of any one person were seldom of concern to many others.

And this was the reality that Jilian Firestoke faced. No one knew where Chane Feldstone had gone, and no one except her really cared, either. However, she was sure now that she knew where Chane had gone, and certain of the mischief her father had engineered.

And so, as was her custom, Jilian made up her own mind.

"I am going outside," she told her neighbor, Silicia Orebrand. "I intend to go and find Chane Feldstone and bring him home. There is just no telling what sort of mess he may be in out there."

The stocky Silicia's eyes went wide with horror. "Outside? Do you mean *outside*, outside?"

"Of course I mean outside," Jilian said. "Chane's dream told him to go and find an old helmet, because Thorbardin was threatened and it was up to him to save it. So I know that's where he went. And my own father, tarnish his whiskers, put him up to it and then betrayed him. I know all about it, you see. So I am going outside to find him."

"But Jilian . . . *outside*? Nobody goes outside! I've never heard of such a thing."

"Tarnish, Silicia. Don't be silly. Of course people go outside. Traders, scouts, metallurgists . . . lots of people go outside. Even Chane has been outside before, helping Rogar Goldbuckle load his packs. He told me about it."

"But *can* you? I mean, go outside? Is it allowed?"

"I asked Ferrous Spikemold. He knows about such things. He said anybody who wants to, can go outside. There is no law against going outside. It's just coming back in that gets sticky."

"Did you tell him that you were thinking about going outside?"

"No, I don't see how that's any of his business. And you know what a gossip he can be. I just asked him in general, about people going outside. He said anybody can, if they want to."

Silicia frowned. "But, Jilian, you've never been outside. I mean . . . out? I bet in your whole life you've never seen the sky except from the Valley of the Thanes. I know I certainly haven't. I've never even dreamed of such a thing. Why, they say there are all sorts of awful things out there—ogres and goblins, warrior elves, humans. By Reorx, they say half the world is overrun with humans these days. Jilian, are you feeling well? I can't imagine thinking such a thing. *Outside*?"

"Outside," Jilian said firmly. "And it will serve my father right if I never come back."

"But, Jilian, dear . . ." Silicia paused, then fired her best shot. "What will people think?"

"Oh, tarnish what people think. I'm going, Silicia, and that's an end to it. All I ask is that you look in on my father from time to time and see that he pays his tap fees when they are due. The old ruster hasn't a brain in his head when it comes to household duties."

"Well, of course I would do that, dear." Silicia still was blinking rapidly, only half-believing what she was hearing. "But how would you even know where to look for your young man, dear? Outside is . . . well, it's just awfully big!" She shuddered, just thinking about it.

"Oh, that. Well, at least I know where to start. I have a map of where he was last seen."

"A map?" Silicia blinked again, awe following awe. "How could you possibly have a map? Did your father. . . ?"

"I haven't even told him about this yet. And I'd appreciate it if you didn't, either. No, I saw the armsmen he sent to drive Chane away. I didn't know who they were at the time, but I remembered later. Then I saw one of them again, at the tinsmith's stall, and I followed him and got him to draw a map for me."

"An armsman? A warren ruffian? Why would he have done that for you? Jilian, you didn't . . ."

"Oh, nothing like that, Silicia. Don't be silly. No, I just followed him until I caught him alone in a cable-shaft, then I crept up behind and hit him in the head with a pry-bar. Then, while he was unconscious, I chained him to a cable-wagon track. When he woke up I told him that if he would draw the map for me I would give him a chisel to cut himself loose. So he drew the map. He was very willing, because we could hear an orewagon coming."

Silicia goggled at her, totally at a loss for words. Finally she shook her head and sighed. "Do you have everything you'll need for such a journey?"

"I have some warm clothing and a pack and waterskin. And my map. I suppose a company of armed fighters might be good to take along, but I can't afford anything like that."

"Well, of course not!" Silicia snapped. "The wages people charge these days, just for single escort through the markets. There's no telling what you'd have to pay to get an escort to go . . . ah . . . *outside*." She looked around at the walls and cabinets of her great room.

Swords and shields, hammers and pikes were displayed and stacked in various places. Her husband, Stonecut Orebrand, prided himself on his collection. "At the very least, I suppose you should take a weapon or two."

"I couldn't take your husband's—"

"Tarnish! He's lost track of what he has, anyway. What he doesn't know, he'll never miss." She went to a corner cabinet and poked around in it, emerging with a small, double-edged sword and a sheathed dagger. "Take these," she said. "My brother gave them to Stoney one time, in a fit of generosity, but I don't think he's even looked at them in years. He doesn't think much of my brother, you know."

Jilian took the sword from her and squinted at it curiously. "This is heavier than a prybar," she noted.

"Have you ever used a sword before, Jilian?"

"Well . . . not really. Have you?"

"No. It can't be very complicated, though. One just swings it, I suppose."

"Like swinging a prybar, do you think?"

"Maybe with two hands, though. The handle is long enough for both of your hands. Here, stand in the middle of the room and swing it around a bit. Then you'll be used to it if you ever want to fight with something."

Jilian helped Silicia slide the furniture out of the way, then placed herself in the cleared area and lifted the sword, gripping it carefully with both hands. Though shorter than most of the swords in Stonecut Orebrand's collection, the weapon still was only six inches shorter than Jilian was, and much of its weight was forward, toward the point, in the dwarven style. Being a sturdy dwarven girl, Jilian had no trouble lifting it, even holding it out at arm's length, but it did tend to off-balance her a bit. "What should I swing it at?" she asked.

Silicia went to a corner and brought back a candlestand with a foot-long taper set in it. "Cut the candle," she suggested.

"All right. Stand back." Jilian placed herself with the candlestand to her left, sighted on it, raised the sword and swung . . . and gasped, then clung for dear life as the sword seemed to take charge. It whisked past the top of the candle and kept going as the momentum of the cut became centrifugal force. Like a spinning top, Jilian twirled around and around, her feet a blur, trying to keep up with the sword in her hands, trying to keep her balance as she spun.

On its second rotation, the sword clove through the candle. On its third it bisected the oakwood candlestand. On its fourth it cut the legs off the stand and took two candles out of a hanging chandelier on the other side of Jilian. Silicia shrieked and dived for cover as the rate of spin increased and the twirling Jilian began to move. Four more revolutions and the sword eviscerated an herb pot, beheaded a chair, bisected a hanging tapestry, and embedded itself firmly in a doorframe. Jilian blinked in amazement, while momentary dizziness subsided, then wrenched the weapon free and stared at it. "Goodness!" she said.

Silicia peeked from behind a stone bench. "Are you finished, do you think?"

"I think so." Jilian looked around. "Oh, rust! Look at the mess I've made."

Silicia came from hiding to gaze in wonder at the sword in Jilian's hand. "I don't think you need any more practice. I believe you've mastered the skill, don't you?"

"I suppose so, but look what we've done to your nice room! Oh, Silicia, I am sorry."

Silicia walked around the room, pursing her lips as she surveyed the damage. "It's not so bad, really. I never liked that candlestand, you know. And that awful tapestry! Honestly, I *have* thought about making a pair of framed needleworks out of it . . ." She came to look at the sword again. "By the lusters, I never realized how much fun a person might have with one of these. I wonder if some of the ladies might like to organize a class."

Jilian nodded. "I believe I will borrow this, if you're sure Stonecut won't mind."

"Not in the slightest. It's as much mine as his, anyway. Now, you take it, and the dagger, too, and you have a nice time with them. We could rent a hall," she continued with her own thoughts, "and practice to music. Some of the girls could certainly use the exercise. . . ."

After her visit with Silicia Orebrand, Jilian went to see the trader, Rogar Goldbuckle.

"You are going *where*?" he squinted at her in disbelief.

"*Outside*," she repeated. "I want to find Chane Feldstone and bring him home. He may be lost and starving, or something."

"You?" the trader still couldn't believe what he was hearing. "You can't go traveling around out there. Don't you know what could happen to you?"

"I plan to take a sword," she said, to put his concerns to rest. "I'm remarkably good with a sword. But what I wondered was . . . well, since you have dealings with people outside, maybe you could tell me who to talk to out there, to help find him."

"Don't talk to anybody outside!" Goldbuckle snapped. "Don't trust anybody or anything out there! Rust and corruption, girl, you have no idea—"

"I have a map," she said. "But it will only show me where he was last seen. He may not be there any more, so I might need to ask about him." A new thought occurred to her. "I don't suppose you have any trading parties going northward, do you? I might just go along with them, as far as the wilderness. That's where I'll start looking."

Goldbuckle eased himself back to a bench and sat down with a thump. The girl before him was as lovely a young dwarf-maiden as he had ever seen, and he had always thought of her as very practical and sensible, the times she had come to shop his bazaar or to deliver purchase orders for her father. But now . . .

"I don't have any parties going that way," he said weakly. "Nobody goes to that wilderness. There hasn't been a trade route through there since before the Cataclysm, and even then it was chancy. Of course, that crazy Wingover has been up that way. He wagered he'd go to Pax Tharkas and back, if I'd give him a commission. Plan of a fool. But, of course, he *is* a fool, to begin with."

"Wingover? What an odd name." Jilian pursed pretty

lips. "Maybe that's who I should talk to. Where can I find him?"

"Well, not anywhere in Thorbardin, certainly. He'd never be allowed within twenty miles of the gate."

"Why on Krynn not? What did he do?"

"You don't understand, girl," Goldbuckle shook his head. "Wingover isn't a dwarf. He's . . . well. I've traded with him a bit and learned to trust him. But he's . . . well. He's a human."

Jilian stared at him, amazed. "What would you trade from humans? I mean, I know there used to be some trade, but aren't humans—?"

"Unreliable, yes. As a rule. Also unstable and generally unpleasant. Of course, one can make some allowances, considering how short-lived they usually are . . . Girl, have you ever *seen* a human?"

"Of course not. I've never been outside of Thorbardin. But I've heard about them. Chane has seen several, when he's gone out to carry reports or messages for you, and he talks about them. He even saw an elf once."

"Yes, I know," Goldbuckle sighed. "All sorts show up at barter camps, but such places are no place for a girl like you. I swear! Why, I shudder to think of—"

"Chane is out there, somewhere. And he's visited these barter camps before, at your employ, after all."

"That's different! Chane can take care of himself. You—"

"That's the other thing I wanted to talk about. He may need the money he earned from you. If you'll give it to me, I'll give it to him . . . when I find him."

Chapter 7

FOR MILES, the black path wound and curved through dense forest. Then, past one final, long curve, it broke out of the forest and extended arrow-straight across a mounded plain where little vegetation grew—only mosses and spindly, scattered shrubs. The light of the moons Lunitari and Solinari—the first nearly overhead, the second just above the crags of Westwall—bathed the scene in eerie red and white highlights beneath a spangled sky.

"More ruins," Chestal Thicketsway declared, pointing about. "There might have been a city here once. Maybe the Cataclysm—"

"Much older than that," Glenshadow the Wanderer said. "Oh, far older than that. Ages old. The legends say it was a city in the Age of Dreams."

"Legends say?" Chane Feldstone growled. "You're a wizard. Don't you know?"

"Not without a powerful spell for time-seeing," the winter voice rasped. "And I'll cast no spells in this place. Strange things happen to magic here."

Near them, somewhere close, something seemed to agree . . . something that lamented the fact.

"It's said there was a city in this valley," the wizard continued. "And in the city was a king, who captured and held in bond the source of all magic. The king's name was Gargath."

"How could he capture the source of magic?" Chess asked, excitedly. "Do you suppose it is still here?"

"No. Only the place where it was once held, and the device that held it. A god-wrought thing called Spellbinder. It still has power, though. Power enough to confuse and bind even the highest orders of spell."

"Misery," something voiceless seemed to say.

"Is that what's wrong with my spell?" Chess asked, looking around. "He's bound?"

The wizard nodded. "Most likely."

"He certainly doesn't seem to be very happy about it," the kender noted.

"*He*?" the dwarf grumped, "What do spells know? They aren't people." He looked up at the wizard. "How much farther do we have to go?"

"Not far," Glenshadow said. "Are you tired so soon?"

"Of course I'm not tired! But I have things to do and I don't see how all this is—"

"It is," Glenshadow assured him. "You want to find the helm, as you dreamed. This is how you must begin."

The dwarf scowled. "What does this have to do with you, though? It's my dream. What makes it important to you?"

"It might be important to a great many people," the wizard sighed. "In ominous times, significances take on new meanings. I have my own reasons for helping you fulfill your destiny, Chane Feldstone . . . if you can fulfill it."

"If it's important to you, then why don't you just go and find the helm, and let me get back to Thorbardin? I'm not fond of having no roof over my head."

"Of course you aren't. You're a mountain dwarf. But it's your dream, Chane Feldstone. Not mine."

"Corrosion," the dwarf muttered. "It's like trying to get a sensible answer from that kender. What do you mean 'ominous times?' "

"There have been omens. Some have interpreted them, and some believe them. Some think that devastation is about to fall on these lands. Some say it has already begun. Invasion. War. The worst of imaginings."

Chane stopped, staring up at the man. "When?"

"Soon," the wizard said. "Some say within five years. Some say within the year."

"But . . . why?"

"I think there will be further omens," Glenshadow said softly, his voice as chill as a winter's night. "Then, perhaps, we will know."

Ahead of them, the path approached what might have been a huge, open gate in a great wall, except that whatever gate might once have been there was long since gone. All that remained was a ragged cleft in a long, high structure of broken stone which ran off to left and right into moon-shadowed distance. An ancient wall, sundered here and there to rubble. Near the wall, just off the dark path, was a separate mound of rubble that looked familiar. It was like the mound they had found back in the forest—a clutter of what might once have been various things all connected together, with stumps and odd shapes protruding from it.

"Another gnome machine?" Chess wondered. "What do you suppose it was for?"

"Old," the wizard nodded.

"Very old," something unseen seemed to agree.

"A siege engine," Glenshadow said. "They kept building them until they got through the wall."

"Who did?"

"Gnomes. Who else?"

"What did they want?"

"What Gargath had. The source of all magic."

"I never heard of a gnome using magic," the kender pointed out.

The wizard frowned and seemed to shudder. "We had better go on," he said.

Beyond the wall the path pitched steeply downward and entered a forest so dense that the light of the moons was only a patchwork through interwoven branches.

"I'd just as soon make camp here," Chane said, then went silent as the singing voice came again, this time much nearer. Someone just ahead was singing in a language none of them knew. The singer's tonal range was tremendous, the voice so utterly lovely that it caught their breaths and tugged at their hearts.

A siren? Chane thought and realized it didn't matter. The voice held him in thrall, and he couldn't have turned away if he had wanted to.

Beyond the trees ahead was a glow of firelight, and the voice seemed to be coming from there. They hurried on. The slope lessened to level ground, and the trees ended abruptly at a circular clearing. The black gravel of the path ended at a clean-swept expanse of black flagstone paving—a circular band of ebony stone nearly one hundred yards across. Thick, short pillars of red granite stood like sentinels around the circle at brief intervals, and within the circle of black was a circle of white, then another of black. The concentric pavings narrowed toward the center, where stood a tall, cone-shaped monolith with a small, dim object at its apex. The firelight came from wood fires set in wide sconces at the four points of the compass, on the inside faces of the surrounding short pillars.

The travelers stood where they had stopped, peering around, trying to see detail in the erratic light.

In the semi-darkness around the circle, shadows moved. "Cats," the dwarf noted. "Dozens of them. They must live here."

The kender peered into the gloom, then straightened and pointed. "Wow! Look at that one!"

Chane looked. A breeze flared one of the flames, and

his eyes widened. Beyond the paved clearing, cats were everywhere. And among them was one, huge even by comparison with the others. Half again the size of the rest, it stood staring directly at the dwarf, great golden eyes thoughtful in a massive indigo head capped by a flowing, snow-white mane.

The wizard seemed to pay no attention. He gazed instead at the monolith, his eyes ranging upward toward its top. The crystal device on his staff no longer looked like a crystal. Its luster was gone, and it was a dull, opaque gray in color. "The temple of Gargath," he muttered. "Where the graygem was entrapped."

"What?" Chane glanced around.

"This is where it happened," Glenshadow said, as though talking to himself. "Up there . . . is the Spellbinder."

"Woe," something voiceless mourned.

The impatient kender had scampered away, out toward the edge of the paving for a better look at the huge, white-maned cat. When it noticed him, he backpedaled, reversed his course, and went to have a closer look at the obelisk. He disappeared beyond it.

"There's somebody here," Chane decided. "Somebody keeps these fires, and somebody made that song." He looked toward the hut beyond the obelisk. "Maybe . . ." Then he turned again, alerted by movement close by. A creature like nothing he had ever seen had stepped onto the pavement. She was far taller than Chane, taller even than the wizard.

Her skin was the color of midnight and caught the light in patterns of indigo and ebony that flowed sensuously over a face and form beautiful almost beyond beauty. Her hair was silver-white, long and flowing, and the single garment she wore—a brief tunic caught at one shoulder and falling to her sleek thighs—seemed to be woven of spider silk.

Chane stared, open-mouthed, stunned by her beauty as he was stunned by her song. Never had he heard such a voice—the power of thunder and the gentleness of summer clouds resonated in perfect balance as she seemed to sing to each of them separately, yet all at once. Never had he heard such a voice, and never had he seen a creature so hauntingly lovely, or radiating such intense, patient power. The dwarf had the feeling that she could crush him with a touch if she chose . . . or could touch as softly as a butterfly landing on a petal.

Behind and above Chane, the wizard whispered, "Irda."

Almost without changing, her song became speech. "Welcome again, man of magic," she crooned, "to the place where magic fails. Is this the one? The Derkin-descendant? Holder of the destiny?" Great eyes in an ebony face turned to Chane, perusing him with a gaze very like the gaze of the great cat moments before.

The dwarf's heart thumped as he realized they were the same eyes. "Shapechanger," he breathed.

"Of course she is a shapechanger," the wizard said. "I told you, she is the Irda. She can take many forms."

"Welcome, small warrior," the Irda crooned. "The moons have promised that you would come, following the path of your—"

Another voice, far less enchanting, shattered the spell: "Come look at the back of this thing!" Chestal Thicketsway called. "There's something like a stairway, and . . . hello? Who is this?" The kender scampered toward them, then stopped and blinked as the Irda turned to regard him. "Wow!" he finished lamely.

"This one is no Hylar kin," the Irda chuckled.

Chess blinked again and gave the tall, stunning creature a slow gaze from top to toe and back. His lips pursed in a low whistle. "Wow," he said again. Then, "Chestal Thicketsway's the name. I'm a kender, from Hylo. What on Krynn are you?"

"Inquisitive," the Irda murmured. "I am Irda, little one."

"I wondered what you'd look like," Chess nodded. "My great-uncle, Tauntry Rimrunner, used to talk about the Irda. I must say, you don't look anything like an ogre."

Chane whirled on the kender, offended and astounded. "What a thing to say!" But a hand on his shoulder stopped him.

"Ogres and the Irda," Glenshadow whispered, leaning close, "a long time ago, they were the same people . . . before ogres became ogrelike and ugly. They aren't at all the same any more."

"The cats are gone," Chess noted suddenly, turning to look all around the clearing.

"They won't bother you again," the Irda said. "They have seen you with me, and I've assured them. They've gone now to patrol the valley. Waykeep likes its privacy."

"Those cats are a pretty effective way of discouraging visitors," Chane noted.

"Come to my home," the Irda beckoned, turning away. "There is sweetnog for refreshment, and we can talk in comfort." She headed for the hut among the trees, and they followed.

Chane paused for a moment as he passed the monolith, and looked up toward its top. A strange feeling gripped him, an intuition that raised the hackles on his neck and sent a shiver down his spine. Just for an instant, he felt as if something atop the monolith had spoken to him . . . something that awaited him, that called out to him. He felt as if he had been here before, though he knew he had not. And the feeling of the place was like the feeling of his dreams.

"Is this the place?" he muttered, to himself. "Is this where I find the helm?"

A large, gentle hand rested on his shoulder, and he jumped, then looked up at the Irda, standing beside him. "What you seek is not here, Chane Feldstone," she crooned. "But here is where you will begin your search."

Again she led the dwarf away, and he noticed that her movements—the sense of great strength in her easy, graceful stride; the lithe, sensuous ripple of smooth muscle beneath shining ebon skin—reminded him of the flowing grace of the great cats that were her companions.

* * * * *

"In ancient times, in the Age of Dreams, this was a

place of men," the Irda told them. "And magic was unknown on Krynn. So say the oldest legends. Then, from the realm of gods, came the graystone gem, and with it magic . . . and chaos. Some say the god Reorx gave to King Gargath the means to trap and hold the graystone. Whether or not that is so, Garath did capture it with a device of two crystals—one to find and hold it, the other to counter its magic."

"That's what the wizard said," Chestal Thicketsway interrupted, sipping from a goblet of warm, sweetnog the Irda had provided. "Only he said there was one crystal—"

"Hush," Glenshadow snapped. "Just listen."

"Gargath held it for a time," the Irda continued. "Then it was lost when the city was besieged by gnomes, with great siege engines."

"So that *is* what those junkheaps are," the kender commented.

This time it was Chane who hushed him. The dwarf reached across the table, grasped the kender's tunic, and lifted him off his stool. "Just shut up and listen!" he demanded.

The Irda continued undaunted. "One legend has it that when the graystone was freed, its magic caused some of the gnomes to become dwarves and kender, thus originating the two races."

"Rubbish," Chess snapped. "No kender's akin to dwarves, and we sure didn't come from gnomes."

"Rust and corruption!" Chane chimed. "Dwarves were here first. Everybody knows that."

"Will the two of you shut up!" Glenshadow rasped, his voice the stuff of blizzards. "Just . . . shut up!"

"But I've been slandered," Chess said.

The wizard's eyes glinted like ice. He pointed his staff at the kender and muttered, *"Thranthalus eghom dit—"* and suddenly went silent. Though Glenshadow's lips continued to move, no sound came out.

"That was a mistake," the Irda said, sympathetically. "The anti-magic in this place is very strong."

"Very strong," something unseen echoed.

The kender stared at the wizard. "What's the matter with him?"

Chane leaned close, seeing the stricken look in the man's eyes. "I think he tried to cast a spell," he suggested. "It must have backfired. He's hushed himself."

The kender cocked his head. "I wonder how long he'll be like this."

"I don't know." Chane shrugged. "It's his spell. Speaking of which, I wish you'd find a way to hush yours."

"My what?"

"Your spell. The one that's following you around. It's spooky to hear something complaining all the time when there's nothing there."

"Be wary of that spell," the Irda said. "Its power is so great that it must happen, eventually."

"You've met my spell?" The kender grinned. "Actually, I guess it isn't mine, but it has become attached to me."

"I know of it," the Irda nodded. "It has been in this valley, waiting to happen, for two hundred years. Ever since dwarves fought near here in the Dwarfgate Wars."

"I'll bet that's where all those frozen dwarves came from," Chess noted.

"This was where Fistandantilus first interceded," the Irda told them.

Chane shuddered. "Fistandantilus? The archmage? He was here?"

"Here first, then at the final battle, two ranges west of here, on the Plains of Dergoth," the Irda told the dwarf.

"That's where Grallen's army was wiped out," Chane noted. "I've heard that story all my life."

"Both armies were wiped out by the fourth and greatest of the elemental spells Fistandantilus cast," the Irda said. "The first three spells were cast in the preliminary battle, here in the Valley of Waykeep. Elemental spells. The first was fire, the second ice . . ."

"Burned forests under ice," the kender breathed. "I saw that. What was the third one?"

"No one knows," the Irda shrugged. "It became entrapped in the anti-magic of this place, and hasn't happened yet."

71

"Woe and misery," something voiceless said.

"You mean him?" Chess looked around, needlessly. "I mean, *it*?"

"Your unexploded spell," she said calmly.

"Wow," was all that Chess could say.

Chane tapped the tabletop with his goblet, growing impatient. "What does all this have to do with me and my dreams?"

The Irda studied him, her eyes luminous. "I told you that there were two crystals in Gargath's device. Only one remains up there now. It is called Spellbinder. Its presence is the reason that magic often fails in this valley. The other crystal, Pathfinder, was found by Prince Grallen of the Hylar—"

"Grallen? But he died in the Dwarfgate War."

"Grallen, son of Duncan, King—the last king—of Thorbardin. The wizard knows of your dreams, Chane Feldstone. What is the thing that you have dreamed of finding?"

"An old helm," the dwarf said. "A battle helmet, with horns and a crown-spire."

"And a crystal at its brow?"

"Well, yes. A sort of green gem."

"That green gem is Pathfinder, Chane. The helm is Grallen's, and your dreams have been more than dreams. Grallen learned something about Thorbardin on his way from here to his last battle, at Zhamen—what is now called Skullcap Peak. He learned that there is a lost entrance to Thorbardin, and had he lived he would have found it and sealed it. But he died. At present, armies are amassing in the north . . . their forward units already invest key areas in many of the nearer lands."

The Irda paused and a shadow crossed her face. "There will be war. The ogres know, and what they know I also know. Very soon, Thorbardin will be surrounded by devastation. That is why you have dreamed, Chane Feldstone. Your dreams are Grallen's spirit, calling to you, trying to tell you what must be done. You are to find Grallen's helm and take up Grallen's quest. You are to seal Thorbardin's lost gate."

The kender smiled, his bright eyes gleaming with excitement. "Wow," he breathed. "I'm really glad I came along."

Chane simply stared at the Irda, at a loss for words. Finally he asked the only question he could think to ask: "Why me?"

Glenshadow tried to speak, rubbed his throat and tried again. "You . . ." the wizard croaked. He coughed, scowled, and tried to clear his throat. In a hoarse voice just above a whisper he said, "Because you are Grallen's kin, Chane Feldstone. You are the last of the line of Duncan, King of Thorbardin."

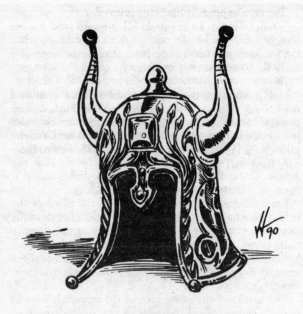

Chapter 8

"Zap," said Chestal Thicketsway, as much to break the silence as for any other reason. Almost a minute had passed since Glenshadow's pronouncement, and nobody had said or done anything since. The three creatures around the kender seemed frozen in place—the dwarf standing stunned, trying to understand what he had just been told; the Irda remote and infinitely patient, waiting; the wizard bleak-eyed and gloomy as though he had spoken the prophecy of his own doom.

When none of them reacted to his word, Chess shrugged and prowled about the little building's interior, looking for anything that might be interesting. "Zap," he said again, to himself. "I'll call him Zap. Good a name as any for a spell that hasn't happened."

"Need to happen," something grieved.

"Well, I'd just as soon you detach yourself from me before you do," the kender said. "I don't even know what kind of spell you are."

"Old," something mourned.

"You've made that clear." Chess peered into a shallow cabinet containing many pigeonhole shelves. Shadows made it hard to see what the shelves contained, and he reached toward them, then withdrew his hand when he felt the Irda's eyes on him. He turned. "Just looking," he grinned. "Maybe I should go outside and look around."

Kenderlike, the thought immediately became the action. Chess strode to the door of the hut, pushed it open, and darted out, closing it behind him.

From his first glimpse of this place, the place of the Irda, Chess had been fascinated by the tall obelisk in the stone-paved clearing. Now he went to it again, directly to its north face where he had found handholds and toeholds leading upward. He had intended to see where they went, but seeing the Irda had made him forget that, momentarily.

The marks in the north face of the monolith weren't really a stairway, only a series of shallow indentations set at regular intervals up the precipitous stone face. For a curious kender, however, they were ladder enough. Chess slung his hoopak on his back and started climbing.

In the distance, in moon-shadowed forest beyond the Irda's clearing, he could hear the rumbling purr of cats on patrol. And somewhere far away, a hint of sound carried back on errant breezes, a raucous bird-voice cawed, "Go away!"

The hand-and toeholds went up and up, and Chess clung and climbed. Near the top, he could look out and see the moon-bathed tops of the forest, the dark walls of the valley beyond to east and west. Then, abruptly, there were no more indentations in the face of the cone. With the top of the monument almost within reach—no more than ten feet above—there was only sheer, smooth stone and nothing to cling to. Chess hunted around for something that his fingers could grasp, his toes brace into, or his hoopak reach. There was nothing. In frustration he clung there for long minutes, then sighed and accepted defeat.

"Isn't that just how things go?" he muttered, beginning a reluctant descent. "Probably the most interesting thing in this whole place is right there on top of this spire, just sitting there waiting to be looked at. Naturally the stairs don't go quite far enough. I wonder what it is, up there . . . might be something valuable, if a person could just reach it. What kind of ladder heads for the top of something and then just stops, just that much short? What kind of sense does that make?"

"All things have reason, little one." The voice was the Irda's voice, low and incredibly sweet. Chess nearly lost his hold, turning to look. She stood just below, watching his descent.

The kender scrambled the rest of the way down the cone, dropped light-footed to the pavement, and turned. "I thought I'd take a look at what's up there," he said. "But I couldn't get to the top. What *is* up there, anyway?"

"Spellbinder," she said.

"Pain and desolation," something seemed to whine.

Chess glanced around, knowing there was no one there to see. "Hush, Zap," he snapped. Then, to the Irda, "Is it something the gods left lying around?"

The Irda only smiled. "Spellbinder has been forgotten." She nodded. "But what the gods discard, eventually find purposes again."

"Woe and misery," Zap's voiceless voice mourned.

The Irda half-turned, raising her head. She seemed to be listening to something Chess couldn't hear. And there was something odd about the light. The fires still flickered in their sconces on the ring of stones, but feebly now, as if their fuel were giving out. The rose and silver glow cast by the moons Solinari and Lunitari had changed, too. The light glistening on the dark, lovely face of the Irda was almost a bloody light.

Chess stepped from her shadow to look into the sky, and saw a sight he had never seen before. The red and silver moons hung above the wall of the valley, only a handspan apart, but the silver moon was only a crescent. As the kender watched, the crescent diminished as though a blackness had come from the north and was eating it away. Narrower and narrower the crescent grew.

"What is it?" Chess wondered. "What's happening?"

Soft light shone from the Irda's hut, and there were footsteps. A moment later the dwarf and the wizard were beside them, also staring at the strange sky. "What's happening to the white moon?" the dwarf rumbled.

Glenshadow raised his staff, useless in this place of anti-magic, and pointed it. "Dragonqueen," he hissed. "The black moon shows itself, and eclipses the white."

"Dragonqueen?" Chess stood on his toes in his excitement, staring. "Do you mean the moon or the goddess?"

"They are the same," the Irda said. "By any name, they are the same. Queen of Darkness, Dragonqueen, Nilat the Corrupter. . . ."

"Tamex the False Metal," Chane growled. "The evil one."

"She of the Many Faces," the kender chirped. "I've never seen the black moon's shape before—only a hole in the sky where it hides stars. It's a disk, like the other two. Look, it's almost covered the white moon. . . . It *has* covered it!"

Where the white moon had been was now only a dim ring of brighter stuff in the sky—a hairline circle of radiance, encompassing darkness. The black moon had covered the white one.

At that instant Glenshadow's staff came to life. The crystal in its head, which normally resembled blue ice but which had looked like dull chalk since entering the Valley of Waykeep, blazed brilliant red as if all the luminance of the red moon had condensed in it. A beam of crimson shot from the staff to burn for an instant on the forehead of the astonished dwarf . . . only for an instant. Then the beam danced away, up the side of the conical tower, right to its top, where it rested, a ruby brilliance at the monolith's peak.

Chane Feldstone stared at the ruby light with eyes not quite the same as his eyes had been before. Without a word he walked to the base of the monolith and found the handholds and toeholds that the kender had found before.

The rest were still staring at the eclipsed white moon, unable to tear their eyes from the omen. Little by little, the dark moon continued its transit, and a crescent of white reappeared—the opposite crescent, emerging.

"The next omen," Glenshadow's voice was as thin and cold as windblown snow. "A portent of great evil."

Something voiceless and terribly sad seemed to say, "The time comes," and Chess glanced around.

"Hush, Zap," the kender said. "Spells should be seen and not heard. Look, Chane . . . now where did the dwarf go?"

Again the Irda tilted her lovely head, as though listening. Glenshadow glanced at her and frowned. "What is it? What do you hear, Irda?"

She shook her head, silver hair dancing in the light that again came from two moons. "Evil," she sang softly. "In the north an evil lives, and one of evil sings. Ogres gloat and goblins march . . . and I hear the sound of wings."

"Where in blazes did that dwarf get off to?" Chestal Thicketsway was prowling the clearing, peering here and there. He looked upward then, and blinked. "Oh. There he is. Chane! You, Chane Feldstone! What are you doing up there? I already tried that. You can't get to the top!"

The others looked, too. High above them, moving with the steady, solid rhythm of a climbing mountain dwarf, Chane was approaching the top of the monolith.

"You're about to run out of ladder!" the kender shouted. "Take my word for it, that's a waste of time. You can't get to the—"

The Irda moved close to him and rested a graceful, powerful dark hand on his head. "Be quiet, small one," she sang softly.

The white moon was whole again, but now the red

moon was diminishing as the black orb began to occlude it. The rose tint of the moonlight dulled, becoming more silvery. Above, Chane Feldstone had reached the last of the fingerholds and hesitated.

Again the crystal on Glenshadow's staff winked alight, this time a cold white light as if the white moon's glow focused in it. A single shaft of white light shot upward, bathing in hard luster the hammer slung on the dwarf's back. Clinging to the cone, Chane loosed the hammer, braced himself and swung its spike-end against the stone above him. He struck again, and a black shard fell, bouncing once on the slight slope of the monolith, ringing as it struck the pavement below.

Snagging the hammer in his belt, the dwarf reached up, found purchase in a new handhold, and retrieved the hammer to cut another one.

"Why didn't I think of that?" the kender chuckled. "Here I was thinking about slings and pulleys or some such."

The red moon was nearly eclipsed now, but still Glenshadow's staff glowed, and strong white light bathed the top of the spire where the dwarf worked. Abruptly, Chestal Thicketsway remembered the nature of his unseen companion—the spell that had somehow associated itself with him. He glanced around nervously. "Wizard, the light . . . does this mean that magic is working here again?"

"No magic of mortals," the wizard breathed. "Nor any that I can sense or understand."

"The gods are not bound by the limits they set," the Irda whispered. "Only Krynn-magic is captured in Spellbinder's net."

"Ashes and woe," something voiceless mourned.

"I'm glad to hear that," the kender sighed. "I'm not in any hurry to find out what happens when Zap gets unbound."

Atop the tall cone, Chane cut another hold, then a final one, and pulled himself up for a look. The top of the monolith was a shallow cup, no more than four feet across, with objects lying in it. The largest was a small, broken statue apparently carved from alabaster—a weathered and eroded representation of a man with a beard, face turned upward, one outthrust arm intact, its hand holding a two-inch oval of dark red crystal. The little statue, which would have stood no more than three feet tall, lay on its back. Part of its other arm lay beside it, but the hand was missing.

The other object in the bowl was a metal ball the size of Chane's fist—deeply rusted, but still showing clearly the dent of ancient impact. A green bronze plate was imbedded in the ball, and Chane bent close. The enhanced light of the white moon showed him part of the inscription: *Size four siege projectile, specific for use with superior flipshot . . .*

Gnomes, he thought.

He swung a leg over the lip of the cup and extended a hand, meaning to set the little statue upright for a better look. But suddenly the red crystal pulsed and hummed, the statue's fingers fell away, and the crystal dropped into his hand. As Chane closed his own fingers around it, it stilled. He knew then, beyond question, why he had climbed the cone. The crystal had called him. He was to take it.

Vaguely, in the dwarf's mind, a face appeared—a face much like his own, the bearded face of a mountain dwarf. But not his own face, though there was a strong resemblance. The face was more stern than Chane's, and bore the scars of battle. And it looked out at him from the curved portal of a studded, horned helmet with a single ornament—a crystal that might have been a twin of the crystal in Chane's hand except for the color. The helmet's stone was green.

"Grallen?" It was his own whisper that asked it.

The face in Chane's mind seemed to nod, to encourage . . . then it faded.

Feeling more confused than ever before in his life, Chane Feldstone secured the red crystal in his pouch, slung his hammer on his back, and eased down to the new holds he had cut. Step by step, hold by hold, he lowered himself down the face of the monolith. Above him, the enhanced light faded and the spire's peak was only that—a stone monolith in moonlight.

At the bottom, they gathered around him, the kender chattering questions, the wizard trying to get a word in, the Irda kneeling to look closely at his face. She peered, then pointed at his forehead. Glenshadow bent to look.

On the dwarf's forehead, above the bridge of his nose, was a red spot, almost the shape and tint of the red moon.

In the Irda's hut, over mugs of spicy drink, Chane told them what he had found. He brought out the crystal to show to them, but when Glenshadow touched it, it burned his fingers. The kender also had been reaching for it, but he withdrew his hand quickly at the wizard's cry of pain.

"I expect you'd better hang on to that," Chess said prudently.

The two visible moons were ordinary moons again, as they had been before the omen, but there was a darkness in the northern sky—an absence of stars where there should have been stars. The black moon hung there, not seeming to move, and Glenshadow shuddered when he looked in that direction. The Irda sat outside her hut, facing northward, her head thrown back as one who listens intently.

The lamplight and the sweetnog were soothing. Chane felt himself nodding, then yawned and lay his head on the table. The kender was already asleep.

* * * * *

Chane and his companions weren't the only ones who watched the omen of the moons. A hundred miles northwest, in the glades of Qualinost, the elves of Qualinesti saw it and sent rangers to spread the word. Something was forecast that demanded study. Evil was afoot.

Eighty miles due west of the Valley of Waykeep, mages at the Tower of High Sorcery also watched the dark moon occlude first the white and then the red. Councils were called—councils at which the wearers of white robes and those who wore red were much more in evidence than the wearers of black.

North of the wilderness, at the great pass city of Pax Tharkas, people lined the battlements to watch the moons in wonder.

And twenty miles from the ancient temple of Gargath, across the ridge line separating Waykeep from the Vale of Respite, ranks of armed goblins spread across the north end of a fertile valley, awaiting orders for their advance southward, where unsuspecting villages lay sleeping among the moonlit fields. Among them, aloof and haughty, were some far larger creatures—ogres who had come from their lairs to join the goblin horde, knowing there would soon be sport for them.

On a brushy rise above the goblins' dark camps a lone figure stood, looking into the sky. Moonlight of two colors shone on a horned helmet and emblazoned black body armor. The faceplate of the many-horned helm was a hideous metal mask, a demon-faced device from which dark, searching eyes peered.

As the occlusion of the visible moons began, the figure unfastened and removed the faceplate. The moonlight revealed the face behind it: a woman's face, stern and dark-eyed. A face that might have been beautiful, had it chosen to be, but that had made other choices from which there had been no turning back.

As the dark moon of Krynn eclipsed the first of the visible moons, the woman drew a thong from beneath her breastplate, a thong from which was suspended a dark, misshapen lump. "Caliban," she said.

The voice that responded was a dry, husky whisper, heard within her ears—an ancient, querulous voice. "Why does she call me now," it breathed. "She does not need me here. There is nothing here that she cannot do for herself."

The woman frowned. "Caliban, the moons. What does it mean?"

"'The moons,' she says," the dry voice had whispered. "She wants to know the story of the moons."

"Tell me!"

"It is another of the Queen's omens," the husky voice

rasped. "She tells the Highlords that the time is almost at hand for their invasion of Ansalon, and she tells whatever gods may notice that she claims this time and this world as hers. She warns them not to interfere."

"Another omen," the armed woman snapped. "Is there a message there for me?"

"Ah," the dry voice said. "She seeks messages for herself."

"Tell me!" the armor-clad woman ordered.

"If there is a message for her, it is only this: she has promised the Highlord that she will take and hold access to the fortress Thorbardin. The Queen will not tolerate any who fail in what they promise on her behalf."

"I will not fail!" the woman said sharply. "Even though I have nothing but . . . these—" she swept her free arm contemptuously, indicating the dark camps of the waiting goblin horde "—to assist me. I asked the Highlord for a strike force. He gave me stinking goblins. But I will succeed. Thorbardin will fall when he is ready."

"She has no need to tell me of this," the dry voice said. "It is her concern, not mine. Now she will let me rest until there is a better reason for me to awaken."

"I will do what I choose!" she started to say, then hissed through clenched teeth as tiny lightnings laced from the dark thing to sting her hand. Quickly, she dropped it back into the shelter of her armor. She could feel it pulsate slightly as it came to rest between her breasts.

"Omens," she muttered. "I need no omens to accomplish what I set out to do."

Her gaze fixed then on the sky, not where the moons were telling their story, but westward, where the line of ridges that formed the valley's east rim stood like jagged teeth against the night sky. There, far in the distance beyond the ridges, was a crimson glow—a light that was neither moonlight nor firelight, but that hung in the sky beyond the mountains like an echo of Lunitari's light.

Between her breasts the dark thing moved, and again she heard the dry, ancient voice. "Ah, but there *is* a message for her, it seems. Someone else is abroad this night, seeking the lost way to Thorbardin."

* * * * *

Full daylight lay on the valley when Chane Feldstone awoke. For an instant he didn't know where he was. He blinked and looked around. The hut was wide open, shutters thrown back and door standing ajar. Cabinets stood open and empty, and the cool breezes of autumn wafted through, carrying the sounds of birdcall and small creatures—sounds that Chane abruptly realized he hadn't heard since coming into this strange valley in the wilderness. Near the door, the wizard Glenshadow lay asleep on a rush mat.

Chane stretched and stood, feeling stiff from sleeping at the table, his hammer still slung on his back. Recalling the night before, he fumbled with the lashing on his pouch and looked inside. The red crystal was there, secure. He touched his forehead, then brought his hammer around, using its polished surface as a mirror. The red spot was still on his face, just above his nose, but it was less vivid now, less noticeable. Still, his mind was full of information that he knew had not been there before.

He looked around at a small sound. The kender was just strolling in through the open door.

"The Irda is gone," the small creature said sadly. "I can't find her anywhere. And I guess she took her kitty cats with her, because I didn't find any of them, either."

"Then I guess she was through here," Chane said, assembling his packs and straps. "It doesn't matter, though. I know which way to go from here."

Part II

WINGOVER'S WAY

Chapter 9

There was a time once, rumor had it, when trade routes had linked the realms of Ansalon in a more or less reliable fashion from Palanthas and Vingaard Keep in the north, through Solamnia, Abanasinia, and Pax Tharkas, all the way south to Thorbardin. And maybe even beyond.

Wingover had heard the stories and felt that they probably were true, though he had never met anyone who could confirm them. He had seen a good bit of the known world in his forty or so years and had dealt with all kinds of people. He knew the value that the elves of Qualinost put on grains and foodstuffs from Solamnia. Mountain-bound Thorbardin traded for grains and spices, as did his own homeland of Abanasinia. And he had seen in Abanasinia and Solamnia—among those who could afford them—plenty of tools and weapons created by the dwarves of Thorbardin, as well as fine textiles from Qualinost.

Fibers and fabrics, feathers and furs . . . comestibles, combustibles, and exotic baubles—every land he had seen in his travels possessed an abundance in some commodities and shortages in others.

Somewhere in the past there had probably been extensive trade all over Ansalon. But trade now—and for all the lifetime Wingover and those he knew could remember—was erratic and hazardous. "It's the way of the world," he himself had said more than once. "There's always someone more determined to make a killing than the rest are to make a living."

"Poor, ravaged Krynn," some poets called the world. But Wingover had no real quarrel with the nature of things. It was the only world he had ever known, and in some respects the very combativeness of its races aided him in his endeavors. Their aloofness, their distrust of one another, made the commodities they all sought even more precious. Sometimes Wingover hired out as a trail guide, sometimes as an escort for traders. And sometimes, as now, he carried a pack himself—usually on a bet.

This time the bet was with the mountain dwarf trader, Rogar Goldbuckle. Over tankards of ale at the Inn of the Flying Pigs in Barter, Goldbuckle had wagered that Wingover could never make it alive from Barter to Pax Tharkas and back, carrying a pack of goods from his agents at Pax Tharkas.

The return on the sealed pack would be small compared to what it would cost Rogar Goldbuckle to pay his gambling debt.

It had been no mean adventure, this journey. Wingover had chosen his routes with care, going north to Pax Tharkas by one route and returning by another to avoid ambushers and other unpleasantries of the wilderness. He had ridden alert and slept with his senses awake, and still there had been incidents—the cave ogre that had almost killed him on a mountain trail somewhere near Wayreth Forest; the landslide that had blocked his path just south of Pax Tharkas; the band of murderous thieves that had picked up his trail on Regret Ridge and pursued until he was forced to teach them some manners; the flooded ford that had forced him to change course. It was that flooded ford that led him into the hidden valley where the bird had screamed a warning at him, and where he had barely escaped with his life when a pack of huge hunting cats chased him.

All that, and goblins, too.

Wingover shook his head now in perplexity. Why were there goblins south of Pax Tharkas? He had never heard of goblins in these lands. Other places, of course, but not here. It reminded him of the talk he had heard in Pax Tharkas—dire rumors, all hazy and confusing, of omens and prophesies, of strange sightings in remote places.

There were even rumors of people somewhere to the north who swore they had seen dragons.

And just the past night—a double eclipse of the moons. Wingover had heard philosophers and stargazers speculate on such things, but he had never before seen such a sight. It had almost cost him his horse and his pack. Geekay had spooked at the sight and pulled loose from his halter, and Wingover had chased the animal for a half-mile before catching him.

Did it mean something? He thought of Garon Wendesthalas and wondered where he was. Elves usually knew more about such phenomena than most people. Maybe he would see the elf in Barter, and could ask him about it then.

Wingover twisted about in his saddle, easing the fatigue of travel, and pulled his elkhide jacket tighter about him. The horse was rounding a bend in the sloping trail, and a fresh wind had sprung up. It was cold at this altitude, even in early autumn.

Cold and—he noticed abruptly—strangely quiet. He looked around. The usual daytime sounds of the mountains, the chittering of small creatures, the myriad calls of cliff-birds, had gone silent. The only sound was the wind sighing forlornly.

Without seeming to have noticed—one learned such skills if one would survive in the wildernesses of Ansalon—Wingover eased his sword around so that its hilt rested across the vent of his saddle, inches from his hand. Eyes that missed little scanned the landscape, searching for anything out of place or out of order.

Wingover's eyes were as pale as the frost on his reddish whiskers, and as alert as those of the darting shoal-kite for which he was named. He studied the rising stonefall to his left, the bouldered slope falling away to the right, the gametrail winding out of sight ahead, and—stretching around as one too long a'saddle—his own backtrail. Nothing caught his eye, nothing out of the ordinary, and yet the silence hung and all his senses responded to it.

Angling near a wide cleft in the stonefall, he reined the horse into cover and stopped, listening. At first there was nothing to hear, then from somewhere came a faint scuffling sound, as of shod feet creeping through gravel. Many shod feet. And now the errant wind carried a smell that alerted him. It was an odor he recognized. A cloying, unpleasant odor.

Wingover frowned, testing the air. Goblins again! What were goblins doing this far south?

Again he heard the furtive, scuffling noises, and this time he heard metallic sounds as well—little clinks as of weapons being drawn. Silently he dismounted, slipping his animal's reins into a crack in the rock. He freed the lashes behind his saddle and righted the flinthide shield there, pulling its strap onto his left arm, gripping the guidon with hard fingers. Sword drawn, Wingover crouched, slipped from the cover of the rocks, and sprinted forward on soft-soled feet, following the gametrail. Just ahead someone was in trouble.

Fifty yards from where the man had dismounted, the dim trail topped a ridge and disappeared. Crawling the last few feet, Wingover looked beyond. The game trail veered away to the right, following a slope. Some distance away it made a switchback turn, angling downward toward a distant, meadowed valley. On the trail below, a single walker strode along—a tall, lithe figure clad in furs and leathers against the cold. Wingover could not see his face, but he knew his race. Distance and angle could not hide the lean, graceful form, the gliding stride of an elf.

The elf turned slightly, surveying the landscape, and Wingover recognized him. An old friend. Garon Wendesthalas. The elf carried a pack and a bow, and Wingover suspected he was going to Barter as he was.

But on the brushy slope between them, crouching in cover and watching the elf approach, were goblins—armed, armored goblins waiting in ambush. He counted eight that he could see and cover where two or three more might be.

Wingover crouched, waiting. There was no question what was about to happen. For whatever reason goblins might have—curiosity about what was in the elf's pack, perhaps, or simply for sport—the goblins were ready to pounce on the elf, to bring him down with their weapons.

Garon Wendesthalas has been taking care of himself for a long time, Wingover told himself, slitted eyes studying the goblins. The goblins may wish they had never met this elf.

Still, he told himself as goblin faces turned toward one another, wide mouths grinning in wicked anticipation, what are friends for, if not to interfere?

With a shrug he got his feet under him, howled a battle cry as wild as any goblin could ever have heard, and plunged down the slope, directly into the crouched goblins' ambush.

With gravity doubling the speed of his long legs, Wingover descended on them and through them, spinning completely around as he pierced their line. His sword was a flashing rage, singing around him, first bright-bladed and then suddenly dark with goblin blood. A goblin head bounced from a rock and rolled down the slope ahead of him. Two more goblins died before they could turn, one severed from shoulder to breastbone, one cloven through the back, through ribs and spine. Another raised an axe and was bowled over by Wingover's flinthide shield. Still another tried to lift a short sword and failed because he had no arm.

In an instant of howling fury, the man was through them and beyond, flailing for balance as he plunged on down the slope. "Goblins!" he shouted. "Ambush!"

Directly below now, the elf dropped his pack, brought around his bow, drew, and let fly. The arrow whisked past Wingover, and somewhere above and behind the man a gurgle and a thud sounded. At a glance he saw the severed head of the first goblin, bouncing merrily along beside him.

A thrown axe sailed past Wingover, embedding itself in loose stone just at the elf's feet. Another of his arrows flew to answer it. On the path, Wingover braced his legs, skidded and somersaulted to a jarring halt . . . then got his feet under him again and dodged as a bronze dart whisked past him from uphill.

"Good morning," he shouted to the elf, then filled his lungs, let loose another battle howl, and headed back up the slope. The elf was right behind him.

The slope above was a confusion of goblins—most of them dead or dying, but some still very much alive. For a moment some of these scrambled, clawing upward, trying to climb the slope. But one, a creature slightly larger than the others and heavily armored, shouted guttural orders and regrouped them.

Going uphill was far slower than coming down had been, and now Wingover and the elf found themselves facing a ready enemy who held the higher ground.

Darts and thrown stones landed about them. Wingover held the lead, wielding his shield to deflect what he could. But a dart scored the human's leg, leaving a bloody gash. Two goblins hoisted a huge stone between them, raising it above their heads.

Behind Wingover, the elf said, "Drop."

He dropped, half-covered by his shield, and the elf loosed an arrow. It took a goblin full in the throat. The second one staggered back under the sudden weight of the stone, and fell.

With a hiss, the goblin leader lifted the fallen creature to his feet and gripped the back of his neck with one strong hand. In the other he held a heavy broadaxe. Pushing his companion ahead of him he charged down on Wingover, who was just scrambling to his feet. Before he could get his shield up, the goblins were on him. His sword impaled one, but the weapon was wrenched aside as the leader flung the expendable one forward and raised his axe in both hands.

Dropping sword and shield, Wingover flung himself upward and grappled the creature. Goblin stench seared his nostrils as he gripped the axehandle, struggling to keep it from completing its swing. Goblin teeth snapped at his throat, grazing the skin. Claws of a goblin hand raked his face, going for his eyes, and a hard-soled boot flailed at his legs. He twisted, thrust, and threw the goblin onto its back, going down with it. Instantly, the locked pair were rolling and bouncing down the slope, grappling and pummeling as they went.

The broadaxe, jarred free, skidded down the slope ahead of them and came to rest on the trail. The rolling combat landed beside it, the goblin on top, going for Wingover's throat. With a heave, Wingover threw the creature over his head, spun, and leaped just as the goblin struggled to hands and knees. Straddling the creature, the man got his toes under the base of its brass chestplate, hooked his fingers under the back-plate, and put all his strength into prying them apart. Held by stout straps, the two pieces of armor closed like a trap around the goblin's neck. Wingover strained harder. Clawing at the man's booted feet, the goblin staggered upright, reeling and struggling to breathe as the clamp tightened at its neck. Its face seemed to swell, its eyes bulged, it staggered and fell, carrying the man with it. A broadaxe descended and crunched into the ground, barely missing both of them, and Wingover's hold slipped. He heard another of the elf's arrows pierce armor somewhere near.

Panting, he stood. On the ground, the goblin gasped for breath, then rolled and came to its feet, wild eyes glaring, taloned fingers reaching.

"I've had enough of this," Wingover decided. With a long stride he ducked the goblin's arms and drove a hard fist full into its face. The creature toppled like a felled tree and lay still.

Stone clattered, and Garon Wendesthalas came down the slope. He glanced at Wingover, then crouched beside the goblin. "Alive," he said. "One of them got away, up the hillside. He was out of reach before I could bring him down."

"I left my horse up there," Wingover panted.

"Well, if that goblin is going to find him, it already has. What are they doing here? I haven't heard of goblins in these lands . . . at least not any time lately." The elf looked up quizzically. "And by the way, good morning to you, too, Wingover."

"Hope you didn't mind my crashing your party," the man said.

"Not at all. There were plenty to go around. Frankly, I'm glad you showed up. I knew they were here—smelled them a ways back—but I didn't know how many, or exactly where they were. But I still can't imagine what they're doing this far south."

"That's what I want to know, too." Wingover squatted on his heels, tilting his head to study the wide, feral face of the unconscious goblin. Dark blood seeped from its nose and mouth. "Maybe he'll tell us about it, if he wakes up."

As though on cue, the goblin stirred and groaned. Garon knelt and lifted one of the creature's eyelids with his thumb. "He's coming around. Let's peel this armor off of him. He'll be more talkative without his shell."

"Whatever you say. You've dealt with goblins."

"When I had to." The elf glanced at Wingover, melancholy elven eyes curious. "I gather you made it to Pax Tharkas?"

"Made it, and the pack I'm bringing back will cost Rogar Goldbuckle a fine purse. But then, the bet was his idea."

"What if he decides to pay you in kind, by freeing you

of your debt of service to him?"

"He won't. Goldbuckle's a wily old dwarf, and he won't put money ahead of collectible service. But then, I don't mind. He staked me when I needed it most . . . I owe him a service whenever he decides to call on me. Probably wind up some day fighting a trader's duel with somebody too big for an old dwarf to handle."

They stripped the goblin of his armor and threw it away. No human or elf would ever willingly put the smelly, tarnished armor next to his own skin.

Garon Wendesthalas used strong rope to bind the creature hand and foot, then drew a slim, needle-pointed dagger and set its hilt in a crack in the stone path, the blade pointing straight up. As the goblin regained consciousness, hissing and cursing, the elf rolled him over onto his belly, dragged him forward, and lifted his head so that his right eye was directly over the dagger's point.

Wingover watched, fascinated. "What are you doing?"

"Creatures of darkness cherish their eyes," the elf said. Holding the goblin's round head in a strong grip, he said, "Tell us now, goblin . . . why are you here? Who sent you?"

"You can fry in molten stone, elf!" The goblin tried to twist away and could not. "I won't tell you anything. I'll—"

Garon shrugged and pushed the head down. The goblin's scream was a shrill hiss, echoing from mountainsides. Matter-of-factly, Garon raised the round head and repositioned it. "This is a little something that elves have learned—the hard way—from goblins," he told Wingover. Then to the goblin he said, "You still have one eye left. Who sent you here?"

The creature writhed and whimpered. "I can't say! I can't!"

Grim-faced, Garon Wendesthalas pushed the creature's head down until eye touched knife-point. "Yes, you can," the elf said. "Who sent you?"

"I can't . . . ahh! Darkmoor! The commander! I answer to the—!" Abruptly the goblin stiffened. Tiny bolts of lightning writhed along its body, twisting in bright weaves around arms and legs, a dancing fabric of blue bolts as fine as spider lace. The bolts lasted only for an instant, then the goblin's pale, flabby body went rigid, the wide spike-toothed mouth opened and heavy, dark smoke gusted from it.

The creature went limp. Garon pulled the body away from the dagger and rolled it over, his long, elven face twisting in disgust. "Dead," he said.

"So I see," Wingover shrugged. "You didn't kill him, though."

"No. He truly couldn't say more. He had a spell upon him, and it killed him rather than let him tell us anything else. Do you know anyone called 'Commander' or 'Darkmoor?' "

Wingover shook his head. "It isn't a goblin name. Doesn't sound dwarven, either. It might be elven, but what kind of elf would associate with goblins?"

"It sounds to me like a human name," Garon said. He glanced at the man, wide eyes thoughtful. "Maybe the question is, what sort of *human* would associate with goblins?"

"I guess I'd better go see about my horse and pack. Are you bound for Barter?"

The elf nodded. "There have been a lot of rumors lately, about trouble in the north. And omens. Did you see the eclipses?"

"Yes. And I thought about you, Garon Wendesthalas. I thought maybe you could tell me what it means."

"Maybe nothing," the elf said. "Or it might mean that something very bad is about to happen." He looked around at the grim carnage of the goblin encounter. "Far worse than this. Maybe we'll learn more at Barter. It's the place to listen, if there is something to be known."

Climbing the slope, Wingover collected his sword and shield, and paused to study some of the dead goblins there. A scouting party, he decided. But scouting for what? And for whom?

The horse was where he had left it, skittish and wild-eyed but still reined within the cleft of rock. Several yards away, though, was the sprawled body of another dead goblin. Its skull had been crushed.

"Don't blame you a bit, Geekay," Wingover reassured the horse. "I don't like goblins, either."

When Wingover came down the trail, Garon Wendesthalas was waiting for him. The human dismounted. "Sling your pack up here with mine," he told the elf. "I'll walk with you."

Wendesthalas tied his pack to Geekay's saddle skirt and turned away, his long stride setting a brisk pace. Wingover walked beside him, leading Geekay, and found himself thinking about the manner of the elf's inquisition of the goblin. He glanced at the lithe, almost-human ranger pacing him. In many ways, it seemed to Wingover, the race of elves could be the gentlest of the people of Krynn. And in many ways the wisest. Yet there was nothing gentle and seemingly little wise in Garon's treatment of the goblin.

Is it possible for me to really understand him or his kind, the man wondered. Can any race ever truly understand any other?

He mulled it over for a few minutes, then decided. Probably not.

Wingover turned his thoughts to another race. He had a gambling debt to collect from Rogar Goldbuckle. Not that the dwarf would try to cheat him. Such was not Goldbuckle's way. Still, dwarves could be full of surprises.

Chapter 10

Though it had started only as a seasonal encampment, a meeting place for those of various races
whose lot it was to go abroad and trade commodities to
supply their various realms, Barter now was a bustling
little town. Resting in a sheltered valley west of Thorbardin, it was a truce village, a place of respite from
whatever conflicts and hostilities might be currently going on around it. A motley collection of low stone
cubicles—favored by the mountain dwarves—log structures where hill dwarves could find comfort, shacks,
shanties, tree houses in the few trees large enough to con-
tain them, mud huts, and a few airy elven lofts, Barter
catered to any who were willing to trade in peace.

Here elves, dwarves, humans, and occasionally kender walked the same paths and sat at the same tables with robed sorcerers and outlaw clerics. Here voices might be—and often were—raised in hot discussion, but outright violence was not condoned. Here even the bitterest of enemies stayed their hands and held their tempers.

For Barter was Barter. As in any place and any time, no matter what grand intrigues may be afoot, no matter what wars might be raging across the lands, still there had to be a means of trade and a place to do it. As in all places and all times, each people had need of what the others had in plenty, if only for the building of weapons to fight against one another.

In Barter, it was said, even an ogre could come and trade—provided he didn't act like an ogre.

Technically, Barter lay within the realm of the dwarves, though whether its origin was from mountain or hill dwarves' settlements none could say. And this was as it should be, for the bands and tribes of humanity had been scattered far and wide, and many were wanderers, while of all the other races the dwarves had the most to trade, the most *need* to trade, and the greatest understanding of how essential trade was. Being in the dwarven realms also gave some measure of protection to the place, as neither mountain nor hill dwarves was amenable to having their lands entered by those who sought trouble.

As they neared the settlement Wingover recalled the simple rules of the place. "Don't kill anybody," he chuckled. "It isn't allowed."

The faint trail they followed wound down into a valley, toward Barter, and within a mile of the village they were among cleared fields on a gentle slope, with the village visible ahead. Wingover pointed toward a large pavilion draped with red and yellow awnings. "The mountain dwarves are here," he said. "That's Goldbuckle's stall."

Just ahead, on the trail, an odd object was moving toward the village—a triangular white thing more than a dozen feet from end to end and half that in width, it had the appearance of a giant spearhead, creeping along on spindly-looking narrow wheels that glinted in the sunlight. Garon Wendesthalas studied the thing ahead, then shook his head and pointed, questioning.

Wingover shrugged. "I haven't the vaguest idea what it is. I've never seen anything like it."

They went on, and within a few minutes were close enough to see more details of the creeping thing. More than a spearhead now, it resembled half a bellows, partially closed. A series of slender ribs extended back from the forward point, all covered over with a layer of white fabric pleated so that each fold at the rear draped at least two feet below the rigid supports. Near the rear was a thing like a wicker basket, two or three feet across, set into the fabric so that only the top of it was clearly visible from behind. Narrow, slightly bowed poles slanted outward below the basket-thing, each tipped with a wheel that was nothing more than a metal ring braced from a hub by thin, gleaming wires. Beyond, someone was walking, only his feet visible, the rest of him hidden by the forward point of the contrivance.

"Maybe it's some kind of a rollable tent," Wingover suggested.

"Half an umbrella?" the elf wondered.

"That big? Nobody would build an umbrella that big. And why does it have wheels?"

"Maybe because it's too big to carry."

They came closer, and a suspicion arose in Wingover's mind. He swung into his saddle, touched heels to the horse, pranced ahead, and pulled up alongside the strange thing. It was longer than he had thought, possibly as much as twenty feet from point to rear, and while its trailing end was no more than three feet high, its long, slim point was well above his head as he sat in his saddle. He walked the horse alongside and leaned down to look below the thing's edge. He sighed and straightened. "Just as I thought," Wingover chuckled. "A gnome."

The thing stopped moving. Its point lowered a bit as a metal shaft swung down to take its weight, and its owner stepped out to look up at the horseman. He stood belly-high to Wingover's horse, and had a bald head surrounded by long white hair that blended into a silvery beard. That trait would have made him look very old . . . had he been human. "Ofcoursel'magnome," he said in a voice that sounded thin and irritated. "That'sonethingtheycan'ttakeawayfromme. Bobbin'sthename. I'meverybitasmuchgnomeasanyofthem,thankyou. Whoareyou?"

The question was so imperious, and came from such a small creature, that Wingover couldn't suppress a smile. "If I understood you correctly, you want my name, which is Wingover," he said. "But don't take it out on me, whatever you're boiling about. It isn't my fault."

"Of course not," the gnome said more slowly as he calmed down. "It isn't anybody's fault. These things just happen. Though they could have been a little kinder about it, in my opinion."

"Who could? And kinder about what?"

"Everybody. The Transportation Guild, the Master Craftsgnome . . . the whole colony. Kinder about getting rid of me, is what they could have been. If it had happened at home, I'd have had my say about it. But no. 'Out in the colonies,' they said, 'this sort of thing can't be tolerated. Good of the colony,' they said. 'Best just to send the poor soul packing off into the howling nowheres, than to chance his infecting anyone else.' So out I went. Kit, klacker, and Krynnbook, as they say. Speaking of which, I sincerely hope my map was right. That's supposed to be the village of Barter just ahead. Is it?"

"It is," Wingover nodded. Garon had come up to them, and the man turned. "I kind of thought there'd be a gnome under this thing," he said. "And here he is. His name's Bobbin." He waved a casual hand. "That's Garon Wendesthalas. He's from Qualinost."

Bobbin nodded curtly, then turned to Wingover again. "How much for the use of your animal?"

"The use of . . . for what?"

"To pull my soarwagon. What else?"

"This thing? You look like you're doing all right, pulling it yourself."

"I don't mean now, I mean later. Does your horse run

fast?"

"As fast as I need him to, when I need him to," Wingover replied cautiously.

"Good," the gnome said, and ducked under his contrivance, then turned and peered up at the human again. "I'll look you up when I need you. I'll supply the rope, so don't worry about that."

Without further conversation, the small creature hoisted the nose of his contraption and trudged on toward Barter, towing the thing as he went, only his feet visible beneath it.

"Did you find out what that thing is?" the elf asked.

"He didn't say, just called it his soarwagon. But it doesn't matter. Whatever it's supposed to do, it probably won't. I've seen gnomish things before."

"Odd," the elf said softly. "I think that's the first time I've ever seen just one gnome. Usually, where there is one there are dozens."

"I gather he's an outcast," Wingover said. "He was part of a colony, but they kicked him out. He isn't too happy about it."

"That explains it, then. But I wonder why." They resumed their pace toward Barter, but the elf remained thoughtful. "Did you notice the wheels on that thing?"

"Yes. Very nicely made. That's a novel idea for wheels, to use wire spokes. Light and practical." Wingover hesitated, then turned. "I see what you mean. Usually if gnomes set out to put wheels under something that weighs ten pounds, they'll wind up using fifteen or twenty wheels and each wheel might weigh a ton . . . then there'll be traction devices, and who knows how many clutch and brake assemblies, and whistles and bells and adjustable levers to adjust the adjustments, and the whole thing won't move an inch under any circumstances."

"Or it might throw itself off a mountain, or dig itself into the ground," the elf added. "Whatever that thing is, it doesn't look like any gnomish thing I've seen."

Barter was busy. First snow shone on the high peaks of the Kharolis Mountains, late harvests were being completed in the valleys, and people everywhere were preparing for winter. The trading taking place now would be the last until spring for most who came, and the village was bustling with activity. Dwarves, elves, gnomes, kender, and humans walked the ways and gathered at stalls and pavilions. Bards, acrobats, jugglers, and elixirhawkers plied their trades. Warriors, farmers, craftsmen, and clerics rubbed shoulders with wizards and rangers, and the usual volatile peace of Barter held sway. At any streetcorner, at any moment, there might be a dozen separate swindlings, thieveries, fair deals and foul going on simultaneously, but weapons were kept sheathed and no blood flowed.

"I see the Inn of the Flying Pigs is still in business," Wingover noted. "I'll be there when I've done my business."

"I'll be around." The elf nodded and started on his way. "Give my regards to Goldbuckle."

Some travelers were staring in fascination at the three pigs above the inn. On flapping wings, they sailed about in lazy circles and figure-eights, as cheerfully content with their lot as any pig with wings might be.

Wingover grinned at a gaping newcomer. "The innkeeper did a favor for a wizard once. No one knows what it was, or who the spellcaster was, but the wizard repaid him by making that unique sign to advertise his place. The pigs fly around up there every afternoon for a few hours, and it's good for his business. Just be a bit careful when you walk beneath them."

Wingover left his horse with a liveryman and made his way to the pavilion of the mountain dwarf trader, Rogar Goldbuckle.

The pavilion, with its red and yellow awnings, was one of the largest in Barter, for Goldbuckle and his party did most of the outside trading commissioned by the Daewar merchants in Thorbardin. The pavilion was a large rectangle, with tended stalls on three sides. There, dwarves wearing Goldbuckle's colors offered the finest of Thorbardin commodities—gemstones of many kinds, pyrites and hewn stone, minerals in powder or granule form, prized funguses famed for their taste, burning-stone to fuel hearths in winter, huge varieties of hand-carved trinkets and decorations, and—of course—some of the finest arms and armor available anywhere in Ansalon.

Within the pavilion's fourth side were the counting tables, and there Wingover found Rogar Goldbuckle. The trader raised a bushy eyebrow at sight of the human and said, "Well, it looks to me as though you are still alive. Did you give up the idea of going to Pax Tharkas by way of the wilderness?"

"Give up, nothing," Wingover chuckled. "I've been there and back, and I'm ready to collect on our wager. But first, it will cost you a mug of ale to hear about it, Rogar Goldbuckle. And none of your trade swill, either. Bring out your own supply."

"Trade swill indeed!" the dwarf snapped. "I handle nothing but the finest, and each barrel better than the rest."

Despite this claim, though, Rogar Goldbuckle brought out his own stock and led the man to a quiet corner where there was a table and benches. He poured golden ale into a pair of fine silver goblets, and for a time they sat together in silence, enjoying the potent beverage. Only when Wingover had drained his goblet and licked his whiskers in appreciation did the dwarf get down to business. "You promised proof," Goldbuckle said. "What kind of proof do you offer?"

With a wink, Wingover slid his pack from beneath his bench, hoisted it, and set it on the plank table between them. "Check the seal," he said. "It's from your own consignee in Pax Tharkas. And it's unbroken."

The dwarf inspected pack and seal, grumbling as he went over it. "It was a stupid wager anyway, and had I been sober at the time you'd not have duped me into it. How much was it, again?"

"You know very well how much it was," Wingover said. "Now pay up. And what do you mean, 'duped?' It was your idea, as I recall."

"I was just trying to do you a good turn," Goldbuckle

snapped. "You had nothing constructive to do, so I thought I'd give you an opportunity for a pleasant outing."

"*Pleasant outing?* When was the last time you tried to cross that wilderness, you old charlatan? I made it there and back, but it's not something I'll do again for a while. What with thieves and waylayers at every turn, and cave-ogres . . . and cats."

"Cats?"

"Cats. Oh, yes. And goblins. Why are there goblins this far south, Rogar? Have you heard anything?"

"You actually saw goblins?" the dwarf's eyes narrowed. "There have been some rumors, of course, but—"

"Not only saw them, but fought them. Garon Wendesthalas and I. He was on his way down from Qualinost, and a band of armed goblins set a trap for him. I happened along and spoiled the party. Half a day from here, or not much farther. Where the trail comes down from Grieving Ridge."

"But—" Goldbuckle's eyes widened. "But that isn't even the wilderness. That's well within Thorbardin's realm."

"That's what I thought. Garon and I think they were a scouting party, but that's about all we could learn. The one that we kept alive—or tried to—had a spell on him. It killed him before he could tell us anything, except a name. Darkmoor. Do you know about anyone by that name? Or anyone called Commander?"

The dwarf shook his head.

Wingover shrugged. "Maybe we'll never know what it's all about. What are these rumors you mentioned?"

"Oh, just odds and ends. Someone said that goblins were seen in upper Dergoth recently, and several people have mentioned seeing more ogres than usual. They said the ogres seemed to be laughing sometimes, as though at a great joke."

"What's a joke to an ogre could be bad news for anyone else," the man noted. "What else?"

"Well . . . they say that some of the plains tribes in the

northern lands have begun migrations southward, with tales of strange happenings in the Khalkists."

"What sort of happenings?"

"Oh, people disappearing and that sort of thing."

"People disappear all the time."

"But not usually whole villages . . . even whole tribes."

"Not usually, no."

"Tarnish," the dwarf rumbled. "It's an uncertain world we live in, Wingover, and troubling times. I've heard a dozen predictions, just since I arrived here, that Ansalon will be overrun by war within two years. Some say less time than that. The seers have been studying omens and comparing notes, along with some of the mages. But not one has any idea who, or what, may be involved in the war if the time should come. Ah, me. What's a poor trader to make of it all?"

Wingover grinned at the dwarf. "Every profit the market will bear, as usual. Speaking of which, I'm ready to collect on our bet, in case you've forgotten." He held out his hand, palm up.

"Corrosion!" Goldbuckle snapped. "That's a lot of money. Do you think all I have to do is snap my fingers and—"

Wingover nodded. "You old skinflint, that's no more than petty coin to you, and you know it. So hand it over, and I'll stand the first round at the Flying Pigs. Garon will meet us there, and we can compare goblin stories and sinister rumors."

Still the dwarf hesitated, and Wingover crossed his arms on the table. "If you're thinking about trying for double or nothing, forget it," the human said. "Of course, now, if you'd like to just keep your coins and cancel my debt of service instead. . . ."

"I can't do that," the dwarf muttered. "Oh, very well!" Without looking around he raised a sturdy arm and snapped his fingers. Within seconds a counting clerk was at his side. The trader whispered to the young dwarf, and the clerk scurried away to return moments later with a fair-sized leather purse. The bag made a resounding, satisfying whack when Goldbuckle slapped it down on the table.

"Ill-gotten gains if ever I saw such," the dwarf rumbled. "But I've never been one not to pay a just debt."

"I never doubted it for a minute," Wingover assured him. "By the way, what's in the pack I brought you?"

"Money," Goldbuckle said, blandly.

"*Money?*"

"A year's accumulated proceeds from my ventures at Pax Tharkas. You'd be amazed at how difficult it is to make shipments of coin these days, Wingover."

The human's mouth hung open in disbelief. "You—you had me set out through the wilderness with your year's fortune in a pack? Do you know how much I'd have charged you to take that responsibility? Even if I took it all?"

"Of course I know," the old dwarf said blandly. "It really was far cheaper to make a bet of it."

"You scoundrel! You . . . you . . ."

"Try, 'bedamned old thieving dwarf,' " the dwarf suggested. "Some good human swearing might make you feel better."

Wingover sputtered, steamed, and finally subsided. There was no way around it. He had been fairly and thoroughly swindled, and had gone along with it wholeheartedly.

Finally he sighed, retrieved his gambling winnings, and thrust them away in his tunic. "Well, at least it's over," he said. "I've had enough of that wilderness to last me for a time."

"About that," Goldbuckle said.

"What about it?"

"Well if you recall, I said I couldn't release you from your debt of service. The reason is, I have assigned your debt to a . . . ah, friend of mine."

"Assigned? To whom?"

"Her." Goldbuckle nodded, looking past the man.

Wingover turned, and his mouth fell open. A yard away, standing patiently, was as stunning a young dwarven girl as he had ever seen. Not much more than four feet tall, she had the wide, strong face of her kind, with large, wide-set eyes and a smallish, full-lipped mouth nicely set between a button nose and a stubborn little chin. And she wore a broadsword strapped to her back.

"This is Jilian," Goldbuckle said. "Jilian Firestoke. Don't bother trying to talk her out of what she has in mind. It can't be done."

Chapter 11

"May the moons fall on me if I ever do business with a dwarf again!" Wingover bellowed as he strode along Barter's main pathway, causing heads to turn in curiosity. Many paused to stare after the tall, angry man who wore the boots and leathers of a ranger or barbarian, but whose sheathed sword and flinthide shield suggested a warrior . . . and at the striking young dwarven girl—hardly more than half his stature—who tagged after him, scampering to keep pace with his long strides.

The sight, to most, was another entertainment in a village that offered many entertainments.

"How you feel about it doesn't matter," the dwarven girl shouted at the man's stiff back. "You *must* take me to find Chane. Rogar Goldbuckle said you would."

"It's a fool's errand," Wingover snapped. "First he cheats me out of an honest fee, then he sends me on a fool's errand. May the curl-winds carry me away if ever I do business with a—"

"It shouldn't be a difficult trip," the girl puffed, wishing he would slow down. "At least, I don't imagine it is. I have a map, you know . . . of where Chane was last seen."

Wingover stopped abruptly and swung around, towering over her. "You're crazy," he snorted. "One lone dwarf—and a girl one at that—out in that wilderness? You wouldn't live an hour. Don't you know what's out there?"

"Not really. I've never been out of Thorbardin before. But how bad could it be? People do go there sometimes, don't they? Oh, look!"

"What?" He glanced around.

"There's a gnome! That is a gnome, isn't it? I've never seen a gnome before. They're very small, aren't they?"

"So it's a gnome," Wingover snapped. "The world is full of gnomes. Just like the world is full of elves, and this part of it is mostly full of dwarves . . . what do you mean, small? That gnome is nearly as tall as you are." He set off again, heading for the Inn of the Flying Pigs. "I'll tell you a few other things the world is full of, that aren't nearly so pleasant. Goblins, for one. And things worse than goblins, too. There are hobgoblins and trolls—"

"I have a sword," the girl pointed out, calmly.

"And ogres," he continued. "Thankfully not as many of those, but there are some. What you should do is go back home and—"

"Oh, look!" she said, interrupting, and pointed. "Look over there!"

Nearby, a dark bird had flapped from the sky, descending to light on the shoulder of a wizard. Now it was talking to him, its beak just at his ear but its voice clearly audible to those around . . . though it spoke a language few among them understood.

The wizard listened intently, then raised his staff and muttered something. Atop the staff a milky globe seemed to swirl with bright color, and a loud hum came from it. It sounded like bees. Abruptly there were other wizards hurrying toward him, pushing and bustling through the crowd. As some of them reached him he said, "The omen is confirmed. It was seen from the Tower of the Orders. Nuitari crossed the orbits of Solinari and Lunitari. Both were eclipsed, each in its turn."

The ensuing babble of excited discussion wasn't limited to the robed sorcerers, but spread rapidly through the crowd.

"What does that mean?" Jilian asked Wingover. "Are they talking about the moons? What did they do?"

"They eclipsed," the man said. He strode on toward the Inn of the Flying Pigs . . . three long strides, then he tripped and sprawled full out on the ground. All around there were cheers and laughter. Wingover raised himself, shaking his head. Jilian stood over him, her sword in both hands. He stared up at her. "Did you trip me?"

"I certainly did," she said, returning the sword to its sling.

He got to his knees and dusted himself off, glaring at her. With him on his knees, they were nearly face to face. "Why?"

The triumphant slight smile on Jilian's wide, pretty face was enough to bring choking sighs from a number of young male dwarves nearby. "Because you have been behaving rudely," she said. "And because if we are to have any sort of discussion, you shall have to slow down."

"There's nothing to discuss," he snapped. "I told you—"

"Well, you really have no choice, anyway. And the sooner you realize that, the happier we both will be."

Wingover muttered horrific curses in several languages, and got to his feet. "If you aren't the most obtuse button I ever—"

"Jilian," she said, coolly.

"What?"

"My name is Jilian. Not Button. But you don't need to apologize. You can call me anything you like, as long as you help me find Chane Feldstone like you promised."

"I didn't promise any such thing!"

"Thereyouare!" a voice behind Wingover said. The human turned as the gnome trotted forward, waving at him. "Thermodynamics,Iheardyoubellowingfromclearacrossthesquare. Ijustwantedtotellyou,I'llbereadywithinthehour."

Wingover stared down at the little creature, blankly.

"It'sme," the gnome said. After noting the confused look on Wingover's face, he took a deep breath and spoke more slowly. "Bobbin. Oh, I know. Humans always say if you've seen one gnome you've seen them all. Somehow I thought you might be above that sort of thing. But it doesn't matter. A deal's a deal, right? All right. There is an open meadow just off there, beyond those huts. Meet me there. And bring your horse, of course. Don't worry about rope. I have some." With that, the gnome turned and hurried away in the direction he had pointed.

Wingover stared after him, feeling dazed.

"What was that all about?" Jilian asked.

"I haven't the vaguest idea."

Somewhat disoriented and thoroughly cranky, Wingover once more headed for the flying pigs, which were just ahead now, gliding in happy circles above the inn. The man walked more slowly, though, and cast cautious glances at the dwarven girl and her sword.

The place was busy, as usual. During trade seasons, Barter was always busy. A few tables back, though, Garon Wendesthalas sat alone. The elf stood as they entered, and beckoned to Wingover. As they approached he said, "Well, did Goldbuckle pay you off without a quarrel?"

"I don't want to talk about it," Wingover snapped. "Did you learn anything about the goblins?"

"Not much. Just a lot of rumors about all sorts of strange things. How about you?"

"About the same. But I have a problem. I'm heading north again tomorrow. Goldbuckle called in his debt."

"More trading packs?" the elf asked.

"Escort service." He turned a surly thumb toward Jilian, who stood just behind his hip. "This is Jilian Firestoke," Wingover said sourly. "I'm to take her out to find a missing dwarf. Jilian, this is Garon Wendesthalas."

"Oh, my." Jilian looked up at the tall, melancholy being. "You're an elf, aren't you? I'm pleased to meet you."

They sat down to mugs of cool ale, and the human and the elf compared what they had heard. Neither had anything definite to report, only various versions of the same stories. Something very ominous was happening somewhere far to the north, but nobody had any very clear idea of what it was.

Jilian listened for a time, then said, "That sounds a little like Chane's dream. It told him that bad times are coming, and that it's his destiny to protect Thorbardin. That's why he's out looking for a helmet."

Garon looked at her, then at Wingover.

The human spread his hands and shook his head. "That's why I'm going back north," he grumped. "Because some dwarf had a dream about a helmet."

"Oh, not just one dream," Jilian corrected. "He's had the same dream for years. It's only lately that it told him what he is supposed to do. It's his destiny."

"Then why do you want to interfere?" the elf asked.

"Oh, I don't want to interfere, just . . . well, he probably needs help. The guards who went with him came back, and I learned they had robbed him and left him alone in the wilderness. But we'll find him, and he'll be all right. Rogar Goldbuckle says Wingover is a very resourceful person . . . even if he is human."

"Resourceful. Hmph!" Wingover snorted dismally. "I'm resourceful, all right. A resource that old villain has mined to its limit."

Someone jostled against Wingover, then tugged at his sleeve. He turned, to find the gnome there, looking peeved.

"I thought you had gone to get your horse," the small one griped in slow clipped words. "My soarwagon is ready and waiting, and we'll lose our light soon. Come along, now. We have to hurry."

"I don't know what you're talking about," Wingover

began.

"What *are* you supposed to be doing?" Jilian asked.

Wingover shrugged. "I don't know. Nobody has told me."

"You're supposed to be pulling my soarwagon with your horse," the gnome explained. "What could be simpler than that? Come along, now. There isn't much time."

"I'll come and watch," the elf said. "Where did you leave your horse?"

Without much choice in the matter, Wingover was hustled from the Inn of the Flying Pigs to the stables where his horse waited, then across town to a clear meadow, where a marvelous thing sat glowing in late sunlight.

When first they had seen the gnome's contraption, it had vaguely resembled a flat parasol, folded. It was no longer folded, now, and no longer resembled a parasol. More than anything else, it looked like a huge, spread-winged seagull sitting on spindly wheels in the meadow. Great, delicate wings of white fabric extended thirty feet on each side of the basketlike contrivance in its center, and its pointed nose had become a square framework of dainty metal rods. Fabric covered four sides of the basket's six, with the front and rear remaining open.

The gnome scampered on ahead of them and was busily tying one end of a long, thin rope to the thing's nose when the dwarf, human, and elf arrived. All around the meadow, but holding their distance, people of several races waited, curious to see what might happen next.

"Polish and shine!" Jilian chattered as she walked around the contrivance. "Isn't this pretty? What is it?"

"It's my soarwagon," the gnome said. "Please stand back. You, bring your horse around here in front, and get mounted. I'm almost ready."

"What is it supposed to do?" Jilian asked.

"It's supposed to fly," the gnome snapped, momentarily losing his composure. He sighed and took a deep breath. "That's why I brought it here. To let people see it fly, so I can sell it and make some more of them. I intend to go into the soarwagon business."

"Well, we know what it *won't* do," Wingover told the elf. "Fly." He did, though, lead his horse to the front of the contrivance, and stepped into the saddle. "Don't worry about it, horse," Wingover muttered. "That thing will fall apart in about ten steps, then we can get on with what we came for." The gnome scampered to him, looped his rope, and raised it. "Here, attach this someplace, but just as a slip. Give me the other end. I'll release it when I want loose from you."

Obediently, with an ironic grin, Wingover slipped the rope through his pommel-clasp and pulled it until the free end came clear, then handed that end back. "Just out of curiosity," he asked the gnome, "why *did* your colony drive you away?"

The gnome glanced up. "Because I'm insane, is why. Insanity can't be tolerated, you know." Bobbin hurried back to his machine, carrying the loose end of the rope, and climbed into the basket between its wings.

"Insane," Wingover told himself. "I should have known."

"Well," the gnome shouted at him, "let's go. Just go as fast as you can, and as soon as I'm airborne I'll unhitch us and take it from there. That's all I need you for."

"Insane," Wingover breathed. "Ye gods." He looked back at the gnome in the fabric-and-metal gull.

"Go!" Bobbin shouted. "Go!"

With an oath, Wingover snapped the reins and dug heels into the horse. The animal surged, took up the slack, and stretched out to a belly-down run. Behind him, Wingover heard a shout, but he didn't look back. The rope sang in his open pommel, and he heard its end snap free. He listened for the sounds of wreckage astern, then ducked as something huge and white whispered past him, just overhead. With another oath, he veered the horse aside, hauled on his reins, and watched in astonishment as Bobbin's soarcraft gathered speed. It receded with distance, then raised its nose and rose into the sky. All around the meadow were cheers, applause, and shouts of surprise.

The soarwagon climbed higher and higher, flashing bright in the slanting sunlight. At some distance it dipped a wing, circled gracefully to the left, came about, and circled above the village, high and tiny in the sun. It looped and soared, dived and turned, as gracefully as a giant eagle riding the air currents of a mountain range.

With his mouth hanging open in disbelief, Wingover walked his horse back to where the others waited, and dismounted. Jilian Firestoke was jumping up and down, clapping with glee as she watched the beautiful machine perform high overhead. Garon Wendesthalas stood in brooding thought.

"I can't believe it," Wingover said, shaking his head. "That thing actually works! It flies!"

"I'm not that surprised," the elf said. "I heard what Bobbin told you, about being insane."

"What does that have to do with it?"

"It's the whole point. He really *is* insane. An insane gnome. What he invents works."

"But they drove him out."

"Well, of course they did. They had to. Can you imagine what might happen if some great, monstrous gnomish engine were to have one part in it that works perfectly, among all those other parts that don't? A thing like that could be devastating. It could wipe out a colony."

Wingover thought about it, staring at the flying machine in the sky. "I see what you mean," he said at last.

For a time the soarwagon cavorted over Barter, then it began to descend and headed back toward the meadow. It slowed, came to within ten feet of the ground, then suddenly shot upward again, climbing away, regaining speed.

Again it approached, and again, and each time it whisked away aloft. On the fourth pass, as it crept by directly overhead, seeming almost to hang in the evening air, Wingover cupped his hands and shouted, "You've proved your point, Bobbin! You can come down now!"

"I can't!" the gnome's exasperated voice came back, growing fainter as the soarwagon once again gained speed and began to climb. "Itgoesupallright,butI-can'tgetittogodown!"

"He may be insane," Wingover told the elf, "but he's still a gnome."

In evening dusk, after giving up on ever seeing the gnome land, the three went back into the village. Jilian had lodgings at Rogar Goldbuckle's camp, and Wingover would sleep in the stable loft.

"You're leaving in the morning?" Garon asked.

"Apparently so," the human said. "On a blamed fool's errand."

"I'll go part way with you," the elf offered. "There's nothing more to learn here, and I've sold my goods."

"Glad to have you along," Wingover told him. "Any special reason?"

"There might be more goblins," the elf said darkly.

Chapter 12

Jilian Firestoke's map—obtained under duress from a ruffian in a Thorbardin tunnel—was not so much a map as a sketch of landmarks with a wavy line meandering among them. When she finally persuaded Wingover to look at it, on their second day of travel northeastward from Barter, he squinted at it, turned it this way and that, then scratched his head.

"Is this all you have to go on?" He turned it again. "You can't find anybody with this. It has no coordinates. Nothing to trace from . . . what is it supposed to be a map of?"

They had stopped to rest on a small meadow that was little more than a wide shelf on the side of a mountain, but a place where Wingover's horse could graze and the travelers could drink from a tiny spring that flowed from porous stone to trickle down the rocky slope where it fed a shallow pool. As usual when they halted, the man and the elf spread along the trail, Wingover going ahead to where he could see for a distance, Garon falling back to keep an eye on the trail behind them. It was an unspoken agreement, simply a thing that two travelers, wise in the ways of wilderness country, would do.

Wingover squatted on his heels and spread Jilian's map on the ground. "It doesn't even have an orientation," he said. "Which way is which?"

She stood behind him, to see over his shoulder. "You can tell that from where the X's are." She pointed. "One of them is the Southgate of Thorbardin, and the other is where those ruffians last saw Chane Feldstone."

"That doesn't tell me anything," Wingover sighed. "Even if we knew which X was which—and we don't— all that would tell us is that this edge of the map—or this opposite one—should face north. But how far apart are the X's?"

"About six inches," Jilian shrugged. "We can measure it if you—"

"I don't mean that. I mean how far is this supposed to represent in real distance?"

"The distance from Southgate to the northern wilderness," she explained, wondering again at the man's inability to remember simple things. "However far that is."

He sighed again, shaking his head. "That might be twenty miles, or it might be fifty. Gods, girl, there isn't a boundary, you know. There isn't some kind of line drawn across the mountains with signs that say, 'This is Thorbardin's realm and that side is wilderness.' The wilderness is anywhere beyond where the latest patrol perimeter happens to be, and that changes all the time. Didn't the person who drew this give you any idea of what to look for . . . or where?"

"He wasn't very happy with me," she admitted. "He had a bump on his head and was shackled to a wagon-track at the time. All he said was, 'This is Southgate and that's where he got away from us. We supposed the cats would get him.' "

"Cats?" Wingover looked up sharply. "What kind of cats?"

"I don't know. He just said cats. Oh, and he said a bird told them to go away, so they went. Does that help?"

"Cats." Wingover opened his pouch and withdrew his own maps, found the one he wanted and studied it. "There is a valley, north of here, that seems to go almost due north and south." He paused and considered the map. "I wandered into it, but I didn't get a chance to explore it. There were cats there. Big, black cats half as high as my horse. If your young dwarf has gone there, I don't expect you'll find him." The human laid the maps side by side, looked at them together, then turned Jilian's map around. "That could be it, I suppose. I saw the valley at the other end, but it would have come out about—" He pointed at his own map "—about here."

"Then that's where we must go," Jilian said. "Is it very far?"

"Not far," the man said. "A day from here, maybe. But that isn't where we're going."

"Why not?"

"Because of the cats. Look, Button, I said I'd help you find that X. But if your dwarf went there, we might as well just turn back."

"But if that's where Chane went, then that's where we must go. You promised, you know."

"How many times do I have to tell you, I promised no such thing?" He stood and put his map away, handing Jilian's back to her. "You know, your father probably has people out looking for you by now . . . or does he even know you're gone?"

"He knows I've gone to look for Chane," Jilian snapped. "I told him I was going to."

"And he didn't stop you? Somehow I can't imagine that, unless—" He looked down at the wide, pretty face, a suspicion dawning. "*Where* does he think you are looking?"

Jilian looked at her feet. "All over Thorbardin, I suppose. I didn't tell him I had talked to his ruffian."

"Ye gods," Wingover breathed. "And Rogar Gold-buckle?"

"Well . . . I told him that I had told my father I was going to look for Chane Feldstone, and that my father said, 'Go right ahead. Look all you want to.' I suppose he might have taken that to mean that it was all right for me go to outside. But what difference does that make? Now that we know where Chane is, all we have to do is go and find him. That valley might be where Chane is, but how will you know for sure if we don't have a good look at it?"

Wingover sighed. "Because of those cats. No one in his right mind would—"

"Oh, rust! Will you stop harping about cats? If that's where Chane went, then I'm sure he has attended to any cats that might be there, so you don't need to worry."

Wingover gritted his teeth. "Talking to you is like talking to a wall! Can't you understand, Button? If one of those cats found your dwarf . . ."

Jilian turned away, then paused. "I see people," she whispered, gesturing toward the edge of the clearing where the mountain fell away. Excitement glowed in her eyes. She pointed again, and Wingover sprinted toward the ledge and dropped flat just short of it, to crawl forward to where he could see beyond. Jilian was right behind him, and he saw at a glance that Garon had spotted the activity and shifted his position to where he could see up and down the trail.

At first, there was nothing in sight below, only steep mountainside dropping away toward the hazy depths of a canyon between slopes. Then he saw movement, and focused on it.

Far below, tiny with distance, a line of creatures moved along a faint trail, going southward. Sunlight flashed on armor, and Wingover's breath became a hiss. Goblins. A small party of them, with a taller figure leading them—a figure wearing dark, glistening armor and what seemed to be a horned helmet. Human? Elf? He couldn't tell. Reaching for his pouch, Wingover brushed an elbow against a stone, which in turn rolled over, balanced for a moment on the shelf's edge, then fell, bouncing down the slope. The human muttered a curse, then found his spyglass and brought it to his eye. Dwarven-made, it was a brass tube with lenses and a quartz prism—not as precise or as delicate as some elven glasses he had seen, but well-crafted and adequate for his purposes.

Adjusting its focus-ring, he sighted on the company below and frowned, trying to count them. Not all of the goblins were in sight at one time since parts of the faint trail were hidden by ridges and features in the mountainside. But there were a dozen or so. And these were better armed and more heavily armored than the ones Wingover and Garon had encountered north of Barter. They moved with a discipline and precision he would not have expected of goblins.

Easing his glass along the line of goblins, Wingover studied the taller figure in front. Dark armor, richly made: lacquered steel breastplate; epaulettes emblazoned in gold; oiled, fine chain; shin-and armguards of polished bronze; a plain black oval shield; embellished sword hilt exposed from bejeweled sheath. The figure carried a light footman's lance or javelin, as well; Wingover could not tell which.

The helmet was multiply horned, and bore a strange and unique mask that was fashioned to resemble an animal's face, but like no animal Wingover had ever seen.

As he looked, the figure halted, raised a hand to halt the goblins following, and turned. The hideous mask turned to watch a pebble bound across the path, then looked up—directly at Wingover.

With a shock, he realized that the being below saw him clearly, that the shadowed eyes behind the grotesque horned-lizard mask were staring at him intently, as though his spyglass worked both ways. Wingover lowered the glass and edged back, away from the ledge, making the girl retreat with him.

"What is it?" Jilian whispered. "Who are those people?"

Garon came and knelt beside him, leaning out just

once for a glance down at the lower path. "Goblins?"

Wingover nodded. "And someone else leading them. Someone taller. We had better be on our way."

The elf glanced down again. "Out of sight now," he said. "Did they see us?"

"The leader did. But it would take a day to get from there to here. That leader . . . I've never seen a face-plate designed like that."

"Describe it," the elf said.

Wingover described it, and the elf listened in thoughtful silence, then nodded. "A dragonmask," he said. "The mask, the helm . . . . the face of a dragon."

"There are no dragons," Wingover said. "That's just old legend."

"There *were* dragons on Krynn," Garon corrected. "Not legends. They were real. And somewhere, I suppose, they still *are* real."

"Well, that was no dragon down there." The man headed for his horse, gathering pack and saddle as he went. "But whoever it was knows we're up here, and those were real goblins. So it's time to move out."

They made camp that night on a mountainside miles away, north and a little east of where they had rested. Wingover made good use of his maps and his skills to put distance behind them, and they were exhausted when finally he called a stop. But it was a good place to rest—a sheltered cove between broken ridges, where a small cookfire would not be seen, but where a guard on the ridgetop above could see for miles in any direction.

Wingover and the elf took turns standing guard. Wingover was not ready yet to trust Jilian Firestoke with such a responsibility.

Morning's sun found the travelers awake, packed, and on their way, threading a narrow ledge-trail. When they stood atop the next pass, Wingover halted them and pointed. "There's your second X, Button. Off there where the peaks still shadow the land between. Just about where those mists begin. That's where Chane Feldstone was seen last, if your armsman was right. A mile or two beyond should be where that valley begins . . . the one with the cats."

"Good," the dwarf said happily. "We can be there in time for lunch."

Wingover started to argue, then stopped. Jilian was standing, hands on hips, gazing up at him with determined bright eyes that held not a hint of compromise.

He sighed. "Oh, all right. We'll go to where the valley begins. You can take a look from there, then we'll circle and search the ridges. But if we see so much as a catwhisker along the way, we turn back."

"I've never met anyone so obsessed with cats," Jilian scoffed. "I think they're sort of cute."

"You haven't seen these cats," Wingover snapped. He took up the horse's reins and led off. When they had covered a mile, the trail pitched steeply downward, dividing just ahead into two faint trails. One ran straight ahead, the other branched off to the right. Wingover glanced at his map.

"That goes to the Vale of Repsite," he said, pointing to the right-hand path. "Two or three days' travel from here. If I were your dwarf, that's where I would be." Probably resting his sore feet in some village over there, the human thought, but did not say it. Probably cozying up to some hill dwarf's daughters . . . if he's still alive.

Garon Wendesthalas stood in thought, looking at the forked trail, then back the way they had come. "I think I'll leave you here, Wingover," he said finally.

"Why?"

"Oh, just to sit and watch the traffic. Maybe we'll meet farther along, somewhere."

Wingover scratched his bearded chin. "It's those goblins, isn't it?"

"They might be coming along here." Garon shrugged, then a cold smile spread across his elven face. "I still have plenty of arrows, and nothing better to do."

"That's why you came, isn't it?" the man said, perhaps a bit sadly. "You said there might be more goblins."

"Have a nice outing, Wingover." The elf turned away. "Maybe we'll meet again." In the somber elven eyes, just as they turned from him, Wingover saw something cold and determined. Something deadly. This elf had a pure hatred for goblins.

"I hope we do meet again," he said.

Another mile down the trail, Wingover turned to look back. There was no sign of the elf . . . but then, there wouldn't be. No one was likely to know he was there until he was ready to show himself.

Distant movement caught Wingover's eye then, and he peered westward. The man shaded his eyes. Far in the distance, something was moving.

As Wingover's eyes adjusted to the distance the object grew from a small speck of white to a bigger speck of white. It was coming rapidly in their direction. Wingover stared, then saw a shadow below the thing and realized that it wasn't on the ground. It was in the air, flying.

It took shape, and its shape was that of a spread-winged gull, soaring aloft on air currents.

"Ye gods," Wingover muttered. "It's that crazy gnome."

Within moments the soarwagon was abreast of Wingover and Jilian, coming about in a wide, graceful turn fifty feet above the trail and a few hundred yards ahead. As it turned it settled and slowed, until it seemed almost to hang in air, fifteen feet above the surface. In that position it crept upslope toward them, rocking gently from side to side. When it was near, they could see the white hair and irritable-looking face of the gnome sitting in its basket.

He peered out at them and raised an arm to wave. "Ho, there! It's me! Bobbin! Do you have anything to eat?"

"We know who you are!" Wingover shouted. "What are you doing way out here?"

"I got caught in a crosswind!" the gnome responded. "I don't know where I am, but I'm hungry! Do you have food?"

"I can make you a nice sandwich!" Jilian called. "Do you like cold roast elk?"

"Did you ever get that thing to land?" Wingover shouted.

The gnome glared at him, fighting to control his rocking craft, now just fifty feet away and no more than twenty feet above. "If I had come down, do you think I'd still be up here? A roast elk sandwich would be just fine, thank you. With raisins, preferably. And I could use some cider, but water will do if that's all you have. I'll drop a line, and you can send it up. Where are you going?"

"We're going to see if Chane Feldstone is in that valley ahead," Jilian told him, pulling food from the travel pack.

"We are not," Wingover snapped. "We're just going to the rim of it. That's all."

"He thinks there are cats in there," Jilian explained to the flying gnome. "He worries all the time about cats."

"Do they have wings, like the innkeeper's pigs?" the gnome wondered.

Jilian giggled. "Of course not. They're just cats."

"Very big cats," Wingover added.

"Seems to me you need a scouting service," the gnome said. "After I eat, I guess I could go fly over the valley and look around for you, if you'll tell me what you're looking for."

"Chane Feldstone," Jilian said. "He's a dwarf, about this tall and very handsome—"

"Cats," Wingover said. "We're on the lookout for cats."

For a moment the gnome didn't answer. An air current had caught his soarwagon, and he was struggling to hold it in place. His controls seemed to consist mostly of strings that ran from the basket to the fabric panels of the thing's boxy nose, strings that controlled the angle and pitch of the panels. The soarwagon rocked, bucked, and settled into position again, twenty feet above them. Bobbin peered down, his gnome-face ridged with irritation.

"I don't mind looking around," he said. "It isn't as though I had anything better to do right now."

Chapter 13

"*I'll bet you never saw anything like this before,*" Chestal Thicketsway said happily, turning full circle to scan the breadth of the ice field with its jumbled, vague shapes, frozen in combat. "Just look at this! Didn't I tell you? Bumps! Ice-bumps, everywhere you look. And inside every bump are frozen dwarves . . . still fighting, except they don't move any more."

Chane Feldstone didn't answer. With haunted eyes he looked around, needing to see what was here but not wanting to. To one raised in the sheltered delves of Thorbardin, the Dwarfgate Wars were just old legend— stories of the defense of Thorbardin's gates in a time of great crisis, tales of heroes who had manned the gates and the pathways beyond, who had fought at King Duncan's order so that Thorbardin could live.

These are some of them, Chane thought, approaching a great, jumbled mound of ice rising from the ice field—a chaotic feature, like a miniature mountain range twice his height and fifty to a hundred feet across in any direction. Within the ice, dark shadows hinted at shapes. He knelt in front of a sheer plane of ice and rubbed at it, smoothing and clearing its face. Polished, the ice was transparent.

The dwarf leaned close, peering within. Just inside, only a few feet away, two dwarves were locked together in combat, hammer against sword, shield to shield, straining each against the other—violence captured just as it had been the instant the ice had covered the combatants. Beyond these two were others, receding into vague translucence. A dwarf on the ground held a shield above him, desperately fending against a slicing blade frozen in descent. Another, arms outspread, flailed motionless for balance, frozen in the act of falling over the body of a dwarf cleft from shoulder to midriff by some lucky blow. Within the ice, the spilled blood remained crimson on the black ash beneath.

These are some of those who went out to defend Thorbardin's gates, the dwarf thought. And these are who they fought. Which are which, though? Did even they know? There might be a hundred or more locked in combat, just within this one mound of ice—dwarves who came out from Thorbardin, and dwarves who fought to go within. All dwarves, and all alike now in frozen silence.

No one ever returned to Thorbardin to tell of this battle, he realized. No one ever went anywhere from here. They are all still here. Encased in ice, with ashes underfoot.

Three spells did Fistandantilus cast. The words echoed in Chane's mind. *The first was fire, the second ice . . .*

Fire and ice. Chane turned away from the ice window, feeling very cold.

"Isn't this great?" The kender hurried past, chattering his enthusiasm. "Dwarfcicles! Imagine! There's one over there you should look at. That little tall lump . . . there are four dwarves really going at it. One of them has an axe and he's fighting the other three. Better hurry . . . but then again, I suppose he'll last as long as the ice lasts, won't he? Wow, this is like a museum of statues, with frosty windows!"

The dwarf turned to glare at the kender, but Chess was already heading off to look at more lumps.

Chane growled, and the growl became a sigh. I don't want to be here, he told himself. I don't want to look at this. And yet, he went on, from mound to mound in the field of frozen death, peering here, kneeling there for a better view within the ice, searching. And through it all he felt the faint tingling of the little red spot on his forehead—the mark of the red moon—driving him on.

None who were on this field when those spells were cast ever left here, Chane thought glumly. They're here still. Yet, according to the old stories, Grallen did not die in this place. The son of King Duncan died in this ancient war, but not here. Somewhere else, sometime later. Another battlefield, somewhere. The place where Fistandantilus cast his last and greatest spell, they said. Chane tried to remember all he had heard of the old legends. Where had that final battle been? He wasn't sure . . . except that it was somewhere other than here. East of here, he seemed to recall. A place called Skullcap.

Grallen, warrior prince of the Hylar, who had learned a secret in his final hours, had learned of a secret way into Thorbardin, too late to find and defend it.

Had Grallen been here, then?

The red spot on Chane's forehead tingled. Yes, he felt, Grallen had been here . . . and gone on. But to where?

Again in his mind he saw the image, of a face not unlike his own, the face that the dream—or the red moon—had shown him. Grallen, son of Duncan. Chane's own ancestor. Could that be true?

Everywhere, ice. Ice whose convoluted shapes contained dwarves frozen in combat. In some of them, the frozen shapes struggled amid dark swirls of smoke that were kept as still as they were. What kind of mage had he been, this Fistandantilus? What kind of sorcery had availed him, that he could have done this? Yet, the legends said, what he had done later was far worse.

The kender skipped past again, as happy as a child with a roomful of new toys. "See anybody you know?" he asked Chane. "Wonder what they were fighting about . . ." He hurried on, toward a new mound that he hadn't yet explored. Then he paused, thoughtfully, and turned back. "Have you thought about taking that hammer and breaking some of them out of the ice? I mean, just to see if they'd go on fighting?"

Chane rounded on him, furious. "I wish you'd just shut up! You might at least show a little respect."

"Then don't break them out." The kender shrugged. "It was just a thought, anyway." He went on his way.

"That kender would rob a graveyard and not think twice about it," the dwarf muttered. Still, the question was intriguing. Were they really dead in there? Or were they only suspended? He thought about it and decided he didn't want to know.

Chane went on, searching this way and that, not sure what he was looking for except that the tingle on his forehead became more pronounced as he worked his way eastward. *Something* here, it suggested, would tell him where Grallen had gone all those long years ago.

As he knelt beside another clustered mound—inside, dwarves with pikes held their ground against dwarves with swords and axes—the kender appeared again from somewhere and stopped beside him. "Find anything yet?" Chess asked.

"More of the same. I don't know what I'm supposed to find. I almost wish that wizard had stayed around. Maybe he would have had an idea."

"If he had, it seems like he'd have mentioned it."

"Did he say anything about where he was going?"

"Up on a mountain. Said he couldn't see down here. He didn't say which mountain, though." The kender shaded his eyes, gazing into the distance. "What do you suppose that is?"

Chane looked up, saw where the kender was pointing,

and gazed in that direction. "I don't see anything."

"I don't either, now. But I thought I saw a big white bird." Chess squinted, then cocked his head. "There it is again. See? Way off there to the north. I wonder what that is."

Chane saw it too, then—a white, winged shape gliding over the forest, miles away. It looked vaguely like a giant seagull. "I don't know," he said. "But whatever it is, it's not what I'm looking for." He stood, glanced around, then headed east again, toward a very large mound of ice some distance away from any others.

Chess watched the distant white thing for a few minutes, then tired of that. He couldn't tell what it was, and it didn't show any sign of coming close enough for a better look. He climbed one of the mounds—beneath his feet, vague dwarf-shapes did perpetual, motionless battle—and looked around. "Now what?" he wondered.

"Go west," something voiceless seemed to say.

"I wasn't talking to you, Zap," Chess scolded. "I was talking to myself. Besides, the only reason you want me to go west is to get far enough from that Spellbinder thing the dwarf has so that you can happen. Right?"

"Right," something mournful agreed.

"I've been west, anyway," Chess added.

"Woe," Zap grieved.

"I wish that dwarf would find what he's looking for," the kender muttered. "I'm ready to go see something new." He started down from the ice-mound, then ducked as a huge shadow swept over him. Clinging to the ice, he looked up. The white thing was no longer far away. It was directly overhead now, spiraling downward, slanted wings carrying it in great descending circles as it came lower and lower. Fifty feet up it leveled out, seemed to stall, then crept toward him and hovered just overhead. A head appeared alongside one wing, and a voice floated down. "Hey! Are you from around here?"

"Of course not!" Chess called back. "I'm just visiting. What is that thing?"

"It's my soarwagon. It still needs a little design modification but I'm working on it. Right now, though, I'm looking for cats. Have you seen any cats?"

"Not lately," the kender admitted. "There were some dandies around here when I first got here, but they've all gone now. Are you going to come down?"

"I can't." The flier shook his head. "Ground effect, I think. Do you have any food?"

"A little. Dried meat and flatbread. Why?"

"How about raisins? Do you have raisins?"

"I don't think so."

"Well, whatever you have will just have to do," the flier called. A rope began to descend from the white thing, with a small basket tied to its end. "How about sending some up?"

Chess dug around in his pack. There were all sorts of things in it, mostly just odds and ends he had picked up, and in most cases he didn't recall where or why. The kender found dried meat and a few flatbreads he had picked up in the Irda's hut. The basket descended on its rope, and when he could reach it Chess deposited some of what he had in it. The food was hauled upward.

"Why are you looking for cats?" Chess called.

"Some people wanted to know about them. Man called Wingover. He's sure this valley is full of cats, so I came to see. I haven't found any."

"They're the Irda's cats. She went away, and I guess they went with her. You're a gnome, aren't you?"

"I am. Bobbin's the name."

"I'm Chestal Thicketsway. Do you know anything about old gnomish engines? Like siege engines from ages back? There are several of those off that direction, but I couldn't tell much about them."

"Neither can I," Bobbin said. "I'm insane."

"Oh. I'm sorry."

"Not your fault. Another thing that Wingover and his bunch asked about was a dwarf. Any dwarves around here?"

"Hundreds," Chess waved his arms around him. "Everywhere you look, but they're frozen under the ice. Been there a long time."

"No, the one I'm looking for is more recent. Dwarf

named, er, Chain something—" The gnome pointed. "Who's that?"

Chane Feldstone had appeared from behind a distant mound, and was hurrying toward the kender and the soarwagon.

"He's a dwarf," Chess said. "He might be the one. Name's Chane Feldstone. What do they want him for?"

"I don't know. Does he always dress like that? What is that outfit? A bunny suit?"

"Catskin," the kender explained.

A vagrant wind whispered across the ice field and made the white bird dip and bobble. The gnome did something, and abruptly the flying thing shot high in the sky, so high that it was only a winged dot overhead. Slowly it seemed to steady, then started going in wide circles.

Chane reached the mound where the kender stood. "Who is that?" he demanded. "What is he doing up there?"

"His name is Bobbin. He's a gnome."

"What is he doing?"

"Looking for cats."

"Up there?" Chane squinted upward, trying to follow the circling path of the flying thing. "What is he riding?"

"Something unreliable, it seems to me," Chess said. "All he said was that some people sent him to look for cats and he hasn't seen any. Oh, and somebody named Wingover asked about you."

"Me?"

"Might be you. Do you know him?"

Chane scratched his beard. The name did sound familiar, as though he might have heard someone mention it sometime. Then he remembered. "Wingover's a human. Rogar Goldbuckle thinks he's crazy."

"No, it's the gnome who's crazy. He said so himself."

"Why would Wingover ask about me? I don't even know him."

"Maybe you're becoming famous," the kender suggested. "Look, the gnome is coming down again. Every time he goes in one of those circles he gets lower. Wow!

That looks like fun."

"Fun," something voiceless said.

Chane jumped and looked around, then clenched his teeth. "I wish that spell would stop talking," he growled. "It makes me nervous."

"Shut up, Zap," the kender said offhandedly. "You just want to get away from the Spellbinder."

"Need to," Zap whispered.

"Oh, he's going away," Chess sighed.

"Your spell?"

"No, the flying gnome. See? He's heading south. Oh, well. Easy come, easy go."

"It doesn't matter," Chane said. "I found something, finally." He walked away, back in the direction he had just come. The kender climbed off the mound and scampered after him.

The large mound was east of all the rest, and well apart from them. It was a grotesquely shaped mound of ice more than a hundred feet long, stretching from north to south in a shallow curve. Even from a distance, the shadowy figures inside were visible as dark silhouettes— a line of armed dwarves in defense position, fighting to hold off a force twice their strength.

"It looks like a rear-guard action," Chess decided.

"It does to me, too. But what I found is beyond it." Chane led the way around one end of the long mound, then part way back along its opposite side. He stopped and pointed. "See?"

The kender looked, blinked and looked again, then shrugged. "See what? The end of the ice field? The slope beyond? That range of peaks?"

"The path," Chane said. "Look. It looks like a faint green trail, heading east. Can't you see it?"

"I don't see anything like that. Are you sure you—" He stopped and stared at Chane. "Do you realize that the red spot on your forehead turned green for a moment?"

Chane raised a tentative hand to touch his forehead. His eyes widened, then he opened his belt pouch and took out the Spellbinder. He took a deep breath. "Well, the gem's still red. I thought for a minute maybe *it* had turned green, too."

The crystal was still red, but something seemed to pulse dimly, deep within the stone. With each pulse the faint green trace of an ancient trail renewed itself to Chane's eyes.

"It's showing me where Grallen went from here," the dwarf said. "He went east."

"Where Pathfinder went," something voiceless whined.

Chane jumped. "I don't think I'll ever get used to that. What did it say?"

"It said, 'where Pathfinder went,' " Chess repeated. "Zap, what are you talking about?"

Where nothing was, something sighed. "Spellbinder's other," the unfired spell whispered.

Chapter 14

High on a mountain slope, where biting winds came down from the snows, Glenshadow the Wanderer paused in his climbing to inspect the head of his sorcerer's staff. No longer chalky, it was again a cold, flawless stone of swirling transparencies.

The wizard pulled his collar tighter against the chill and raised the staff a foot or so. He muttered a word, and the stone burst into cold, bright light. He nodded, doused it with a word, and looked around. Some distance away, a large, serrated stone lay against a jagged cliff, half-buried in wind-blown snow. He raised the staff, pointed it at the stone, and uttered other words. A tight beam of silver light shot from the gem and struck the boulder, which exploded into shards, some of them bounding away down the mountainside.

Satisfied, Glenshadow climbed again until he came to a high place where patches of ice lay like white pools in the weathered stone.

He gazed into a small ice-covered pool. "Master of the tower," Glenshadow said in a voice as cold as winter's winds, "Grallen's descendant has the Spellbinder, and has begun his search for the helm. Is there word of the outlaw?"

"The Black One lives," said the ice-image that formed on the frozen pool. "Though he was certainly put to death long ago, there is no doubt now that he lives. His magic is known. Other searchers have tasted it, just in recent days."

"Can you tell me where he is, then, or must I continue to follow the dwarf?"

"He is somewhere to the east," the hooded image said. "Nearer to you than you are to me, but though his magic is sensed he goes hidden . . . shielded somehow from our seekings. If you would find him, you must go with the dwarf."

"Does the outlaw know yet of the dwarf and his quest?"

"We think he knows that something is amiss." The ice-image told him. "The Black One is pledged to a quest against the dwarven realm of Thorbardin. This much we know, from those of our order in the Khalkist Mountains. Two died and a third was horribly burned just to bring us the information. Tell me, does the dwarf know his purpose?"

"To go where the Hylar Grallen went." Glenshadow said and nodded. "To seek the helm of his ancestor, which alone might save Thorbardin from infiltration by its enemies. He has an artifact—an ancient god-stone, the twin of the one his ancestor wore on his helm. One stone will lead him to the other, and thus to the helm."

"And should he find this helm . . . will he then know where Thorbardin's weakness lies?"

"If his ancestor Grallen saw the secret gate, then the stone in the helm may also show it to its next wearer.

Both are god-stones, as was suspected. Their magic is beyond sorcery."

"Then the thread is not frail," the ice-pool said. "If the dwarf poses a threat, the Black One will know it. He sees more clearly now than when he was alive . . . before he was put to death. Follow the dwarf, Wanderer, if you would find the Black One; the Black One will surely seek him. Follow the dwarf toward shattered Zhaman, if you would seek again to destroy the outlaw mage." A pause, and then the faint voice asked, "Did you see the omen, the eclipse of the moons?"

"I saw it. What does it mean?"

"None knows for sure," the voice said. "But all the omens point to a great darkness from the north. Evil has its pawns a'play, and moves across the gaming board. Beware."

The pool darkened, cleared, and was simply a pool of ice. Glenshadow shivered, drew his bison cloak more tightly around his shoulders, and again touched the ice with his staff. This time the image that appeared was of the valley from which he had come. Chane Feldstone and the kender stood at the edge of a patterned ice-field and looked eastward.

"Toward shattered Zhaman," the mage whispered. "He follows Grallen's path, toward the resting place of Grallen's helm."

He started to turn away from the pool, then stopped. Another vision had formed there, coming without call. In inky blackness swirled indistinct shapes, coalescing at the center in a pattern that become a face . . . or not quite a face, just the ghostly outline of one, but one that Glenshadow had seen before, long years ago.

And a voice as dry as dust—a voice that seemed shriveled with hatred and age—hissed from the image. "He seeks me, does he?" it said. "The puny red-robe would try again to do what he thought he had done before? Hee-hee. He asks the ice whether I know there is an obstacle in my way. A puny obstacle it is, too. A dwarf. Only a dwarf. Did I know before, he wonders? No matter. I know now." Giggling, the dry voice faded and the ice cleared. Long after the vision was gone, Glenshadow knelt by the ice, shaken and unsure.

"Caliban," he muttered. "Caliban."

*   *   *   *   *

Viewed from the south, the valley was a long, deep cut among towering mountains. Miles wide and many more miles long, deep enough that fall foliage still livened the forests below, it swept away to the north. The valley was straighter than most Wingover had explored, and interesting to his explorer's mind because, while its sides were crested by precipitous cliffs, its approach from due south was a long, fairly gentle slope.

It seemed to almost offer itself as a route, and Wingover found that irritating. He had seen the great cats who lived in this valley, and he knew the valley was a trap. He wondered if any who had entered there had ever come out again.

The man was moody and irritable as the hours passed, tired of waiting for a crazy gnome in a sailing contrivance, who probably would never return anyway. He brooded upon the fates that had brought him to be here, back out in the wilderness again, pursuing an impossible quest—to find one lost dwarf in ten thousand square miles of barely explored territory.

It didn't help Wingover's attitude that Jilian Firestoke seemed to have decided that it was her responsibility to fill the idle hours with constant chatter. He had heard a dozen times now about Chane Feldstone's dream, and at least a half-dozen times about the perfidy and downright churlishness of Jilian's father, Slag Firestoke. He had been belabored by gossip—most of it meaningless to him—about the feud between the Tinturner and Ironstrike families, which had kept the fifth level downshaft neighborhood of Daewar in an uproar for months; about how Silicia Orebrand's sister was not on speaking terms with any of the Silverfest Society members; about the uncouth mannerisms of Daergar dwarves who seemed to think they owned the Fourteenth Road; and about the scandal that had risen when Furth Undermine accused the East Warren overseers of bribing the executor of the Council of Thanes.

"Far stars, Button," Wingover finally erupted, "doesn't anybody get along with anybody in Thorbardin? To hear you talk, I'd think the intrigues and hostilities outnumber the population by five to one."

She blinked in surprise. "Oh, it isn't like that at all," she said. "Thorbardin is the nicest place imaginable. Really. I've just been telling you the juicy stuff because that's what most people prefer to hear. But then, most people—at least most people I know—are dwarves. What do humans like to hear?"

"Silence, occasionally," he snapped.

For long minutes, he had his wish. Jilian sat facing away from him, her sturdy little back arrow-straight. She had tried to entertain him. Now she made a point of ignoring him, which, for his part, Wingover liked better.

Soon, though, she asked, "Do you mind if I tell you one other thing?"

"I knew it was too good to last," he said. "What?"

She pointed. "The gnome is coming back."

He saw it, then—the gliding, erratic flight of the gnome's machine, coming toward them, low over the valley's forested floor.

"It's about time," Wingover snorted.

The white kite came closer, rising as it neared the climbing slope, seeming to shoot upward on wind currents until it was a tiny thing far overhead. Then it dipped its wing and began the wide circling that they had seen before. It seemed that, once up, the only way the gnome could come down again was by this tedious procedure.

The soarwagon circled and descended, circled and descended, and finally crept to a halt hovering just a few yards up—but in the wrong place. It was a quarter of a mile from them, above a jagged cliff where the valley's west wall began.

"What is he doing?" Wingover growled. "Why doesn't he come over here?"

"He's probably trying to," Jilian said. "I don't think his

machine really works all that well."

"It's a wonder it works at all," Wingover pointed out.

For a moment, the soarwagon hovered where it was. Then with a shudder it shot upward again, and the circling began all over. This time the gnome seemed to have corrected his navigation, and when next the thing hovered it was just above Wingover and Jilian.

Bobbin leaned out, his face pinched with irritation. He looked from one to another of them, then settled on Wingover. "I'm back," he announced. "It's me . . . Bobbin. I'm here."

"I know you're here," Wingover called back. "I can see you. Did you find anything?"

"Quite a lot of valley, with various things in it. Several miles north, there's a ring of stones with a thing in the center that looks like a really big thermodynamic inflector, though I'm sure it isn't that. There's a sort of little, broken statue on top of it, and paving all around. Then there's a hut, though if anyone lives there he wasn't at home, and there is a winding black path that goes off in both directions from it. I saw a river and enough trees to make a woodnymph think she'd gone to paradise, and several nice meadows that I could have landed in . . . if I could land. And an ice field covered with lumpy shapes, and what's left of an old wall—older than I can calculate from up here, but I imagine it was old before anybody I know was old enough to understand old—"

"How about cats?" Wingover called.

"How about what?"

"Cats! That's what you went to look for. Cats!"

"No. No cats. One kender, but no cats. Though I did see someone wearing a bunny suit made out of cathide, if you can believe anything a kender tells you. What do you want cats for?"

"I don't want cats! I just wanted to know if you saw any!"

"Well, I didn't. Some bison, here and there, and a few elk, though . . ."

"How about Chane Feldstone?" Jilian called. "Did you see him?"

"Does he wear a bunny suit?"

Jilian had started to shout something else at the gnome, but suddenly his invention was off again, shooting away in a sharp climb that carried it toward the distant peaks to the west.

The girl sighed, then slung her pack and her sword. "I guess that settles that," she said. "We'll just have to look for ourselves. Are you ready?"

"Hold on, there, Button," Wingover snapped. "I'm in charge here, remember? I decide where and when we go."

"Then decide," she said and headed for the valley.

They camped that evening in a clearing well within the valley, where a chuckling little river flowed cold from the mountains to the west, and a strange, black-gravel path wound aimlessly northward through deepening forest.

At day's final hour, Wingover scouted ahead and found nothing to alarm him except an odd emptiness about the valley. "It's strange," he told Jilian when he returned. "It's as if this place has been lived in—but isn't now. Recently vacated. I had the same feeling once when I stumbled across a village of the Parwind people on the plains. At least it had been one of their villages; the tents had all been folded and the people were gone. That place felt the way this place feels. It's as though the area had accustomed itself to being home to someone, and now it doesn't quite know what to do with itself."

Jilian gazed at the man thoughtfully, then shrugged. "Humans are very strange people," she decided, and set about cooking their supper.

A shadow flitted across the twilight clearing and a sharp, high-pitched voice called from overhead, "I'm hungry! How about sending up some supper?"

Bobbin and his soarwagon were with them again. Wingover looked at the contrivance hovering above the camp and shook his head. He had seen gnomes from time to time, but he had never encountered a mad one. He cupped his hands and called, "I want to know about this valley."

"What about it?" the gnome called back.

"Everything that you see that might be useful to me.

Like how far north does it go, and are there dangers ahead, and where does it come out?"

"It's a big place. I haven't seen the whole thing."

"How about scouting for dangers, then?"

"I can do that, if you ask me nicely. What sort of dangers are you looking for?"

"Any that might be there. Like cats."

"There aren't any cats. I already told you that, but I don't suppose you remember. There's a wizard on a mountainside off there somewhere, but he's miles and miles away. And a kender and a dwarf in a funny suit, east of where you are . . . or north, I'm not sure. And way off over there I saw a bunch of people crossing over from the next valley. They're really a mess, all cut up like they've been in a fight, and carrying their wounded. Really a mess, it looked to me. I—"

The soarwagon pitched, nosed up, and shot toward the sky, the exasperated shout of the gnome trailing back from it, "Save me some supper!"

*　*　*　*　*

Bloody, battered, stripped, and staked out on the cold ground, Garon Wendesthalas was only vaguely aware of those who stood over him. For hours, the goblins had tormented him while the one in the lacquered armor— their leader—stood quietly and watched. Torture after torture they had applied, gleeful in their sport, stopping just short of breaking his bones or drawing enough blood to kill him. The leader wanted information from him. Did he know of a mountain dwarf somewhere near, a dwarf who might have Hylar features? Where was the dwarven girl they had seen traveling with him? And the human, who—and where—was he?

The elf had not uttered a sound throughout. Nor had he let his attention fix on the pain they inflicted. Instead, he drifted in his mind, remote and aloof, savoring memories, recalling pleasant times . . . remote and unreachable. He had removed himself to such distance that he was barely aware of the goblins around him. But he knew the leader now. A human female, Kolanda Darkmoor. Commander, the goblins called her. And he knew that someone—or something—else was with her, though he had seen no one. Distantly, he had heard bits of their conversation . . . the woman's voice impatient and querulous, the other's a dry, shriveled husk of a voice that whispered in tones of venom and mockery. He had heard her call the other's name. Caliban.

Garon shut out all other awarenesses. In his mind he walked the patterned forests of the Qualinesti, drank cool water from a brook, listened to the songs of elves in a nearby glade. . . .

"We're learning nothing here," Kolanda Darkmoor snapped, beckoning to an armored hobgoblin. "We've wasted enough time. This elf will tell us nothing."

"Kill him now?" the creature asked hopefully.

"No, bring him along. He's strong. He will make a good slave."

"Elf," the hobgoblin snarled. "Make trouble. Run away, sure—"

Kolanda turned fierce eyes on him. "Did I ask for your opinion, Thog?"

The hobgoblin stepped back quickly, then lowered his face in submission. "Forgive, Commander."

"Assemble your patrol, Thog. Or what's left of it. We're going back to Respite. The valley should be reduced by now, and there are things to do. Bring the elf, but first cut the tendons in his legs. Then he won't run away. When we rejoin, put him to work tending one of the carts."

She turned away, cold and angry. No elf would ever make a worthwhile slave, but this one would live long enough to serve her. He had killed nearly half of her patrol before they brought him down.

Chapter 15

As the sunset shadows of Westwall climbed the slopes of the ridge above the Valley of Waykeep, Chane Feldstone cut a final hold in a rock cliff, pulled himself up and over the lip of a ledge, and gawked at the kender sitting there idly, waiting for him. The sound he had been hearing for the past half-hour, virtually since he had begun to ascend the sheer cliff, was louder and nearer now—a wailing, keening, heart-rending song of misery with no apparent source.

"You always do everything the hard way," Chestal Thicketsway chided him. "I guess it's just the nature of dwarves, to tackle everything headlong no matter how difficult it is. Do you suppose you just can't help being that way?"

"How did you get up here?" the dwarf puffed. "It's taken me half an hour to climb this cliff. How did you do it so fast?"

"I didn't," the kender shrugged. "I went around. There's a perfectly good by-path just over there. Easy climbing, for anybody who'd take the trouble to find it. I brought your sword and your pack, too. They're over there on that rock. Do you want to camp here for the night, or do you want to scale the next cliff? If you want to do that, I've found another by-path so I can meet you up there."

Chane shook his head. "What is that awful noise? It sounds like somebody in pain."

"Oh, that's just Zap." The kender looked around, then shrugged again, remembering that Zap wasn't really anywhere to be seen. "It's his latest talent, wailing like a stricken soul. He's been doing it for quite a while now."

"I know. I've heard him most of the way up. Can you get him to hush?"

"I don't know how. I don't even know what he's wailing about. Maybe he misses the valley or the frozen dwarf place. That's where I found him, originally."

"Well, I wish you'd shut him up. He gets on my nerves."

Chess turned. "Zap! Shut up!"

The eerie, voiceless wailing faltered, then began again with new enthusiasm—only now it added occasional sobs to its repertoire.

"That's even worse," the dwarf growled. "How come he's following you, anyway? I mean, *it*. That isn't a person, you know. It's just an old spell that never happened."

"I don't know why he follows me, but he . . . *it* does. Zap! I do wish you'd be quiet!"

The wailing, sobbing almost-sound continued. Chane sighed, stood, and looked around. They were on a wide, rubbly ledge with another wall of shorn stone ahead. But, as the kender had pointed out, the wall diminished a short distance away and a path began there, angling upward. Abruptly evening had come, with the setting of the sun beyond the valley's other rim, but there still was lingering twilight.

"We have time to go on a little farther," Chane decided. "I wonder if we're anywhere near that green path."

"The one I can't see?" Chess spread his hands. "I haven't the vaguest idea."

Chane looked one way, then the other, along the mountain's slope. He rubbed his forehead, feeling the tingle there, but saw no green trail. Still, he knew from last sighting that he was somewhere near it. From a distance, it had appeared there was a shallow pass between peaks above, and the dwarf had assumed that the trail was going there. But by what route? He went to his pack, fumbled around inside it, then looked up. "Where's my gem?"

"Your what?"

"Spellbinder! Where is it?"

The kender looked thoughtful, then snapped his fingers and reached into his own pouch. "Do you mean this?" He pulled out the red stone, which pulsed with a steady rhythm as the dwarf reached an angry hand to take it. "You must have dropped that somewhere," the kender said innocently. "I guess I picked it up for you. Don't bother to thank me."

"What else do you have in that pouch that isn't yours?" Chane growled.

Chess peered into his pouch. "I don't know. I lose track. Here's a marble of some kind that I found on that old battlefield. And some nice pebbles, and a toad's skull . . . a couple of candles, some twine, an earring, a twig. What's this? Oh, a pair of nice cat-tooth daggers." He pulled out one of the daggers. "Didn't you used to have one like this?"

"I had *two* like that," the dwarf rumbled.

"Did you? What did you do with them?"

"Give me that!" Chane growled.

Chess handed over the dagger, then closed his pouch. "If you're going to expect me to replace everything you lose—"

"Oh, shut up!" Chane stopped abruptly and looked

around. "Well, one good thing. Your spell has stopped wailing."

The kender listened for a moment, then grinned. "He has, hasn't he? Thank you, Zap."

"Agony," something voiceless mourned.

With the Spellbinder gem in his hand, Chane pointed. "There it is. The green line. It goes up the by-path." He hoisted pack, sword, and hammer. "Are you ready?"

"Look at that!" The kender pointed upward. Overhead, great flocks of birds flew, coming from the high peaks, winging toward the valley. Birds of all sorts, a migration of panic.

Chane watched them, wave after wave coming past. "What do you suppose caused that?" he wondered aloud.

"Whatever it was, the birds are in a hurry," the kender said. "See those out ahead? Those are pigeons. And mountain kites, and jays, and ducks, and . . . stand back!" Chess swiftly pulled a pebble from his pouch, fitted the sling to his staff, placed the pebble, aimed, and let go. The pebble streaked skyward, and an instant later a large bird crumpled in flight and fell, thudding to the shelf almost at Chane's feet.

"Goose," the kender explained. "I'm getting tired of dried cat. We'll have this for supper."

Chane gaped at him. "How did you do that?"

"With a pebble. I thought you saw." He picked up the goose and slung it over his shoulder. "See if you can find some berries along the way. Snowberries will do. They're the yellow ones on the thorny vines. Snowberries go good with goose." Chess started up the path, and the dwarf followed, still glancing in awe at the smaller creature's forked hoopak.

Overhead, the waves of fleeing birds continued to pass. And now Chess and Chane had company on the slope. The kender and the dwarf dodged aside as a lithe, furred creature with sharp horns bounded past them. A few yards farther along they hugged the stone wall as a line of other creatures, these with heavy coats of thick wool, surged past them, bleating in panic. At the higher ledge, where the trail cut back toward the peaks, the two dived for cover as a pair of panting wolves loped down the path, followed by several elk.

"Do you suppose winter is coming early this year?" The kender stepped out on the trail to look after the strange procession, then dodged back as more of the woolly creatures charged past him.

"They're running from something," Chane said. "I guess that settles it. We'll camp here. A person could get hurt going up that path, with everything else coming down."

Two huge highland bison charged past the ledge and veered away, following the downward path. Another elk was right behind them, cavorting in desperation as the heavier animals blocked its way. Then more of the woolly creatures. One of them wore a collar with a bell.

"Somebody's sheep," Chess noted. "I'll bet there's a pretty unhappy herder up there somewhere."

"I think we'd better get a little farther from this path," Chane decided. "Camping here would be like trying to sleep in a tunnelwagon turnaround. Rust, but the traffic is heavy."

They trudged along the ledge, away from the path, rounded a sheer bend, and saw a rubble-slope ahead. After testing it, Chane began to climb. The kender followed, carrying his goose. The bird was almost as big as he was.

They were climbing by moonlight when they reached a quiet swale higher up—well beyond and above the noisy switchback with its stampeding animals. "This will do," Chane said. "I'll make a cookfire back there, behind that outcrop. You can cook the goose."

"Did you get some snowberries?" Chess asked hopefully.

"I haven't had a chance. We'll do without."

By the time the goose was roasted, both the white moon and the red stood above the peaks, giving their dichromatic glow to the steep slopes and the forest-tops of the distant valley. The two ate in silence, except for occasional outbursts of commentary and chatter by the kender, most of which Chane Feldstone chose to ignore. The dwarf sat deep in thought, occasionally rubbing his forehead, which tingled when the light of the red moon touched it. A secret way into Thorbardin, and Grallen had learned of it. Like a third gate, he thought. One that nobody knew about.

He thought of Thorbardin, exploring in his mind all of the myriad ways and working clusters of the undermountain kingdom—as much of it as he had seen and could recall. Clearest to him in memory were the city of the Daewar, the only home he had ever known, and the warrens where he had worked for his keep from time to time—first tending fields, then helping with the constant delving by which the dwarves sought to expand their underground crop lands. Clearly he recalled Twelfth Road, which he had passed so often as a child. Less distinctly he knew the Tenth, Eleventh, Thirteenth, and Fourteenth Roads, by which Daewar conducted commerce with other cities of Thorbardin.

Dimly, from one brief visit, he recalled the awesome Life-Tree, home of the Hylar. Their city was delved into a giant stalactite above the great, subterranean Urkhan Sea. As an orphan Chane had possessed the appearance of Hylar in his build and features, and later even in the manner in which his beard lay back against his cheeks rather than hanging resignedly downward. The Hylar, he had thought as a child, had a fierce and noble appearance—and undoubtedly some among them had such qualities, though there were plenty of Hylar who in practice were no more noble than the average Daewar.

Still, Chane's beard grew in the Hylar manner, and it did not displease him that it made him look as though he were standing sturdy and proud, facing down a strong wind.

The Valley of the Thanes, noblest place in all of Thorbardin, Chane had seen only once. He wondered briefly if the supposed "secret way" could lead there. The valley was sacred to the dwarves, for it contained a magical floating tomb—final resting place of the great King Duncan, some said. And the tomb of Grallen, which lay nearby on the lakeshore, was, after all, the only place in Thorbardin that was open to the sky. Yet the only accesses to the Valley of the Thanes were three roads from within Thorbardin itself. And certainly if there were the slightest passage-point through the Guardian Walls, *somebody* within would have noticed it.

Not the Valley of the Thanes then, Chane decided.

And not Southgate, which was the common entrance to Thorbardin since the Cataclysm, nor likely the mostly abandoned Northgate, with its shattered portal ledge. Northgate might be unused, Chane told himself, but it's not undefended. It was equipped for the same impenetrable defenses as Southgate.

Possibly some long-forgotten tunnel or shielded pass breaking through into one of the warrens, or one of the lower cities? Kiar, Theiwar . . . Daergar? It didn't seem likely to him. Surely *someone* would have noticed.

"There's a creature with long, flexible arms and not a bone in its body."

Chane looked up. "What? Where?"

"In the Sirrion Sea," the kender said. "Aren't you paying attention? That's what I'm talking about. The Sirrion Sea. They also say that there is a gigantic island out there, just far enough from the Isle of Sancrist to be out of sight, that isn't an island at all. It's really a gnomish ship, hundreds and hundreds of years old, that was supposed to drive itself by a geared rod with a weight atop it. The reason it's in the sea, they say, is because the gnomes who built it set out westward and that was as far as they got before the falling rod buried itself in the ocean floor. They've been working on it ever since, trying to iron out all the bugs, and it just keeps getting bigger and bigger."

With a low growl, Chane Feldstone returned to his own thoughts. The First Road? One of the Halls of Justice? There was so much to Thorbardin, so many different parts and places in the kingdom beneath the Kharolis Mountains. Chane Feldstone had seen so few of them, and almost none of the outside perimeters and capping peaks that protected the dwarven kingdom.

Chane sighed and tried another tack.

Grallen had learned . . . so the Irda said . . . that there was a secret entrance, and that Thorbardin would be threatened by invasion because of that entrance. But where was it? Grallen had not been in Thorbardin when he learned of that; he had been outside, fighting in the Dwarfgate Wars. Grallen had not returned alive, but he had tried—or at least intended—to find the secret passage and block it somehow.

The dwarf rubbed his chin. Where, then, did Grallen go? Using his crystal, Chane could see a green line that he intended to follow. It was, he trusted, Grallen's path. And yet, where did it lead?

"Five unicorns," Chestal Thicketsway said.

Again the dwarf glanced around, startled. "Where?"

"What?"

"You said 'five unicorns.' Where?"

"Oh, all over," the kender shrugged. "I'm not even sure I believe him, you know. Capstick Heelfeather has been known to exaggerate. But that's what he says. He says he has personally seen five unicorns. So far, I've only seen one."

"I wish that wizard would come back," the dwarf muttered.

"Why? I thought you didn't like him."

"I don't. I wouldn't trust that mage as far as I can spit, but he knows a lot of things about outside that I don't know."

"Is that all?" The kender brightened. "I've been outside all my life. What do you want to know?"

"Well, to begin with, where exactly was Grallen when he died?"

"I haven't the foggiest notion," Chess said happily. "Ask me something else."

Shaking his head in exasperation, Chane went back to his puzzle. How am I supposed to find a secret entrance if no one has a clue to its location? he wondered. And even if there *is* a secret entrance, and I find it, what am I supposed to do about it? Apparently the only one who ever knew anything about any of this was Grallen, and he died a long, long time ago and never told anybody . . . did he?

Chane shook his head. If Grallen did tell someone about the entrance, why didn't somebody do something about it back then? Or since? *Why me?*

"Dwarves and humans," the kender said. "At least that's what I—"

"Will you please be quiet?" Chane stormed. "Can't you see I'm trying to think?"

"I'm just trying to tell you, there are dwarves and humans down there."

"Where?"

"On the path, where all the animals were. But the animals are mostly past now, and there are people over there, going down that path as fast as they can. Some of them are bleeding, too. I wonder what's going on."

Chapter 16

FROM THE TOP OF A ROCK OUTCROP, CHANE AND Chess had a view of the path. It was below, and some distance away, and the moonlight cast eerie shadows where the slopes rose above it. But it was a view, and Chane crouched there, staring in wonder at the dark shapes moving down the cutback slope. Dozens were in view, people of all sizes. Some were dwarves, and some were taller—humans, perhaps. Some scampered along the downward path, turning often to look back. Some moved more slowly, clinging to one another; some supporting others, some being carried.

Behind the first wave of refugees came a small knot of figures brandishing spears and swords, moving slowly. A few were shouting at those ahead, urging them on.

Others at the rear faced back up the path, their weapons at the ready.

"Somebody's chasing them," Chess said. "That's their rear guard. I wonder who's after them."

Slowly the fleeing people made their way down the angled by-path, disappearing by twos and threes as they reached the cutback below and rounded the shoulder there. Shouts and cries carried upward, distorted by the spires and tumbles of the mountainside and by distance.

"Let's get closer," Chane decided. "I can't tell anything from here." He rose and turned to find the kender already gone, scrambling across tumble-slopes, leaping from stone to stone, heading for a better view of the path. Chane hurried after him.

For long moments the dwarf and the kender were out of sight of the path, but then they emerged on a ledge directly above it and looked down the length of the sloping angle between cutbacks. The path was empty now, as far as they could see. But just opposite the two, in a shadowed canyon from which the path emerged, something was moving, coming toward the turn. Heavy footfalls crunched in the rubble of the path. Footfalls . . . and a deep, harsh voice that broke into cruel laughter.

"See 'em run!" the voice rumbled up from the shadows. "Blood an' gore. Me, I go an' find me more. Bash 'ere skulls an' break 'ere bones! Let 'em go? Haw! Not me. Not Loam!"

The figure that emerged from the darkness was huge— a massive, wide-bodied thing that loped down the path on bowed, gnarled legs. It carried a huge club in one hand, which it flailed as though it were a twig.

"Make 'em run!" the thing bellowed as it passed directly below the dwarf and the kender. "Make 'em flee! Make 'em die . . . in agony. Hee, hee!"

It skidded in the rubble, faltered for just an instant, and changed course, heading down the cutback where the fleeing people had gone.

"What in tarnish is that?" Chane whispered.

"Ugly, isn't it?" the kender said. "They're even uglier in front. Here, I'll show you."

Before Chane could react, the kender stood, drew his hoopak-sling, and sent a large pebble flying after the monster. The pebble bounced off the thing's skull with a distant thud. Howling, the monster slapped a massive hand to its insulted head and spun around. Moon-red eyes in a massive, heavy-browed face darted this way and that, then came to rest on the dwarf and the kender.

"Oops," Chess said.

With a roar that reverberated off the mountain peaks, the great creature started up the path toward them, swinging its club.

"Anyway," Chess said, "now you have a better look at it. I'll bet you've never seen an ogre before. Have you?"

"Puny things!" the ogre roared, gaining momentum. "Throw rock at me? Loam last thing you will see!"

"What did you do that for?" the dwarf growled. "Now look what—"

"I didn't expect him to be quite so cranky," Chess explained, interrupting. His hoopak-sling sang and another pebble—this one larger—smashed into the advancing ogre's face, full on his wide nose. Dark blood spurted, then dripped downward, veiling the thing's grotesque mouth. The ogre roared again and sprinted toward them.

"I think he's really angry," the kender said. "This one's yours. I'd better look around and see if there are others."

"What?" Chane turned, but the kender was already gone, leaping nimbly from one rock to another, upslope, pausing here and there to peer down into the shadowed pathway below.

"Rust and tarnish!" Chane stared at the advancing monster. The thing was tall enough to reach him with its club, even from the path below the rock where he still crouched. And it was coming fast. He fingered the hilt of his sword, then decided against it and unslung his hammer.

"Kharas aid me now," the dwarf breathed.

Backing up a step from the edge of the rock, Chane glanced quickly at its moonlit top, then knelt and swung. He struck stone with the spike-end of his hammer. Again he swung. Then the dwarf ducked as a hand the size of his back appeared above the stone and swung a massive club that whuffed over him.

Chane's hammer rang again on the surface of the stone, and again. The great club rose above him and descended, crunching into the stone beside him with a sound of thunder. Again the cudgel was raised aloft, and this time Chane had to throw himself to one side as it smashed down where he had been. He rolled, righted himself, and swung his hammer again. The weapon's spike sank into stone, making another hole in a precise line of holes that—he hoped—followed a faint flaw line in the rock.

Just beyond and below the rock outcrop, the ogre leaped upward. For an instant its eyes were level with Chane's. The dwarf dodged, and the club descended again, raising a cloud of stonepowder. The ogre's roar was a rising, echoing thunder of rage. The club thudded here and there, searching for Chane . . . then paused. The sounds beyond told the dwarf that the monster was climbing. He sighted on the fault line and swung again.

The top of the ogre's head came into view, then its eyes. The creature bellowed in huge pleasure when it saw that the dwarf was trapped there with sheer cliff at his back and no place to go. The ogre clung to the stone and raised its massive club. Chane scooped stone dust and threw it into the huge, grinning, bloody face.

The ogre roared in rage, lost its hold, and dropped from view. Quickly, though, it started climbing again. Chane's hammer rang. The sound of its impact was different now, a slight, hollow echo accompanying each stroke. And the spike sank deeper into the stone with each swing. Again the massive hand appeared with its club, and descended a blow that would have flattened and crushed the dwarf, had it found him. Chane panted, concentrating on his work. The scrabbling sounds of clumsy climbing began again, and the ogre's head came into view.

Chane raised his hammer one last time, whispered, "Reorx, guide my maul," and brought it down against the stone. The sound of the impact seemed to go on and on, the ringing strike becoming a deep, low grinding sound as the fault opened . . . a hair line that became an inch, then another inch . . . then a cleft a foot across, that widened abruptly and crashed away into the walled pathway below, carrying the ogre with it. Chane crept to the newly sheared edge of the outcrop and looked down. The pathway beneath was a jumble of fallen stone, its walled opening filled halfway to the top. A cloud of stone dust hung above it, veiling the moons' light.

Slinging his hammer, Chane took his sword in hand and bounded down to the rockfall, searching for openings. He found a wide slit, thrust his sword into it, and prodded as far as the blade would go. Somewhere underfoot, distant-sounding and muffled, the ogre howled in outrage. Chane went looking for wider fissures.

He was still darting back and forth across the tumble of slab-stone when the kender reappeared, just above, crouched on the sheared ledge. "What did you do with your ogre?" the smaller one asked. "I hear him, but I don't see him."

"He's under these rocks," the dwarf snapped. "I can't reach him."

"Well, that's not so bad," Chess shrugged. "That means he can't reach you, either. Of course, if you'd killed him first, *then* buried him, you wouldn't have this sort of problem. Don't you know *anything* about ogres?"

"This is the first one I ever saw," Chane growled, prodding into another crack with his sword. Beneath the rocks something yelped, and the pile of stone shuddered.

"Well, you may have the chance to see some more, if that's what you want. There's something else up there— quite a distance away, but definitely up the path. It might be another ogre . . . maybe several. They tend to come in bunches, you know."

"No, I didn't know."

"Kind of like goblins," the kender said. "You hardly ever find one goblin without finding a lot of goblins. Which reminds me, I thought for a minute up there that I could smell goblins. Have you ever smelled goblins?"

"Not intentionally. What do they smell like?"

"Oh, I don't know." The kender pondered it, finding the challenge interesting. "They smell like, uh, maybe a sort of a mixture of fresh manure and dead frogs. I don't know. Goblins smell like goblins. Anyway, you don't generally find ogres and goblins in the same place at the same time. That's why I was surprised to smell goblins."

Chane made a final pass from one end of the rockfall to the other, but found no opening large enough to reach the buried ogre with more than just the tip of his sword. The kender, watching him, went to one of the cracks the dwarf had already tried and inserted the butt-end of his hoopak, then plunged it downward as hard and as deep as he was able. Beneath their feet, the pile of stones rumbled and quaked, and a trilling bellow emerged from various crevices.

"I think he's ticklish," Chess observed.

"I think we should get out of here before he really becomes irritated," Chane said. Thoughtfully, he reached into his pack and touched the hard, warm facets of Spellbinder. Instantly, the faint, green guideline was there, leading up the switchback trail, heading for the pass high above. Yet the kender said there were more ogres up there, and maybe goblins, as well. Chane realized that he had never seen a goblin either. He didn't relish the idea of meeting some of them just now, though. The ordeal with the ogre had left him shaken.

"Maybe the thing to do," he told himself, "is to go after those people who were running down the path and find out what they know about what's waiting above."

Chess looked around, frowning. "Don't you want to see for yourself? I do."

"I'd just as soon know what I'm getting myself into before I get into it," Chane decided aloud. "I'm going to talk to some of those people. You can go on up there if you want to."

"Good idea," something soundless seemed to say. "Let's go."

"Hush, Zap," the kender said. "I know what you're trying to do."

"Misery," the spell mourned.

The dwarf glanced around. He was growing accustomed to the ditherings of the kender's companion, but it still bothered him.

"Zap thinks if I take him far enough away from you and Spellbinder, that he can happen," Chess said with a shrug.

The dwarf had already started back down the zigzag trail, so the kender followed him. Chess looked back toward the distant heights now and then and wished the old spell hadn't attached itself to him.

Full morning lay on the valley by the time Chane and the kender rounded a bluff on the mountain's long slope and saw people ahead. Where a stream came down from the heights, two rough camps had been established, a few hundred yards apart. The larger camp, and farthest from the rising mountain, was of dwarves. The nearer, smaller camp—no more than a few cookfires and bits of bedding where injured people rested—held a few dozen humans.

As the dwarf and the kender neared, those humans capable of holding weapons came out part way and formed a defensive line, watching the newcomers carefully. In the dwarf camp beyond, people scurried here and there; twenty or thirty dwarves soon came at a run to join the human fighters.

When they were near enough, Chane cupped his hands at his cheeks and called, "Hello there! Can we join you? We're peaceful!"

There was hesitation, then a burly human with a full beard stepped out of the line and called, "Who are you?"

"I'm Chane Feldstone," the dwarf returned. "That's Chestal Thicketsway. We were on our way up the mountain when you passed us. I want to talk to you."

"There were ogres and goblins behind us," the man said, shading his eyes against the morning sun. "If you came from there, how did you get past them?"

"We only saw one ogre," Chane called, "and no goblins, though there may have been some higher up."

"How did you get past the ogre you saw?"

Chestal Thicketsway danced forward, past Chane. "Chane Feldstone is a famous warrior," he shouted. "He dumped rocks on your ogre and buried him."

"I'm not famous," Chane hissed at the beaming kender. He turned his attention to the people ahead. Closer now, he could see them clearly. Many of them had fresh, bound wounds, and those huddling in the two camps beyond were in a sorry shape. "Who are you people?" he called. "Where have you come from?"

The humans and dwarves—and women among them, Chane noted, of both races—relaxed visibly as the two strangers came near and they saw that they weren't goblins. The burly man lowered his pike and tapped himself on the chest with a grimy thumb. "I'm Camber Meld. That's Fleece Ironhill over there." He pointed toward a gray-bearded hill dwarf standing just ahead of a phalanx of armed soldiers. "We're chiefs of our people. We have—er, *had*—villages a mile apart in the Vale of Respite. That's the next valley over. His people are herders. Mine are growers. Or were." He looked around, blank-eyed. "I guess what you see is all that are left."

Chane stopped just a few paces from the leaders, looking from one to the other. "What happened?"

"They fell on us just at daybreak," the dwarven chief said. "An army of goblins and several ogres. First my village, then Camber's. We didn't have a chance."

"We fought," the man corrected. "For three days, we fought, first in the villages, then retreating up the slopes. But there were too many of them, and we weren't prepared for defense. There haven't ever been goblins around here, and not many ogres."

"But there are now," Fleece growled.

Chane stared at them bewildered. "What did they want? Why did they attack you?"

"Base for the Commander," the dwarven chief said. "One of my herders hid in a ravine and heard some of them talking. That's what they said. 'The Vale of Respite would serve as a base for the Commander.' And they were taking slaves."

"Is that why they followed you over the ridge?" Chane

asked.

"Ogres followed," the dwarven chief muttered. "Two of them, at least, though one may have stopped to torture a few of our people who fell behind. The other one was right behind us."

"Why do ogres follow anyone?" the human leader snarled at Chane. "To torture, to mutilate, to kill." He looked at Chane curiously. "But you got him, huh?"

"I didn't kill him," Chane said. "I tried to, but all I managed was to bury him under some rock."

"We irritated him, though," Chess said helpfully.

The dwarven chief also was gazing at Chane, studying him. "You don't look like a hill dwarf," he said.

"I'm not. I'm from Thorbardin."

The hill dwarf sucked in his breath, his eyes narrowing to slits. He half-raised the axe he carried, then shrugged and let it down. "Mountain dwarf," he rumbled. "But I guess that war was over a long time ago."

Chane thought abruptly of the ice-field—only a few miles away—where two kinds of dwarves remained frozen in bloody, ancient conflict. "I hope so," he said.

Chapter 17

The dwarf and the kender rested that night in the humans' camp. Despite Fleece Ironhill's concession, a mountain dwarf still was more welcome among humans than among hill dwarves. What remained in their packs—a few pounds of dried cat, some rolls of goose, and a piece of flatbread—they shared. The humans in turn shared some of the meager provisions they had carried in their retreat from the goblin marauders.

It was a sad and sorry camp, as was the dwarf camp just beyond. Everywhere, there were injured people. And everywhere there was grief.

Chane sat apart for a time, talking with the human chief, Camber Meld. Then he curled up and went to sleep, wondering how he was to follow the path of the old warrior, Grallen, if that path led right into a fresh nest of armed goblins and bloodthirsty ogres.

Chestal Thicketsway, still wide awake and excited by the rate at which new adventures were coming along, roamed about the two camps for a time, then climbed a hill and sat on top of it, watching the moons creep across the sky.

In the distance, he could see the hooded fires of the refugee camps, where Chane Feldstone slept. The kender felt at his side and frowned. He didn't have his pouch with him. He had left it with his pack, back there at the camp. And he had his hoopak, but no pebbles. Immediately Chess scouted around and found several good pebbles. He then felt much more comfortable.

It was oddly quiet, he noticed. Not so much as a whimper from Zap. Chess's eyes widened, and he whirled to look again at the distant fires, abruptly realizing that he was a long way from Spellbinder. "Whoops," he muttered. Turning full circle, slowly, speaking distinctly, he said, "Now, listen, Zap, I think we ought to talk about this. I'm sure we can find a civilized way to. . . . Zap? Are you listening? I'd really just as soon you behave yourself for a while longer. There's no reason to go off half . . . Zap? Zap! Where are you, anyway?"

Nothing responded. There was not the slightest hint of the old spell's presence.

"Zap, are you hiding from me?" The kender peered all about even though he knew that there would be nothing to see. "Look, if you're tired of following me around, that's all right with me. No problem at all. I never could figure out why you were tagging after me in the first place." He paused and listened again. "If you want to just head out on your own, I certainly won't hold a grudge. In fact, that might be the best thing you could do. Just go along by yourself—the farther the better, of course, and do your destiny, whatever that is. You might get a real bang out of that, don't you think?" The kender frowned at the absolute lack of response. "Zap! I know you're around somewhere. Where are you?"

Still there was no answer. The kender sat on a rock,

deep in thought. Maybe the spell had come up with a new tactic, he reasoned. Maybe it would try to convince him that it was gone, to lull him into taking it to where it could explode. On the other hand, maybe this was already far enough away for it to explode.

Then again, maybe it wasn't here at all. But if not, where was it? It had been attached to him since the day on the old battlefield where he had first met it. How could it be unattached now? Unless. . . .

Chess snapped his fingers and grinned. He had left his pouch and his pack at the humans' camp. Maybe it wasn't him that Zap was attached to, but his belongings. Maybe it was attached to his pouch! That could explain the awful wailing the spell had been doing, up on the mountainside. If it was attached to his pouch and Spellbinder had been *in* his pouch . . . well, he could see how Zap might have been pretty unhappy about that.

With a grin, Chestal Thicketsway realized that he had found a solution to a problem. If Zap was attached to his pouch, all he needed to do was make a new pouch and go off and leave the old one. Then he'd be rid of the pesky spell once and for all. He began to think about the materials he would need for a pouch.

"Hellothere," a voice said. "Isthatyou?"

Chess jumped to his feet, spinning around.

"Up here," the voice said more slowly. "It's me, Bobbin. Do you have any raisins?"

Overhead, the wide-winged soarwagon floated, shadowy in the light of the two moons. Chess waved, and the gnome did something to his controls, bringing the machine lower still.

"I don't have any raisins," the kender said. "Sorry. What are you doing here?"

"Scouting," Bobbin explained. "I've sort of signed on as chief scout for the Wingover company . . . since I have nothing better to do. I'm looking for danger. Do you have any?"

"Not right now," Chess admitted. "I had an ogre a while back, though. That's pretty dangerous. And from what I hear, there's plenty of danger beyond those peaks, over in the Vale of Respite. Goblins and ogres have taken the place over. Those people out there by the fires are refugees. Why don't you talk to them?"

"I've been trying to," Bobbin snapped, "but my soarwagon needs some adjustment of its aerodynamic equivalences . . . which I will attend to if I ever get back on the ground. I've been trying since early evening to get to that camp, but I keep winding up somewhere else. I guess you'll have to give me my report. Goblins and ogres, you say? And you actually met one of the ogres? What's his side of the story?"

"I don't know. I didn't stop to chat."

"Well, where's the ogre now?"

"He's up on the mountain, buried under several tons of rock. Chane Feldstone buried him."

"Chane Feldstone? I've heard that name."

"I wouldn't be surprised. He's famous, you know. Not rich, but well on his way to being famous. I'm helping him." The kender grinned proudly. "You can help, too, if you'll spread the word. Just tell anybody you happen to see that Chane Feldstone is a famous warrior."

"I suppose I can do that," the gnome agreed. "Where is Chane Feldstone?"

"He's over there where those people are camped. He's asleep, though. Burying ogres is tiring work."

"Well, Wingover wants to know what's going on. I wonder—" The gnome paused, thinking, then said, "Maybe we could offset the lateral drift ratio in this thing, if you'd help."

"What do you want me to do?" the kender asked doubtfully.

"I'll drop a line. You grab it, and maybe you can tow me over to where those people are."

A length of stout rope snaked downward from the underside of the soarwagon. Chess dutifully slung his hoopak on his back and grasped the rope in both hands. "Now what?" the kender called.

"Now just start walking, and I'll try to follow along."

Chess shrugged, hauled the rope tight, and started to walk. For a dozen steps, the gnome's craft crept along above him, obediently. Then it stalled in a draft and edged to one side. The kender took a tighter grip and hauled it back toward the proper course.

"This may work out," the gnome called down. "Just keep going and hold tight to that line, and . . . oh, cross-current! Hang on!"

Chess clung to the line as the soarwagon nosed up, and suddenly realized that his feet were no longer on the ground. He looked down. The hill where he had rested was falling away below, as was the rest of the world. Moonlit landscapes widened beneath him, shrinking away to miniature forests, streams, trails, and ridges. Higher and higher the soarwagon soared, the bit in its teeth now and the winds of altitude under its wings.

"Would you look at that," the kender breathed. "Wow! What a view!"

Above him, the gnome muttered and swore, working at his controls. "Linkjoint!" he said in obvious annoyance. "The zag and the zig have reversed again. I thought I had that fixed." He leaned out from his basket, squinting as he peered downward. "Are you still there?"

"I certainly hope so," Chess assured him. "Otherwise I'm in a lot of trouble."

"Well, don't just hang there gawking! Come up here and help me. You can hand me my tools."

"How do I get up there?" Chess asked.

"Just a minute. When I get my hands free, I'll winch you up. Don't go away."

"I wouldn't dream of it," the kender assured him.

Moments passed, then Chess felt the rope inching upward toward the belly of the gnome's invention. Winchteeth rattled above, and the great, shadowy wings seemed to close down on the kender like storm clouds descending. He rotated slowly as he rose, and suddenly there was a wickerwork surface before him.

"Climb in," Bobbin ordered. "Then hand me that wobble-wrench. I have to readjust the nose attitude."

Chess climbed into the basket, found and handed over a strange-looking tool, then resumed his sightseeing. "Where are we going?"

"I don't know," the gnome snapped. "How should I know? I never know where I'm going from one minute to the next. I spend all my time just trying to get from where I didn't want to go back to where I shouldn't have been in the first place. Hand me the washer-pull."

An hour passed, and then another, while the gnome did things to his controls and the kender passed tools. Rising mountainscapes crept by below, cliffs and crags, moonlit steeps and shadowy canyons. Then high peaks appeared to either side. Finally, another landscape, which fell away toward a distant wide valley where fires burned and smoke clung like fog in the lower reaches, spread below them.

"I'll bet that's where all those goblins are," Chess said. "I'll bet that's the Vale of Respite."

The gnome paused to look. "Is there danger there?"

"From what I hear, there is."

"Then I'd better tell Wingover about it—ah! There, now. Here, Chess, you hold these two strings. Just hang on to them, and don't let them slip. I think I can turn around now."

Bobbin drew a pair of strings and let several others slacken. The soarwagon tipped its wings and soared into a wide turn, spanning several miles of valley below in the process.

"Can we go down for a better look?" Chess wondered aloud.

"What do you want to look at?"

"Whatever's down there. Let's go see." In his excitement the kender eased his hold on the two strings, and the soarwagon's nose pitched downward. Abruptly they were in a screaming dive, straight down, with terrain rising to meet them.

"Oh, let me have those!" Bobbin leaned over, took the strings away from the kender, and pulled on them. The dive flattened out, and the flying machine raced over the tops of leafless trees toward a pall of smoke just ahead.

"This is a lot better," Chess observed, leaning far out from the basket for a better view.

The smoke was a thick darkness underlit by the flames

of many fires—burning houses, burning sheds, huts ablaze, and haystacks smoldering. An entire village was burning, and in the distance another lay in ash and embers. As the flying machine swept over the fires, Chess saw dozens of goblins below, tending the fires and bringing things to throw upon them. A few slit-mouthed faces turned upward as the soarwagon passed, and gaped at the contrivance sailing through the smokes. Something struck the soarwagon's frame and glanced away. The basket twanged, and Chess glanced around to find a bronze dart protruding through the wicker, inches from his thigh.

"Do you suppose we've seen enough?" he asked Bobbin.

A flaming bolt arced upward ahead of them, and the gnome veered his machine to the right. "If those people set my wings afire—"

"Those aren't people. Those are goblins."

Another bolt whisked by. Without hesitation, Chess unslung his hoopak, dug a pebble from his tunic, and twisted around in the basket to send the stone zinging on its way. Below and behind them, a goblin howled in pain.

Bobbin glanced at the hoopak thoughtfully. "I wish I'd thought to mount something like that on the soarwagon," he said.

The kender shrugged. "It's just a hoopak."

They were past the burning village then, and closing on the second village, which was little more than glowing sparks wafting from piles of ash. Chess pointed ahead. "Aha!" he said. "Ogres."

"Where?" Bobbin leaned to look, and the soarwagon executed a barrel roll at treetop level. The kender clung to the basket as the gnome worked frantically to get the contrivance right side up again. When finally it was flying upright and level, Bobbin said, "Sorry about that."

Chess shook his head. "I have an idea. . . . You tend to the navigation, and I'll do the sightseeing."

"How many ogres did you see?"

"Three, I think. Can you turn around and go over

again? I'll count them."

"Never mind," the gnome said. "In certain circumstances an informed estimate is as acceptable as quantitative data. I'm going to try to—"

The soarwagon's nose lofted, and the Vale of Respite fell away behind them as the machine headed for the sky. Bobbin wrestled with his control strings and muttered to himself: "Don't know why it does that . . . only trying for a reasonable rate of ascent . . . something about the angle of trim on the horizontal vanes, I suppose."

When he succeeded in leveling the soarwagon out, it was approaching the peaks again, heading more or less west.

"Would you classify what we saw back there as danger?" Bobbin asked.

"It certainly looked dangerous to me," Chess said brightly.

"Then I expect I should tell Wingover about it. I agreed to do that, you know."

"Do you suppose you can drop me off on the way?"

"I'll try." The gnome manipulated strings, and the soarwagon sailed over moonlit ridgetops, then down toward the refugee camps a few miles beyond the slopes. "I think we can—"

A crosswind fluttered the box-kite nose of the contrivance, and it veered aside, then nosed up and headed for the sky again, straight up and gaining speed. "Oh, no. Link failure!" the gnome cursed.

Chapter 18

"This is Chane's," Jilian stated, turning the rough hammer over in her hands. "I'm positive it is."

It was a crude tool, obviously wrought by someone who had almost nothing to work with. Wingover crouched beside the primitive stone forge and brushed his hand across the cold ashes in its firepit, then turned his attention to a mudstone thing beside it, puzzling over what it might be. A piece of rock—tough, flaky mudstone that had been shaped into a rough oval with a flat top—its sides were bound with sapling withes. Wingover glanced at the firepit forge again, then realized that the mudstone thing, bound as it was atop a fallen log, had served as an anvil. A contrivance beside the forge might have served as a bellows. Flakes of stone fallen around the makeshift anvil indicated that someone had done something here recently.

"Interesting," the man muttered. "Whoever was here certainly made do with what was at hand. But how can you be sure it was Chane?"

"He made this hammer," Jilian said cheerfully. "See, it has his mark on it. CF. Just like on his nickeliron dagger."

She handed the tool back to Wingover, and he studied it. "I thought it might be a hammer," he said. "So we can suppose that Chane Feldstone *did* stop here and make himself a hammer. Why would he have gone off and left it?"

"Oh, Chane wouldn't have wanted anything as crude as that," the girl explained, wondering again at the vagaries of the human mind. This human seemed quite intelligent in many ways, but there were some things he just didn't seem to grasp. Things any dwarf would understand immediately.

The man stood and frowned at her. "Well, if he made it and didn't want to keep it, what did he do with it?"

"He used it to make another hammer, of course."

Wingover sighed and shook his head. Jilian was probably right, he decided. It sounded like good dwarven logic.

"The inscription is right there." She pointed. "Right on top. Here . . ." Opening her small pack, Jilian brought out a beautiful dagger with a mirror-bright blade and a grip of ebony and brass. "Here, see the inscription on this blade? It's the same as the one on that hammer. I imagine we'll find him just any time now. Don't you think so?"

Wingover didn't answer. He was walking slowly around the forge site, looking at the ground. He circled it twice, stopped, and squatted for a closer look at something. Then he circled it again and stopped to look again, in a different place. "There's no clear trail," he said finally. "He might have gone anywhere from here. But he wasn't alone. There were others with him—at least one, maybe more. One was a human, about my size."

She blinked up at him. "How do you know that?"

"The same way you know this thing is Chane's hammer, I guess. I know what to look for. It's called reading signs."

"Outside certainly is different from Thorbardin," Jilian observed. "In Thorbardin, signs are written on planks or linen and hung on walls for people to see. They say things like, 'Trespassers Will Be Mutilated,' or 'Gorlum's Friendly Furs,' or 'No Aghar Allowed.' "

"Those are signs," the man said. "This is a *sign* . . . in this case, footprints. But they've been here a while, so I can't tell where the trail leads from here."

"Then let's keep going the way we were going and see what else we can find," Jilian decided.

He shrugged and stepped toward the horse. "Come on, then. I'll help you up onto Geekay," Wingover said. "I'll walk and lead for a while. Maybe I can pick up a trail."

"I'll walk, too," the dwarf said, backing away a step. "I've had enough riding for a while."

"Geekay doesn't mind," he told her. "Ride if you like."

"He may not, but I do. I hurt."

"You hurt?" He glanced around at her. "Where?"

"That's none of your business," the dwarven girl snapped, her cheeks turning pink.

"Oh, I see," he grinned. "Saddle sores, huh? It won't last long. I'll bet this is the first horse you ever rode."

"I never even saw a horse until I left Thorbardin," she admitted. "I don't mean the people there don't have horses, of course. A lot do, but they don't bring them into Thorbardin. They keep them outside, in the pastures beyond Southgate."

"I know that," he said a little testily. He took up Geekay's reins and led off, heading north. Jilian followed, grateful to have her feet on solid ground again instead of bouncing along on her bottom, behind Wingover in his hard saddle. Riding a horse was just one of thousands of interesting new experiences she would have to tell Silicia about when she returned to Thorbardin.

They had gone nearly two miles and had come into open, rolling land when Wingover glanced westward, shaded his eyes, and then pointed. Above distant tree-tops, wide wings tilted in a descending turn. Bobbin was back.

Jilian squinted, shading her eyes as Wingover had done. "I think he has someone with him," she said.

The flying thing closed until it was directly overhead, sixty feet above. Two heads appeared at the wicker rail, silhouettes against bright sky. The one farthest aft cupped his hands and called, "Do you have any raisins yet?"

"Sorry!" Wingover shouted. "Still no raisins, but we have some other food." He beckoned to Jilian. "Can you get something together to send up to him?"

She nodded and began opening packs. "Right away."

Wingover shouted aloft, "What do you have to report?"

There was hesitation above, then the gnome replied, "Chane Feldstone is a famous warrior!" More dimly, they heard him ask his passenger, "How was that?"

"Perfect," another voice said aloft. "Tell enough people that, and he'll be really famous in no time at all. Then all he has to worry about is how to get rich."

"That's a kender," Wingover noted. "Where in Krynn did that gnome get a kender?" he asked, not really expecting an answer. "And what kind of report is that?"

He started to repeat his question, but Jilian Firestoke had jumped to her feet, dancing with excitement. "Have you seen Chane Feldstone?" she shouted. "That's who we're looking for!"

"All I know is, he's famous!" Bobbin responded. "Oh, yes, and we saw danger. If that food is ready, I'll try to let down a line." Without warning the soarwagon lurched, nosed upward, and shot away, straight up into the bright sky. In a moment it was a tiny dot, circling wildly, this way and that.

An hour passed, and part of another, before the flying thing approached Wingover and Jilian again. This time, as it completed its final pass, a rope descended from beneath it and a small figure slid down to the end of the rope and clung there. He touched down on nimble feet as the soarwagon again hovered just overhead.

Jilian ran to meet the newcomer, took the rope from him, and attached a parcel of food to it. A winch creaked over their heads, and the rope rose as it was reeled in. Jilian gaped at the newcomer. She had never seen a kender before. He was no taller than herself and slight of build. His clothing was strangely colored, and he had a forked stick slung at his back. He grinned at her—a friendly, open grin on a childlike face that was neither human nor elf and certainly not dwarf—but was not so very different from any of them. What she had first thought was a beard, she now realized was a great mane of hair coiled and looped around his neck, resembling a fur collar.

"I'll bet you're Jilian," the kender said. "That dwarf—ah, I mean Chane—has mentioned you several times." He executed a slight, courtly bow. "I'm Chestal Thicketsway. I've been helping Chane become rich and famous so he can go back to Thorbardin and do unpleasant things to your father."

"Where is he?" she managed to say.

"Your father? I don't know. I haven't seen him. Oh, you mean Chane? He's out there a few miles . . . kind of that direction . . . camping with a bunch of refugees from the Vale of Respite. I'll bet you won't even recognize him in his new suit. Does he know you're coming? He didn't mention that to me."

Wingover hurried to them and glanced at Chess. "A kender," he muttered. Throwing back his head, he shouted at the gnome above. "What was that about danger? What kind of danger?"

"Ask him!" Bobbin shouted back. "He knows more about it than I do. I don't suppose you have a number eleven sprocket on you, do you? I think I'll try to modify the trim-bracing to see if that will—oh, gearslip! Here it goes again!"

With a shudder, the soarwagon edged off to one side, dropped its nose, and ran straight at those on the ground. As one, Wingover, Jilian, and Chess sprawled face-down. The soarwagon's wire wheels whisked over them. It leveled out just above the ground and sped toward the base of a tall tree a hundred yards away. At the last moment it nosed up and climbed, clipping twigs as it shaved the treetop and headed for distant skies. A stream of angry words drifted back on the breeze.

Those on the ground got to their feet and stared after the contrivance. "What was that he was shouting?" Jilian asked. "What kind of words were those?"

"Gnomenclature," the human sighed. He turned to the enthralled kender. "My name is Wingover," he said. "I'm in charge of this expedition . . . or at least I keep telling myself that. And I guess if we're to learn anything, it will have to be from you."

* * * * *

The refugees from the Vale of Respite had moved farther west, deeper into Waykeep Valley. Pens were being built for livestock, and a few huts had been erected for the sick and injured. Exploring parties were ranging outward, followed by gatherers gleaning field and forest for supplies to help last out the winter. And a strong guard perimeter was maintained to the east, though there had been no evidence of any further pursuit.

Though he was anxious to be on his way, Chane Feldstone had put off his quest long enough to build a sturdy pit-forge and begin the making of tools that the refugees would need. Scavengers from both the human and dwarven camps were sifting through the ruins of nearby ancient gnomish artifacts, recovering metal to be fired and beaten into tools and weapons to replace things they had left behind when the goblin force attacked.

Chane was shaping a serviceable anvil and showing some of the younger hill dwarves how to cut blade-stock when the hum of conversation around him died, and he looked up. And gawked.

Jilian Firestoke stood before him, staring in profound disbelief. Jilian Firestoke, who was supposed to be safely home in the Daewar district of Thorbardin. She stood just yards away, here in the wilderness, dressed in rugged trail garb and sturdy boots, with a broadsword slung at her back. Still, beyond all doubt she was the same Jilian Firestoke who so often filled his dreams. Morning sun danced in her hair and gleamed in her bright eyes, and Chane simply stared at her.

"What on Krynn are you doing?" she asked. "Those clothes . . . I never saw anything like those. And your cheeks are ruddier than before. You look older, too. What is *that?*" She pointed at his face.

Chane groped for words and found none.

"That spot on his head?" the grinning kender beside Jilian asked. "The red moon gave him that. It has something to do with the crystal he has. The Spellbinder."

Chane tried again. "J—Jilian?"

"I told you he'd be surprised," the kender chatted.

"Surprised?" A tall man with sword and flinthide shield came into Chane's shocked and narrowed view. "I'd say he's speechless."

"Wh—What are you . . . ah . . . Jilian?"

"Of course I'm Jilian." The dwarven girl shook her head. "Chane, you look so strange. Where did you get that clothing?"

"He hollowed out a kitty cat." The kender giggled. "It was his first step toward becoming rich and famous."

The words crowding and jostling each other at Chane's lips finally sorted themselves out. In a roar that stunned those facing him and set them back a step, he said, "*Jilian, what are you doing here?*"

"Why . . ." She blinked large, startled eyes. "Why, I came to find you. I found out what my father did, and I thought you might be in trouble."

Chane's mouth hung open for a long moment, then he closed it with a snap. His eyes blazing, Chane came around the forge. He strode to Jilian and pointed a shaking finger at her nose. "That is the stupidest thing I ever heard! Of all the. . . . Don't you know it's dangerous out here? You could be hurt! You could be . . . Jilian, for Reorx's sake! You have no business outside, much less out here in the wilderness!"

Her voice shook and her eyes blinked rapidly as she pointed out, "*You're* here."

"That's different! I can take care of myself!"

Jilian was silent for a moment, the set of her face changing from bewilderment to a smoldering anger. She threw back her shoulders and planted her hands on her hips. "Well, by all that's rustproof, *so can I.*"

Chane glanced at the kender. "Where did you find her?"

Chess indicated the man with the flinthide shield. "She was with him."

Chane pivoted toward the man and raised his hammer. "You brought her here? By what right—"

"Don't shake that thing at me," Wingover warned. His hand was at the hilt of his sword.

"I'm here by my own doing, Chane Feldstone," Jilian snapped. "I thought you'd be glad to see me."

Chane turned from the human. "I am glad to see you," he admitted. "But, Jilian, you don't belong here. You belong in Thorbardin, where you're safe."

"I'm safe here," she said. "You're here. Besides, I brought you something. I thought you might need it."

"What?"

"This." She drew a dagger from her tunic and handed it to him, hilt-first.

Chane held the dagger, turning it in his hands, barely seeing it as a sudden, embarrassing moisture clouded his eyes. It was his nickeliron knife—the very one he had cherished for so long, then had lost to the toughs who routed him from the realm of Thorbardin. "You . . . came all this way to bring me this?"

"Well, yes. You always said it was important to you."

Chestal Thicketsway stepped close to look at the ornate dagger. "That's pretty," he said.

Chane glared at him. "You keep your hands off of it. It's mine."

"I wouldn't doubt it for a minute," the kender said innocently. "Besides, I don't need it. I have a matched pair of nice cat-tooth daggers. Why would I need another dagger?"

Quite a crowd seemed to have gathered, Chane noticed. Fleece Ironhill and Camber Meld were nearby, with a number of their people from the refugee camps. Also, there was a horse.

"Speaking of daggers," the kender chattered, "I hope you took care of my pouch while I was gone, because I think that's what Zap is attached to."

"That thing has been hanging around ever since you left," Chane noted absently. "So maybe it *is* your pouch it's attached to."

"Well, I plan to get rid of that pouch," Chess said.

Near at hand, something silent seemed to say, "Yes, do. Please."

Several of those present jumped, and some turned full circle, searching.

"What was that?" Jilian Firestoke asked.

"That was Zap." Chess shrugged. "Spooky, isn't he?"

"It's an unexploded spell," Chane told the girl. "Chess accumulated it somewhere."

"He wants to happen," Chess explained, "but he can't because he's too close to Chane, and Chane has the Spellbinder."

"Well, when we come to someplace harmless, you can throw away your pouch and that should put an end to that," the dwarf said.

"Soon, please," Zap's soundless voice sounded.

"All right," the kender agreed. "But you'll have to wait until I make a new pouch to keep all my things in. I've got some pretty good stuff in that pouch, and I don't want to lose any of it."

For a moment there was silence, then the silence seemed to weep a thin, bitter wail of frustration.

"Look, I don't know what all this is about," Wingover said, "but I'd sure like to have a serious talk with somebody."

"You will." A new voice spoke—a voice as cold as winter's frost. "'Tis time you knew where you're going, man of the far places. Not that you've a choice, any more than anyone else."

No one, apparently, had seen him arrive. But he stood among them now, tall and thin, leaning on his staff. Beneath his bison cloak, the hem of his faded red robe identified him.

"A wizard," Wingover muttered.

"There you are," the kender grinned.

"Glenshadow," Chane Feldstone growled.

By reflex, Wingover's flinthide shield drew across his breast, and the wilderness man glared at the wizard across its notched edge. "What's that about having no choice? I make my choices, wizard."

"The moons have made an omen," Glenshadow breathed. "One here has a mission, stamped upon him by Lunitari. Others are chosen to accompany him, and a magic beyond magic binds the bargain." He looked around, his eyes falling upon the kender, then on Jilian, and again on Wingover. Finally the wizard raised his eyes and gazed into the high distances. Far off, against the face of a mountain peak, Bobbin the gnome's soar-wagon glided in great circles.

"An odd assortment," the wizard muttered. "Very odd, indeed."

* * * * * *

Through waning day and into evening, there were councils. News was exchanged, stories told and plans discussed. Camber Meld and Fleece Ironhill recounted again what had happened in the Vale of Respite, beyond the Eastwall peaks. An army of goblins, they said. And ogres among them. Camber Meld's eyes were moist as he described the sudden, all-out attack on the human village of Harvest—the slaughter, the rout of survivors unprepared for battle, the blood and the burning. Old Fleece Ironhill's voice was a cold growl as he told of the similar struggle at the hill dwarf village of Herdlinger. The dwarves had been slightly better prepared. They had seen the smoke above Harvest. But except for the fighting lasting a bit longer, the story of Herdlinger's fall was the same.

Chane Feldstone recounted the pursuit of the refugees by ogres, as he had seen it, and Chestal Thicketsway told with glee of the mountain dwarf's defeat of the ogre beneath. The kender also told of what he had seen from aloft, in the Vale of Respite. Camber Meld and Fleece Ironhill glanced at each other, their faces stricken. Nothing was left of the places they and their people had called home. There was nothing to go back to.

"How many were there?" Wingover asked. "You say an army. How much of an army was it?"

Camber Meld shrugged. "Two hundred. Five hundred. We couldn't tell."

"Nearly eight hundred," a cold voice from outside the circle put in. Everyone turned. "I saw it from the mountain," Glenshadow added. "Possibly eight hundred goblins, at least a dozen ogres among them . . . and a human leader."

"Where were you, to see all that?" Chane Feldstone frowned.

The wizard lifted his staff. "When I am away from you—and that accursed stone you carry—I have eyes far better than my own."

"Chane has the Spellbinder," Chess told Jilian. "Magic doesn't work when it's around."

"A *human* leader?" Wingover was leaning toward the wizard, frowning. "What can you tell me of him?"

"Darkmoor," the wizard spoke almost in a whisper. "Commander of goblins."

"What can you tell us of him, wizard?" Wingover asked again.

"Not *him*," Glenshadow said slowly. "*Her.* Kolanda Darkmoor. This much the mirror of the ice could tell me. This much, and one thing more, the thing the moons in omen told. It is the intent of someone—who, I do not know—that the wilderness between Thorbardin and Pax Tharkas be occupied and held."

"They will come here, then? The goblins?" Fleece Ironhill looked at Camber Meld, then at the rest. "My people—our people—will flee no more. But how can we fight them when they come? We have so few weapons. . . ."

Chane Feldstone stood, looking like one who had come to a difficult decision. "There are weapons here," he said. "I will show you where . . . or he can." He nodded at Chestal Thicketsway. "You will have to break them out of ice, but they will serve." He indicated the old sword slung to his back. "This is one of them. There are many more. But I demand a thing of you, on your honor."

"And that is?" Camber Meld asked.

"Those you find there, with the weapons, are to be treated gently and with respect. They have had enough of fighting."

HEROES II

Part III

A FORCE OF GOBLINS

Chapter 19

ON A WINDING TRAIL HIGH ON A MOUNTAINSIDE, the group halted its climb at a place where broken rock was strewn across a hundred yards of trail and onto the rises above.

"He's gone," Chane Feldstone said. "This is where I left him, but he isn't here now."

"You should have killed him," Wingover said. "Burying an ogre doesn't mean he'll die. Earth is their natural element. Probably another one came along and dug him out. You'll have to be very watchful now. Ogres don't forget a slight or a defeat. This one won't forget you, Chane."

"Loam," the dwarf muttered. "His name is Loam."

"His buddy's name is Cleft," Chestal Thicketsway offered. "I saw him farther up, that day. But I didn't know ogres helped each other."

"Against anyone else, they will," the man told him. "They are not pleasant to have as enemies."

Jilian clung closely to Chane, her wide eyes alert and darting about the mountainscape. She had never seen an ogre, but she had heard of the creatures. If Chane had ogres after him, she had a feeling he would need all the help he could find.

Wingover scanned the skies, wishing abruptly that Bobbin and his flying whatzit would show up. "You can never find a gnome when you need one," he muttered.

Chane glanced around. "Why do you need the gnome?"

"It would be nice to have some idea what's beyond the next turn," the man said. "I still think he could scout for us, if he would just stick around."

"He doesn't have much control of the soarwagon," Chess pointed out. "It just sort of goes where it pleases most of the time."

Wingover busied himself with trying to calm Geekay. He kept a firm grip on the animal's lead, scratched its ears and stroked its nose. The horse had been skittish for the past hour, and Wingover wasn't sure whether it was the recent presence here of an ogre, or possibly some distant scent of goblins that worried him. Geekay shared one characteristic with the elf, Garon Wendesthalas. Geekay simply did not like goblins.

Thinking of the elf, Wingover wondered where he was. Probably on his way back to Qualinost by now, he decided.

With Geekay somewhat mollified, Wingover got out one of his maps and studied it, then put it away. "We had better go on," he told them. "There should be a goat-trail up ahead somewhere, leading off to the south. We'll follow that until we find a better path. I'd guess we're about three days from safety."

Chane glanced around at him again. "Safety?"

"Thorbardin," Wingover said. "If we make good time and stay to the high ground, it should be no more than three days until we run into a border patrol. From there, it's an easy trip home for you two, and I can head for Barter and start spending Rogar Goldbuckle's money."

"I'm not going to Thorbardin," Chane said levelly. "I told you, I have something I have to do first."

"Then I'll just take Jilian home." Wingover shrugged. "Either way, I'll have kept my pledge."

"You won't do anything of the kind," the girl snapped. "I'm going where Chane goes, and you're supposed to go along with us."

"Now look, Button, all I agreed to do was to escort you into the wilderness to look for Chane Feldstone, then to get you home safely. All right. We've been to the wilderness. We found Chane Feldstone. Now it's time to go home. It's as simple as that."

Nearby, the wizard Glenshadow sat on a rock, listening. At Wingover's statement, he shook his head slowly, but said nothing.

Jilian glared at the man. "You made a debt of service. Do you intend to break your pledge?"

Wingover frowned. "I intend to keep it. I just told you that."

"Well, then, you'll have to wait a while longer because Chane has to find Grallen's helm. It's his destiny."

The man stared at the dwarven girl, then at the bearded young dwarf behind her. Two of a kind, he thought. Each one more stubborn than the other. He turned to Glenshadow, sitting on his rock. "You talk to them," he said.

"What about?" the wizard asked, his voice hardly more than a whisper. "She's right. Chane does have a destiny. And as I said, you have no choice in the matter."

"Well, as *I* said, I make my own choices," Wingover growled. "East across this ridge is a valley swarming with hostiles. A person would have to be crazy to go there."

Jilian stepped back and took Chane's hand in hers. "Then I release you from your pledge," she told the man. "We will go on without you, and you owe us nothing more. Good-bye."

Geekay tossed his head, broke his reins free from Wingover's grip, and pranced a few steps up the path,

past the glowering dwarves. He stood there, facing upward and away, snorting and pawing at the rock path.

"You, too?" Wingover snapped. He pointed a stern finger at Chane. "You're going to get everyone killed," he
warned. "And for what? A dream."

"The dream was real," Chane said, his voice level.
"Grallen called me to go and find his helm. Thorbardin is
at stake, and the power to protect the kingdom is in that
helm. But you heard Jilian. You're free to go wherever
you want to go. We don't need you."

"And where do you intend to go from here?"

"Where Grallen went. I have the Spellbinder. It shows
me the way."

Wingover took a deep breath, then released it in a
sigh. "That's how it is, then." He strode past them, recov-
ered Geekay's lead, and started on without looking back,
though he could hear them following.

After a time, the old trail wound to the right along a
shoulder of the ridge, then switched back, climbing. At
the turn, a faint trail parted from it, leading southward.
The goat-trail. Wingover turned south, leading a reluctant Geekay, and walked a hundred yards before turning
to see the others going away, following the climbing trail
upward. At that distance, they looked very small. Two
dwarves, a robed mage, and a kender. Of them all, only
the kender turned to look back at Wingover; Chess gave
him a sad wave of the hand.

"Crazy," Wingover muttered. "They're all crazy."

He shrugged, put a toe in a stirrup, and swung into his
saddle. Ahead lay three days of wilderness, then the relative security of the dwarven realm and the road back to
Barter. And he was free now of the debt of service. He
had been released. It would be good to get back to Barter,
to rest a bit, carouse a bit and spend Rogar Goldbuckle's
wager money. . . .

Wingover turned in his saddle for another look back.
Far off on the climbing slope, Chane Feldstone and Jilian
Firestoke were just disappearing around a shoulder of
rockfall, the wizard plodding along behind them. Higher
up on the slope, the kender was scampering off ahead,

looking for whatever kender looked for.

"By all the moons," Wingover muttered, "I must be as crazy as they are." He reined Geekay around, touched heels to the animal, and went to catch up to the others.

When he finally came up to them, near the crest of the ridge, he reined in. Dismounting, Wingover pointed a demanding finger at Glenshadow. "There's just one thing I want to know," he said. "What is your interest in all this? Why are you with these people?"

"I have my own reasons," the wizard said.

"That's not good enough," Wingover growled. "If I'm to face danger with someone, I want to know why he is there."

Chane Feldstone rubbed his whiskers. "That sounds like a fair question to me," he noted. Wide-set dwarven eyes studied the wizard. "What's in it for you, anyway?"

Glenshadow sighed and slumped, leaning on his staff. "A long time ago," he said slowly, "there was a renegade mage. A wizard of the black who rejected the robes and the order. Three of us went in search of him. One of each order. We went to find him, to . . . deal with him."

"Deal with him?" Jilian raised a pert brow. "What does that mean?"

"A rogue mage cannot be tolerated," Glenshadow said. "He must be persuaded to return to one of the orders . . . or he must be eliminated. We tried to persuade him." He paused, staring off into the distance. "We tried. And of the three who went out, only I came back. Caliban's powers were greater than we had known."

Glenshadow paused again, then added, "Caliban died in the conflict, as well. And yet, somehow Caliban still lives. I have set myself the task of completing what I thought was through back then. Caliban lives, and he is with those who oppose Chane Feldstone and his quest. I seek Caliban."

Wingover looked at the mage with hooded eyes. "To kill him?"

"If I can."

*　*　*　*　*

Sunlight lingered on the peaks when the group came down through a meandering pass and looked out across the Vale of Respite. In the distance, smoke trailed above two burned-out villages—no longer the smoke of destruction, but now the smoke of cookfires where an army rested, occupying what had been a peaceful valley.

Chane stepped into the lead, raised a hand to halt the column, and gazed into the distance. His hand closed around the pulsing crystal in his pack. For a time he simply stood there, the high-mountain wind ruffling his beard. Then he turned away, and the others gathered around him.

"Grallen's path leads east," he said. "On and on . . . through the valley, and up the mountains beyond. I had hoped it—wherever I have to go—would be closer."

"Toward Skullcap," Wingover said. "I thought as much."

Chane gasped. "You know where Grallen went?"

"I've heard the stories," the man said. "From Rogar Goldbuckle, and others. Grallen died at Shaman, or somewhere nearby. It's called Skullcap, now. That would be roughly northeast from here." He turned to see the last of sunlight above the peaks to the west, then turned back. "Point where it goes, this green trail of yours."

Chane pointed, due east across the valley.

"Well, that doesn't tell us much," Wingover sighed. "There's an easy path through the mountains over there. But it's farther north. Where you're pointing—that highest peak off there, that's called Sky's End. My map doesn't show a trail there."

"I can only see what the stone shows me," Chane admitted. "We'll have to cross over, and look from there."

"Easy enough to say," Wingover snorted. "Just cross over. Of course, there's a little matter of several hundred goblins and some ogres between here and there. Do you have any ideas on that score?"

"We have the element of surprise," Chane suggested uncertainly.

"That's the ticket," Chess said. "We'll slip up on them

and catch them off guard."

"That seems like a lot of goblins for us to attack," Jilian pointed out. "Maybe it would be better if we just went around them."

"If we can figure out where 'around them' is," Wingover noted. He turned to the wizard. "Don't you have powers that might help us out?"

"Not here," Glenshadow said. "Not in the presence of Spellbinder. Here I have only my eyes."

"Your magic doesn't work at all?" Wingover asked.

"It might or might not. And if it did, it would be unreliable."

"A little invisibility might come in handy," the kender said. "I saw a lot of invisibility at Hylo the time the bird came from . . . well, I didn't *see* it, exactly. What I did was *not* see it. That's what invisibility does."

"I wish we had the gnome here now," Wingover said. "I wonder where he is."

"Right here," a voice came from aloft. Wingover stared up at the flying contraption, barely ten feet overhead. "It's me," the gnome said. "Bobbin. Do you remember?"

"Of course I remember! Where have you been?"

"I'm not quite sure. Somewhere northwest, I think. Where are you going?"

"Across that valley," Wingover shouted. "I'd like for you to scout for us."

"All right, if that's what you want. But I don't think it's such a good idea to go across there. There are surly people all over the place. Look here." He tossed something over the side of the basket. It rang against stone, and Chane picked it up. It was a bronze dart.

"Somebody shot me in the hub with that thing," Bobbin griped. "Would have cost me a wheel, if I still had my wheels."

Wingover blinked, realizing for the first time that the flying craft no longer had its delicate silver-wire wheels. "What did you do with your wheels?"

"While I was in the northwest, I found some people— elves, I think—with raisins. I traded them my wheels for a half-bushel of raisins. Fat lot of good wheels do me up here, anyway."

"Take a look at this," Chane handed the goblin-dart to Wingover.

The man looked at the object closely. It was a slim bolt, about eighteen inches long, with a broad, sharp head and airfoils of shaved wood. Darts were a favorite weapon of goblins, and they often fired them from short, stiff crossbows. Wingover started to shrug, then looked more closely. "This isn't sand-cast," he said. "It looks as though it has been forged, or turned on a wheel." He handed the dart to Glenshadow.

"Not goblin work," the wizard judged.

"Well, it was a goblin that flung it at me," Bobbin called down.

"I'd like to see a few more of these," Chane said. "If I could compare some of them, I'd know whether they were forge-turned or ground on a cold lathe."

Chestal Thicketsway snapped his fingers and opened his large pack. "Like these?" He drew out two more goblin-bolts.

"Where did you get those?"

"The other night, when I was flying with Bobbin, these came along. I'd forgotten that I had them." He dug deeper into his pack, lifting out various other things one by one, to look at them. "I have some pretty good stuff in here. I should check it more often."

"Lathe-turned," Chane Feldstone pronounced, comparing the darts. "No goblin ever made these. I wonder who did."

"Somebody whose purpose was to turn out a lot of them in a hurry," Wingover said.

"Somebody equipping an army?" Chane asked.

"Somebody who isn't a goblin, outfitting goblins? That's crazy," Wingover scoffed.

Chane shook his head. "No crazier than the idea of a human—a human *female*—being in command of a goblin force."

"Speaking of females," Wingover said as he looked around, "where's Jilian?"

Chapter 20

Jilian was tired and cold. While the others discussed plans and situations, she wandered about the area, looking for a place to rest out of the wind. The pass here was a snow-dusted trough between rising peaks, with little cover from the wind's biting teeth. Not far away, though, an outcropping had sheared away in some bygone age, forming a mazelike rockfall where slabs of stone lay against one another and dark crevices beckoned.

She stooped to peer into one of these, a shadowy cave where slate walls broke the wind. The cave was deeper than it appeared, and another, darker opening, offset and aslant, lay beyond it. The wind gusted again as Jilian stepped into the shelter, leaning down to avoid the rock above. It was cold within, but not as sharply so as outside, where the relentless wind played. Her back to the deeper cave, she crouched there, watching the rest of the group. She hoped they would make up their minds soon. It would be a relief to get off this cold mountain pass, to be moving downward for a time, instead of toiling and climbing.

Mountain winds sang around the opening in the rocks, then died abruptly. In the silence Jilian heard a furtive sound. As she started to turn, the dwarven girl was seized by massive hard hands. She tried to struggle, but the strength of whatever held her was immense. She tried to scream . . . and could not. She was hauled backward, beyond the crevice and into the dark cave. A huge, leering face appeared directly above Jilian—a face twice the size of any she had ever seen, with a wide, grinning mouth and little glittering eyes set close beside a great snout of a nose.

"Pretty toy," the thing whispered, a low rumble of sound at her ear. "Nice for Cleft. Maybe Loam can have what's left." Crouching, the thing turned and headed down into darkness, carrying Jilian as a child would carry a doll.

Jilian's dwarven eyes adjusted quickly to darkness. Even in her shock and panic, she noted that the tunnel along which she was carried was of dwarven design. Like the load-shafts in Thorbardin that led from one level to another, it was a long, delved curve, spiraling downward, turn after turn.

She tried to struggle against the hands that held her, but it was no use. The monster's hands completely encircled her, binding her arms to her sides so that all she could move was her head and her feet. The pressure of the thing's grip was crushing. Jilian fought desperately just to breathe, and her spinning mind registered spiral after spiral of descending tunnel, its walls echoing to the thud of the creature's feet.

After a time, the girl twisted her head around, trying to get her teeth into a huge thumb. The thing glanced down at her, saw what she was trying to do, and chuckled, a deep, evil rumble of mirth. It shifted its grip slightly and increased the pressure. Jilian felt as though her ribs were breaking. Ogre, she thought. This is an ogre! Maybe the same ogre that has a grudge against Chane. Maybe it's doing this to get even with him . . . or maybe to lure him into a trap!

Jilian made herself hold very still. After she pretended to go limp, the creature's grip eased slightly. There was a little more light now, and she could see that the tunnel widened out, then widened again, becoming a vaulted cavern twenty or thirty feet across.

A staging area, she thought. Whatever dwarves had delved this place, in some bygone time, had crafted a cavern here—a place to store and sort things to be carried up or down the spiral shaft. A resting place. She had seen such places in Thorbardin. Dim marks on the floor might even have been the bases of ancient cable-track, though there was no hardware in the place now. All this she noticed in an instant, as the ogre slowed its pace and raised her higher in the dim light.

"Far enough," the creature rumbled. A mouth like a yawning slit revealed spike teeth. "Well underground. Let's see what pretty thing I have found."

Jilian lay limp in its grasp, and let her head loll to one side, feigning unconsciousness. Higher she was lifted as the ogre peered at her in the dim shaft-light, turning her this way and that. It relaxed its grip, holding her now with one hand while the other poked her with large fingers. Finally, the ogre took hold of her tunic and started to tear it away. Close enough, Jilian decided. With a heave, she freed herself from some of the fingers, twisted around, and delivered a solid kick, directly into a leering eye.

The ogre roared as it staggered back and dropped Jilian. She hit the cavern floor and scooted away on hands and knees. Suddenly, though, she remembered that her borrowed sword was still slung on her back. Ignoring the monster's roars, she got to her feet and loosed the sword, then ducked as the ogre's hand whisked past her. She turned and ran into the descending tunnel beyond the staging cavern.

In this lower spiral there was no light at all.

Surrounded by complete darkness, Jilian ran as she had never run before, counting her steps, trusting her dwarven instincts and the skills of the tunnelers who had built this place long ago. The lower spiral would be a twin of the upper . . . she hoped. She put her faith in the dwarven passion for symmetry and ran. The thudding footfalls of the ogre echoed off walls around her, and its rumbling curses were thunder in her ears. The monster was no more than a half-turn behind, and she wondered for a moment how something that big could move so quickly in a black tunnel. Then she recalled something Wingover had said about ogres. Ogres are at home underground. It's their natural element.

Well, it's mine, too, Jilian thought fiercely. And no ogre built this place. Dwarves did. "You don't belong here, you ugly rust-heap!" she shouted. "You aren't fit to use a good delving!"

Behind her the ogre roared again and quickened its pace.

Again counting her steps, and putting blind faith in the good judgment of dwarven delvers, she sprinted another dozen paces, then stopped, turned to her right, and scurried forward. In the upper spiral there had been a small cubicle opening to the left. In the lower tunnel, midway, there should be one to the right.

It was there. Jilian found the opening and scurried through, holding her breath as the ogre raced past . . . and stopped. For a long moment there was silence, then she heard its rasping breath, returning. It knew she had eluded it, and it was coming back to search.

Quickly, Jilian felt around on the floor. Her hand closed on a small, flat stone. She eased herself to the portal, edged partway into the tunnel, and threw the stone upshaft, toward the staging room. The stone rang against rock wall, and the ogre chuckled in the darkness. Jilian ducked into the cubicle again as it charged past, heading back up the tunnel. Then the girl darted out into the tunnel and ran.

She hadn't gained much. Within seconds the ogre was in pursuit again and closing. She ran and let dwarven instinct guide her flying feet.

Abruptly, she realized that she could see the walls. There was light ahead, and it was growing. The lower end of the spiral-shaft was ahead.

Another hundred yards and the tunnel bent slightly to the left, straightened, and ended. Jilian sprinted between fallen stones and emerged on a cleared shelf on the side of a mountain—a shelf that once had been the terminus of a path. But there was no path now. It had sheared away in some long-ago rockfall. It would be a tedious climb, to get down to better ground, but at least now there was light.

"So far, so good," Jilian panted, then turned as a thunderous growl erupted behind her. Only yards away, the ogre had emerged from the tunnel. It still held a hand over one eye.

"I'm warning you," Jilian shouted, "I'm getting very tired of this. You'd better go away and leave me alone."

The ogre growled again and started for her. Jilian picked up a rock and flung it, aiming for the thing's other eye. The rock bounced off the monster's nose.

"Oh, rust," Jilian swore. "That's only made things worse." She hefted her sword and squared her stance sideways to the approaching ogre. "I didn't want to have to do this," she muttered.

As the monster charged, Jilian braced her feet and swung the sword with all her strength.

Chapter 21

Atop the pass, the others had split up. Wingover sent Bobbin sailing off westward to have a look at the backtrail, then swung into his saddle and spurred his horse down the twisting, perilous path that led away into the Vale of Respite. Chane Feldstone started after him, then glanced aside and recognized the cavern behind the rockfall. "Tunneling," he muttered. Without a backward look, he dashed into the cavern and ran, his hammer at the ready. Within a few yards, his nostrils caught the earthy scent of ogre, and he gritted his teeth. "Jilian," he whispered. "Ah, Reorx. Jilian. . . ."

Chestal Thicketsway was right behind the dwarf, followed by a whining, complaining, voiceless voice that seemed to object fiercely to being dragged through subterranean places.

The wizard Glenshadow watched them go, then chose a peak and began to climb. He noticed almost immediately that the crystal atop his staff had cleared as soon as Chane Feldstone went underground. It was something important to remember, regarding Spellbinder. Glenshadow climbed, seeking an ice pool that would give him seeing eyes.

Down and down the searchers went, the dwarf and the kender pounding down a long, corkscrew spiral in the heart of the mountain; the mounted man descending the slope, looking everywhere, trying to see everything.

In the cavern with the light shaft, Chane found prints in the dust on the stone floor and paused, then hurried on. Jilian was ahead somewhere, with the ogre in pursuit.

As one, Chane and Chess darted into the far tunnel and continued downward, running as fast as they could in the darkness. The kender's natural balance and simple luck were all that kept him abreast of the tunnel-wise dwarf.

The downward slope eased, and the tunnel began to straighten. Chane put on more speed. Just ahead, he knew, the shaft should emerge into open air. And if Jilian had managed to escape the ogre in the tunnel—how, he couldn't imagine—her fate would be sealed when the monster had room to maneuver. Outside, she would have no chance.

The tunnel wound slightly to the left, and then there was light ahead . . . light and an abrupt, heart-stopping sound. A shrill, agonized scream reverberated back into the tunnel from just beyond its end.

Chane put his head down, filled his aching lungs, and plunged ahead into the evening light. Off to one side, he heard a horseman coming downslope, rocks clattering beneath charging hooves.

The dwarf raised his hammer. As Chane skidded to a halt, the kender bumped into him from behind, then dashed aside to wield his hoopak.

But there was nothing to attack. Chane and Chess gathered there, staring in wonder.

Jilian was a spinning top, just beginning to run down—a flashing, tilting, dancing blur spewing blood from the point of an extended sword. Cloven carnage was just collapsing, almost at her twirling feet. The head and shoulders of an ogre thudded down on top of a tangled pile of bloody parts, just as the dwarven girl's sword flashed around again and took off the top of its skull, above its eyes.

"By the Hammer of Kharas," Chane swore.

"Yuk," Chestal Thicketsway said.

"What in the name of all the gods?" Wingover's voice came from just upslope. "Jilian? Are you . . . are you all right?"

Jilian pivoted a few more times, then got her balance. Wordlessly the girl lowered the point of her sword and rested on its hilt as she tried to catch her breath. She stared at the pile of sliced ogre, then turned away, wrinkling her nose. At the sight of Chane, she ran to him. "I knew you'd come," she puffed, "but that . . . he didn't give me any time to wait for you."

Chane simply stared at the dismembered ogre, speechless.

"He was rude," Jilian explained. "He wasn't behaving well at all."

Chane began to shake his head, slowly.

"That's Cleft," Jilian introduced, pointing at the stack of ogre parts.

"That's one way to put it," Chess noted. "Although 'sliced' would be a better word. Wow! Look at that! Feet . . . shins . . . knees . . . hands . . . thighs . . . nothing is connected together. Even his head's in two pieces. Wow!"

Wingover had dismounted, and now he, too, stood and stared.

"I never realized that ogres had two stomachs," Chess remarked, poking around in the gore of the monster with a stick.

Chane took Jilian's sword and began to clean it, still shaking his head. "Where did you learn to use a sword?" he asked dazedly.

"In Silicia Orebrand's parlor," she said. "It didn't take

200

much practice. I seem to be a natural. Now aren't you glad I came looking for you?" She strode to Wingover's horse, led the animal a few yards away, positioned it beside a boulder, and said, "Excuse me for a minute, please." Dropping its reins, she climbed up on the rock and began unlashing one of the packs.

Wingover was still gawking at the cloven ogre, but now he noticed Jilian with his horse, and hurried across. "What are you doing? Those things are mine."

"Then make yourself useful and convince your animal to stand still," she said. "He keeps sidling away."

Wingover stilled the horse, caught up its reins, and scowled across the saddle at the dwarven girl. "Those are my private things. What are you doing?"

Rummaging deep in the open pack, Jilian drew out a long garment of stained white linen. It was longer than she was tall, but by holding it high and turning to the edge of the rock, she could study it full-length. "This will do, I suppose," she decided. "What is it?"

Wingover tried to reach across the saddle, to grab the garment out of her hand, but couldn't reach it. "Put that back," he demanded.

"That ogre ripped my clothing," Jilian said. "But what is this thing, anyway?"

"It's a cleric's robe," Wingover snapped. "I traded some deerhides for it."

"Why? What did you want it for?"

"I intend to sleep in it! Sometime, if ever I find a quiet room in a civilized place. Now, let's drop the subject. If you can use it, go ahead, I guess. Do you want me to—?"

"I think I can tend to the fitting." Jilian smiled, folding the robe and turning back to the open pack to see what else might be useful. She had help now. The kender had lost interest in ogre internals and was up on the boulder, helping her rummage.

"You have some nice stuff in here," Chess told the man.

"There are goblins or something all over down there," Chane said, peering down at the valley. "They're out in squadrons, patrolling all over the place. We won't be able to go around them."

"Through them, then?" Chess asked, looking up from a saddlebag.

"I wish we had Bobbin to sort out a route for us," the man said. "But he went the other way, and there's no telling when he might show up again. By the way, where's the wizard? I haven't seen him since we came down from the pass."

"He went up," Chane said.

"I guess we'll just have to find our way, then." Wingover looked at the sky. "Daylight will be gone in an hour. I guess we can try to cross by night. It's only a few miles, straight across . . . unless we decided to change our minds and just make for Thorbardin." He had their attention, and the expressions forming on various faces brought a grin to his own. "Just checking," he said. "I wouldn't want to try to slip through a valley full of goblins unless I was pretty sure everybody with me is as determined as I am."

Chane Feldstone's thoughtful frown didn't relax. The dwarf stepped closer to the human, looked up into his eyes, and held his gaze. "I never wanted to get involved in anything like this. I didn't want to wind up in the wilderness, or fight ogres and goblins, or be singled out to finish some task that was begun before ever I was born. But I won't turn back now. I wouldn't if I could. Do you know why? It's because something very bad is happening . . . or is going to happen. I happen to be here, and I happen to have a chance to do something about it. If I don't, then who is going to?"

"I wouldn't miss it for anything," Chestal Thicketsway assured Wingover. "And I think that goes for Zap, too." He glanced around at nothing in particular. "Doesn't it, Zap?"

"Misery and confusion," something silent seemed to say.

The kender grinned. "That means he can hardly wait to see what happens next."

Jilian Firestoke peered out from behind a screen of mountain brush, where she was doing something. "What Chane said goes for me, too," she said.

"Any further doubts?" Chane asked the man.

Wingover shook his head. "Not a single one."

"Then let's stop talking about it and go on," Chane snapped.

"Someone is coming." The kender pointed. A moment later brush parted on the rising slope and the wizard Glenshadow came into view. He looked haggard and cold, but his steps were firm.

"The valley is full of goblins," Chane told him. "We are going to try to cross at night."

"I've seen them," Glenshadow said. "They are all over, and they're moving around. Where is the crystal? Where is Spellbinder?"

"Right here." Chane reached into his belt-pouch. As his fingers touched the artifact it pulsed warmly, and again he saw the luminous green path leading away across the Vale of Respite, toward the slopes beyond. He drew it out. It glowed, rosy in the half-light.

"Put it in a hole," the wizard said.

"Why?"

"Because I'm curious about something. Don't worry, I won't trick you. There. That hole in the rock, put it there."

Suspiciously, Chane squatted beside the indicated hole. It was little more than a foot deep, just a pocket where erosion had widened a crack on the stone. The others gathered around, curious.

"Go ahead," the wizard insisted. "Put it in there. You can take it out again in a moment."

Chane lowered the crystal into the hole, rested it on the bottom, then stood and stepped back. Glenshadow backed away, his eyes nearly closed. The crystal device on his staff glowed feebly. "There is an effect," he muttered. "It makes a difference."

Chestal Thicketsway blinked and looked up. A drop of rain had fallen on his head.

"Are you finished?" Chane asked the wizard. "It's time to go."

"Yes," Glenshadow noted thoughtfully. "It is time to go."

"What was that all about?" Wingover asked. But the wizard had turned away.

Chane retrieved the crystal, put it away, and lashed his pack. Jilian came from the screen of brush, now clad in a tunic of stained white linen, scaled down to fit her by a series of clever tucks, folds, and ties. She handed most of the once-robe back to the human.

Wingover stared at her. "I don't know why I ever thought that old robe was for me," he said.

Chane took the lead, and they started down the darkening slopes, toward the Vale of Respite, where goblins now occupied what had once been a vale of peace.

When they were gone, something massive came from the rocks and paused to look at the heap of chilling gore that once had been an ogre.

He prodded the mess with his toes, then stepped over it and went to where the dim trail led downward. He growled, a noise that rumbled like distant thunder.

"Cleft was careless," he muttered. "Cleft is dead. Should have waited for Loam, instead. But puny ones are still in sight. Loam will have a sport this night."

Without looking back, the ogre took the trail where the searchers had gone.

ChapteR 22

Full night lay on the valley, a night of moons in crescent pale above the smoke that hung like a layer of smudgy cloud just at the treetops. Bonfires, dozens of them, glowed at ragged intervals along the course of the winding stream that fed the valley from the south. Out in the meadows, near the treelines that marked the grazing fields and burned-over stubbles, other fires marked a perimeter. And through it all, suffusing the acrid pall of smoke, was goblin-stench.

Mounted, Wingover ranged out on the forward flanks of the little band of travelers—first warning and first defense for the group, should they be discovered. He went silently, keeping to shadows where he could. Chane Feldstone led the rest, his hammer ready in his hand, the ancient path of Grallen visible before him as a faint green mist.

Chestal Thicketsway was a small, darting shadow, sometimes among them and sometimes not, but never far away. The kender's sheer, wide-eyed excitement and curiosity was a source of real concern to the rest, but there was little enough anyone could do to curb him. A kender was always a kender.

Had Chess been as tall as a goblin, Wingover might well have chopped off his head when the kender appeared unexpectedly in shadows beside him and said, "I—"

The sharp sword that whisked past the top of Chess's head would have taken a goblin at the gullet.

"Oops," the kender said. "Did I startle you? Sorry."

"Keep your voice down!" Wingover whispered. "What are you doing here?"

"I'm part of this group, remember?" Chess held it to a whisper now. "I just wanted to tell you, there are goblins moving back and forth among the fires. I saw a handful of them right over there, just a minute ago."

"A handful?"

"Five. They have a dead sheep."

"I wish you'd stay with the dwarves," Wingover hissed. But there was no answer. Chess was gone again, off on some adventure of his own. At least, Wingover reassured himself, the little creature could move silently when he felt like it.

They were nearly a mile into the valley when Wingover saw movement near the end of a hedgerow a hundred yards away. He signaled, a downward thrust of his spread hand, and reined into shadow. The stench of goblin and smoke was everywhere, and the sky above was a low, drifting fabric with fireglow on its belly. Only rarely was any trace of the moons beyond visible.

Crouching in silence, Wingover chanced a glance back and saw that the rest were out of sight. They had seen the signal and faded into a clump of trees at the edge of a field.

At first there was nothing to see, then there was movement just ahead. Dark shapes appeared, coming over a low knoll, directly toward Chane's party. Wingover counted three silhouettes with wide, round heads, wearing inverted-bowl helmets. The glint of weapons showed amongst them.

The shadows came on, moving quietly, their only sound an occasional muted clank of metal on metal. Wingover dismounted and raised his shield an inch, peering over the top of it, his sword ready. The goblins were so close that the man could hear their guttural voices:

". . . not much farther. Don't get too close. Want to ring them, not run into them." A few steps more and they stopped. Wingover saw a tiny flare of light made by a hooded lamp, its top lifted an inch to light a straw.

They had torches! Suddenly Wingover realized what they were doing. They were part of an encirclement, preparing to flare torches.

Somewhere a hoopak whistled, and one of the goblin shadows stiffened, gurgled, and fell. The human didn't hesitate. Still crouching, he launched himself at the remaining two, clenching his teeth to stifle the battle cry that built in his throat. Like a darker shadow, Wingover was on them, and his sword sang softly as it clove between the helm and collar of the nearest one.

Without stopping, Wingover thrust at the remaining goblin, and his blade rang on metal. In the fitful light he saw its glittering eyes, wide with surprise, saw its mouth open to shout alarm. He clubbed the goblin with the edge of his shield. It crumpled at his feet. Before the hooded lantern could strike the ground, Wingover caught and covered it. Then he took a quick look around, raised himself slightly, and signaled.

In moments the others were with him.

"They know we're here," Chane said.

"They know, all right. Stay close and follow me—straight out across that field. And hurry!"

They moved, trusting to no more than luck to see them to the next cover. The searchers crept across a narrow field of stubble, where dead things they could not make out were beginning to rot, then down a slope into a gully that would carry seasonal runoff toward the main flowing stream.

"Lead," Wingover whispered to Chane. "We need distance, quick!"

The dwarf went ahead silently, and they increased their pace, staying low in the gully.

Wingover glanced back, looking over the cut just where it deepened. There, where they had been, torches were springing alight by twos and threes—a wide ring of lights that would have bathed them in glowing fire had they been there.

He went on, catching up to the rest, counting them as he passed. There was no sign of the kender. Chane eased back to cover the rear now, and Wingover led, choosing the best and most silent route down through the gully.

"How do they know we're here?" Jilian whispered.

"Worse than that, they knew exactly where," Wingover pointed out. "They may find us again." He motioned ahead. "This cut winds around farther on. There could be an ambush. One of us should scout ahead."

"I'll go," Jilian said, then paused. Just ahead a small figure was running toward them. It was the kender.

Chess reached them and pointed back the way he had come. "There are goblins ahead, waiting," he whispered. "I think they know we're here."

Somewhere behind, there were guttural shouts.

"They've found the dead ones," Wingover said. "If they didn't know before—which they probably did— they certainly know now. How many are ahead?"

"I don't know." Chess shrugged. "A bunch."

"Hold up here," the man hissed, and Chane came forward to see what was happening.

"There's an ambush ahead," Wingover said. "They've found us, and now they'll close in."

Chane turned to the wizard, who had remained silent for much of the trek. "Do you have any ideas?"

"I can't rely on magic here," Glenshadow rasped. "Not with you carrying that crystal."

"Not even a little spell?" Chess suggested. "Just something innocent, like conjuring fifty or sixty armed fighters to back us, or—"

"Make us invisible," Chane said. "Can you do that?"

"A spell of invisibility? Easily . . . except for Spellbinder. I don't know what would happen."

"You had the dwarf put that thing in a hole earlier," Wingover said. "How about trying it that way? I saw your staff glow when he did."

"I'm going back down there to look at those goblins," the kender said. "Let me know what you decide." He was gone before anyone could stop him.

"It might not work," Glenshadow said. "Spellbinder's power is—"

"We'll try it," Chane decided. He looked around, then crawled on hands and knees to the edge of the gully, explored there for a second, and whispered, "Here's something. Like a small animal's burrow. It's—ouch!"

"What happened?" Jilian asked.

"Something bit me, then ran up my arm and across my head. It's gone now, though. This hole is . . . uh! . . . arm's length. I'm putting Spellbinder in here! Try it, wizard. It's our only chance."

A fat drop of rain splatted into the dust at the wizard's feet, then several more. Faint thunder rumbled overhead, and the murk deepened. "I'll try," Glenshadow decided. He raised his staff, its own crystal device glowing faintly, and spoke sharp words in a language that meant nothing to the rest.

For a long moment, nothing happened. Then Wingover looked around and drew a sharp breath. Nearby, Jilian had begun to glow—a rosy pink light emanated from her, haloed about her. And beyond, the others glowed, too. Even the horse had a fine gray patina that reflected off the walls of the gully. The man looked at his own hands. He, too, was shining—a distinct yellow-gold glow. Even the wizard was lit . . . had a glow on, Wingover corrected. Glenshadow shone a deep ruby-red, as though light came from within him and carried the color of his blood.

Down the gully, guttural voices were raised, and something small and bright green came racing toward them from that direction. "You call this invisible?" The kender's exasperated cry echoed ahead of him. He skidded to a stop. "Wow! You look like lanterns with legs!" he said, pointing back down the gully. "They'll be here in a minute. They're yours to play with. I'll go see if I can find some others."

Like a small, green torch, Chess bounded to the wall of the gully, up it to the top, and away across open land. Shouts of pursuit came from where he had gone.

The sprinkling rain that had started moments before had eased, but now, abruptly, it came again, a soaking curtain of rain with winds behind it. High lightnings danced, and thunder rolled.

"Now that's more like it," Wingover snapped at the wizard. "Come on, we have to get out of this gully. Here, I'll take the horse. Where's Chane? Chane?"

"I'm right here beside you," the dwarf said. "Go on, Jilian. I'm right behind you."

Of them all, only Chane was not aglow. He had never released his grip on Spellbinder.

The rain came harder, a blinding, driving downpour that began to fill the gully as they climbed to its high bank. Through the noise of the storm, Chane and the others heard the voices of goblins coming up the cut, then the sounds of splashing in water and mud.

Clouds had rolled in above the lingering smoke, hiding the dim moons. The rain doused the goblins' fires. Within moments, the only light in the valley was the bright glows from the heroes themselves.

"I wish you'd done the second spell first and just skipped the first one," Wingover told the wizard.

"My spell recoiled," Glenshadow said. "Spellbinder is too powerful."

"I mean the rain," the man said, hurrying them along. "If we can get a little distance, the downpour might help us."

"I didn't bring the rain," Glenshadow admitted.

"You mean it just happened?" Chane Feldstone

growled, a shadow among glowing people. "I don't believe it."

Glenshadow shook his head. "No, it didn't just happen. It's magic . . . but not mine."

"There are goblins coming from both directions in that cut." Wingover pointed back. "When they meet, they're going to come out. Even in this rain, they'll see us, the way we're shining. Come on, we'd better run for it."

He lifted Geekay's reins, turned to run, and stopped. He listened. "I hear something," he said.

The rest turned, listening intently. Rain hissed and thunders rolled overhead, and through it came the splashing, shouting menace of goblins converging in the gully. For a moment there was nothing more, then the others heard it.

Below the other sounds, lower-pitched and barely audible, a rumbling grew, coming from their right, from higher ground.

"What is it?" Jilian hissed. "That sound."

Then Wingover knew, and he arched a thoughtful brow. Flash flood. Massed waters filling the lowlands upstream, overtopping the deep gully, rushing down toward the stream somewhere below.

"Floodwaters," he said.

"The goblins in the gully," Jilian added.

"They're wearing armor," Chane concluded.

Wingover dropped his reins and ran back toward the gully. He heard the others coming behind him. By the light of his own glow he saw the gully's rim, saw heads coming up over it, and saw a pair of hasty bolts flick past as he halted, just a few yards from the edge. A flung stone toppled a goblin backward into the dark cut he had just left. The rumble had become a roar, and was coming closer.

Wingover felt a bronze bolt tear at his shield, ducked a second missile, and howled a chilling war cry as he charged down on the shadowy figures coming over the edge. His sword, glowing with golden light, traced rapid patterns up and down and around, clattering against armor and blades, darkening itself with goblin blood.

Two creatures fell before Wingover, and four more took their places, coming up from the roaring, water-filled gully. He fended the strokes of two with his blade, took another cut on his shield, and saw the dark, furred shape of Chane Feldstone as the dwarf's hammer pierced a goblin's helmet.

At Chane's side, Jilian was a rosy blur in the dark, a whirling blade with a spinning top at its axis.

The roar from the gully became a crashing, tearing screech of sound, and a wall of spray swept down the draw, sparkling in the light of the glowing fighters as it passed. After the wall of water passed, there seemed to be nothing left to fight.

How many goblins had there been, there in the cut? Wingover wondered silently. There was no way to know. They were gone, drowned and carried away toward the main watercourse.

On the bank, a shadow moved and another, darker shadow sprang toward it. Chane's hammer went up, and the dwarf rolled another goblin into the torrent. He stood, staggering, and Jilian caught him as he started to fall. The dwarven girl raised her glowing face, wide-eyed, and beckoned to Wingover. He reached the two in two steps and knelt.

Chane was down, his teeth gritted with pain, and by their own light they saw the bronze bolt standing in his shoulder. Jilian reached for it, but a glowing, red hand stopped her.

"Let me," Glenshadow said. "I know what to do."

With Chane's own nickeliron dagger, the wizard cut out the goblin-bolt, then peeled back the dwarf's fur tunic to cut away the rag of linen beneath. He studied the wound. Setting his thumbs at each side of the gash, he squeezed it closed. "Get me a flame," he told Wingover.

The man fumbled in his pouch for his fire-maker, a cunning device obtained from hill dwarves long ago. He fumbled again, then peered into his pouch. "It isn't here," he said.

"Never mind," the wizard said. "Jilian, see how I'm holding the puncture? Can you do that?"

Jilian took Glenshadow's place, and the wizard reached into his own belt-pouch and brought out a small, silver object with a lid. "Phosphors," he said. "It will do as well."

"Phosphors," Wingover muttered, an idea dawning. But there wasn't time to consider it now.

Glenshadow smeared a bit of paste from the container over the hole in Chane's shoulder, then took another, darker substance and knelt beside Jilian. "Let go now, and get back," he said.

She withdrew her hands, and Glenshadow touched the second paste to the first with a knife-blade. Suddenly a brilliance flared on the dwarf's shoulder, and Chane moaned.

The light subsided as quickly as it had flared. A puff of white smoke, lifting away to be dispersed by the pounding rain, rose into the air.

"Bandage him," Wingover said grimly. "We have to move on. It's still a long way across this valley."

Chapter 23

WHEN CHESTAL THICKETSWAY WENT LOOKING FOR
more goblins, it didn't take him long to find them. Unfor-
tunately, he had momentarily overlooked the fact that he
was glowing bright green.

By the time the kender saw the double platoon of
armed hostiles coming at him across a field, they had already seen him. All he could do was run. Rain danced
and sizzled around him as he fled, every step taking him
farther from his friends and deeper into enemy territory.
He tried dodging into a hedgerow, and realized there was
nowhere for him to hide. In the thickening blackness of
the rainy night, he shone like a green beacon. Even
shielded by the pouring rain, which increased steadily as
he fled from a growing pursuit, his light gave him away.

Sure evidence of that was the sheer number of metal bolts that whisked and sang around him, coming from various directions.

The goblins couldn't see him well enough to aim carefully, Chess realized—at lease if he kept moving and managed to evade close contact with any of them. But the bolts kept coming, and he had to admit that simple luck would guide some of them his direction.

"This may not have been a very good idea," he told himself, diving into a wash half-filled with dark, racing water. A pair of bronze bolts slapped water into the kender's face, and he ducked. Soon Chess was fighting an increasing current. It carried him one hundred yards downstream before he made it to the far bank.

His glow preceded him, and as he clambered out of the wash a grinning goblin charged into the light, brandishing a sword. Chess braced his hoopak, thumped the butt end of it into the creature's face, then brought it around full-circle. The shaft struck the goblin across the back of the neck and laid it out.

Chess grabbed up the creature's sword, and his nostrils twitched at the smell of goblin. He changed his mind and flung the sword from him, point-first. In the darkness somewhere close, a goblin gurgled and fell, pierced between breastplate and buckler. Chess didn't wait to see what would happen next. He turned and ran, following the course of the filling wash.

All about him was storm—pouring rain and driving winds, sheet lightning and rumbling thunder. Chess ran, and something hung with him, something that was part of the storm. It seemed to expand, to flex invisible muscles. A voice that was no voice said, "Ah!"

"Ah?" Chess panted. "What do you mean, *ah?* Do you have something to do with this . . . aha! You do! Well, nice going, Zap. Just keep it up, will you?"

"More," something seemed to demand. "Much more."

"Just behave yourself!" The kender dodged through a small wooded lot, where trees exploded into fiery kindling as great bolts of lightning struck them. The thunder was deafening. Goblin feet pounded behind Chess, pur-

suing the globe of bright green light. A bronze bolt
zipped past the kender's ear and buried itself in a tree
trunk.

As Chess dodged past a clump of brush, lightning revealed a wedge of goblin-warriors coming at the kender
from ahead, only yards away. Crossbows went up, and
Chess went down, diving flat onto a sheet of water
inches deep. Bolts sang over him and found targets
among the goblins pursuing. Chess rolled aside and set
off at right angles, cursing the bright green glow that
shone about him. "Invisibility," he hissed. "That's some
wizard we found!"

Hazy boles of trees danced past the kender, reflecting
his own green light through the pouring rain, then he was
in a cleared field and someone was just ahead. Chess
skidded to a halt, soupy mud sheeting from his feet.
More goblins . . . and something else. A creature taller
than goblins, wearing dark armor with intricate designs
and a grotesque barbed helmet with a hideous mask. The
creature raised a sword, beckoned, and the goblins
around it charged.

"If you have any more tricks, Zap," Chess breathed,
"now's the time."

"Much more," something silent said.

Lightning crashed and crescendoed, huge brilliant
bolts striking all around. The kender's long hair fell from
around his neck, unraveled itself, and seemed to stand
straight out from his head, a huge crown of dark bristle.
Bolt after bolt of lightning cracked and seared, before
Chess and behind, and in the flashes he saw goblins tumbling through the air, falling here and there; goblins
thrown aloft; goblins that smoked and sizzled and fried.
A wind smacked Chess aside. The kender's racing feet
barely touched the ground as he flew.

"Wow," he whispered, nearly blinded by his own
streaming hair.

Somewhere behind, he heard a voice—authoritative
and furious—shouting orders. She sounds cross, he told
himself. Better keep going.

Driven by a howling wind that seemed to try to lift

him from the ground, lashed by huge drops of rain that stung his back as they flew in almost horizontal sheets, blinded by his streaming hair and deafened by thunders, the kender gripped his hoopak and leaped high over a tapering rock ledge. Through the tunnel of his hair he saw trees ahead, lit by stuttering flashes and his own green glow. He bounded down a sloping bank toward heavy growth and tried to slow himself, without much success.

Then directly ahead, something huge and ugly raised itself and spread wide arms, bracing itself against the screaming wind. An ogre. Chess even recognized the huge, grimacing features.

Loam.

At gale speed the kender closed on the brute, his eyes wide. At the last instant, he thrust out his hoopak, dropped its butt, and vaulted. A tumbling leap carried him up and past the creature's crushing hands, almost high enough to clear its head.

Almost, but not quite. Instead, the kender's feet smacked the ogre's jutting brow. Chess's free hand caught a tangle of Loam's hair, and the kender completed his flip upright, standing on top of the ogre's head.

"I can't wait to tell them about this at Hylo," he muttered. "Of course, they're never going to believe it."

Before the ogre could react, wind hit them like a fist and Chess was thrown tumbling, into a grove of trees. He got his feet under him and dodged among the trees, downslope. Behind him he heard a crash and an angry roar. Loam had run into a tree.

Among the trees, the wind was diffused a little, and the kender slowed a bit. But then he was in the open again, on a broad, shoaling bank with raging floodwaters beyond. Wind swept down on him, caught him, and threw him head over heels into the churning maelstrom.

Tumbling and fighting, the kender bobbed away downstream. Above him a voice that was not there seemed to moan, "No-o-o! Other way-y-y!"

* * * * *

Four brightly shining figures and one dark one fled across storm-blown fields in a murk lighted only by staccato flares from above. Sheets of rain hissed around them, and thunder reverberated. The ground was a flowing morass of runoff.

Chane Feldstone led now, holding to the slim green trace that was their only means of direction in the turbulent darkness. The dwarf was a blackness against the dark, staggering sometimes from weakness. He was supported by the rosy-glowing Jilian, who refused to leave his side. The golden brightness of Wingover, leading a glowing gray horse, and the ruby-red Glenshadow, struggled along after the dark dwarven shape.

The worst of the storm seemed to be to the south, a few miles away at most. The curtained darkness in that direction was broken by a constant blaze of lightning, and the gale winds swirling from there carried the sharp, sweet breath of ozone.

They had tried to persuade the dwarf to ride, but he would have none of it. Wingover suspected that Chane, like many of his race, simply disliked horses. Some dwarves were excellent riders, but not all.

Since leaving the gully, they had seen no goblins—or any other living thing. Possibly the kender, going off alone as he had, had led the main forces away. If so, Wingover thought, then the gods help the little creature. He would never stand a chance out there alone.

Two miles of travel brought them to a descending slope with forest beyond, and beyond that the sound of a torrent raging. The valley's stream would be out of its banks by now, a rushing beast that no one could cross.

While Chane rested, with the attentive Jilian chattering at his side, Wingover scouted. When he returned, he had news. Upstream a half-mile was a well-worn path going east. If there was a bridge, it should be there.

"And if the alert went out, that's where the goblins on the other side will be waiting," the wizard pointed out.

Chane got to his feet. "We'll weld that joint when we find it," he said gruffly.

Wingover shrugged. "Then lead on, Grallen-kin," he

said.

Again, then, they were on the move. The path Wingover had found veered eastward, downslope and into forest, beyond which the torrent raged. The little stream that Camber Meld had called Respite River was, in normal conditions, a tame and pretty brook. Now, though, it was rushing, whitecapped black water nearly a hundred yards across—but spanned yet by a raised footbridge wide enough to allow carts to pass from one side to the other.

Beyond the stream was rainy darkness.

"I'll go first." Chane took a deep breath, drawing himself up. "I'm the only one who might get a look at the other side before he's spotted."

Without waiting for argument, the dwarf trotted down the streaming bank, waded through knee-deep water to the bridge's ramp, and disappeared in pouring darkness. He was back a short time later, appearing out of the darkness like a black-furred shadow with a glinting hammer in its hand.

"The bridge is sound," he told them. "There have been goblins on the path beyond, but they aren't there now. I took a good look around. Maybe the rain drove them to shelter."

"I've heard that goblins have no love of clean water," Wingover noted.

With Chane leading, pale but clear-eyed, they started across. The bridge shivered with the force of the torrent below it, and creaked and groaned when the horse was led onto it, but it seemed secure. The searchers were halfway across when they noticed that the wind had died and the pouring rain was letting up. The storm was dissolving as quickly as it had begun, and through clouds above, the visible moons could be seen in crescent.

"Our shine is outlasting our shield," Wingover growled, not looking at the wizard. In a way, he felt the blame had to be shared. The mage had at least *tried* to give them cover.

Jilian stopped and raised a hand, pointing upstream. "Look," she said.

Far up the stream, a greenness glowed—a widening point of light that sparkled the torrent's surface and glimmered along both banks. Even as they watched, the green glow grew, coming toward them rapidly.

"The kender?" Chane wondered.

"Oh, rust," Jilian said. "I hope it isn't the poor little thing's corpse."

"He's still shining," Wingover reassured her.

As Wingover made that hopeful statement, the approaching green light winked out and there was only darkness on the stream. Jilian gasped.

And gasped again as her own rosy glow dimmed and failed.

"We're losing our glow," Jilian said.

Wingover's gold radiance held for a moment more, then blinked off abruptly. Now they were only huddled shadows on a dark bridge, highlighted by a glowing horse and a radiant red wizard. The horse's light dimmed, lingered for a moment, and was gone.

The dark torrent raged beneath the footbridge, and now there were specks of light upstream. A blaze of torches was coming along the bank, on the side they had left. Wingover pointed. "They were following the kender."

"I think it would be a good idea if you doused yourself," Jilian Firestoke told Glenshadow. Still the wizard shone with a bright ruby glow.

"Come on," Chane urged. "Let's get across. They're coming."

"How about somebody giving me a hand?"

The voice that came from below the bridge was high-pitched and excited. Chane and Wingover hurried to the edge and peered down into dark, rushing water. They quickly stepped across to the other side. Just below, barely visible, Chestal Thicketsway clung to a hoopak jammed between bridge pilings.

"Give us some light here," Wingover ordered, pulling Glenshadow to the edge of the bridge. Ruby glow lit rushing dark waters and the childlike face, grinning up at them. Chane Feldstone started to crouch above the kender, then winced as his wounded arm took his weight.

"Get back," Wingover snapped, pushing the dwarf aside. "I'll get him." Kneeling, clinging to a bridge support, the man reached down and lifted the drenched kender, hoopak and all, to set him on his feet on the structure. The others stared at Chess. His hair falling around him, the kender looked like nothing more than a dark mushroom with a forked stick.

He pulled back long, soggy hair, shook it aside, and grinned at them. "Hello," he said cheerfully, water cascading from him. "Did you know there are just a heck of a lot of goblins out there? I'm glad we stopped shining." He looked at the wizard critically. "If you intend to go on doing that, maybe you should go somewhere else."

After watching the torches come closer for a moment, Chane and his allies could see goblins . . . and creatures that were taller. Dragging the glowing wizard with them, trying to keep him shielded behind the horse, the searchers scurried for the far end of the bridge and the darkness beyond. When they were clear, Wingover waved the rest ahead, except for Glenshadow. "Your phosphors gave me an idea," he told the wizard. "I think it's time to try it."

Wingover dug into one of his packs and brought out a pair of hand-length cylinders that glowed silvery in the faint, murky moonlight. "Phosphor flares," he explained. "I got them from a Qualinesti traveler, Garon Wendesthalas." He dug deeper into the pack. "I still can't find my oil striker. Can you light these with that phosphor thing?"

"I can try. What do I light?"

"This thing here, on each one. It's a fuse." Wingover hurried to the foot of the bridge and placed a flare on each side, at the main supports. "Hurry," he said.

The wizard knelt at first one and then the other of the flares, preparing the wicks. His glow was dimming slightly, and he squinted in the gloom.

"Will this help?" It was Chess, coming back to see what they were doing. The kender held a small metal object, which he manipulated with his thumb. A merry little fire appeared above his hand. But the wizard set the flares then. Harsh, bright sparks spewed forth, and

Wingover said. "All right, get back!"

They retreated a dozen paces, then several more as bronze bolts sang past them from beyond the stream. Suddenly the flares erupted in furious blinding brilliance, beyond which a flood of armed goblins were running up the far ramp, onto the bridge.

Another bronze dart flew past, and Wingover snapped, "Put out that light." Then he turned to the kender as the little flame went out. "Where did you get that?"

Chess shrugged. "I don't know. Found it somewhere. What is it?"

"It's my oil striker!" Wingover growled.

"Is that what it is? Why do I have it, then?"

"I don't know why you have it. Give it back!"

Chess handed the thing over. "You must have dropped it along the way. Lucky I found it for you. Looks a lot handier than flint and steel."

"It *is* flint and steel. With a wick. And oil. I—"

Wingover stopped and stared. The flares on the bridge had done their job. The bridge blazed merrily now, a wall of fire from edge to edge, barring passage from the other side. A few wooden planks were even falling away to hiss in the dark waters below. But on the other side, a person had pushed through the clamoring crowd of goblins—a taller person, wearing gleaming black, ornamented armor and a horned helmet with a beaten mask. As Wingover, and now the others, stared across the fire, the person removed the mask. The wilderness man caught his breath. For the first time, he saw the face of Kolanda Darkmoor.

The hideous mask across the bridge was lowered, and the woman behind it was—no, might have been—stunningly beautiful. But she was something else instead. Wingover sensed absolute evil there. She only glanced at him, though, for her gaze swiftly locked on Chane Feldstone. She put her hand to her throat and lifted something from her breastplate.

Chapter 24

"How could you let them get away?" the woman shouted. "I set a net across this valley, and you . . . you sniveling excuse for a troopleader . . . you let them slip through!"

Thog, a particularly ugly hobgoblin, and six goblins cowered before the Commander, afraid to respond.

"Two platoons dead or missing!" The horned helmet turned from one to another of them, its dragon facemask seeming to boom with each syllable. "Did any of you even see them clearly? Do you know how many there were?"

Thog scuffed his toe and raised his eyes. "Five of the lighted ones, Commander . . . but one of them was a horse."

Furious eyes blazed at the hobgoblin from behind the mask. "Five, but one was a horse. There were six! Counting the horse. I counted them. Why couldn't you?"

When there was no answer, the Commander paused a moment, shaking with fury.

"Double shifts!" she said then. "Double shifts for everyone until further ordered. Now, get out of my sight!"

The hobgoblin and the goblins turned and hurried away, almost scrambling in their haste. When they were gone, she muttered, "And you . . . I found the dwarf for you. All you had to do was destroy him. Why didn't you?"

A dry, twisted voice that seemed to come from within the Commander's armor said, "Ah . . . she questions me? Does she dare?"

"I dare question you, yes," Kolanda hissed. "Why didn't you strike down that dwarf? Why didn't you strike them all down? I gave you the chance!"

"Magic failed," the voice said. "But there will be another chance. Glenshadow knows."

"Glenshadow?"

"Glenshadow," the thin voice repeated bitterly. "He knows I will kill him when next we meet."

Kolanda Darkmoor walked to a high, clear ridge to oversee the reorganization of her troops. Though it was unthinkable that the dwarf with the knowledge of Thorbardin's secret—and his companions—had somehow managed to get past all her defenses, she let her fury subside somewhat and resumed her planning. The dwarf had to be stopped. She turned and looked at the range of mountains to the east.

Goblin trackers had reported at morning's first light. The group had gone almost straight east across the valley . . . at least as far as they had been able to track them. Someone with the group, it seemed, was skilled at covering trail. But they had gone east, and due east lay the soaring peak of Sky's End. Kolanda knew from her scouts that there was an old, climbing trail that curved around the mountain's slopes, but it would be a tedious and difficult journey. It would have been far better for them to take the pass road, farther north. It crossed heights more scalable than giant Sky's End, and there was a bridge beyond that crossed the chasm and led toward the Plains of Dergoth. And it was to those plains that the dwarf must be going, because it was there that Grallen fell.

Kolanda smiled. Several of the captured humans and dwarves had died in the process of their inquisition, but she had a serviceable map and a great deal of information as a result.

The northern pass would place her on Dergoth well ahead of the fleeing group.

There was still one other matter to attend to here. The refugees who had crossed the ridge into the next valley to the west were still at large, and she wanted them. Only a small force would be necessary for that.

When the troops were assembled, Kolanda Darkmoor sent a group to find the fugitives from Harvest and Herdlinger, and bring back all those fit to be put to work. The unfit would simply be killed.

"Go south a few miles," she told them, "then cross over into Waykeep and turn northward. Trap them, subdue them, and bring back slaves."

*　*　*　*　*

Bobbin was growing more and more irritated as the days passed. He was irritated with himself, irritated with his soarwagon, and irritated with the world in general. And much of his irritation came of being bored. Except for sightseeing, there was hardly anything to do when one was stuck aloft in a contrivance powered by the very air currents on which it floated. And the soarwagon was far more responsive to the wind's vagaries than to the feeble controls the gnome had managed to build into its structure.

For the past day or so, there hadn't even been anyone to talk to. Since leaving the pass between Waykeep and Respite, Bobbin had tried any number of times to return, but the soarwagon wouldn't go. He kept winding up in other places, or over familiar places but too high in the sky to make contact with anyone. And he was running low on raisins.

In a way, that could be a blessing, he realized, because it was the half-bushel of raisins that had caused his present set of problems. The raisin basket—resting just in front of him in the soarwagon's wicker cab—had shifted and fouled his control lines, and so far he had been unable to correct them. His lateral and pitch pulls were crisscrossed in some fashion, somewhere beyond his reach. The result was that he could gain altitude more or less at will. To descend, however, he had to wait for the air currents to make proper adjustments on the vehicle's forward foils, and hope that the positioning would hold long enough to get near the ground again before it reversed itself and climbed. Worse still, he could not turn left. Only right.

The dilemma was symptomatic of the basic control problem in the soarwagon's design. In building it, Bobbin had underestimated the craft's buoyancy and misjudged the sensitivity of its control surfaces.

The other gnomes were right, he told himself. I *am* insane. Had this contrivance been built in proper gnomish fashion—designed by a committee, sublet out among several guilds, and then assembled by a task force, it wouldn't have these problems. But then, it wouldn't fly at all.

The problem of the airfoils and their controls wasn't insoluble. Within the first week of his plight, Bobbin had deduced what was wrong and how it could be corrected. Part of it was the result of something unforeseen, a phenomenon that Bobbin simply had not known existed. The air near the ground was denser and more turbulent than that higher up, and all drafts within twenty or thirty feet of the ground were updrafts.

Obvious enough, now that he understood it. But he hadn't known about such things when he had designed the soarwagon. His assumption had been that air was air, anywhere.

He had even named the phenomenon of the near-surface currents. Ground effect, he called it. And he had worked out the control requirements to correct for it. Only one problem remained. The soarwagon couldn't be repaired in flight. He would have to land first.

And he couldn't land until it was repaired.

Feeling grumpier by the minute, Bobbin tugged his strings and helped himself to some more raisins. He wished he had some cider to go with them. Raisins without cider were like a sundial without a pointer. Adequate, but hardly timely.

Through a long morning he had been drifting in wide right-hand circles, while the soarwagon descended from an abrupt, screaming climb to an estimated twenty thousand feet—a maneuver executed entirely without Bobbin's assistance. Once at that lofty altitude, the device had seemed satisfied to begin a slow, languid descent. Bobbin had set the soarwagon in an easy right-hand pitch and spent the intervening hours dozing, fuming, and eating raisins.

After Bobbin finished his breakfast and washed it down with rainwater collected during the previous night's storm, he looked over the side of his wicker cab to see if he could identify where he was. He frowned and shook his head in disgust. A half-mile below was that same valley he had been trying to leave when his raisins shifted: the long, wooded valley between ridges, the one those people had called Waykeep. The place with the winding black road.

Off to Bobbin's left was the smoke of the refugee camps, the people who had come across from the next valley, fleeing an invasion of goblins. Ahead, just a few miles, was the textured ice-field where he had first met the kender, Chestal Thicketsway.

An old battleground, the creature had said. The lumps of ice on the field contained fighting dwarves, frozen in place. Bobbin saw no reason to doubt it, though why it mattered was beyond him.

There were people out there now, on the ice. People moving around. He squinted. Dwarves . . . and either humans or elves. From such a distance, it was hard to tell, except that some of them seemed to have beards.

Humans, then, he decided. Elves don't have beards.

Other movement caught the gnome's attention then, far off to his right, to the south. He squinted, trying to see details. A large group of . . . something . . . crossing a clearing between stands of forest, coming north. Sunlight glinted on metal. Armor?

The soarwagon's lazy circle brought it over the edge of the ice field, and Bobbin leaned out to wave. "Somebody'scomingyourway!" he shouted excitedly, waving his arms and pointing. But he was too high. The people down there, dwarves and humans, obviously from the refugee camps, were intent on the ice itself, and what was under it. No one looked up, and within moments the soarwagon was past them, continuing its descending spiral.

Long minutes passed, then the other group was in sight again below, now dead ahead. The gnome leaned out to squint at them. He saw them clearly now. Armored goblins, a company of them marching in rough phalanx order, with a slightly larger figure in the lead—a waddling, greenish-colored thing in bright misfitting armor. Bobbin had never seen a hobgoblin before, though he knew what they were. If anything, he decided, hobgoblins were even uglier than ordinary goblins. Without its bright garb, the thing would have resembled a big, misshapen frog.

The soarwagon closed on the marching company below, lower now, only a few hundred yards up.

Well, Bobbin told himself, I'll circle over those other people again pretty soon. I can tell them then that there are goblins coming. None of my business, I suppose, but then nobody needs goblins.

As he sailed over the marching goblins, Bobbin heard their shouts and leaned out to look down at them. Crossbows and blades were brandished at him, and guttural taunts drifted upward. On impulse, the gnome looked around for something unpleasant that he could drop on them. The only thing that came to hand was an empty line-spool wedged between the raisin basket and the lateral courses. He gripped it, pulled it loose . . . then grabbed the rails of his cab and hung on for dear life as the snagged tilt controls of the soarwagon suddenly broke free and the vehicle responded.

The left wing dipped sharply, the nose went up, and Bobbin's contrivance came around in a hard turn, climbing. Righting itself, the soarwagon pointed its nose at the sky and shot straight up, then completed a perfect roll and reversed itself in a blistering dive, directly at the goblins below. They stared, shouted, and began to run in all directions. Bobbin cursed as he fought his lines and eased the dive. But the craft had a mind of its own and responded with a neat half-roll.

Upside down and frantic, Bobbin shot over the heads of the goblin troops, raining raisins down upon them. By the time he managed to turn the soarwagon right side up, he was four miles south and climbing, again coming about in a wide right-hand turn.

Bobbin clung to his lines, pounded his wicker rail with a frustrated fist. "Gearslip!" he cursed. "Threadbind and metal fatigue! You misassembled piece of junk, can't you behave yourself just once? Stress analysis and critical path! If I ever get my feet on solid ground again, I'm going to take you apart and make camel davits out of you!"

At a half-mile relative altitude, the soarwagon soared serenely over the scattered force of goblins, over the intervening forests, over the ice field where humans and dwarves worked to gather old weapons. Finally, it passed over the huddled encampment beyond, where refugees tended their children and wounded companions, then raised its nose and climbed.

Bobbin closed his eyes and shook his head. Things were bad before. Now he was out of raisins.

High above the ridge that separated two wilderness valleys, and miles north of the pass, the gnome repaired and rerouted his control lines and prepared to come about one more time. At least now he had controls again, after a fashion. He could turn east, then south, and possibly find the people he had lost at the mountain crossing.

Then movement of an entirely different sort caught

Bobbin's eye, and he raised himself high in his wicker to peer dead ahead. Something was coming from the north, coming toward him, a speck against the horizon but definitely coming his way . . . and flying. Where exasperation had been, hope surged forward, brightening the gnome's gaze.

Flying! Someone else is up here in another flying machine, Bobbin thought gleefully. I'm not alone. Grinning eagerly, he settled into his wicker seat and lowered the nose of the soarwagon gently, aiming for the approaching flier. Someone to compare notes with! Someone who might have an answer to my dilemma! Someone else in the sky!

At a mile's distance, the gnome studied the stranger. Red in color—bright, crimson red—with movable wings that flapped rhythmically, and a long, trailing appendage of some sort. And legs? Yes, definitely legs. Not wheels or runners, but jointed legs, like an animal's.

And who was flying it? Bobbin could not see a cockpit or basket, not even someone mounted on a bench.

Closer still, Bobbin moved. Then his eyes began to widen in incredulous astonishment. The thing looked—he would have sworn it—like a flying dragon.

Ridiculous, he told himself. There are no dragons on Krynn. There were dragons once, they said. Ages ago. But not now. Not in the memory of anyone living had there been reports of dragons.

Closer and closer the two fliers came, and more and more Bobbin had to admit that it *did* look like a dragon. A huge, red, flying dragon, coming along the line of peaks, coming directly toward him.

Fear washed up and down the gnome's spine, a compelling, sweating fear that was like cold fingers gripped him. Then a voice spoke to him. "Who are you?" it asked, seeming to be right there beside him.

Bobbin gasped and looked around, this way and that, trying to see who had spoken. The dragon was a half-mile away now, and there was no doubt in the gnome's mind that it was, indeed, a dragon. Again the voice at the gnome's shoulder asked, "Who are you?"

"Who are *you?*" the gnome shouted. "*Where* are you?"

"You're looking at me," the voice said. "Yes. Me. And yes, little creature, I am what you think I am. Now, calm down and tell me who you are?"

"Bobbin," Bobbin said. "I . . . I'm a gnome. Are you *really* a . . . But of course you are. You wouldn't say so if you weren't, would you?"

"Bobbin," the voice seemed to purr in his ear. "Just keep coming, Bobbin. You will have no further doubts, in a moment or so."

Whether it was Bobbin's own numb hands trembling at the control strings, or some vagrant current of air, the soarwagon chose that instant to slip to the right, stall, and go into a nosedive. Suddenly the gnome saw spinning mountaintops straight ahead, and somewhere behind him the air crackled with fire.

"Oh, gearslip!" he muttered, struggling with his controls.

"Aha," the voice at his shoulder chuckled. "A fine dodge, gnome. You were lucky that time. But you won't be so lucky again. I can't let you live, you know."

"Why not?" Bobbin tugged strings, wrestling the plunging soarwagon out of its spin.

"Because you have seen me," the calm voice said. "That is your misfortune. None who see me must live to tell of it . . . not yet, anyway. You see, that could spoil the Highlord's plan."

"I wouldn't want to do that, I suppose." Bobbin hauled on his lines, and the soarwagon's nose edged a few degrees down. Bobbin glanced back and gasped. The red dragon was less than a hundred yards back, wings folded, gaping jaws displaying ranks of glittering teeth.

The soarwagon screamed into a dive, strained its fabrics, and flattened out of the descent, its wake currents spewing a small snowstorm from the icy top of a rock peak. Behind the contraption the dragon spread great wings and dodged the pinnacle.

"That was a nice stunt," the deep voice said in Bobbin's mind. "But awfully chancy."

"I'm insane," the gnome explained.

"What a shame," the dragon voice purred. "Well, you won't have to worry about that much longer."

Bobbin glanced around again. He had gained some lead, but now the dragon was winging around, making for him in a flanking attack. The creature was huge, far larger in both length and wingspan than Bobbin's soarwagon. It fairly radiated power and dominance and a mastery of the air. Its very presence was enough to inspire an awful fear, like nothing the gnome had felt before.

"I don't suppose we could come to some . . . ah . . . less terminal agreement?" Bobbin suggested, throwing the soarwagon into a side slip that plunged it directly below the dragon. He soared into a climb beyond his pursuer.

"Don't be ridiculous," the dragon voice was tinged with anger now . . . and something else that tingled just beyond the gnome's understanding. "You might as well stop this dancing around. You don't have a chance of escaping, you know."

"I'm sorry," Bobbin said. "No offense intended, of course, but self-preservation is a difficult habit to break." He increased the soarwagon's pitch and reached for the sky. Behind him, the red dragon beat great wings, powerful in full pursuit. Yet, somehow, the beast seemed a trifle sluggish.

Could the creature be tired? the gnome wondered. The hint in the voice, that subtle something . . . could it be fatigue?

"Stop this, now!" the dragon commanded. "I don't have all day."

"I'm wrestling with my instincts," Bobbin assured it. "I suppose you've come quite a long way."

"Nearly five hundred miles," the dragon snapped. "Not that it's any of your business."

"Aerodynamics," Bobbin muttered. "Mass and energy coefficients."

"Stop babbling and come back here!"

"You certainly are big," the gnome remarked, his mind racing. "I'll bet you weigh a ton."

"Closer to three," the dragon voice sneered.

"Five hundred miles, you said?" He dug out a carbon marker and did rapid calculations on the trailing edge of his wing. "At say . . . twenty knots? That means you've been in the air for more than twenty-four hours. That's a long time. Do you have far to go?"

"Not much farther. Now let's get this over with. Turn around!"

"I'm still having problems with my autonomic responses," the gnome apologized. Glancing around one more time, he readjusted his lines, dropping the craft's nose in a sudden forty-five degree dive. He wondered how much longer he could stay out of the dragon's reach.

Chapter 25

CAMBER MELD AND FLEECE IRONHILL STOOD at the center of a ragged, determined line of refugees, watching goblins advance across the ice. Twenty-eight fighters formed the motley line, dwarves and humans, most of them male but with a few females among them. A few held weapons of recent make, but most were armed with ancient blades, hammers, axes, and shields broken from the smoking ice—weapons that had been dropped or cast aside by those still under the ice. The two chieftains looked each way along their ragged battle line, then glanced at each other. There was nothing more to say, and nothing now to do except wait for the attack and hold the line for as long as possible while the helpless ones—those in the refugee camps—made their escape.

It was all they could do. The refugees were outnumbered four to one, poorly armed and poorly equipped, a handful of herders and planters against a force of goblins. They all knew that the best they might achieve would be a little time.

The refugees had been exploring the ice field when they saw the goblins coming from the south, no more than a mile away. There had been time to do no more than send a runner to warn the camps, and break out as many weapons and shields as they could find under the shallow ice. Wisps of ancient dark smoke, trapped from trees and grasses caught blazing by the ice, had drifted from the breaks with each new crack.

Now they waited as grinning goblins, a hobgoblin leading them, surged across the ice, eager for slaughter. Crossbows were aimed, and a deadly rain of bronze darts lashed out at the defenders. Shields took most of the missiles, but two dwarves and a gray-haired man fell. The goblins shouted as they slung their bows, raised swords and pikes, and charged.

All along the line, blades struck from behind shields as the foes closed, and goblin blood steamed and stank on the ice, mingling here and there with the crimson blood of humans and dwarves.

The little line of defenders took the first assault and turned it back, then closed ranks and retreated slowly, drawing the barely disciplined goblins out of their formation and into single—or more often double or triple—combat. For long minutes, the skill and sheer desperation of the defending line held the field. But the goblins were too many, and the refugee army retreated again . . . and again. Camber Meld and Fleece Ironhill found themselves fighting side by side, and knew that this would be the final strategy. Hold and retreat, hold and retreat, until none were left to face the goblins. It was, simply, a buying of time.

At the edge of the ice field they retreated yet again, no more than a dozen of them now against at least seventy goblins. The goblins formed another charge, then halted. Goblin mouths dropped open, and goblin eyes stared aloft, beyond and above the line of defenders.

Fleece Ironhill glanced around just as something very fast skimmed over his head and swept upward on wide, pale wings. He didn't see what it was, nor did he try to follow it with his eyes. Instead he stared at the second flying thing, plunging down from above. A huge red dragon, its mouth opened wide and a rush of fire coming from it. The dragon flared its wings and soared over the line of battle.

Without warning, the dragon's fire-breath smote the ice field behind the goblins.

* * * * *

Bobbin was in trouble. For a brief time, he had held his distance ahead of the dragon, the soarwagon diving earthward on rippling wings. But he had waited too long, gone too low, and lost his edge. The dragon had managed to get above him, and now was closing with deadly speed. The gnome heard the long, deep rumble of in-drawn breath and knew what it meant.

"Thermodynamics," the gnome muttered, praying that his final calculation was correct, that the same ground effect that had been his undoing might just this once work to his advantage. How many times since he had gone aloft had the soarwagon abruptly shot skyward in a screaming climb, propelled by the extra buoyancy of the near-ground air?

"Don't change your ways just yet," Bobbin muttered, taking a firm hold on his lateral controls. The ice field sped by just a few yards below.

Closing his eyes, he pulled the strings. Behind and beneath the soarwagon's tail, a torrent of terrible flame seared the air and flowed in waves of heat across the ice field, which seemed to explode in great clouds of steam and soot.

The soarwagon went nearly straight up, a pale sliver flung by its own dynamics and given added speed by up-rushing air currents ahead of the rising clouds of steam. Bobbin opened his eyes and looked around. Behind him was a tiny, distant landscape, where finger ridges of mountains lay like furrows in a field. And barely visible, far below, was the red dragon, just coming out of its dive and beginning to circle to the east.

"How did you do that?" The dragon voice in his ears seemed genuinely impressed.

"I bounced off the ground effect," the gnome explained. "It's nothing especially new. I've been bouncing off it for weeks."

"Ground effect?" The voice seemed fainter now.

"That's what I call it. The air near the ground is denser than the air higher up. It's why I can't land."

"You can't land? You mean you can't get down?"

"No, blast it! I can get near the ground, but I can't quite reach it. Uh . . . are you coming after me again? I'd rather you didn't. I have enough troubles without you."

The diminishing voice in Bobbin's ear seemed to chuckle. "I've heard of gnomes being standoffish, but you're the first one I've found who was actually stuck up! But I have no more time for you, so I suppose this is your lucky day. Goodbye, Bobbin." Again there was a fading chuckle, then the voice was gone.

The gnome had managed to level out his climb, and he looked over the wicker rail. In the distance below, the red dragon was winging for the mountains east of Waykeep. Bobbin circled and watched until the mythical beast cleared the peaks there and descended into the smoky mists beyond. Then he sighed and tugged on his descent strings. He was cold and hungry, and ready to go down. Apparently the soarwagon was, too. At the slightest pressure on its vanes, it dropped its nose and plummeted straight down, its wings rippling and whining.

"Stress and derailment!" the gnome swore, and began another adjustment on his controls.

*　*　*　*　*

When dragonfire rolled over the frozen battlefield, the effects were instantaneous. Ice splintered and fell away, becoming great spreading clouds of steam mixed with ancient smoke. Gray mist roiled outward, obscuring the goblins and the defenders beyond, then drifted upward on heated drafts. A wide, thick cloud shadowed a fore-shortened land where everything seemed to writhe and rumble. Goblins retreated, wide-eyed, then turned and retreated again when the blades of the handful of human and dwarf refugees drew blood.

The evil minions fell back, turned again, and stopped in confusion. From the rolling clouds came dwarves, hundreds of dwarves. Dwarves armed and armored. Mountain dwarves and hill dwarves with dead eyes in frozen faces that had not known change in more than two centuries—faces that grimaced and twisted in the exact ways they had when they fought against one another in a burning forest at the instant the spell of ice had been cast by an archmage.

But they were not fighting among themselves now. Mountain dwarves and hill dwarves stood shoulder to shoulder, spread out beneath the dark plume of choking steam. They were silent and relentless, and fell on the panicked goblins without a hesitation or a sound.

The hobgoblin leader screamed, turned to run, and fell, his helm pierced by Fleece Ironhill's spiked hammer. Two jibbering goblins following him died under the sword of Camber Meld. The cooling cloud of dark steam above was descending now, settling as a dense fog streaked with ash, slanting before a wind that came across the old battlefield, carrying the dry scent of ages.

For long minutes there was only silence and the blinding mist. Then, slowly, the cloud thinned. Five humans and six hill dwarves, the last of the combined fighting force led by Camber Meld and Fleece Ironhill, stood alone at the edge of a great, blackened plain littered with bodies, dropped arms and ancient burned stumps. Most of the strewn bodies were goblins, many of them still pierced by the weapons that had killed them. And everywhere, among and around them, were little heaps of clothing and armor—all that remained of the dwarves of Waykeep, fighters released from an ancient spell for one last cut, one last thrust, at an enemy.

The refugees looked around in awe. Nothing moved

except the wind . . . the wind, and a sliver of white far to the east, something that flew like a bird with still wings, riding on the air. Something going away.

* * * * *

On a forest-shrouded knoll in the Vale of Respite, some distance south of the encampments of the goblins, a red dragon burrowed into leaf-mold and slept the sleep of exhaustion. Even the most powerful of creatures had its limits, and this one had been in flight for nearly thirty hours and more than five hundred miles. It had flown from a lair deep in the Khalkist Mountains to a secret place near Sanction, then had spanned the entire width of Newsea, past Pax Tharkas, and now lay in the wilderness ranges between Qualinost and Thorbardin, in the Kharolis Mountains of western Ansalon.

It had chosen the knoll, sent a mind-call northward, then burrowed in and slept. Through the remainder of that day it rested, and through the night and most of the next day. The sleep restored its strength, and the dragon dreamed the comfortable dreams of one who by birthright can be absolute lord over anyone or anything that it cares to dominate . . . except others like itself, and one beyond, the one the dragon called the Dark Queen.

The dragon slept for twenty-eight hours, then awoke briefly to be aware of its surroundings.

The one it had called was there, waiting. The dragon went back to sleep and dozed for another three hours.

Finally, when it was rested, the red dragon stirred, shook away the forest leaves, and lifted its huge head. Its long, sinuous body moved, and the beast stretched its wings deliciously. The dragon felt renewed, restored.

Nearby, a small fire burned, and the person beside it came to her feet. "Have you slept enough?" she asked sourly.

"I always sleep enough," the dragon said. "It is you who should worry about sleep. The Highlord would be displeased if you should fail in your mission."

"I have not failed," the woman said. "All of the lands between Pax Tharkas and Thorbardin are in my control

. . . or will be by the coming of spring. My goblins are in place, and all that remains is the gathering of slaves to build some decent fortifications."

The dragon's gaze was mocking. "If that is all that remains, why are you aligning your troops to cross over into the Plains of Dergoth beyond the mountains?"

"A minor matter," she snapped. "It would not interest the Highlord."

"It might," the dragon purred. "Or would you rather I just report that you didn't care to discuss it?"

"It's nothing! There is a dwarf who has learned of the invasion gate to Thorbardin and thinks he can block it. I simply intend to eliminate him."

"Interesting," the dragon said. "As I recall, you told the Highlord that no one except you and your . . . ah, co-inhabitant . . . knew of the lost gate. You assured the Highlord that Thorbardin will stand open to him when he comes, and that he can make it his base of operations."

"So I did, and so it will be. Do you doubt me?"

"So many of the best-laid plans," the dragon chuckled. "Especially those of humans. . . ."

"I will not fail!"

"I wouldn't, if I were you," the dragon whispered. "Is there anything you would like reported to the Highlord?"

"Report what you have seen," Kolanda snarled. "I'm doing my job, so I assume you can do yours."

The woman glared at the dragon, then turned without a word and walked away. The horned mask under her arm stared back at the lizard through hollow eyes.

The red dragon watched her go, then stretched luxuriously. It would be time soon to spread great wings and begin the long flight back to the region of Sanction. The Highlord would be waiting for his report.

The Highlord. One of many Highlords in the north now, amassing armies, sending out spies and patrols, plotting and securing lines of march, organizing systems . . . petty, mortal creatures preparing for the day the Dark Queen would unleash them across Ansalon and beyond. They would then secure for her—once and for all—the world she wanted and was fit to rule.

The dragon pondered for a moment whether to report the gnome in the flying thing who had seen him and somehow escaped. He thought about it, but decided that there was nothing to be gained. It was, after all, only a gnome.

* * * * *

Two days' foot-travel to the east of the dragon's resting place, Chane Feldstone led a tired and dusty little group along a winding ledge. Mountain winds sang in towering crags above them, and mists hid the depths below.

"Do you know where we are?" Wingover asked the dwarf for the second or third time in an hour.

"Why don't you leave him alone?" Jilian Firestoke snapped. "Can't you see he's tired?"

Wingover nodded. It was obvious the dwarf was tired. Still weak from his shoulder wound, he sometimes stumbled and rarely spoke, though he pushed on with grim determination. Chane was following—the rest could only assume—the green line that marked the path where Grallen had gone centuries before.

In fact, Chane's weakened state was why Wingover kept questioning him. The dwarf was showing signs that to the wilderness man spelled sheer exhaustion—a flat-eyed stare that never seemed to blink; paleness that came and went; a rolling, almost drunken pace.

Wingover knew that it was time to stop and rest, and for the past day or more the man had been looking for a place to do that. The problem was, except for a pair of wide places on the trail where bitter winds had chilled them and the last of their provisions had run out, there had simply been no place to rest.

Their current trail along the mountainside was one Wingover had never explored. The human marveled at the idea that a dwarven prince had once led armies this way, heading for the final battle of his final war on what most men called the Plains of Dergoth, though dwarves more often called the region the Plains of Death.

Wingover snorted as the dwarf in the lead stumbled

again. He handed his horse's lead to Jilian and caught Chane's good shoulder in a firm hand. "Are you all right?" he asked, looking into the dwarf's exhausted eyes.

"I'm all right," Chane growled. "We have to keep going."

"Do you know where we are?"

"I know where I'm going. The path is clear."

"Yes, but do you know where we are?"

"Not exactly. Where?"

"I didn't think so," the man said gently. "Look off across there . . . across the gorge, over on the face of the next peak."

Chane looked, his eyes blank. There was a feature over there, tiny in the distance but somehow familiar. "What is it?"

"I don't suppose you've ever seen it," Wingover said. "At least not from this side, but I thought you might want to know what you're looking at. That's Northgate."

"North . . . You mean . . . ?"

"Exactly," the man told him. "That is the Northgate of Thorbardin."

"But the green line doesn't go there," Chane said. "It goes east . . . I think that's east, anyway. Out there, across those plains. Toward that lone mountain, whatever that is."

"Skullcap," Wingover breathed. "The ruins of what was once the most feared tower of sorcery, Zhaman, lie there."

Chane sighed. "Then that is where Grallen went. But the line . . . it doesn't seem to go all the way. I can't really see what it does. We have to go on. We have to get closer."

"We have to rest," Wingover said flatly. He shielded his eyes, peering ahead. Somewhere near, there should be a place safe to rest. He squinted, then his eyes widened and breath hissed through his teeth. On the trail ahead, just where it wound out of sight, a large, black cat stood, looking back at them. Even as Wingover saw it, the animal turned languidly and slunk out of sight.

Chapter 26

"Cats!"

With a visible shudder, Wingover drew his sword, gripped his shield, and eased past the weakened dwarf. He had seen the great black cats of Waykeep only once. But once was enough. On stiff legs he started toward the bend, certain that at any moment a bounding, snarling pack of the giant creatures would appear there, coming for him. And it would be up to him to defend the others. Glenshadow's magic would not work in Spellbinder's presence. Chane Feldstone was hardly strong enough to stand off cats. Still, Jilian might make an accounting of herself with that sword she carried. After seeing the remains of her ogre, the man was willing to believe almost anything.

Small feet scuffed just behind Wingover, and Chestal Thicketsway's voice said cheerfully, "What are you doing?"

"Stay back," the man snapped. "There are cats ahead."

"Cats? Kitty cats or the Irda's cats?"

"Just stay back, out of the way." Wingover shot a quick glance back, felt something brush past his legs, and turned to shout, "Come back here!"

"I'll just take a quick look," the kender said, scampering ahead. "If they're like the Irda's cats, I've seen a lot of those."

"Ye gods," the man swore and quickened his pace, willing the rest to stay where they were. Ahead of Wingover, the curious kender disappeared around the bend.

Wingover ran, then stopped. Just past the bend, the trail widened, then widened again, and became a deep, sheltered cove in the mountainside. Clear, cold water flowed from a tiny spring and pooled before overflowing its rock tank and disappearing again into crevices in the mountain. Conifers grew in abundance, and rich, chill-bleached grass was everywhere. Beside the pool were several bundles, all securely wrapped in sacking, and the kender knelt beside the nearest one, untying its straps. He glanced up, grinned, and pointed. "Look."

High on a rock ridge beyond the cove, several of the big, dark cats were climbing, going away. Some of them turned to look back, feral eyes seeming to glow in the pale light. But they only hesitated, then went on. Within seconds, they were gone.

"Food!" the kender chirped. "Look at this. Biscuits! And honey, and oats, and cabbage . . . wow!" With one pack open, he went on to the next one.

Wingover heard the thump of a staff and turned. Glenshadow stood a few paces back, cold eyes peering from the shadows of his bison cloak. "The Irda," he said. "She has provided for us. She said that would be done."

"But those cats—"

"Are hers. In a way, I suppose they *are* her."

"Where is she, then, this Irda?"

The wizard gazed at him for a moment, then shrugged

and turned away. "She is an Irda. I suppose she is wher-ever she chooses to be."

"Irda," Wingover breathed. "Irdas are ogres, from what I've heard."

Glenshadow shook his head. "No. The Irda is what ogres may once have been. They are not the same."

"You'd know that if you'd seen her," the kender said. "Look at this! Raisins. How about that? And cider."

The others had appeared, Jilian helping Chane and leading Wingover's horse. At the cove, they all stopped and stared. Jilian nodded. "This is more like it. Let's get a fire going, and I'll make tea. And soup. Don't you think some soup would taste good, Chane? Here, you sit down over here. Eat a biscuit while I'm cooking."

"There is danger ahead of us, then," the wizard noted ominously. "The Irda knows."

"How does she know any such thing?" Wingover spun toward Glenshadow, tired and angry, confused and feel-ing as though everyone but himself had a hand in this sit-uation. "Does she use magic?"

"Only a little . . . of the kind I use, when I can use it at all," Glenshadow said. "The kind you so despise, though it is a part of your world and not always to your disad-vantage. The Irda is a shapechanger. That much is magic, though natural to her kind. And she is a singer. Some have said the Irda carry magic in their voices, though I think now it is simply that they have . . . such voices." He paused and considered the point for a mo-ment. "Perhaps they have another magic that is outside the magic of Krynn. I believe they do, but who can say for certain. If they do, then it is used entirely for their own purposes and not for or against any other being. It is the nature of the Irda."

"You haven't answered my question," Wingover snorted. "How could such a creature—as you say—know that there is danger ahead for us?"

"She listens." Glenshadow shrugged. "The world has many voices, and eyes everywhere. The world itself knows what passes upon it. It speaks of it to itself, and the Irda listens. How else could she do what she does . . .

observe the purposes of the gods' things, the ones that the gods themselves no longer observe? Who else could inform the Irda, except the world itself?"

Wingover shook his head, wondering if the mage was in fact deranged. What he said almost made sense . . . sometimes, but not in any way that Wingover could see. He turned away and went to start unpacking his horse.

"Don't do that," Chane Feldstone shouted, getting to his feet. "We have to go on."

"We aren't going anywhere for a while," Wingover told him. "We are going to rest here until we're fit to travel."

"But I see the path now," the dwarf said, his face going pale again. "I see where Grallen went, and I have to go there. Spellbinder—"

Jilian Firestoke was at Chane's side then, bracing him with strong little hands. "The man is right, Chane," she said gently. "You must rest. Then we can go on. Please, sit down."

A sheen of sweat had erupted on Chane's forehead, and his eyes seemed glazed. Still, he tried to struggle free. "Can't you see the path? Can't any of you see it? It goes down this mountain and out onto the plain, then it doubles back . . . just out there. It turns back and stops. See? Why can't any of you see?" The dwarf slumped and let himself be eased down to a sitting position.

"Jilian?" Chane murmured. "Jilian, I think your father was right. I don't deserve you. But he was wrong, too. He was wrong in . . . deciding he could decide. It is for you to decide, Jilian . . ."

Chane's voice trailed off, and quickly he was asleep. Jilian covered him gently with a wrap from her own pack, and when she looked up her eyes were moist. "He's so tired," she said.

Wingover knelt beside the dwarf and touched a palm to the sweating forehead. Then he stood, nodding. "It was the goblin dart. It has sickened him. He needs rest." To Jilian he added, "Chane will be all right. If the wound were going to kill him, it would have before now."

Leaving Jilian hovering over the sleeping dwarf, Wingover walked to where the wizard stood, looking eastward. The mage raised his hand and pointed.

Far out in the distance, where the slopes ended and a flatter land began, there was movement. Wingover and Glenshadow were too far away to be sure, but they suspected who was there. The Commander of Goblins was ahead of them, and with her was her army.

"They know we're here," Wingover growled. "But if they didn't follow us, how did they find us?"

"Maybe they don't know exactly where we are," the bison-robed wizard offered, lowering his hand. "But they know which way we were going. And they know why."

"The mage?" Wingover muttered. "The one who died, but didn't?"

Glenshadow only nodded.

A flash of white in the distance flickered above the gorge where the path bent around the mountain slope. It wasn't bright, but the flash was enough to catch Wingover's eyes. He turned. "It's that gnome," he growled, pointing. "Where has he been, anyway?"

The soarwagon neared the mountainside, skimmed away, and did a wide turn. As the gnomish contraption came about for another approach, Jilian Firestoke waved and Chestal Thicketsway ran to the ledge to watch.

"Tell him to come in and lower his line," the kender said. "Tell him we have raisins. And cider."

The flying thing approached carefully this time, finally hovering on updrafts just above the cove. The gnome in the wicker seat leaned out and waved. "Hello!" he called. "Do you remember me? I'm Bobbin."

"I remember you!" Wingover shouted. "What news do you have?"

"About what? . . . Ah, yes! You're the one who's looking for cats. Well, I saw some, up the mountain from where you are. But they're going the other way."

Wingover scowled. "We know about the cats! Anything else?"

"Well, I saw a dragon. A big, red one. He weighs nearly three tons and had flown five hundred miles." The gnome frowned. "He wasn't very friendly."

"A dragon?" The kender danced about in his excitement. "A real dragon? Where?"

Wingover shook his head in disgust. There was no telling what the gnome had actually seen . . . if anything.

Part IV

GRALLEN'S HELM

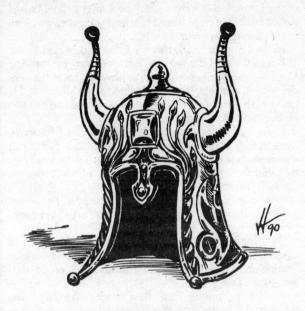

Chapter 27

Solinari and Lunitari had set hours ago. *Beside* a small fire, set far back in a mountain cove, Chane Feldstone lay in peaceful sleep for the first time in several days. For the moment, the red spot on his forehead was so dim that it was barely noticeable. Better still, the firelight reflecting on his cheeks above his beard revealed a healthy, ruddy color that Jilian attributed to two days of rest and good food, though among the others were some who suspected other cures as well.

Glenshadow the wizard had made it clear that, in his opinion, the dwarf had been in no danger, despite his illness. The red moon, the wizard said, had set Chane a task.

Glenshadow had been silent after that. He had gone

off by himself to sit in thought. Then, after a time, he had pulled his bison cloak about him and wandered away on some path of his own.

He had not returned, though a day had passed.

But as Chane Feldstone lay now, sleeping by the little fire, Jilian hovering beside him as always, it was the kender who saw a thing that needed no reconsideration. He came with twigs to feed the fire and paused there. Then he beckoned to Wingover and pointed.

Jilian had fallen asleep. Her head nodded forward, then rested, moving slightly with her even breathing as she slept. In the shadows between the two dwarves, their two hands lay clasped, Jilian's little hand resting in Chane's larger one.

Wingover grinned. "Yes," he whispered. "That very likely is what is curing him. Some comforts have more power than people know."

"Not for me," something seemed to say wistfully, and Chestal Thicketsway looked up from the new task he had begun, which was trimming branches off a long, thin sapling he had found.

"Quit complaining, Zap," the kender said testily. "You never had it better than this. I'll bet you never expected to travel."

"No," the disembodied non-voice seemed to mourn, "just to happen."

"Well, you weren't happening where you were, either. So what's the difference?"

Wingover glanced at the kender, curious to see what the little person was doing. It was the first time he had seen Chestal Thicketsway concentrate on anything for more than one hour. Yet, Chess had been working on his sapling for most of the day. With all of its branches gone and most of its bark peeled away, it was a slim pole of fresh wood more than twenty feet long.

With the last of the trimming done, the kender laid the sapling down near the ledge and looked around. "I need some string," he said.

The man arched a curious brow. "Do you plan to go fishing?"

"I don't think so," the kender said distractedly. "But I need . . . ah, excuse me." He trotted away, heading for the stacked packs and equipment.

After a time he returned, heading for the ledge. "I found some thongs," he said. "They're not string, but they'll do."

Wingover looked after Chess, then called softly, "What are you making over there?"

"A supply stick," Chess called back. "Gnomes aren't the only ones who can invent good stuff, you know."

"A supply stick," Wingover muttered, wondering what it was all about. Then it came to him, and he grinned. Raisins for Bobbin, of course. The gnome had shown up twice since they had been here, both times cursing in gnomic and trying desperately to bring his craft close enough to the ledge for someone to reach his lowered line. He kept jabbering about something called "ground effect," and "ninety degrees to the grade," and "the gearstripping tiltyness of mountains."

They had raisins for him, and cider—which seemed to delight him—but so far they hadn't been able to deliver the goods to his supply line. At its nearest, the line had dangled fifteen feet beyond the sheer ledge.

Bobbin was probably getting hungry up there, wherever he was.

"Supply stick," Wingover said again. "Well, it just might work."

"What might?"

The deep voice, strong and quiet, startled him. Chane Feldstone hadn't moved, but he was awake. His eyes were bright in the firelight, looking from Wingover to the dozing Jilian.

"Are you feeling better?" Wingover got to his knees and leaned for a better look at the dwarf.

"I feel fine." Chane looked around, careful not to disturb Jilian. "How long have we been here? I thought we had gone to . . . no, it was only a dream, wasn't it?"

"Couple of days," Wingover told him. "You were pretty sick. How does your shoulder feel?"

Chane shifted, winced, and sat up, still holding Jilian's

hand. "A little stiff, but it's all right. Are we all here?"

"The wizard's gone off someplace again. I don't think he cares for the company around here. Chess is over there, by the ledge, rigging a pole so we can feed the gnome when he shows up again . . . if he shows up again."

Chane looked at Jilian, his eyes softening. "How long has she been sitting here?" Carefully, he eased her down into a sleeping position, still holding her hand. Then he freed himself and stood.

"She hasn't been away from your side for more than a few minutes since we got here," the man said. "But if you're ready, we need to talk about where we go from here. Those troops are ahead of us, out there on that plain. They're waiting for us."

"Maybe it wasn't all a dream, then," Chane muttered. "I dreamed the soldiers were there, waiting across a ravaged plain, where the stump of a melted peak rises. A peak that looks like a giant death's-head."

"It's called Skullcap," Wingover said. "Have you seen it?"

"No, but now I have. We—in the dream—we came around the mountain and stopped here. This very place. The air was clear, and in the distance we could see the spire of Zhaman, about ten miles away on the steppes of Dergoth. It was so clear. It glittered in the sunlight, a high, fortified tower standing alone out there, beyond where our army was gathered . . . and theirs.

"There were fourteen of us here on the mountainside. Derek was here, and Carn and Hodar, and old Callan Rockreave . . . old Callan." Chane's voice broke, then steadied. "He was my father's most stalwart friend, always at my side as he had pledged to the king. And the Daewar brothers, Hasp and Hoven Fire—" He paused again and glanced at the sleeping Jilian. "Firestoke. They were of her family. I wonder if she knows that my family and hers once were . . . no," Chane shook his head. "She couldn't have known that. Or about me, because she wasn't born then. Even her father's father wasn't born then. Odd, isn't it?"

Wingover squatted on his heels, staring at the dwarf, astonished.

"We were here," Chane sighed. "Then we went from here, across a stone bridge and onto the steppes of Dergoth, where our armies waited for us . . . and their armies, too. And we fought. Were we in the right? I didn't even wonder, then. My father had set our course, and we fought. I led my troops; I can still hear their shouts when we charged. 'On Grallen,' they shouted. 'For Thorbardin!' You see, human? In my dream I was Grallen, on the field at Zhaman. Why are you staring at me like that?"

"The spot on your forehead," Wingover pointed. "It glows."

"It has done that before." Chane looked up at the red moon Lunitari. "At least now I know exactly why I wear it."

"But . . . it glows like red crystal. Like Spellbinder itself."

"In the dream I wore its other self, just here," he touched the glowing circle between his brows. "But on my helm, embedded just above the noseguard. They said it glowed too, when I . . . when Grallen wore it. But not red. Pathfinder is green. The trace I follow is where Pathfinder went." He looked toward where Jilian slept beside the fire. "I'd like to see her safely home, you know. But home will never be safe, for her or anyone, unless I do what Grallen intended. The secret has already been sold."

"Sold?"

"Yes, according to the dream. A human has learned of the hidden way, and traded knowledge for power. There was a voice in the dream that told me that. It was as though Spellbinder itself spoke to me . . . right here, on my forehead."

"If you've seen Grallen—" The man rubbed his whiskers thoughtfully "—then you know why he was here on Sky's End. I've wondered about that. I've heard the tale, you know, from Rogar Goldbuckle and others. But they said that Grallen and his army went north, from

Northgate, and across the Plains of Dergoth to meet Fistandantilus in the final battle. What was he doing over here, so far west?"

Chane nodded. "His army went north and awaited the archmage on the plains. But I . . . Grallen, I mean, and a small force went west first, to unite the skirmishers of Coal Delvish and the border guards under Melden Coppershield. Grallen had word from the king's spies that a massed army of hill dwarves was preparing to march from southern Abanasinia. They had to be stopped. Otherwise the mountain dwarf army at Dergoth would have been caught between two enemies.

"Somehow Fistandantilus was there, at Waykeep, and joined the battle, casting spells of fire and ice. Those who came this way were all that remained from that battle."

"And nobody in Thorbardin knew of that, since nobody came home after Zhaman," Wingover muttered. "What else did you see? In your dream, I mean?"

The dwarf's eyes narrowed. "Another battle. A greater one taking place across Dergoth toward the old fortress standing there. I knew, Wingover. I knew . . . did I know then? Did *he* know that it was the last battle?

"Callan Rockreave led the main assault. I wonder if any in Thorbardin know that. And Derek Hammerthane carried the king's pennant. Others joined us, too . . . joined *them*, I mean. Some humans among them, who fought courageously alongside Grallen and the others.

"I . . . Grallen, I mean. In the dream, he actually took the tower, then confronted the old wizard in his lair. He intended to exact an oath from Fistandantilus . . . or to kill him. The prince was in a hurry, though, and distracted. He wanted to finish the fight and get back to Thorbardin because of something the gem above his noseguard had revealed to him. He was worried, and he underestimated the old wizard."

Chane paused and closed his eyes. "I saw it in the dream. The wizard was in a rage. His eyes . . . there is no way to describe such eyes. They were not the eyes of any living thing. They were . . . evil. Then the wizard smiled and set loose his final magic. And Grallen . . . and everyone and everything . . . were gone."

Chane's voice had gone soft as he spoke, and was barely audible in the final words. As he opened his eyes a tear welled in one of them and started to trickle down his cheek. He snorted, shook his head, and brushed it away. "Everything ended there, you know. They all died."

The dwarf sighed heavily, glancing around as though he were just awakening. The kender had come to listen and was holding one end of a long pole with leather loops on it. Chane realized this was probably the first time he had ever seen the kender speechless.

"But you said you saw Skullcap," Wingover persisted. "Grallen couldn't have seen that."

"No. It was as well that he never saw it. It was like the mountain . . . melted, changed into something hideous. Grallen didn't see it, Wingover, but I did. In the dream." He tapped his forehead. "The stone in Grallen's helm— Pathfinder—saw it, and I've seen what Pathfinder saw.

"Grallen must have put his helm aside . . . or lost it in the tower or something. But I know where it is now, and why the green trace out there looks so odd, as though it doubles back on itself." He walked to the ledge and pointed, not toward distant Skullcap, but south of there. "Zhaman's spire," he said. "It was blown entirely away from the tower, and bits of the upper portions with it. Grallen's helm—and Pathfinder—are there, where the wreckage fell."

* * * * *

Morning sun was on the peaks of Sky's End when the soarwagon appeared again, spiraling down from high above in a series of precipitous loops and tumbles—for all the world like a stricken bird falling away from a raptor. And as it tumbled closer, Chane and his allies squinted at it. The contrivance seemed to have added something since its last visit. Thrust upward from its top side was a slim thing like a narrow mast.

Over the gorge, just out from the cove, the soarwagon leveled out and its nose-vanes shifted. It hovered on rising mists while Bobbin leaned out to shout, "Get the supplies ready! I've solved the problem!"

"What do you mean, *you've* solved the problem?" Chess called back. "I worked all day on solving the problem."

"Hurry!" Bobbin tugged the control lines, ignoring the kender, and eased the soarwagon toward the ledge. As it had done before, the contraption began to tilt, aligning itself to the slope of the mountain steeps above. Closer it came, and closer, and the slender mastlike thing began to extend from its underside, toward the cove. Chess and the others could see what it was: Bobbin's rope. But somehow it was stiff, snaking toward the ledge at an angle.

"Hurry!" the gnome shouted. "And don't forget the cider!"

Chess danced about the ledge, his eyes bright with excitement. "Look at that! He's made the rope stiff. It's coming right to us."

Bobbin worked his controls and continued feeding out the rope, doing all he could to settle the soarwagon in close to the ledge.

"How did you do that?" Chess shouted. "That's really something! Come on! The raisins and cider are right here, all lashed together. All we have to do is hook them . . . oops!"

The rope had come within five feet of the ledge, almost within reach. Then, abruptly, it sagged and went limp. The rope dangled from the flying craft, its hook swinging fifteen feet out from the cliff.

"Oh, breakdown!" the gnome cursed. "It melted!"

"Melted?"

"Right. I used up the last of my water, soaking it, then spent the night at least ten thousand feet up, freezing it. I thought that would work."

"Well, don't worry," the kender called. "Just try to hold still."

Strutting with pride, Chess brought out his supply pole—twenty feet of slim sapling, with loops at its ends. He attached the narrow-end loop to the raisin-and-cider pack and lifted it, then began to feed out pole toward

Bobbin's dangling hook.

Leaning over his wicker rail, the gnome watched with worried eyes. "That isn't going to work," he said. "You can't lever that much weight that far out without a counterbalance."

Chess braced himself, struggling to feed out the pole. The weight of the supplies seemed to double with each foot of extension. "I may need some help," he admitted.

The others had gathered around him, watching with a mixture of amusement and disbelief.

"You need more than help," Wingover advised. "There isn't enough pole there."

"This just has to work," the kender panted, beginning to stagger at the leveraged weight of the supply pole. "It's the only idea I have."

With the last of his strength, Chess hauled the supplies back to the ledge. He carried the pack twenty feet to the left and ran back. Lifting the butt-end of the pole, the kender put his shoulder to it.

"Don't!" Wingover started.

"Wait!" Chane shouted.

"Youcan'tdothat!" Bobbin called.

But the kender already had. With a tremendous heave, Chess swung the pack off the ledge, trying to hoist it out to the soarwagon's hook. Pack, pole, and kender disappeared over the edge. Jilian screamed.

Instantly Wingover loosed his sword, plunged its blade deep into a crack in the rock, and swung himself outward and down. Chane Feldstone jumped over him, cleared the ledge, and scrambled down the man's length. The dwarf hung from Wingover's ankle and grabbed Chess's free hand just as the kender lost his grip on a snag.

"Got him!" Chane called. "Pull us back up!"

Wingover pulled, but nothing happened. His grip on his sword held them suspended—man, dwarf, kender, pole and pack hanging over the misted gorge—but no amount of muscle-wrenching effort would lift them.

"I thought I was the one who was crazy," Bobbin called from the hovering soarwagon.

Just at the cliff's edge, Jilian had her feet braced and both hands on Wingover's forearm. Her nails bit into his skin as she pulled. "Let go!" he shouted at her. "You're making it worse!"

"Somebody get a rope!" Chane called from below.

"I have a rope," Bobbin mentioned. "A fat lot of good it does me, now that it's melted."

Jilian scrambled back from the ledge, then turned and ran, returning with Wingover's horse and a length of rope from his packs. Working quickly, the girl secured the rope to the saddle, carried its free end to the ledge, and leaned over to tie it around Wingover's arm.

With Jilian pulling on its headstall, the horse braced itself and hauled. Wingover appeared at the ledge and was dragged to safety, snatching up his sword as he came. Then came Chane and finally the kender. Chess had one hand firmly grasped in the dwarf's fingers; the other held the pole's loop.

"Remarkable," Bobbin sighed, watching from the limit of ground effect.

When finally the pole and packs were safe, Chane Feldstone released his grips on the man's ankle and the kender's hand. The dwarf stood up, brushed himself off, and took the pole away from Chess. "Get out of the way," he growled.

Angrily, the dwarf reversed the pole and thrust its butt-loop out toward the gnome's dangling hook, hand over hand.

Chess watched for a moment, then shook his head. "That won't work," he said.

"Why not?" Chane kept feeding out the pole.

"Because then I'll lose my supply pole!"

"What do you want it for?"

"Well, it's for sending raisins and cider out to where Bobbin can get them."

"And when he has the pole, he'll have the supplies, too," the dwarf rumbled. "Mercy!"

"Oh." Chess backed off, considering the logic of it. "Well, there is that."

Using the supply pack as a counterweight, Chane fed

the pole out and neatly dropped its loop over Bobbin's hook. The gnome began to winch in his line, and the pack slid off the ledge and fell. The heavy bundle of supplies swung at pole's end, making the soarwagon dance in its hover. The contraption held for a moment, then sensitive vanes reacted to the shifting currents and it soared away over the gorge, circling and climbing as Bobbin's angry voice trailed away.

"You're welcome!" Chess shouted, watching soarwagon, rope, supply pole, and raisin-and-cider pack diminish into the distance.

"At least he has provisions," Jilian pointed out. "I'm sure he was getting hungry."

Chapter 28

High on a chill slope, where whining winds drove scudding clouds below and whipped snow from peaks above, the wizard Glenshadow knelt beside a pool of ice. The hooded face looking up at him was grim. "Only a few days ago you were within an arrow-shot of the Dark One, Wanderer. Did you see him?"

"I saw something," Glenshadow replied. "The warrior-woman lifted something from beneath her breastplate. Something small and dark, it seemed, like an amulet."

"It was the Dark One," the face told him. "You could have killed him then . . . or he you."

Glenshadow shook his head. "His magic would no more work for him than mine for me," he said. "Not in the presence of Spellbinder."

"The dwarf still carries the stone, then," the voice muttered. "Has he seen where it directs him?"

"He sees the trail of Pathfinder, and thus the way to Grallen's helm. He may know soon where it lies, for he is on the east face of Sky's End now. All of Dergoth is visible beyond the chasm."

"All of Dergoth . . . and the woman, Darkmoor. The Dark One is with her. They are ahead of you, Wanderer. They await you."

"Then so it must be," Glenshadow rasped, his voice as chill as the whining winds on the mountain. "Tell me, has the riddle been tested? The omen of the moons?"

"We think it means there will be war," the ice-face said. "A war like none Krynn has ever known."

"When?"

"Soon. The preliminary games are in play even now . . . as you have seen."

"But, a war of the moons? What kind of war must that be?"

"Of the moons, Wanderer? Or of the gods? We believe the omens mean a war for dominion. Some say a contest among gods, to once and for all determine which of the triad alignments shall rule on Krynn . . . But, of course, there are always those who speak of ultimates and finalities. Even so, those of the dark robes are gleeful these days, while those of the white are silent and anxious." The figure in the ice seemed to shrug. "We shall see what comes of it all. Most of us are not overly concerned."

The ice faded, went blank. The mirror surface reflected only cold sky above—that, and the cold, thoughtful face of the wizard who knelt beside it.

"Not overly concerned," he muttered, and his cold words were carried away by the wind. "Not concerned? It was not only the white moon that was eclipsed, but the red, as well."

Glenshadow passed the glowing tip of his staff over the ice pool, and again it shifted. He knew from past trials that it would show him nothing of Chane Feldstone and his companions. It was, after all, only magic. It could not see within the realm of Spellbinder. But it would show him other things, in other places.

A scene emerged: a sundered plain where goblins marched, and in the background the blind, leering death's-head of Skullcap, hideous monument to the power of magics drawn from Nuitari, the black moon.

"Chislev!" the wizard said.

The ice scene flowed, spanned across miles, and refocused on a barren hillside. There, a figure stood motionless—a curious, oddly-jointed thing that might have been a horse . . . or some woodcarver's interpretation of a horse. It was obviously a carven figure, wooden with pin-hinged joints like a child's toy. As the ice eye closed on the figure its carved head turned. Painted eyes looked at the wizard.

"Which are you?" Glenshadow asked the ice.

"I am Hobby," the carved horse told him. "What wish do you have?"

"The helm of the dwarven prince, Grallen. Do you know where it is?"

"I know nothing except what Chislev wills," Hobby said.

. "And I have called upon Chislev and found you. Therefore it is the will of Chislev. Hobby, where is Grallen's helm?"

The carved horse turned away, seeming to look about uncertainly. Suddenly its hinged joints came alive, and it sprang away, running at an awkward, loose-legged gallop that seemed slow—except for the blur of landscape flashing past. Hobby ran, and the ice image followed it. Hills sped past, and wild steppes where raw wind flattened scrub. The torn and savaged land was seen just in glimpses by the mage.

The carved horse ran, then slowed and halted atop another hill. "There," it said. "Hobby has found it."

The wooden horse looked away, and the ice image followed its steady gaze. At the foot of the hill was a tumble of rocks. Great boulders lay here and there in a field of smaller, broken stones, which stretched across a quarter-mile of barren waste. Only here and there among the rocks was there indication that they had once been part of a structure—a squared corner, a wedge-cut face of flat stone.

Hobby's gaze narrowed, and so did the scene in the ice pool. Among the stones, a point jutted up, tilted at a slight angle, its lower parts buried under sand and debris. It was a piece of what must once have been a mighty structure, now only wreckage among rubble.

A wide crack ran from the covered base part way toward the upright point, and Hobby's painted eyes focused on that crack. In the shadows within the fissure, something glowed for a moment.

"The helm is there," Hobby said. "Chislev knows where everything is. Chislev is everywhere that there are eyes to see." Slowly, the carved wooden head turned to the right, and in the ice pool the landscape slithered past: a place of broken lands; a wide, cold marsh with mountains beyond. Only a few miles away, a range of giant peaks rose above the sheer wall of a great cliff hundreds of feet high, a cliff that soared upward from a misted gorge. And just at the top of the cliff, facing on a narrow ledge, was a massive, closed gate.

The great northern gate of the undermountain realm of Thorbardin, still intact though its approaches had been sheared away for centuries.

Abruptly the picture vanished, and the carved wooden face of Hobby was again in the ice. "Hobby has shown what you wanted to see," the horse said.

Glenshadow drew his staff across the ice, and again it was only ice. He stood, wind whipping the fringes of his bison cloak, rippling the hems of the faded red robes beneath.

Far out across the plain, tiny with distance, plumes of dust arose where armies moved. Glenshadow watched these, deep in thought. Out there, somehow joined to the woman who led the invaders, was Caliban.

Caliban, the renegade black-robed mage Glenshadow and two others had hunted down years before . . . Caliban, who chose to fight them rather than accept the rules of the robed orders . . . Caliban, whose magic destroyed two of the three before he himself died.

Glenshadow's cold eyes were as bleak as a winter storm as he remembered. Caliban had died, but not at Glenshadow's hand. He had killed himself, rather than accept defeat. Glenshadow had seen the manner of it. The black-robed mage, with his own two hands, had torn out his own heart.

Even across the miles now, he felt eyes upon him and knew that he was seen. Caliban's magic lived, and was at work.

The wizard on the mountain raised his eyes toward the skies. "Hear me Gilean, gate of souls," he said, his voice like the mountain wind. "Hear me Sirrion Firemaster. Hear me Chislev, whose carven creatures see what is to see. World-tree Zivilyn, and Shinare by whose color the wilderness man shone, hear me. Hear me all who seek balance in a struggling world, who yearn for order in a plane whose name is chaos. Two things more do I ask in this life: to see the death of he who died before . . . and first, to see what Chane Feldstone sees when he holds Spellbinder and Pathfinder and looks toward Thorbardin."

Sighing, the mage looked across distances toward the place where the dust plumes blew. He knew what the thing was that Kolanda Darkmoor had raised from her breastplate—the thing he had thought was an amulet. It was what remained of Caliban. It was the wizard's heart.

The Wanderer felt eyes upon him, and sensed a building of magics. He turned his eyes toward the place the wooden horse had shown him, and muttered a transport spell.

Winds whipped about him on the mountainside, and then there was only the wind.

* * * * *

In the final four miles of approach, with Skullcap fully and horribly visible ahead, Kolanda Darkmoor had fanned her goblin troops out in three long lines. They had swept the plains for a sign of anyone having passed as she waited for the reports to come back. Within hours, a front several miles long had been combed. It was clear that no one had passed this way recently.

Thoughtfully, then, Kolanda looked back the way she had come. Due west, the bulk of Sky's End rose somber against the sky. To the south, just visible across the miles, was the massive mountain wall of Thorbardin, the great north gate tiny above a sheer cliff of huge proportion. Northgate was almost never used now because of its nearly impossible access—even by the dwarves who lived beyond it.

Her eyes, shadowed within the grotesque horned mask that was the faceplate of her helmet, rested on Northgate for a time. Then they roved downward, seeking something she knew was there but had never seen—the thing her career with the Highlord's forces was based upon, the thing that would assure her the power she craved when the Highlords began their campaigns. That thing was the secret way into Thorbardin.

Command of Thorbardin was to be Kolanda Darkmoor's reward—provided she remained in the good graces of the Highlord of Neraka. She would have command of defeated and occupied Thorbardin, and first share of the treasures of the realm.

Kolanda could not see the hidden entrance. No one could, now. But it was there, and she knew the way to it. It was that information that had gained her the interim rank of Commander.

She wished she could see the hidden gate now. It would feel good, she thought, to see the route by which she would lead forces to penetrate and conquer the kingdom of the western dwarves of Ansalon.

It's there, she thought, scanning with her eyes. Just there . . . and unknown to those within.

But there was one who posed a threat: a dwarf who had the means to thwart her plans. He must be destroyed. But where was he? Not here yet, certainly. Back there somewhere, she realized, but coming this way. But where? The plains were vast, with no significant feature except the ruined fortress of Zhaman . . . now Skullcap. He *would* be coming to Skullcap, wouldn't he? Where else would he seek that which he sought?

Shadowed eyes in a hideous mask roved the slopes of Sky's End. Up there? Where?

It was time to ask Caliban. She turned away, looking for one of her hobgoblin marshals. None were near, and the only goblins within call were stupid brutes—a dozen or so greasy swamp goblins good only for carrying packs and spears, and for combing the field after combat to dispatch the wounded. A pair of ogres squatted nearby, though, two of four that had come south with her force. The other two had been missing for at least a week.

She approached the pair and pointed at the nearest one. "You, go and tell the marshals to form here and await orders."

The huge creature stared at her with cruel, close-set eyes—eyes that were above her own even though the ogre was squatting on its heels. It yawned, baring great slabs of yellow teeth, and looked away.

Raising her faceplate Kolanda stepped closer and barked, "You heard me! Do as I say!"

The two ogres grinned at each other, then the one she had addressed spat on the ground. "Don't feel like it," it rumbled. "Do it yourself."

With rising fury in her eyes, Kolanda Darkmoor drew her sword and swatted the ogre across the face with the flat of her blade. "Obey me!" she hissed.

The grin disappeared from the huge, leering face. The ogre stood, rubbing its cheek with a hand that was eighteen inches across. It towered over the woman. "Puny human," it rumbled. "Go too far. Maybe I squash you where you are."

Kolanda reached to her throat and drew a leather thong from beneath the lacquered metal of her breastplate. At its end dangled a black, misshapen thing that resembled a shriveled pear. "Caliban," she said.

A rush of heat sprang from the thing, a tangible force that made the air around it sizzle. Fire shot from it and struck the ogre in the chest. The creature was thrown backward a dozen yards. It tumbled, rolled, and sprawled, then lay still. Vile smoke curled upward from its midsection, and dead eyes stared at the sky.

Kolanda dropped the dark thing back into her breast-plate and pointed at the second ogre. "You heard my order," she said. "*You* do it."

Growling deep in its massive chest, the monster scrambled to its feet, glaring at the woman. It paused for a moment over the smoking body of its partner, shot a murderous glance back at Kolanda, then went to do her bidding. After watching the ogre move off, the Commander beckoned to some of the swamp goblins. "Bring the slaves," she ordered. "Set my pavilion here."

When she was alone, she pulled the dark thing from her breastplate again, where an angry heat had developed between her breasts. She held it up, gazing at it with revulsion.

"Why did she wake me?" the thing asked, its voice a dry, husky whisper in her ear. "Does she need *me* to deal with ogres?"

"You didn't have to kill it," Kolanda said. "It might have proven useful."

"She criticizes me," the thing whispered. "What does she want?"

"I need you to tell me where my quarry is," she said.

"Ah? Needs me, does she? Hee-hee!" The ancient, wizened voice was a whispered cackle. "Needs Caliban, she does. Very well, Caliban is awake. But she knows the price."

With a shudder of revulsion, Kolanda dropped to her knees and held the wrinkled thing before her face. Lowering her head the woman said, "Caliban lives forever. Caliban's power goes beyond death. Caliban will never die again. Caliban offered me his help . . ." Her voice trailed off in a choking whisper.

"Hee-hee!" the dark thing rasped. "She has to say it all."

"Caliban offered me his help," she continued, "and I accepted. I sealed the bargain with the blood of my own brother, and thus Caliban owns my soul."

In her ear, the wispy voice chortled and cackled. "Very good. She always remembers . . . as she must. What does she ask of me now?"

"I cannot see my prey, Caliban," Kolanda said. "See them for me, and tell me where they are."

"She wants to know where people are," the voice breathed. "Kiss me, Kolanda."

With a shudder, she brought the thing to her lips and kissed it, then held it against her forehead and looked again toward Sky's End. She could see them—the dwarf and his companions—across the miles but as if they were only a few feet away. Caliban's magic magnified the scene, and she counted them there. A pair of dwarves, one male and one female; a rangy, bearded man dressed as a ranger or forester; a horse carrying packs; a kender. There was something odd about the kender, almost as though someone else walked beside him, but there was no one else there to see. They were coming down a steep trail, toward the gorge that faced the plains. A stone bridge arched across, just ahead of them.

"They are near the lost gate," she whispered. "But they aren't all there. Where is the wizard?"

Kolanda raised her eyes and saw him. High on the side of Sky's End, he stood alone, a cloaked wizard of the red robes.

The heart of Caliban became hot against her skin. "Glenshadow!" the husky voice rasped. There was a sizzling sound, a ringing in the air, a massing of powers to be unleashed. The figure on the mountain raised his staff and vanished.

Puzzled, Kolanda Darkmoor withdrew the wrinkled black thing from her brow and gazed at it. "What is it?" she asked. "Why were you so . . . ah. Aha, I think I see. He was one of them, wasn't he! One of those who killed you?"

The husky voice no longer chortled. Now its whisper breathed of deadly hatred. "She must hold me aloft now. I will find him again. I will kill him."

Quickly, Kolanda lowered Caliban. She dropped the thing back beneath her breastplate and smiled, a cruel smile on a face that should have been beautiful. "I owe you no favors, sorcerer," she said. "Our accounts are square. Go back to sleep."

Caliban stirred for a moment between her breasts, and then became still. She shuddered in revulsion as she always did. Years before, Kolanda had made her pact, a pact between herself and the withered heart of an old renegade wizard, hunted down by wizards of the various orders. Caliban was a black-robe who had set himself beyond the bounds and had paid the price. But Caliban was also a mage who even in death had somehow torn out his own heart with his two hands, and willed his spirit into it.

This was Caliban, and this was the pact between them. As long as she lived, she would keep and use the thing that owned her.

The slaves had been brought forward to set up the Commander's pavilion. They were mostly hill dwarves, with a few other creatures among them—a few miserable Aghar, an elf shackled and mutilated almost beyond recognition, a few humans. Kolanda Darkmoor watched the work, wrinkling her nose. So pitifully few, they were. But there would be more. One day she would have all the slaves she wanted, to use as she wished.

It was a thing she had learned from Caliban, or maybe had always known. People are of value only if they are owned.

She glanced at the slaves again. Among them, the lone elf was clinging to the rails of a forage cart, staring at her. Both legs made useless by cut tendons, still he clung to stay upright and looked at her with eyes that held no expression at all. Drivers goaded him, marked him with whips, and he ignored them. I should kill him, she thought. But this was the one who had ambushed her scouting party—had cost her half her escort—and she wanted him to live and suffer for that.

Among the wounds the elf carried were recent ones. His face had been battered, and one of his ears was gone. Bitten off, by the look of it.

Kolanda looked around for Thog, one of her hobgoblins, and summoned him. "The elf has been beaten again." She pointed at the slave accusingly. "I want him alive."

"Tried to 'scape," Thog growled. "Han's an' knees, an' he brained one of th' drivers wi' a rock."

"All right," she said. "Just see that he isn't killed. I'm not ready to release him yet."

When the hobgoblin was gone, Kolanda once again drew the withered wizard-heart from her breast and said, "Caliban."

Instantly he was awake.

"You can tell me where that wizard is now," she ordered. "But after that we do things my way. And no more ritual grovel, do you understand? Don't forget, I'm all that keeps you alive."

"She is arrogant," the thing whispered. "But for now, I agree. For now."

She held the old heart against her forehead and looked into the distance.

Later, when the slaves had erected her pavilion, Kolanda Darkmoor called for Thog again. "Have them take it down and pack it away," she said. "And get your troops together. We're moving out."

Chapter 29

The stone bridge across the gorge, at its narrowest point near the foot of Sky's End, was old. Not truly ancient, in the sense that Gargath's monolith and such constructs as Pax Tharkas and the ruins of Zhaman were ancient, but it was old. Obviously, it had been built since the Cataclysm, because prior to that there was no gorge between the mountain peaks and the Plains of Dergoth.

And obviously, it was of dwarven construction. A high-arched bridge, it was built entirely of stone—huge blocks of cut and shaped granite rising a hundred feet or more in its center as it spanned three hundred yards of abyss. Its floor was a precise nine feet in width. That was the same width as the cable-cart tunnels in Thorbardin.

As he approached the structure, Wingover studied it intently. "I hope you know what you're doing," he told Chane. "Once we cross the gorge, we're going away from Thorbardin, not toward it. And there are some very unfriendly goblins over there somewhere."

"At least I know where to look for Pathfinder," the dwarf noted. "It's just at the edge of the plains, on a hillside. Probably not more than three miles from here."

"When you have it, it will lead you back toward Thorbardin," Wingover noted. "The bridge will be between us and the city, then. I can't think of a better place for those goblins to trap us."

"That's why I'm going on alone, after we cross the bridge," Chane said. "The rest of you can wait at the other abutment, to make sure we can come back."

"I'll do no such thing, Chane Feldstone," Jilian snapped. "If you go out there, then I'm going too."

"I don't have much choice about it," Chestal Thicketsway pointed out. "I'm with you, Chane. At least until I do something about Zap."

"I'll leave Spellbinder here," the dwarf said. "Wingover can hold it for me. That way you can stay here, too, Chess. I don't know, you might be handy to have around if Chane has to hold the bridge. I've seen you use that hoopak."

"Yeah, I'm pretty good with it, don't you think?"

"Isn't that what I just said?"

"No. You said you'd seen me use it."

"You're good with it, so stay here."

"I don't have much choice, if Spellbinder's here. Unless . . . I don't suppose you'd want *me* to hang on to Spellbinder until you get back. That way I could—"

"No-o-o!" something that wasn't exactly a voice seemed to wail.

"Oh, yeah," the kender remembered. "I don't want to have to listen to that again. Of course, I could leave my pouch, but then what would I use to carry hoopak pebbles?"

"Stay!" Chane growled. "All the rest of you, too. I know where I'm going, and I'll go faster alone."

But Wingover was ignoring the dwarf. Quickly, the man stripped the packs from his horse, down to just saddle and gear. As he swung aboard, he snugged his flinthide shield to his left forearm in riding mode. Wingover then pulled his sword around, ready to hand, and looked down at the glowering dwarf. "When it comes to traveling fast, you're about the worst choice we have at the moment. So it's up to me. Where is that hillside?"

Chane glared up at him. "How do I know you'll come back?"

"How do you know *you* would?" the man bristled. "Do you want my help or not?"

"I never asked for your help," Chane grumbled. "Jilian did."

Wingover leaned down to match the dwarf's pugnacious glare with one of his own. "I believe you could aggravate the horns off a minotaur, dwarf, but I don't think you're stupid. Tell me where to find that helm of yours, or I'll go search for it anyway."

Jilian tugged the sleeve of Chane's black fur coat. "Tell him, Chane. He'll bring it back."

"How do you know he . . . ?" Chane looked around and paused. "Oh. Well, I suppose you're right. It's just that humans are so hard to trust."

"Well?" Wingover asked.

"Beyond the bridge is a broken slope, with a trail winding down through rock outcrop for about half a mile. The trail is easy to see . . . or it used to be, anyway, when I . . .I mean when Grallen saw it. After you get out of the breaks, you'll see a few low hills ahead, and the trail will fork around the first one. Take the left fork. The right leads to the bog." He paused, and Wingover nodded.

"Past that hill you'll see two more a mile or so away— little hills that look alike, with a gap between and the sundered plains beyond. The right-hand hill is where Grallen's helm is, with Pathfinder. The hillside faces Skullcap, and the helm's near the foot of the hill. There's rubble there, so I guess you'll just have to search through it."

"What if it's buried or something?"

"It isn't buried. But it's in a dark place with a tall, tilted opening—like a crack. Jagged, kind of. And where it is, it can't see Thorbardin."

"How do you know that?" Wingover asked.

Chane shrugged. "Because it wants to, and it can't. I don't know. The Irda said the two gems are god-things, left over from something a god did. Maybe they are interested in whatever that god is concerned about."

"And what god is that?" Wingover said with a frown. "Assuming, of course, that there really are gods. I'm not sure I believe any of that."

"I don't know if I do, either," the dwarf admitted. "But the Irda did. And Reorx is the highest of the gods . . . if there are any."

"Reorx?" Wingover scoffed. "What about Gilean? And Paladine, and Kiri-Jolith? Reorx isn't any higher than them!"

"Who?"

"Gilean."

The dwarf nodded. "He's all right, I suppose. I meant Reorx was greater than those other two you named. I've never even heard of them."

"You never heard of Paladine? He's the highest-ranking of—"

"He means Thak and Kijo," Chess butted in, grinning. "A lot of people call them Paladine and Kiri-Jolith."

They both looked at the kender. Chane frowned and snapped, "What are you grinning about?"

"Oh, I was just thinking, for two people who don't believe there are gods, you both certainly have your favorites."

"And how do you know so much about it?"

"I listen a lot."

"Pure superstition, anyway," Wingover snorted, straightening in his saddle. He looked at the rising stone bridge ahead and lifted his reins.

"I'll be back," he said. "Just hold the bridge for me if trouble comes."

He touched heels to the horse and trotted it to the foot

of the stone bridge. The horse abruptly turned tail and tried to throw him off. He clung, cursing, and finally got the animal under control.

"Maybe he's afraid of the bridge," Chane suggested.

"Geekay has never been afraid of a bridge in his life!" Wingover shouted. "Or a goblin, either! He's just full of vinegar from not being exercised."

"Geekay? Is that his name? What does it mean?"

"He named himself. It's Goblin Killer." Wingover hauled the reins. The horse spun, dug in haunches-down, and hit the bridge at a full gallop. Wingover's diminishing voice came back to them: "Blast it, horse! Not so fast!"

In seconds the thundering horse had topped out at the crown of the high-curved span and was out of sight. A moment later the ring of hooves on stone faded to a distant clatter, beyond the gorge.

"Well, the bridge is still there," Chestal Thicketsway decided. "I guess it's safe to cross."

"Of course it's safe," Chane growled. "It's dwarven work." Picking up his pack, he started up the bridge, the others following after him.

"If a gnome can fly," the kender muttered, "then I guess a dwarf might miscalculate rocks and things from time to time."

* * * * *

By the time Wingover got the bridge-spooked horse under tight rein, they were through the breaks and into rolling, open country. Holding Geekay to a steady trot, the wilderness man scanned the lands ahead. A few low hills lay ahead, about a half-mile away, just as Chane had said. Wingover eased the reins and headed for them, looking for signs of a trail.

At first there was none, then in a low place that might once have been a mudflat he saw tracks. They were old tracks, but still clear—at least three horses, and the short, wide prints of dwarven boots. The trail disappeared short of the hill, but Wingover made left and circled around it, his eyes roving the landscape. Sometimes he raised his shield to eye-level and peered over the top edge of it. An old trick, it was a way to see distinct movement that might otherwise lose itself in mirage. So far he had seen nothing, but vagrant breezes carried the stink of goblins. Wingover knew they were out there somewhere.

As much as he watched the land around him, he watched the ears of his horse. The animal smelled goblins, too, and was wary. Its ears swiveled this way and that, pausing sometimes. When they did, Wingover scanned in their direction.

The hill was a smooth mound, and as Wingover passed it he saw two more, just as the dwarf had described. They lay about a mile ahead, with some draws and gullys lacing the lower ground between.

Geekay's ears turned, fixed on a direction ahead and to the left, and a tremor ran along its mane. Wingover lifted his shield, peering over its edge. Atop a narrow draw, barely a hundred yards away, something moved. It looked like a twig twitching in the wind . . . except that twigs twitch rhythmically, and this one didn't. It moved, disappeared below the rim of the draw, and reappeared a few yards away. Its direction was toward the point where his own path would cross the draw.

So they're waiting for me there, he decided. But how many?

Wingover reined a little to the left, holding hard against the bit, then let Geekay have his head. The horse had never been trained as a warhorse—not as some he had seen, great steeds in armor, ridden by men in armor, silent men who had come down from Solamnia once many years before in search of a fugitive—but Wingover and Geekay had traveled far together and had been in some scrapes.

With the bit eased and the scent of goblins in his nostrils, and with the tug to the left from his rider, Geekay took the lead. As the horse gathered himself, Wingover jumped to the ground and headed for the draw at a crouching run, angling to the right. Behind him, Geekay whinnied shrilly and galloped away to the left. Fifty yards . . . one hundred . . . then he turned and headed for the draw.

In the ravine, four goblin scouts paused, puzzled at the sudden change in approaching sounds. One started to raise his head and another swatted him down. "Don' look," he growled. "Get us seen. Listen!"

"Runnin' away," another said, pointing back the way they had come. "That way."

The goblins turned to follow the hoofbeats, but a blood-freezing howl erupted just behind them. The rear-most goblin didn't even have time to turn. Wingover's sword flashed across his back from shoulder to waist, and dark blood spurted. The second turned, tried to raise his dart-bow, and had it knocked from his hand. With his sword, the goblin barely countered the human's fol-lowing thrust with a low, chopping swing at his legs. Metal rang on metal.

The third goblin had his blade out, but the fourth caught his arm. "Back up," he hissed. "Get room. Use darts."

They scrambled back, setting darts to their crossbows. The first dart ricocheted off Wingover's flinthide shield. The second buried itself in the back of a goblin flung from the point of a sword. The last two set darts again, then their eyes widened as the sound of thunder bore down on them from behind. One turned, screamed, and bounced off the other as the flashing hooves of a horse named Goblin Killer descended upon him. The remain-ing goblin was still scrambling to his feet when Geekay swapped ends and kicked. Crushed like a turtle in its shell, the goblin flew over Wingover's head and re-bounded off a wall of the gully.

"Not bad," Wingover breathed, catching up the reins of the excited, wild-eyed horse. "Now let's move. It stinks here."

He scrambled into his saddle. Geekay cleared the rim at a bound and headed for the right-hand hill ahead, Wingover wondered where the rest of the goblins were. He knew there were at least a hundred more, and among them possibly ogres—as well as a woman in a hideous armor mask that hid a face that should have been beautiful.

Atop the hill was a bright green statue of a wizard, both arms extended to their full length, a motionless staff in one hand. Wingover blinked at it, then headed for it. Even from the foot of the hill, he recognized Glenshadow the Wanderer . . . even though he was bright green and motionless.

The wilderness man reined in beside the wizard, gaping at him. Even his clothing and his hair were bright green. Leaning from his saddle, he asked, "What happened to you?"

"Take . . . it," the wizard gasped.

"Take what?" He looked the mage over and noticed that one hand was balled into a tight fist. Wingover pried it open. In the wizard's hand was a crystal, the twin of Spellbinder, except for its color. As red as Spellbinder was, so was Pathfinder green.

Wingover took the crystal, and the green color faded from the mage.

Glenshadow slumped, trembling. "I—I shouldn't have touched it," he rasped. "Should have known. Spellbinder binds magic, turns it against itself. Pathfinder freezes it, holds it in stasis. It was how Gargath held and controlled the graystone."

Wingover flipped the crystal over in his hand. "Very pretty," he said. "All right, they're waiting for us at the bridge. Can you ride?"

"Can't get through," the wizard said, still trembling. "The goblins . . . they're behind you, heading for the bridge. I saw them from up here. With Pathfinder, I couldn't move. But I could see . . . everything. The dwarf was right. Thorbardin is breached. Here."

Glenshadow stooped and picked up something Wingover had not noticed until then—an old dwarven helmet, not elaborate but of fine craft. It was a horned and spired helm of burnished metal with skirts and a carven nosepiece. Above the noseguard was a setting.

"The gem belongs here," Glenshadow said. "Please put it back in place."

Wingover took the helmet and turned it, wonder in his eyes. Grallen's helm. There was no doubt of it. The dwarven prince of old had been here. He had been inside the fortress of Zhaman, and only this helm had survived to tell of it. And it had called out to Chane Feldstone in dreams.

Carefully Wingover reset Pathfinder in the helm's setting. His hard, but gentle fingers refit the brass prongs that had held it, and for a moment Wingover was tempted to put it on his head. It would fit, and it might speak to him . . . then he changed his mind. This is Chane's to do with as he must, he told himself. And if there is one lesson I can learn from this wizard here, it is not to fiddle with things that are beyond me.

Wingover bound the old helmet with thongs and hung it from his saddle, then reached a hand to Glenshadow. "Come up," he said. "The horse can carry double. We've got to get back to the bridge."

Chapter 30

BECAUSE THE GOBLIN ARMY WAS SO WIDELY SPREAD, fanned across the plains in three troops, miles apart, Kolanda Darkmoor decided to move against the people at the bridge. Even though the wizard might be with them, the defenders were still only a handful. She ordered Thog to gather the main force on the central plain to await her signal.

Thus, when Wingover made his dash from the breaks to the fork-trail hill, spotters saw him from less than a mile away. The word of his sighting was relayed immediately.

"We got foragers workin' those gully-washes," the runner said. "They'll get him there."

"Groups of four?"

"Like you said," the sprinter noted, "he won' get through. Jus' one man . . . they'll get him."

Yet, moments later, the rider was seen again, farther away and past the washes, heading for the more distant of the twin hills. Kolanda swore, halted her platoon, and pulled Caliban from beneath her breastplate. "Caliban!" she snapped. "See for me now." She held the withered heart to her forehead without ceremony.

"She is arrogant," the whispering voice said. "She will require special attention when . . . ah?" The voice became a hiss. "Glenshadow!"

"See for me!" Kolanda ordered. "The man on the horse, what is he doing?"

The view closed on the distant rider, who was swerving to climb the hill, then shifted to the hilltop. Kolanda stiffened. The wizard there stood immobile, arms outstretched, and shone with a green glare that seemed to burn through her skin. She jerked Caliban away from her forehead. "What is that?"

"She doesn't know what has hurt us," the feathery voice whispered. The heart vibrated in the Commander's hand, the air sizzled and trembled, and Caliban loosed a bolt of pure energy across the miles, aimed at the wizard on the hill. Then Caliban went cold in Kolanda's palm. "An element protects him," it whispered. "I could not reach him."

"Is his magic more powerful than yours?" the woman snapped.

"She doesn't understand," Caliban whispered. "It is not his magic. It is something else. Wait . . . ah. The man has taken it. Now Glenshadow is revealed. Now I can fight him. Hold me up. I must draw power from you."

"Wait," Kolanda commanded. "The thing he had, that the rider has now, is that what the dwarf is seeking?"

"She plays at riddles," the dry voice grated. "Hold me up."

Kolanda felt the familiar tingling in her skin as Caliban started to restore his energy for another attack, drawing from her own reserves. Abruptly she dropped the withered thing, letting it hang on its thong outside her breastplate. "You will obey me," she commanded. "Obey or find no source for your magic. Without me, you are nothing. We do this my way. Do you agree?"

"She oversteps," the voice whispered, distant and dry. "She will pay when the time is right. It must be so."

"Another time, we can discuss it," she said. "But now, do you agree?"

"How can we fight as two?" the ancient voice insinuated. "When I am at rest her armor hides me, and hides all from me except her. When I am in use, she must hold me in contact with her; she can do nothing else."

"Do you agree?" Kolanda demanded.

"I agree," the distant, evil voice said. "For now. But how?"

"Like this," she said. Reaching behind her, the Commander loosed the lacings on her breastplate, then pulled it off and threw it aside for the slaves to pick up and place in the cart. The blouse beneath it she tore from neck to waist, exposing her breasts. Caliban hung now in the cleft between them, and his voice was no longer distant.

"I can draw from her heart to fight, as well as from her head," it admitted.

Immediately, Kolanda felt the tingling again, this time through her chest, and the surrounding air seemed to sizzle. "My way," she reminded. "You can have the wizard, but not at risk of the man and the thing he carries." The distant vision came again, but only vaguely now that Caliban was not at her eyes. Still, it was enough.

The wizard was mounting the horse, swinging up behind its rider.

Kolanda beckoned a hobgoblin. "Noll," she commanded, "take the platoon at double-time and go to the bridge. Take those you find there. Kill them if they resist." She motioned the troops forward, and they lined out at a run, followed by the cart drawn by slaves and by the swamp goblins searing them with whips to get more speed from them.

Only Kolanda and her personal guard of six selected fighting goblins remained. With them at her heels, she set off at a steady trot toward the edge of the breaks. Where the trail emerged, she would wait for the two riders coming from the hills. Caliban could have his revenge on the wizard. He could have the other man, too, as far as she was concerned, but intuition told her that the thing he carried with him must not reach the dwarf at the bridge. It must not reach Thorbardin, of course, but more than that she herself must have it.

Whatever it was, it had the power to punish Caliban.

The two men on the horse were still nearly a mile away when Kolanda Darkmoor and her guards took up ambush positions along the trail, just where it entered the broken lands.

Half a mile to the west, Noll and his platoon of goblin warriors crept through narrow ways among heaped boulders, approaching the abutment of Sky's End Bridge. Behind them came the cart, pulled by slaves. In the same cart Kolanda Darkmoor's lacquered steel breastplate lay atop bundles of lathed bronze darts, foraged weapons and supplies, and bits of booty picked up along the trail. Where it lay, it almost hid a sleek longbow of elven design and a single arrow . . . the last arrow of Garon Wendesthalas.

Weak and battered, beaten and mutilated, the elf clung to the side of the cart for support as swamp goblins harried the slaves along. He clung, and his hand was never far from the bow and the single arrow.

* * * * *

Wingover was long since out of sight by the time Chane and the others had crossed the arched bridge, and they settled in to wait between a pair of pillars that might once have been guard towers, flanking the east end of the bridge. Guard towers or, Chane thought, possibly counting towers for inspection of wares in transit. Idly, the dwarf found himself thinking: this might once have been a trade road. Wingover had spoken of trade roads. Probably there had been such a road, going out from Thorbardin to points north by way of Pax Tharkas. Obviously there had once been a lot of trade between the undermountain kingdom and other realms—far more than the modest efforts of Rogar Goldbuckle and other traders produced now.

Thorbardin itself was full of things not dwarven. Elvenwares of great beauty were treasured under the mountains, as were tapestries and feather arrangements, cunning table services of carved wood made by humans somewhere, toys and folding screens, vine-laced frames for paintings, small bits of treasured ivory. Chane had seen such things all his life in Thorbardin, but had never thought much about them. Now he realized that they were relics of some long-ago time when the gates had been open and roads had been in use for caravans to come and go upon them. Chane thought of it, and felt as though some grand thing had been lost along the way. Wars and hostilities and conflicts among peoples had destroyed the roads, and put an end to the commerce they had represented.

This very bridge, this soaring arch across a misted gorge, might have been part of that same old route from Thorbardin to Pax Tharkas to the lands of Abanasinia . . . destroyed in the Dwarfgate Wars. The bridge might have been a point of registry for dwarven goods outbound, and a point of inspection for the treasures of other places, coming to the dwarven realm. The broken lands beyond would have made ideal trading grounds. A hundred camps could be set up within a half-mile, each in its private corner, and all interconnected by the maze of stone-walled paths. It would have been a trading bazaar like nothing ever seen in Thorbardin, even in the great centers of the Daewar city.

It was a pity, that such things no longer were.

"If ever there is peace," Chane muttered, "real peace and cooperation, it will be warriors and fighters who bring it. For they are the ones who have seen the most of chaos."

Chess glanced around at him. "You sound like an elf."

"Or a human," Jilian observed. "That does sound awfully human, Chane."

"I wonder," he said. "I wonder if there's that much difference."

"I think I'll take a look around," Chess said. "Things are getting dull around here."

Before he could turn away, though, the kender looked up and grinned. "Things may perk up a little, I guess. Bobbin's back."

Like a speck against the mountainside, rapidly growing, the soarwagon dipped and tumbled toward Chane, Jilian, and Chess. The kender's supply pole dangled below it, horizontal, attached to the hook on Bobbin's lifeline. They walked a few steps out on the bridge to watch its approach, and Chane's foot bumped something protruding from the bridge rail. He knelt for a better look. It was a metal ring the size of the palm of his hand, just inches above the bridge's floor. He raised his eyes, searching along the rail. There was another a few yards away, and another beyond that . . . and the same along the base of the south rail. Metal rings were set in the stone at intervals, as far up the bridge as Chane could see. He knew what they were. Every cable-cart tunnel in Thorbardin had such rings at every change in grade. Such winch rings were used for the hoisting and lowering of laden carts along slopes, by use of pulleys.

Just like in Thorbardin.

But why equip an open-road bridge with winch-rings? Unless. . . .

Chane stood, gazing past the rising bridge, across the gorge at the sheer face of Sky's End. They had come down from a high ledge, along a narrow switchback trail that approached the bridge from a sharp angle. No straight approach from the west was possible, because the bridge footings ran nearly to the sheer, clifflike face of the cutaway mountain. It had, now that Chane thought of it, seemed odd that a bridge should end at right angles to the foot of a cliff, but he had other things on his mind when they'd first encountered it.

Chane took a deep breath and nodded. Intuition so strong it was beyond question poured through him.

"I know where it is," he muttered.

Beyond the west end of the bridge, at the foot of Sky's End's towering cliff, was a rockfall. And behind the rockfall . . . it had to be. An ancient tradeway, under the mountain. A tradeway that would lead to the warrens.

The forgotten entrance to Thorbardin. Forgotten because an old war had brought an end to trade.

"Hello!"

Chane blinked and turned. Just a few yards away, level with the bridge, the soarwagon hovered over the gorge. The gnome waved at them. "Do you want this pole back?" he called. "I don't have any use for it, and it's a clumsy thing to carry around."

"Why don't you just drop it?" the kender asked.

"It's a nice pole, and you might want to send over some more raisins some time. Why don't you keep it?"

Chess smiled. "All right. Let it down, and I'll keep it."

"Not here," Bobbin said. "I'm afraid to get too close to that bridge. But I can let it down just past those towers."

The soarwagon edged upward, dipped, and soared out over the gorge in a wide circle. It settled to a hover again just past the foot of the bridge.

"I'll go get the pole," the kender said.

Bobbin began lowering the horizontal pole, working his winch, then paused, looking toward the breaks. He cupped his hands and shouted, "Did you know there are goblins here?"

In the instant the gnome took his hand from the winch, the pole dropped free. In that same instant a company of armed goblins surged out of hiding just beyond the bridge abutments and charged.

The pole and the lead hobgoblin arrived at the gap between the pillars at exactly the same time. The creature's midsection hit the pole, jamming it against the pillars, and he flipped over it and fell. Several goblins fell over him, and others over them; the pole splintered, and Bobbin's line broke free. The soarwagon bobbed skyward as Chestal Thicketsway turned and ran, back up the rise of the bridge.

"Goblins!" Chess shouted needlessly, for the sprawling, shouting mass of creatures behind him would have been difficult to overlook.

Chane leaped to Jilian's side, grabbed her arm, and

pulled her to the nearest vertical riser on the bridge rail. Without a word, he thrust her down behind it.

Chess turned and drew his hoopak sling. As the hobgoblin tried to get to his feet, spilling goblins around him, the kender bounced a rock off his helmet, knocking it askew.

Momentarily blinded, the hobgoblin waved his sword and screeched, "Rush 'em! Cut'm down!"

A goblin free of the rest started to charge, and a whining pebble took him in the eye. He went over backward, screaming.

Jilian Firestoke had no intention of hiding behind a vertical pillar of a bridge rail, when there were things to be done. Holding her sword in launch position she rushed past Chane and headed for the enemy.

Chane started to shout at her, then saw one of the goblins beyond her raise a crossbow. He drew his sword and threw it, as hard as he could. End over end, it flashed in the sunlight . . . over Jilian's head and downward. Point first it hit the goblin's breast armor, and the sheer weight of it drove it through. The goblin fell, skewered through the brisket, and his dart sailed out over the gorge.

Jilian swung at the nearest goblin, missed, and spun around, clinging to her centrifugal blade. The creature's laugh was cut short as the sword came around again, this time full across his leering face.

Chane hoisted his hammer and waded in, following Jilian.

"Fall back!" the hobgoblin shouted. "Fall back! Use th' darts!" He sprinted for cover as Jilian whirled toward him. Her blade took the tassel off his helmet, the stock off his crossbow, and the tail off his kilt before he got out of range.

For a moment there was scrambling, fleeing goblins everywhere, then the bridge was clear. Chane dived under Jilian's flashing sword to keep from being beheaded. "Stop now!" he roared, catching her around the waist in a diving tackle. They tumbled across a dead goblin and rolled against the bridge rail.

"I said, stop," Chane panted.

Jilian picked herself up and smoothed her hair. "I was trying to. You didn't have to be so grabby about it. Honestly!"

A bronze dart ricocheted off stone beside the dwarven girl. Chane glanced around, then grabbed her hand and headed up the bridge, seeking cover. Darts zipped around them, and pebbles flew in answer.

The kender was dodging in and out of the cover of stone uprights, stepping out to use his weapon, then darting back to cover to reload. But as the dwarves piled in behind him, he reached into his pouch and his hand came out empty. He was out of pebbles, and there was nothing on the bridge to throw.

Chess dug deeper into the pouch. "I've probably got some things in here that I can shoot."

He searched, found something, and slipped it into the hoopak's sling just as a goblin peered around one of the bridge spires. The kender let fly, and his missile burst and splattered on the creature's face.

"What was that?" Chane called.

"Pigeon egg," the kender admitted. "Not a very good choice, I guess."

Darts continued to fly and zing around the defenders.

"We'd better retreat," Chane rumbled. "Come on. Follow me across the bridge."

Chess glanced around, and his eyes widened. "I don't think so," he said. "Look."

Above and behind them on the bridge stood an ogre with a huge club in his fist. As the dwarves turned and saw him, the creature grinned. He pointed his club at Chane Feldstone. "You see me, dwarf?" he thundered. "I see you, too. You think Loam don't remember you?"

The darts stopped flying, and goblin cheers sounded below. The ogre stood, gloating, his stance nearly spanning the width of the bridge.

"Maybe I can slice him," Jilian offered, but Chane pushed her back. The dwarf stood, balancing his hammer for combat. In return, the ogre licked its lips, grinned again, and came for him.

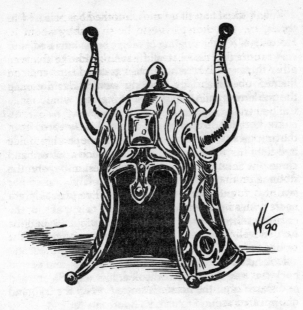

Chapter 31

Out on the plains, Thog had gathered the sepa-
rate segments of Kolanda's command, and was marching
toward the breaks. From the bridge-trail gap, Kolanda
saw the troops funneling between the distant hills, and
knew there would be little for them to do. It would all be
over before they arrived. Already, she could hear the
hoofbeats of the approaching horse. Edging back into
the shadows of a stone slab, the Commander waved her
six guards farther back into their hiding places across the
trail. In moments, the riders would be between them.

"You can have the wizard, Caliban," she muttered.
"The goblins and I will deal with the barbarian."

"Glenshadow," the withered thing at her breast whispered. "Caliban has waited a very long time. Glensha-

---

291

dow will die many times now, before he is released to death."

Kolanda felt the tingling of magic being amassed, and was satisfied. Caliban would have no time to think of other things until he was through taking his revenge on the red-robed mage. By then, she would have the thing the wilderness man carried, the thing that would make Caliban truly her slave.

The horse's hooves clopped on stone, only yards from the ambushers, and the Commander gripped her blade and held her breath, counting the seconds. Closer and closer the sounds came. There was motion beyond the stone, and a horse's head appeared. Kolanda raised her sword . . . and stopped. There were no riders, only a horse with an empty saddle. Looking straight ahead, the creature trotted on, seeing none of them . . . though its ears swiveled toward the goblin guards in hiding as it passed.

Kolanda stepped out from her hiding place and peered back the way the horse had come. Nothing. She turned and stared after the horse. It trotted on up the trail and disappeared around a turn, its hoofbeats fading.

"They've tricked me," Kolanda breathed. "Well, we'll see who gets the last trick." She waved at her guards. "Come out! Follow me, on the double!"

They fell in behind her, glancing at one another in confusion, and headed up the trail. At a dark cleft in the broken stone, the rearmost goblin saw the others pass by ahead of him, then paused as something seemed to move in the cleft. Slowing, he approached and stepped close to the darkness. It was the last thing he ever did. Hard hooves lashed out, with great haunches driving them. One caught the goblin in the face, the other in the chest.

Geekay stepped out of his hidey-hole, pawed at the dead thing on the trail, twitched his ears in revulsion, and looked up the trail where the others had gone. At an easy trot, he followed.

* * * * *

"It's a thing a man picks up, traveling wilderness,"

Wingover explained, helping Glenshadow over a fissure. "Never backtrack yourself without a diversion of some kind. You don't know what might be waiting for you."

"And you might lose your horse," the wizard rasped.

"Better him than me." Wingover shrugged. "But it's not likely. We've been around a while. He knows what to do." The wilderness man paused and sniffed. "I smell goblins."

"And I sense evil," Glenshadow said. "Magic and evil. I wish I could see."

The man looked at him, peering into his eyes. "You mean you can't see?"

"I don't mean just with my eyes. There are better ways, you know." He sighed. "It seems I've been blind forever. The cursed Spellbinder."

Wingover turned the helmet, indicating the green gem inside. "What about this one? Pathfinder. What does it do to you?"

"Nothing . . . unless I touch it. You saw what it does then."

"Is that because you're a wizard?"

Glenshadow nodded. "The two gems react to magic. Pathfinder holds it in place; Spellbinder confuses it, turns it upon itself. It is how Gargath trapped the graystone. At least, such is the legend. I believe it now."

Abruptly Wingover turned away, holding up his hand. "Hush," he whispered. "Listen!"

Ahead of them, not far away, there was a clamor of voices. Goblins cheered and cackled.

"They're at the bridge," Wingover said. "Let's go." With a bound he hurried on, leaving Glenshadow to follow as best he could. Running, sprinting, leaping from stone to stone atop the broken zone, Wingover rounded a shoulder and saw the bridge ahead. Goblins in force pressed forward at the foot of it, and a huge ogre with a club stood halfway up its slope, facing down. Between were the two dwarves and the kender.

Even at this distance, Wingover saw Chane Feldstone brace himself for battle . . . a tiny creature, not half as tall as the monster he faced, and armed only with a hammer. Above it all, the crazy gnome circled in the air on the wings of a sailcloth kite.

Wingover slung the dwarven helmet at his back, tightened the straps on his shield, and raised his sword. By the time he hit the lower trail, he was moving at a run. His war cry was a howl of fury as he burst upon the goblin platoon.

* * * * *

Loam advanced slowly toward the waiting dwarf, enjoying the moment, drawing out the sweet satisfaction of destroying the small creature who had humiliated him. For long days and long miles, the ridicule Cleft had heaped upon him after digging him out from the fallen stone, had rung in his ears. His fury had fermented into a deep hatred for the dwarf with the cat-fur garments. Cleft was dead now, and Loam felt no regret, but still the harsh glee of his fellow's taunts lingered to haunt the ogre.

Many times in his life, Loam had killed dwarves—as well as humans and other lesser creatures. He had even killed two elves, purely for the sport of it. But this kill would be the sweetest of all. He wanted to make it last.

Just within reach of the smaller being, he feinted suddenly, thrusting his club forward. The dwarf's frenzied dodge delighted him, and he chuckled, a deep rumble like distant thunder. Again Loam jabbed, prodding with the huge club, this time grazing Chane's head as the dwarf backpedaled. Was that panic in the little creature's eyes? Loam's pleasure deepened. He held the club out, waving it lazily from side to side, taunting, and beckoned with his other hand. "Little fighter," he chuckled. "See how brave! Can't even make his knees behave. Think your hammer worries me? Come and try it, then you'll see."

From the corner of his eye Loam saw the little kender sidling along the bridge rail, trying to flank him. With his empty hand he reached out, swatted casually, and sent the small thing tumbling. "Friends can't help the fighting one," he rumbled. "Dwarf must deal with Loam alone."

He raised his club higher, threatening, and suddenly the dwarf darted under it. Loam roared as the creature's hammer cracked against his kneecap.

Chane ducked between the ogre's legs, whirled around, and went between again as the monster turned, getting in another blow at the same kneecap. The ogre's roar was deafening. Chess darted past, swatting the ogre across the knuckles with the heavy end of his hoopak and chattering at the top of his lungs, hurling taunts and insults that fairly summarized the misbegotten nature of ogredom.

A tide of goblins had started to flow up the bridge, but they now hesitated. Beyond the bridge spires a blood-chilling howl sounded, and goblins scattered in panic as Wingover charged among them, shield pummeling, sword flashing. A few goblins at the foot of the bridge turned and tried to form a defense, but were cut down by Jilian in full spin.

At the ogre's feet, Chane managed one more solid blow with his hammer, this time at Loam's midriff. The dwarf was then knocked flat by the massive club. He lay stunned, trying to breathe, and Loam stepped to him. Ignoring the kender's prodding hoopak, the ogre raised his club to crush the dwarf.

Chess flailed at the ogre's back, then blinked as something fell across his arm . . . a metal hook, attached to a rope. He dropped his hoopak and grabbed the rope. After throwing it around the ogre's massive ankle, the kender set the hook to the rope in one motion. Finally, Chess straightened and pulled down on the rope as hard as he could.

Overhead, the soarwagon's sensitive vanes reacted to the tug. They instantly realigned themselves, and the craft nosed up, seeking the sky.

Loam's club descended as his feet went out from under him. The blow rang against stone a foot from Chane's head, and the dwarf looked up, trying to see clearly. Just above the bridge, a flailing ogre dangled upside down from Bobbin's supply line, while overhead the soarwagon shivered and trembled, fighting for altitude. The gnome's voice was a screech: "Get that creature off my line! He's too heavy!"

Chestal Thicketsway picked up his hoopak and dug into his pouch desperately. The only thing that came to hand was a small glass ball, something he had picked up on the old, frozen battlefield in the Valley of Waykeep.

He set it in the hoopak's sling-pocket and sighted at the hook holding the rope to the ogre's ankle. "Maybe I can shoot him loose," he called reassuringly.

The glass ball flew, ricocheted off Loam's foot, and zoomed upward to imbed itself in the wicker of Bobbin's cab. In the air above Chess, something voiceless seemed to say, "Ah. Much better."

The kender stared up and around. "Zap? Was that you?"

Enraged and frothing, Loam dropped his club, curled his body upward, and began clawing at the rope that held him. The ogre's huge hand grasped it, then hand over hand, he pulled himself upright and began to climb.

Chess cupped his hands and shouted, "Watch out, Bobbin! The ogre's coming up your rope! I missed my shot!"

"Drat and threadbind," the gnome's irritated voice answered. "If you want something done right, you have to do it yourself, I suppose. Now where did I put that wrench? Ah, here it is."

The struggling, bucking soarwagon had edged away from the bridge and was beginning, little by little, to fall toward the gorge. Bobbin worked feverishly, loosing first one lug and then the next, then drew back as his winch mount broke loose, taking a piece of the soarwagon with it. Ogre, supply line, and winch plummeted away, into the mists of the great gorge. The soarwagon, suddenly free of the creature's weight, shot upward like a winged arrow. High above it did a tight barrel roll, looped about, and headed out over the breaks, toward the plains.

Chess danced on tiptoes, shouting, "Come back! You've got Zap!" But it was far too late for his words to be heard.

Wingover cut and slashed his way through a gaggle of panicked goblins at the foot of the bridge, the stench of goblin blood a miasma around him. His battle howl still echoing from the stone walls of the breaks, he clove through them, wading in dark gore. Stab, slash, and cut, his blade was a dancing tongue of death, his shield a dark battering ram. Goblins fell, and goblins fled. A pain like searing fire lanced through Wingover's shoulder and down his shield arm. He lunged forward and spun around.

An armored hobgoblin faced Wingover, its sword red with blood and poised to strike again. The human tried to raise his shield, but couldn't. He dodged aside instead, barely escaping the thrust. The hobgoblin hissed, feinted, and thrust again. Wingover felt the cut on his thigh as his own blade descended, leaving a deep dent in the creature's helmet.

A random thought teased Wingover: the hobgoblin was hiding. It waited and got behind me.

Again the hobgoblin struck. Wingover managed to deflect the cut with his shield, and lunged forward, blade extended. The point ground against metal breastplate and slid away, and Wingover felt blood dripping down his cheek. He realized dimly that he wasn't standing any more. He sat spread-legged and dazed, and the hobgoblin's wide mouth split in a sharp-toothed leer. Raising its sword above its head, the creature charged, then stiffened and gurgled as Wingover's blade slid between its breastplate and its buckler.

Slowly, shaking his head to clear the mists, the man got to his feet and pulled his sword free. Someone was beside him, helping him. It was Jilian, her eyes wide and excited. Wingover staggered, then stood. All around was stench and carnage . . . and silence. Nothing moved, and the only sound was an odd, distant singing as of great winds building aloft.

The air felt still and heavy. Where is the sunlight, the wilderness man wondered vaguely. Why is it so dark?

Feeling dizzy from shock, Wingover raised his head. Heavy clouds were forming above—dense, swirling clouds to the east, above the Plains of Dergoth; dark ropes of cloud sweeping outward from the slopes of Sky's End. Odd, he thought. Odd weather. But his wounds put thoughts of the clouds aside. He was hurt, he knew. But how hurt? Jilian tugged at him and pointed.

Beyond the bridge, someone was coming. Shadows from the swirling clouds interefered, then Wingover saw clearly. Kolanda Darkmoor. The Commander. Bare-breasted, her woman's body contrasted strangely with the hideous helmet and the weapons she carried. Goblins ran beside her. Five of them that he could see, better-armed than the ones he had fought on the bridge. More disciplined. Crack troops.

Partway up the bridge, Chane met them. Wingover had to lay down his sword to remove the dwarven helm from its sling at his back. It was smeared with blood—his own, he knew.

He handed it to Chane Feldstone. "Here's your ancestor's hat," he said gruffly. "Jewel and all. I hope it's worth it."

Chane turned the helm in his hands, studying it.

"Well, don't just stand there," Wingover gritted. "Use it."

"You're hurt," the dwarf said.

"It's nothing much. I'll be all right. But we don't have time to discuss it. *Use the helmet!*"

Chane pushed back the cat-eared hood of his black cloak, and Chess gaped at him. Somehow, he hadn't noticed how much the dwarf had changed. The dwarf's swept-back beard, his intense, wide-set eyes were the same, but Chane was different now. Somehow the kender couldn't see him now as an amusing dwarf in a bunny suit. He might almost have been someone else entirely. Chess wondered if the old warrior, Grallen, had looked like this.

The dwarf set the helm on his head. It fit as though it had been made for him, and seemed as though none other had ever been intended to wear it. Grallen's helm settled over Chane's head, and the green stone above the noseguard began to glow.

Chane seemed to stiffen. His eyes closed, and when he spoke his voice had changed.

"I, Grallen," he said, "son of King Duncan, rode forth on the morning of the last battle in the great charge of the Hylar dwarves. From the Northgate of Thorbardin we had come, then westward to where the roving companies encamped, then across Sky's End to the Plains of Dergoth, to join the main force of Hylar. My troop assaulted the mountain home of the wizard there. My brothers fought with courage and valor; many fell with honor at my side."

They stared at him in wonder. Even Jilian had backed away, her eyes wide.

"Yet when the tide of battle turned in our favor," Chane recited, "and I confronted the wizard in his lair, he smiled, and a great magic rushed from his being: a flame of power and horror that broke through stone and steel.

"Thus in his rage and despair, he destroyed both his allies and his enemies.

"Thus did I die, and thus now I am doomed to live in the remains of the fortress, now known as Skullcap Mountain, until the day when someone will take my helm and return it to the land of my fathers so that I may find rest."

Clouds seethed and churned overhead, darkening the land. Whining winds aloft echoed in the chasm below. Chane stood a moment longer as one entranced, then shuddered and opened his eyes. "Grallen," he said.

He turned to stare at the massive face of Sky's End across the bridge, and a green light glowed there among the fallen stone. It looked to the dwarf like light coming from an open door.

"Go," Wingover said. "I'll hold them here as long as I can. Go and do what we came for . . . whatever that is."

Chane hesitated, then nodded. "It is what we came for," he said. Abruptly he held out his hand. "Good luck, human."

Wingover took the hand in his good one. "Good journey, dwarf."

Chane turned toward the crown of the bridge and the

mystery beyond, Jilian following. Chess looked after them, started to tag along, but changed his mind.

"He's probably about to become rich and famous," the kender muttered. "And probably insufferable. I think I'll stay."

Just beyond the foot of the bridge, Kolanda Darkmoor stood, looking up at them. Her stance was a warrior's stance. A victor's stance. Her eyes behind her steel mask glittered with anticipation, and something between her breasts glowed darkly. A faint, sizzling sound lingered in the air.

And then there was no more time. Out past the breaks, goblin troops raced toward Chane and his companions, and just beyond the foot of the bridge Kolanda Darkmoor signaled her guard to advance. Wingover picked up his sword and braced himself, estimating how long it would take for the dwarves to reach safety under the mountain.

Chapter 32

AN EERIE DARKNESS WALKED ACROSS THE LAND, a darkness of writhing black clouds that swirled and coiled, defeating the sunlight. West of the bridge, Sky's End was veiled, its slopes immersed in flowing darkness. To the east, the breaks, the low hills, and the vast plains beyond were a dancing mosaic of deepening shadow. Toward Skullcap the clouds circled and tumbled in upon themselves, twisting in clockwise rotation as the descending belly of the storm dropped lower and lower, becoming a funnel miles across. Above the gorge winds swept down from mountain passes and howled in murky glee.

Wingover set his sword upright against a stone and used his right hand to lift his left arm, shield and all, until

301

the flinthide's edge was just below his eyes. With a strip of fabric from his tunic he tied the useless arm in place, then retrieved his sword.

The woman in the horned helmet gazed up at him, her pose arrogant, speculative. After a moment she called, "I want the thing you brought from Dergoth! Give it to me!"

Wingover waited.

"You won't kill me," the woman called. "You can't." Her laughter cut across the wind as she lifted the hideous mask, letting Wingover see her face.

"I don't know what you want," Wingover shouted.

"You know," the woman laughed. "The thing your wizard had. The thing you brought here. Give it to me!"

Wingover faced Kolanda, trying to hold her gaze, counting silently. It was only three hundred yards to the rockfall beyond the bridge. The dwarves should reach it any moment. Once within that hidden portal, they might be safe. He didn't know how he knew that, but he knew.

"You've come too late for that," he shouted. "It's gone."

"Gone? Gone where?"

Above and just beyond the woman and the goblins, a figure appeared on top of a rock. It was Glenshadow. Bison cloak whipping in the wind, long hair and beard streaming, he leaned for a moment on his staff, then stood erect as the staff's crystal cap winked to life. A clear crimson beacon blinked to life in the darkening murk.

"They made it," Wingover muttered. "Spellbinder is beneath the ground."

On the flat top of a sundered stone the wizard Glenshadow raised his glowing staff and shouted, "I know you, Caliban!" His voice carried on the wind like flung ice, and a brilliant flare of crimson shot out from his staff toward Kolanda Darkmoor—shot out, and stopped just short of reaching her, swallowed up in a darkness that had a voice of its own.

The sibilant, withered voice said, "And I know you, Glenshadow. You are the last." Blinding light blazed where the crimson beam ended, and crackling thunder rolled.

Glenshadow's beam receded, swallowed by a wave of darkness that rushed toward Glenshadow. Rushed, then hesitated. Wingover's mind reeled. Which Glenshadow? There wasn't just one any more. There were three. Then five. Then a dozen, and more. Myriad Glenshadows, everywhere, all moving in perfect unison as they willed their magics back upon the darkness centered at Kolanda's breast.

"Trickster!" the withered voice rasped. "Red-robe, you'd fight me with illusion?" Blacknesses writhed outward, seeking all the Glenshadows. "Die," the voice whispered.

The blacknesses snaked out, and one by one the image mages were gone . . . except one. As Wingover watched that one grew to gigantic size. Hundreds of feet tall, his stance spanning the nearby breaks, Glenshadow absorbed the blackness cast at him. It pierced him here, there, searching, and lost itself in his vastness.

"Illusion," the withered voice hissed. "Can you do no better than that?" The winds swirled, sizzling, and the searching blackness grew. Great dark holes appeared in the fabric of Glenshadow's massive image, and it seemed to flutter in the wind, dissolving. From one tiny corner of it a beam of crimson lanced out and smote the thing at Kolanda's breast, making it shriek and writhe. It fought back, then, and again the span between them was colliding energies, crimson and black with blinding glare between.

Somewhere beyond the bridge, greater thunders erupted. The stone bridge trembled, keened, and swayed. Somewhere across the gorge a piece of the mountain was falling.

"Where is the thing I want?" Kolanda shouted again, her voice rising in anger.

"It's where you can never reach it now," Wingover called and started forward, limping. A goblin dart thumped into his shield, clung for an instant, and dropped away. A pigeon egg splattered on the armor of a goblin, then a pewter mug took the creature full in the face. One beside it screeched as a dagger made from a cat's tooth whistled from the kender's hoopak and lodged in its throat.

"I've had enough of this," Kolanda Darkmoor spat. She stooped, retrieved a set and loaded crossbow, and trained it for an instant on Wingover. "It ends now! Caliban, finish it!"

Massed darknesses welled outward, seeking Glenshadow. The dark magics reached out, then hesitated and swiftly faded. The crossbow faltered as Kolanda Darkmoor looked down at the arrow standing in her breast, piercing the withered heart of Caliban, linking it forever to her own heart by a common shaft of hickory wood.

Beside the north spire Garon Wendesthalas slumped, a goblin's blade piercing his throat. Slowly he sprawled, his bow sliding from nerveless fingers to lie beside him. He turned his head and looked up the bridge rise, then raised a battered hand in final salute to his old friend, Wingover. He didn't move again.

The winds howled, and hailstones battered the land. Lightning like spider legs walked across the Plains of Dergoth and the nearer hills, striking among the goblin troops there. Staccato and brilliance, darkness and storm, the bolts danced on winds that screamed and sang and buffeted the swaying stone bridge.

Chestal Thicketsway clung to a bridge rail and shouted, "It's Zap! He's happening!"

His shield to the raging wind, Wingover fought his way to the foot of the bridge with the kender clinging to him. They fell, rolled, and sought shelter in a storm like no storm ever seen on Ansalon . . . at least since the Cataclysm.

"Three spells cast Fistandantilus," the Irda had said, "in the Valley of Waykeep. The first was fire, the second ice. The third has not yet happened."

Now, the sundered Plains of Dergoth were washed by storm, as Zap fulfilled his destiny.

* * * * *

Rockfall had hidden the old trade portal. What once had been an iron-framed gate, nine feet wide and twenty feet high, with cable-cart stays and transfer platforms, now was a forgotten gap behind hundreds of tons of tumbled stone. Hidden, but not closed.

With Jilian following, Chane Feldstone crawled through a cleft among the rocks and entered a tunnel, which was more a maze that only a dwarf or a curious kender might have riddled out. Behind them, faint now, was the rolling thunder of the storm. Chane eased around a hairpin turn between boulders, then crawled over a buried slab and under another, following the green light that seemed to speak to the gem set in the old helm he wore. On and on they went, and everywhere was dark, fallen stone with only the green trace to guide them. Pathfinder pulsed and glowed as the stone maze wound on dimly. In the pouch at Chane's belt, Spellbinder throbbed a silent song.

Jilian's cheeks were moist with wiped-away tears, her throat tight with dread and regret. People she had come to love were now left behind. They would probably die so that the mission of Grallen and of Chane's dream could be completed. She had looked back just once, from the top of the bridge, and felt as though her heart might break. The two had seemed so small back there, so helpless—a bleeding man and a bright-eyed kender with his hair coiled around his throat. Just those two, facing . . . Jilian had not looked back again.

For the first time in her life, Jilian felt the weight of mountains above her, the press of the stone through which they made their way. "Maybe we can go back and help them," she whispered. "I mean, when you've done whatever it is you are supposed to do."

Ahead of her Chane squeezed his broad shoulders through a narrow crevice and took another turn, pausing only to make sure that she followed. He said nothing, though she knew he ached for their friends just as she did.

Another tight, jagged opening between tumbled slabs, another turn, and Jilian heard Chane's breath catch in his throat. He clawed and pulled through a crack, and when he was beyond it he turned to give her his hand. Greenish light flooded about him and lit up the cavern he had discovered. Chane and Jilian looked around. The light they saw was Pathfinder's glow, reflecting back from the delved walls and ceiling of a wide, hewn space. A few bits of rubble lay scattered among neat mounds of piled stone. Nearby, an old cable-cart lay on its side.

"A transfer terminal," Chane said. He pointed to the left. A clean, unshattered tunnel led away there, into darkness. Pathfinder pulsed, and the narrow trail of green light appeared again, on the dusty floor. It led straight to a mound of crushed stone, up the side of it to the top, and stopped at a little cone of green light, with a red center.

Chane walked to the mound, head-high to him, and stood a moment, listening to something that only he could hear. Then he took Spellbinder from his pouch. The red gem pulsed warmly, its glow the color of Lunitari's light. Reaching out, he placed the gem on the pile of stone, where the spot of red shone.

From behind the dwarves, from the buried gate they had traversed, came a sound of distant, rolling thunder. Spellbinder's light grew in power, flared brilliantly in the cavern, then settled into a steady, warm glow that seemed to fill the air with tiny music.

"Come." Chane took Jilian's hand. "Pathfinder has brought Spellbinder home. Now we must hurry."

"Can we go back?" she asked.

As though in answer, the thunder grew beyond the gate and the cavern quaked ominously. Chane headed for the left tunnel at a run, pulling Jilian along with him. The thunder mounted behind them.

Once beyond the cavern, Pathfinder's steady green glow lighted a cable-way long forgotten, a finely-delved tunnel that seemed to go on ahead of them unobstructed. "Hurry," Chane said. Behind them, the thunder became the roar of solid stone shearing and the chatter of rockfall. A cloud of dust obscured the opening of the cavern, and the faint red light winked out.

"It's sealed," Chane rumbled. "And locked against magic. That was what Grallen intended to do."

"Where does this go?" Jilian pointed ahead, down the cable-way.

"It goes where it always went," Chane Feldstone said. "It goes to Thorbardin."

Once more Jilian looked back. "I'd like to see outside again . . . sometime. Do you suppose we ever will?"

"We'll see it," Chane replied softly. "Maybe we'll even see . . . them . . . again sometime."

At his brow, Pathfinder throbbed a clear green pulse of reassurance. Chane felt as though Grallen's helm had just given him a promise.

Chapter 33

ON a bright spring day, a man came down from the wilderness ranges. He rode a sturdy, battle-wise horse and had the look of far places about him. In the main square at the crossroads of Barter he reined in and dismounted. Not far away, winged pigs circled contentedly above an inn. Some distance beyond, pavilions spread their bright expanses, a sign of the spring trading season. Among them was a large, red-and-gold pavilion that stood amidst myriad stalls and showing tables.

"Goldbuckle is here," the man noted, talking to himself and his horse in the way of one who has been afar and long alone. He smiled a sardonic smile, unlashing a pack from behind his saddle. Inside was Abanasinian ivory, an exquisite collection of the finest carvings. "That old

308

thief is going to drool all over himself when he sees this," he told the horse. "But it's going to cost him plenty to get his hands on it."

Leading the horse, he started for the trade pavilion of the Daewar merchant, then stopped when a high-pitched, excited voice shouted, "Hey! Look who's here!"

Chestal Thicketsway pushed through a crowd of traders and ran toward him. "Wingover! I thought you were dead or something!" He skidded to a stop, beaming up at the man. "And Geekay made it, too. Wow! Did you hear about Chane Feldstone? He's rich and famous, just like I said he'd be. The Thorbardin traders talk about him all the time. Rogar Goldbuckle has been strutting around here ever since he arrived, telling everybody how he's a personal friend of Chane Feldstone. He has the trading sanction for the Hylar now, too. Gee, everybody thought you were dead, though. How did you survive that storm?"

"I—" Wingover started.

"Did you ever see such a storm in all your life? Wow! What a wind! I saw a boulder as big as a house, just rolling along with the wind pushing it. I never saw anything like that storm. Most people don't believe me when I talk about it, but that's all right. What did you do, find a hiding place? After we got separated, I mean? That's what I did. I just crawled into a hole and stayed there until Zap got it out of his system."

"I—" Wingover attempted.

"I'll bet you didn't expect to find me here, either, did you? I wouldn't be, except that Bobbin couldn't find his way back without a guide. Every place he'd seen was from the air, and after Zap knocked him down everything looked different. He got lost! Did I tell you . . . no, I didn't yet, did I? . . . Bobbin's building a new invention. It's kind of like an iron fish, and I don't know much about it. You know how gnomes are. Either they don't tell you anything, or you can't get a word in edgewise. He says he wants to go and find an ocean as soon as he gets it ready. Are you going to see Rogar Goldbuckle? He's here, you know. That's his place over—"

"Chess, I—"

"—there, with all the red-and-yellow drapings. There's some really neat stuff in there. I found a—"

"Chess—"

"—whole sack of bright beads that somebody had dropped or something, but the dwarves at the gate made me leave it. That's all right, though. I found some other things, too, and I can go back and look some more any time I want to, no matter what they say about—"

"Chestal Thicketsway!"

The kender blinked, startled. "Ah . . . yes?"

"You haven't changed a bit."

FOR THE BEST IN PAPERBACKS, LOOK FOR THE

In every corner of the world, on every subject under the sun, Penguin represents quality and variety – the very best in publishing today.

For complete information about books available from Penguin – including Puffins, Penguin Classics and Arkana – and how to order them, write to us at the appropriate address below. Please note that for copyright reasons the selection of books varies from country to country.

In the United Kingdom: Please write to *Dept E.P., Penguin Books Ltd, Harmondsworth, Middlesex, UB7 0DA.*

If you have any difficulty in obtaining a title, please send your order with the correct money, plus ten per cent for postage and packaging, to *PO Box No 11, West Drayton, Middlesex*

In the United States: Please write to *Dept BA, Penguin, 299 Murray Hill Parkway, East Rutherford, New Jersey 07073*

In Canada: Please write to *Penguin Books Canada Ltd, 2801 John Street, Markham, Ontario L3R 1B4*

In Australia: Please write to the *Marketing Department, Penguin Books Australia Ltd, P.O. Box 257, Ringwood, Victoria 3134*

In New Zealand: Please write to the *Marketing Department, Penguin Books (NZ) Ltd, Private Bag, Takapuna, Auckland 9*

In India: Please write to *Penguin Overseas Ltd, 706 Eros Apartments, 56 Nehru Place, New Delhi, 110019*

In the Netherlands: Please write to *Penguin Books Netherlands B.V., Postbus 3507, 1001 AH, Amsterdam*

In West Germany: Please write to *Penguin Books Ltd, Friedrichstrasse 10–12, D–6000 Frankfurt/Main 1*

In Spain: Please write to *Alhambra Longman S.A., Fernandez de la Hoz 9, E–28010 Madrid*

In Italy: Please write to *Penguin Italia s.r.l., Via Como 4, I-20096 Pioltello (Milano)*

In France: Please write to *Penguin Books Ltd, 39 Rue de Montmorency, F-75003 Paris*

In Japan: Please write to *Longman Penguin Japan Co Ltd, Yamaguchi Building, 2-12-9 Kanda Jimbocho, Chiyoda-Ku, Tokyo 101*